HEROES
OF THE
EMPIRE

BOOK 3: THE EMPEROR

HEROES OF THE EMPIRE

ISRAH AZIZI

Published in the United States of America by PageTurnerPress LLC. Visit page-turner-press.com

Title: Heroes of the Empire/Israh Azizi

Other titles: The Emperor

Cover design by Damonza

Identifiers: Library of Congress Control Number: 2024914205

ISBN: 978-1-958688-06-9 (Hardback)

ISBN: 978-1-958688-05-2 (Paperback)

ISBN: 978-1-958688-07-6 (ebook)

Printed in the United States of America

10 9 8 7 6 5 4 3 2 1

First Edition

For anyone who doubted themselves and was
afraid of the beasts hungering to tear them
down. Pick up your sword and slay them.

PRONUNCIATION AND CHARACTER GUIDE

Adelania (eda-lay-nee-ya) — former Ondalarian princess

Alesto (eh-les-toh) — Queen Coralie's advisor

Aria (ah-ree-ya) — Boltrex's daughter

Asilles (es-sill-lees) — Ondalarian shieldmaiden

Aylis (EYE-less) — Savorian, Svorgin's sister

Bear (bay-er) — Velamir's former mentor

Boltrex Vaz (bol-TREX) — deceased general of Verin, Velamir's father

Bronus (BRO-nis) — Honzio's decoy and bodyguard, deceased

Cerel (SER-rill) — True Manos in the Grand Palace

Clion (klee-own) — the proprietor of an inn in Hearcross

Coralie (cora-LEE) — Queen of Verin

Cores-na (core-es-na) — Coralie's birth name

Cselnsor (SELLIN-soar) — Mordon's birth name

Dale (DAY-ell) — deceased king of Verin, Coralie's uncle

Draven Valent (DRAY-ven VALL-ont) — former prince of Ayleth

Dunya (doon-yuh) — head of the Elders

Finnean Colleda (FINN-ee-ahn COLE-eda) — Verin soldier

Gallaxos (gall-axe-us) — Ondalarian king

Galva Desor Blayton (BLAY-ten) — Latimus's father, deceased

Genvor (Jen-vore) — Ondalarian High Lord

Grongar-ja (gron-gar-ja) — Uluzar/Savagelander

Hesten Hartinza (HES-tin HEART-inza) — Natassa's older brother, deceased

Honzio Hartinza (HON-zee-oh HEART-inza) — crown prince of Karalik Empire, Natassa's older brother

Inat (ee-knot) — alpha rumlok Mordon bonded with

Irox (EYE-rocks) — deceased prince of Verin, King Dale's brother, Coralie's adoptive father

Jaxon Tana (JAX-en tan-nuh) — Shadow Manos, Velamir's closest friend

Jinong-ja (jih-nong-ja) — Uluzar chief

Joster (JAW-ster) — former king of Ayleth, Draven's father

Kasdeya Vosta (kas-DAY-a VOZ-ta) — Natassa's former decoy and handmaiden, Krealyn's twin, deceased

Kolesta-na Zurg (coal-esta-na Zoo-org) — Uluzar, former king of Ayleth's courtesan, Coralie's birth mother

Korso (Core-soh) — shieldmaiden trainer

Koseer-ja (KOH-seer-jah) — Uluzar/Savagelander

Krealyn Vosta (KREE-ah-lin VOZ-ta) — Natassa's decoy and handmaiden, Kasdeya's twin, deceased

Lady Blayton (BLAY-ten) — Latimus's mother

Latimus (LAT-ih-miss) — Verin captain, Blayton's son

Lilly (lil-lee) — Jax's cousin

Lissa (LISS-ah) — graduate of the Chishman Academy, deceased

Lore Blayton (LO-ore) — Latimus's younger brother

Malus Hartinza (MAL-us HEART-inza) — former emperor of Karalik Empire

Marcella (MAR-sell-uh) — Shadow Manos in Ayleth

Mari (MAR-ee) — late Verin princess, Coralie's adoptive mother

Moralis Vane (MORE-al-less vein) — Honzio's cousin, Galvasir

Mordon Vaz (MORE-dawn) — Winston's son

Natassa Hartinza (NAT-ossa HEART-inza) — princess of Karalik Empire

Ovi (OH-vee) — Natassa's late mother

Prolus (PRO-lus) — the lord of Tariqi

Quintus (Qu-win-tis) — Chishma

Rost (roh-ist) — Elder member

Sardala (SAR-doll-ah) — Lord Genvor's daughter

Salvador (SAL-va-door) — Vykus's henchman

Saphira (sef-ira) — Winston's wife

Serana (sir-ronna) — Boltrex's deceased wife

Silopar (SEE-lo-par) — Handler

Sovor-ja (SAV-oar-jah) — Uluzar/Savagelander

Svorgin (sa-vor-gin) — Aylis's brother

Thorsten Hartinza (thor-stin HEART-inza) — Natassa and Honzio's late brother

Vandal (VAAN-del) — Velamir's horse

Velamir (vel-uh-meer) — Winston's adopted son, the Cavalier

Vykus (VI-kiss) — renowned mercenary king

Winston Raga (win-ston raw-ga) — Dark Lord Prolus

Yalnos (yull-nose) — man who abducted Natassa

Xan-ja (zaan-jah) — Uluzar Chief

Zenrelius (ZEN-rel-ee-us) — Ondalarian general

IMPORTANT LOCATIONS AND TERMS

(the) Awal (OW-aal) — the Tariqin Army, filled with
   deedans

Alaris (UH-lar-rus) — the afterlife, eternal bliss

Ayleth (EYE-leth) — one of the four kingdoms

(the) Borderlands — once a defensive stronghold against
   the Tariqins

Chirokhe Mordeh (che-rogh-eh more-deh) — ceremony
   for the dead

Calestor (KEL-es-tore) — Tariqin captain title

Chishma (chish-muh) — Prolus's elite soldiers and
   graduates of the Chishman Academy

Clovensgate (clo-vens-gate) — General Boltrex's
   conquered fortress

Deedans (DEED-aans) — soldiers in the Awal, rejected
   from the Chishman Academy

Devorin (DEH-vorin) — one of the four kingdoms

(the) Docks — lawless city containing mercenaries and
   illegal trading ports

Galvasir (GAAL-vasir) — high-ranking soldier in the
   Empire

Hearcross (HEER-cross) — capital of Karalik Empire

Karalik Empire (KAARA-lik) — land of the remaining four kingdoms

Lagrima Sea (la-ree-ma) — body of water bordering Savoria

Mavaalin (MOV-aw-lin) — Savorian farewell meaning *wind in your sails*

Ondalar (on-DUH-laar) — one of the four kingdoms

Rumlok (RUM-lock) — wolf/bearlike creature

Savagelands — also called Uluz, an arid environment housing tribal groups

Savoria (SAAV-oria) — large island conquered by Prolus

Shikista (shi-kis-ta) — castle in Ayleth

Sirchoba (sir-cho-bah) — messenger bird

Sok (so-uk) — main city in Devorin

Tariqi (TO-RIH-qee) — realm consisting of nine kingdoms, eight of which used to belong to Karalik Empire

True Manos — Imperial healer

Verin (VER-in) — one of the four kingdoms

Veyer (Vay-yer) — a paste used for wedding ceremonies

Zamanin Sulari (ZAAMON-in SOOL-ari) — waters of time, a swift traveling serum

Zat (ZAAT) — crimson wine-like drink

Zelont (ZEL-lont) — Imperial for *monster*

SHADOW MANOS ABILITIES

Shadow Manos — an individual marked with a phoenix birthmark, retaining a type of shadow
Doer — common Shadow Manos ability, crafter and able to enhance poison with their blood
Lure — rarest Shadow Manos skill, able to bend a person(s) to their will
Seer — rare Shadow Manos ability, able to see, past, present, and future

A depiction of
Karalik Empire
and surrounding
territories.
As drawn by
Imperial Cartographer
Master Jowsha

Savoria
Lagrima Sea
Ondalar
Port of Ayleth
Ayleth
Castle Shikista
Karakan
Zarosari
Wallington
The Pit
The Ja Sea
The Savagelan
The Ja Desert
Po
Cas
Flond

The Red Bridge
Realm of Tariqi
Mines
Topragar Fortress
Kalea Acadamy
The Qistool
Awal Military Base
t of Savoria
Red Eagle Forest
ress Vadigar
Verin
e Verin
Namaar
Raga Manor
Verintown
Castle Yakh
Devorin
n Woods
Savastown
Sok Town
Hearcross
Mines
Karalik Palace
S
Whispering Woods
The Docks

PROLOGUE

Honzio touched his face. A large handprint marked the burning on his cheek. Emperor Malus towered over him, fury blazing from his eyes.

"One would think you are younger than twelve years! How else can you explain that senseless action in the dining hall?"

It was a rhetorical question. Honzio had learned from previous encounters that any defense on his part would lead to nothing but further torment. His lips clamped together, and his hands fisted at his sides. His eyes were level with his father's silk doublet and the golden medals dripping from his chest—medals that were meaningless to those who looked past the extravagant façade the emperor presented. He blinded those he wished to with gold beyond their wildest dreams to hide the corrupt business he committed in the dark.

"Speaking with a lesser lord's son." Malus scoffed, rubbing a ring-adorned hand over his clean-shaven face. "You single-handedly sank our family's reputation by associating with them. I thought I was clear when I told you whom you can mingle with. As a prince, you do not cower before those who solely wish to gain from the Hartinza line. And you most definitely do not extend them a hand of friendship. But what did you do? You offered our True Manos for some simple ailment? Are you a fool?"

Honzio winced. It was far more than a simple ailment. More like the certain death of the lord's son in question. But that wouldn't matter to Malus.

The emperor's hand shot out, squeezing Honzio's chin and forcing his head up. Honzio swallowed, unblinking as his father examined him with a frosty glare.

"It is clear you will not learn this way."

Honzio shook his head, panic shooting through him as the emperor grabbed hold of his arm and shoved him out of his bedchamber. Guards on hallway patrol stared as Honzio was dragged past. Emperor Malus's bruising pace did not relent until they reached the kitchens. Tears streamed freely down Honzio's face. The kitchen staff froze in their work, watching with apprehension.

"Away with you," the emperor ordered, and they shuffled out.

"Please, Your Majesty!" Honzio begged as his father shoved him toward the large tandoor ovens.

Honzio's fear boiled over as he fought against his father's unyielding grip. The ovens had been specially made for the palace, intended to cook the most lavish of breads and meats. They were said to be the largest ever built, taking up half of the kitchen space. Five stood alongside each other. Emperor Malus stopped at the last one—the one Honzio had become acquainted with at the age of six years. When he had laughed during the birth ceremony of his little brother, Thorsten. A joyful laugh at the sight of Thorsten's tiny fingers waving through the air, but it had been enough to warrant a punishment from the emperor. Honzio wished he could go back in time, when his father had seemed to be a different man. A kinder man.

"Get in," Malus bit out.

"Your Majesty, please!" Honzio addressed him with the forced formality his father required of his children through broken sobs.

Malus grabbed his collar and hoisted him over the rim of the tandoor oven. Honzio's breath left his lungs as he slammed onto the sooty charcoal bottom. The coals were still warm, stinging the palms of his hands as he shoved himself up. He stared upward at his father.

"Please, let me out! Father, please."

But the metal cover that prevented rats and other creatures from entering the oven when not in use slid over the top, sealing Honzio within and taking with it the last sliver of light. Honzio was left alone with the torment of his thoughts. *Just a few hours.* He whispered a hoarse prayer for that time to quicken. He would get through it. Like always.

Honzio reached out with a shaking hand, his fingers trailing the markings in the warm stone enclosing him. The heels of his boots dug the coals into ash beneath his feet. The fire had been out for hours, but the smoky scent lingered, watering his eyes and clutching his throat. He coughed.

Honzio had thought he was safe, preserved from the duties chained to his elder brother, Hesten, but he was no longer just the spare once the crown prince's ailment had been revealed. Even a scrape could kill Hesten and also make Honzio heir. Honzio pried his knife loose and slashed against the wall, marking a new entry in the dark journal holding him captive. It wasn't long after that his hold on fear relented and the panic poured in, raising the hairs on his arms. The confining prison crept closer, tangling around his throat and stealing his breath. He grasped at his chest, struggling to gulp a lungful of air. The space was too small, too dark. He wouldn't make it. He would die in that tiny decrepit hole.

Then he heard footsteps and the heave of the metal cover. Light poured in. Like every other time, his mother, Ovi, appeared like an angel from above, rescuing him from certain death. He was numb as she pulled him out. He slumped in her arms, shivering and shaking. She held him for endless minutes, offering assurances in the form of words he could not decipher, for the fright still paralyzed him. Her fingers traced his face, wiping away trails of soot that clung to his skin. He was terrified to lose her, even for a minute, for how could he see the way forward if his lantern gave out? But he couldn't cling to her because there were Thorsten and Natassa. They took her far too often, claiming so much of her attention, and Honzio grew envious of the time he couldn't have.

The punishments continued, worsening after Hesten's death. Emperor Malus demanded Honzio be the crown prince he claimed the Empire needed. So Honzio gave in. He became a tool, a puppet, everything he once fought against. And when he sank into that dark hole, even that light that had once aided him faded.

MOTHER. IT WAS Honzio's first thought when he jerked awake. It had been years since he'd seen her, but she was still his source of protection, his safe place. And since he was in an actual dungeon and not in the small prisons of his father's making, he needed a savior more than ever. Honzio groaned, touching his neck gingerly to ease the tension created by the strange position he'd fallen asleep in. He stretched his arms, lifting his right one as high as it allowed him.

A soft chuckle drifted to him. Draven reclined on the stone wall across from him, his legs splayed out on the grimy floor. Honzio had never

seen him so disheveled in all the years of tolerating his presence. If there was one thing the former prince-king of Ayleth fixated on, it was his appearance. His beard, which Honzio had thought him incapable of growing, hugged the sharp lines of his jaw, and his white-blond hair was streaked with dirt and blood and who knows what other filth he'd collected from their cell. Honzio shuddered, and the temporary emperor of a few brief hours, who was half the reason they were in the dungeon, smirked at him.

"We haven't been here two days, and you are already screaming for your mother? Try to be a bit original."

Honzio's reply stuck in his throat as a grunt broke through the thick tension between them. He glanced at the bunk, where the faintest line of a muscled arm could be seen.

"Leave him be, *Lsrar*. We all have horrors to contend with and losses that haunt us." Svorgin's deep accented voice held a note of warning.

Honzio could hardly believe he was still drawing breath after mentioning the Savorian's sister earlier. Svorgin had released him with a brutal stare after nearly breaking his neck. On the bright side, Honzio had accomplished one thing in his completely disastrous plan of retaking the palace: he'd found Aylis's brother. Once he reunited them, perhaps he would see her smile, a true smile, for the first time. She deserved a bit of joy after everything she'd been through. Thoughts of her brought to mind the small slip of paper crumpled in his hand. He'd managed to keep the note hidden from Draven, though the man had been far too curious when the True Manos Cerel had come to pay Honzio a visit. Honzio couldn't explain the relief he'd felt at seeing a trusted ally alive. She hadn't stayed long but gave him a reassuring nod and the note before fading away, sending the torchlight flickering as she retreated.

Little Cousin, Madame Clion's Inn is a lovely place.

A strange note but one Honzio had deciphered at once. Moralis was well. His cousin had found shelter and was giving him a destination to escape to. But first, Honzio had to break past those iron bars.

A grumble brought his gaze back to Draven. The man's face darkened, eyes resembling dark pits of despair. *Losses that haunt us.* Despite what a monster Draven was, it seemed his past affected him as well. He caught Honzio's stare, and his expression shifted to a sneer. His fingers gripped the clay bowl in his hands before he tossed it aside, spilling the mush by his boots. A drop landed on Honzio's face. He wiped it off roughly, holding back the insult on the tip of his tongue.

"These meals have no flavor," Draven muttered.

"What did you expect, a princely cuisine to be served to prisoners? Besides, our hosts are Uluzar. Their prized meals comprise arms and legs. *Human* arms and legs," Honzio said.

Draven's head thunked back against the wall. "How kind of you to remind me of that horrific detail."

A sigh rose from the bunk before Svorgin dropped down and evaluated them with a less-than-pleased frown. His attention lowered to Draven's discarded meal. "A shame to waste that."

"It's not edible," Draven replied without care.

The Savorian bent over till his midnight-blue eyes were level with Draven's. Honzio shifted, slightly alarmed at the anger seeping out of the Savorian's gaze. He pitied anyone on the receiving end of such a look.

"You call this inedible, *Lsrar*." Svorgin scooped the chunks of mush with his fingers. "You toss this aside without a blink because you wouldn't understand its worth unless you were without sustenance for days. Unless you were starving in the streets, broken and cold, hoping for even a crumb to fill your belly. You haven't known true hunger."

Draven's mouth parted, fury and a good amount of what Honzio estimated was shock keeping him frozen.

"If you truly knew hunger, not only would this be edible, but you would lick the ground for every drop."

Honzio's head lowered to his own bowl resting untouched beside him. His life had been a privileged one. He'd never had to worry about where his next meal was coming from.

"And I assume you do?" Words emerged from Draven. "A day ago, you wouldn't have dared to speak to me in such a manner. No one would."

"A day ago, you weren't in the dungeon," Honzio said. "It's an unfamiliar experience for us all."

"Not for me." Svorgin crossed his arms over his broad chest. "This is the fifth dungeon I've been jailed in."

"You must be an important prisoner," Draven said, scanning him over, "to have been transported so many times."

As the single living soul who knew the whereabouts

of the legendary Golden Crown, Svorgin might very well be the most important prisoner in the Empire. Honzio recalled overhearing his late father, former Emperor Malus, plotting different torture methods to extract its location from the Savorian. Svorgin's secret was the key to his survival.

"Not transported. I broke out of the other dungeons."

"Broke out," Honzio repeated. "How?"

Draven narrowed his icy gray eyes on the Savorian, the same question emanating from his posture.

Svorgin shrugged. "It's simple."

"You are insinuating you could escape this dungeon as well?" Draven pushed to his feet. "Then what are you waiting for?"

Svorgin scoffed, meeting Draven's stare dead-on. "I had countless chances to escape. Do you think I would do so on account of you being here?"

"You remained here and accepted the torture when you had the opportunity to break out. Have you lost your mind?"

Honzio rose as well, wincing at the creak in his joints.

"I would have been hunted wherever I went and eventually trapped somewhere. The torture is worse in the beginning. At least here I have a bed." He motioned to the bunk. "And food."

"Then it seems you won't mind if I add a few more scars to your back," Draven spat.

Svorgin's nostrils flared. His scars weren't up for discussion. Honzio wasn't exactly thankful for the reminder of them either. The endless marks and open wounds welling with irritation on the Savorian's back were enough to make him turn for nights without a wink of sleep. Honzio placed his arm between them before a fight broke out.

"Aid us, and we will return the favor. When I'm emperor, you will live a free life."

Draven cleared his throat. "When *I* reclaim my rightful position as emperor, I shall reward you. Gold, jewels, name your price."

Svorgin watched them with disgust. "I am not a man to be bought. I don't want your tainted jewels and gold. And the word of nobility is worth less than dirt. I can never trust either of you."

Honzio grasped for his final card. "Then have faith in your sister's judgment."

Svorgin's gaze sharpened, and his jaw clenched.

"Aylis trusted me to find you. I will keep my word, whatever it is you want," Honzio promised, ensuring his face was earnest.

Draven stepped back, surrendering as his eyes darted between them. Svorgin hesitated. A moment turned to two and then three.

"I want my people freed from Prolus's reign. I want Savoria liberated. Can you do that?"

"With whatever power I have, once I reclaim the throne, I will march to Savoria and free your people."

"If you break your word, know that I will not rest till I spear you through."

"Fair enough," Honzio said. The moment seemed to miss something, some kind of finality. Honzio spat into his hand and extended it to Svorgin.

The Savorian's lips tugged downward, his eyes riveted on the saliva trickling down Honzio's palm.

"I know it is the left hand, but . . ." Honzio motioned toward his other marred arm.

Draven's chuckle filled the strained silence. "I see our dear prince has finally taken leave of his faculties." He grimaced, slapping Honzio's shoulder, and then hissed in a low voice, "What in the four kingdoms are you doing?"

"Sealing the agreement?" Honzio said, his hand still lingering in the air. "The Uluzar did this."

Svorgin's face cleared. "I see." He motioned Honzio forward.

Honzio neared, and Svorgin's calloused hand settled on his neck. Honzio found himself inadvertently leaning away. Svorgin yanked him close and knocked his head into Honzio's. Honzio groaned, agony momentarily blinding him.

"That is how we seal matters in my homeland."

"How pleasant." Honzio leaned over, taking deep breaths to ease out the pain. Draven's snickers were audible but out of focus. When his surroundings cleared, he saw Svorgin watching him.

"Are you prepared?"

"For what?" Honzio grumbled.

"To escape."

NATASSA
KARALIK EMPIRE

EXHAUSTION PULLED AT her limbs. Natassa's every breath was squeezed out of her as if a rock were pressed down on her chest. The tight rope around her wrists hauled her forward after the others. Bright sunlight shone through the gaps in the outstretching branches of the towering trees. Natassa searched for the light, holding on to the hope it provided. Her face was lifted upward, the glowing rays brushing across her skin. Her aching feet stumbled over a root obscured by the melting snow, and she gasped, returning to the world of misery and endless moss-green trees. A hand righted her, fingers drifting around her forearm and remaining there.

"Careful."

Natassa peered at the speaker. He was looking worse than before, but perhaps he continued to grow viler in her sight with every passing moment. His dark eyes glinted and were separated by a wide nose that rested over thick lips. He was smiling, seemingly attempting to put her at ease. His efforts were in vain. Natassa had no intention of interacting with the man who was the reason she was currently being dragged to the nearest market to be sold as a slave. She wrenched her arm out of her captor's grip.

"Don't touch me, you serpent."

He held up his hands in surrender, but his smile widened, revealing his fairly normal-looking teeth. She had been examining her captors during the never-ending trek, evaluating them, counting them, searching for a way or a moment to break free. There were fifteen Savagelanders, each one armed to the teeth, which themselves were sharpened to points. Most of them spoke in Savese. Just their leader, Sovor-ja, and the infuriating man glued to her side spoke the common Imperial dialect. And of those two, only the latter's Imperial was polished and without accent. And since she had seen his unsharpened teeth, she knew he differed from the others. He wasn't a Savagelander.

"Serpent?" An eyebrow tilted up. "I would prefer if you called me by my name. Yalnos."

"I only call those I consider human by their names."

He laughed, angling his head back. She wished she had her knives. She could have easily sliced open the large expanse of neck he revealed. Natassa blinked, her stomach turning at the thought. When had she become so prone to violent notions?

"Well, well, not only am I a serpent, but I am also

not deserving of a name?" He was purposely shortening his strides to match her pace.

Sweat trailed down Natassa's face despite the cold still lingering in the air. Strands of her hair dangled before her eyes. She blew at them but didn't succeed in moving them. Yalnos leaned in, his long fingers tucking the strands back. Natassa jerked away, alarmed by his touch and the fear of him seeing her Shadow Mark.

"Stay back," she hissed.

The crack of a whip echoed ahead of them. "Silence!"

Sovor-ja's sharp command was followed by cries of pain as the whips continued falling, slashing into the backs of the helpless prisoners. Natassa quickened her pace. She couldn't hold up the line. Whenever the prisoners' speed lessened, the whips would rise and snap down without mercy.

Time continued to pass. Natassa was unfortunate enough to have Yalnos rooted to her side. She ignored any more of his attempts to converse. She had seen him in her vision before. Natassa wondered if her shadows had been attempting to tell her something. Perhaps they'd been warning her as well as giving her an escape route by showing him. If she could use her shadows to manipulate him . . . Natassa grimaced, squeezing her eyes shut. Twisting people to her will was something that disgusted her to no end. Though she had done it for years in the past, she had done it unknowingly. But currently, it would be different. She would be purposely toying with emotions and thoughts. Every time she used her shadows, she felt like she lost parts of herself.

A cry snagged her attention. She leaned forward to

peer over shoulders. A woman huddled on the ground, forcing the rest of them to a stop. She gripped her ankle, and tears rolled down her dirt-streaked face. A man dropped to his knees before her, his eyes pleading with her.

"My heart, you must stand." He attempted to heft her up.

"I cannot." She wept. "I cannot go farther."

Natassa's chest ached at the despair lining their features. She scanned the surrounding Savagelanders. Their amused chuckles drifted around as they watched the distressed couple. Sovor-ja barked in Savese and stormed to the couple.

"Get moving," he snarled in Imperial.

The woman bit her lip, her chest heaving with the sob she was trying to contain. Sovor-ja lifted his whip. The leather was slick with blood. The man dove, covering the woman just as the whip came down. Natassa flinched when it connected with the torn fabric of his dirtied tunic. She saw his wince and could imagine the burning sting.

"You want to rest? Is that it?" Sovor-ja asked the shaking woman.

She sobbed. "Please . . ."

"In return for your demand, we will take something."

Fear circulated in her eyes. The man spoke instead. "Whatever your punishment is, take it from me."

Sovor-ja eyed him, his gaze calculating before he barked orders in Savese. Savagelanders grouped around the man, hauled him to his feet, and freed him from the rope connecting him to the others. Natassa watched uneasily, trepidation rising with every moment.

"No! What are you doing with him?" the woman screamed.

As he was dragged away, the man's fingers brushed her tearstained face. They forced him to a tree ahead. Natassa's breath hitched. She glanced at Yalnos. He was peering at her, completely unconcerned with the scene before them.

"What are they doing?" she asked, horrified.

He didn't respond. The Savagelanders bound the man to the tree, with his arms tied to the thick branches above him. Natassa and the others were shoved forward until they were a short distance behind the man. His back was to them, muscles tense with unease. Sovor-ja tossed his whip to another Savagelander.

Time seemed to slow as the Savagelander raised the whip and lashed it across the bound man's back. Another lash followed and then another. Natassa's ears buzzed. She heard distant screams and shouts, but she couldn't look away from the torture before her. She'd seen whippings before—her father had been very fond of them—but that didn't change the pain she felt for the innocents who paid the price. A tear slipped down her cheek. The man was stoic at first, but on the twentieth lash, he let out a roar filled with such anguish, Natassa could have sworn the leaves on the trees trembled. She could no longer hold herself back.

Natassa broke out of the line, heedless of the ropes binding her wrists. One step, then another. Arms circled her middle and dragged her back. She turned and slammed her bound fists on a chest, looking up to meet Yalnos's dark eyes. He shook his head, his silvery-brown hair falling over his forehead.

"Don't try it," he said, and she saw real worry in his gaze.

"Let go of me."

Her furious whisper was answered only by his grip tightening. Down the line, the other prisoners held the woman back. She was barely standing on her feet, sobs racking her form. Natassa's eyes shuttered closed, praying it would end. Another tear slipped from her lashes. The strikes continued until the screams of agony ceased. Sovor-ja shouted in Savese before switching to Imperial. The menacing smile on his lips told Natassa he wanted them to understand his next words.

"He is useless now. No one will spend a coin on him. Throw him in the road and let the scavengers feast."

The Savagelanders cheered and dragged the man away. Through Natassa's blurry gaze, she made out the bloody pulp that made up the man's back. They pulled him across dead leaves and snow, leaving a trail of red behind. Sovor-ja turned to face the prisoners.

"You have gotten your request," he told the woman, who stared ahead with a blank numbness. "We will camp here for the night."

Yalnos relinquished his hold, and Natassa sank to her knees. She couldn't wait on some wishful hope that she would be found. She had to save herself.

Honzio
Karalik Empire
The Grand Palace
Dungeons

THE COLD STONE beneath Honzio seeped into his thin linen shirt. He lay flat on his back, focusing on keeping his body still and holding his breath. His eyes were squeezed shut, and his lips formed a line as he concentrated. The sounds around him came into focus. Chains in the cell across from him rattled as prisoners were led out. Their cries of alarm rose within the compressed dungeon walls as they fought against the Uluzar dragging them up and out of the dungeon. They were either being taken to be executed or released; otherwise, who knew what the Uluzar had planned for them. Honzio's focus returned to appearing motionless as Svorgin and Draven called for assistance, yelling at the Uluzar. The dungeon door slammed closed, and a hand smacked against the iron bars, then came a familiar curse. Honzio's eyes flew open, finding Svorgin peering down at him before glancing at Draven gripping the cell door.

Honzio sighed. "This will not work."

"The act isn't very convincing. They didn't even look. Do you have another escape plan, Savorian?" Draven asked.

"The name is Svorgin. If you cannot manage that, Barinson works fine. And we have plenty of time to test other routes," Svorgin muttered. "Try again, *Mosori*."

"*Mosori*," Honzio repeated, tasting the feel of the foreign word on his tongue and wondering about its meaning.

"*Brother*," Draven answered before Svorgin could speak, and both their faces swiveled toward him. He shrugged. "I learned a few words. And I know you were referring to me as a prince sarcastically when you called me *Lsrar*."

"Draven, you surprise me," Honzio said. "There's more to you than what meets the eye."

Draven scoffed, turning away. A recollection struck Honzio. Draven's mother had been Savorian. He examined the former prince, who was staring out between the cell bars, his fingers tight around the metal. So there *was* a part of him that hadn't been lost to the dark. The man was holding on to the past. Perhaps the memory of his mother was the thing keeping him from fully turning into the monster he presented. Honzio pitied him, but he couldn't allow any more sympathy than that. He couldn't forgive the terrible crimes Draven had committed. Countless actions that had ended lives in gruesome ways. Hesten, Natassa's decoy. Hell, even his father.

"Try to breathe in slowly and hold your breath," Svorgin said. "Focus on something that keeps you calm."

Calm. The word echoed in his mind. Manos Xeni, his childhood tutor and a former True Manos at the palace, had listened as Honzio confessed his burdens and shared his fears. The old man had gifted him with a beaded necklace. The cool beads had rested against Honzio's skin beneath his shirt ever since.

When you are agitated, this will help. Each bead represents a breath.

Honzio had caressed the beads so much that the lacquered surfaces had dulled. They aided him in keeping his panic at bay when he was in enclosed areas.

"That's better," Svorgin said lowly.

Honzio remained silent, his lashes tangled together as he kept himself composed. Long moments passed as he continued to work on the act. The dungeon door creaked open, and the thud of boots approached.

"What's going on here?" The thick Uluzar accent garbled the words.

A boot nudged Honzio's side. A cue to remain still.

"He suddenly collapsed." Concern flooded Draven's voice. He added a contrived stutter to reinforce the worry.

Honzio contained a smile at the false emperor's false sincerity.

Somebody touched his neck, and then he heard Svorgin speak. "I can't feel a pulse."

The Uluzar muttered in his own language before switching to Imperial. "Don't fool around."

"This is a life and death matter."

The footsteps receded. Honzio blinked, his eyes half-lidded, taking in the blurry view of the Uluzar turning away.

Svorgin launched himself at the cell door, calling after him in a desperate last attempt. "What will you tell your chief when he learns you allowed Prince Honzio to die?"

The Uluzar paused. Honzio clamped his eyes shut as the man turned. Moments of breathless silence elapsed, and then the jingle of keys sounded. The cell door swung open with a groan.

A shadow fell over Honzio's face. He heard a sniff and felt stares burning into him. An itch probed his upper lip, and he nearly groaned with annoyance. Out of all blasted moments, it had chosen that one. He fought to ignore it, but he couldn't stop his lip from moving. The Uluzar released a startled yelp. Honzio opened his eyes and scrambled to his feet. The Uluzar retreated while reaching for his sword. But his exit was blocked.

Draven wrapped a thick arm around the Uluzar's neck and dragged him to the side. An audible snap followed. Honzio flinched as the man crumpled to the ground at Draven's feet, his neck twisted at an unnatural angle. Draven pulled the sword free, and Honzio could swear he heard three hearts beating as they all stared at each other. Svorgin's fists were clenched, his eyes darting between Draven and Honzio. Honzio glanced at the open cell door. Draven was the closest to it, and he had the upper hand. He could gut them both and escape alone. But then he lowered the blade.

"Well, Barinson, show us the way out."

The tension seeped from Honzio's shoulders. Svorgin nodded, his hands loosening, though he still moved past Draven with caution. They followed Svorgin out of the cell. They were nearing the stairs that led out of the dungeon when someone shouted in Savese. The words were vicious and rough. The sound of rushing footsteps neared, and the dungeon door crashed open. Torchlight flickered into view. Honzio turned, heading deeper into the dungeon with the others paces behind.

"*Goshsta*," Svorgin muttered, slipping into his native language under duress, and continued muttering what Honzio estimated were not pleasant phrases.

More Uluzar appeared at the top steps. Honzio retreated farther, wincing when angry Savese blared through the dungeon. The Uluzar had discovered their lifeless comrade. Honzio's outstretched hand hit a solid wall. They were at a dead end. The escape route was through the swarm of Uluzar on the verge of hunting them down. Honzio's fingers slammed against something cold. Metal. Then he smiled. The second entrance to the underground tunnels.

"Gentlemen," he began, his voice low, "I believe I've found our way out."

Velamir
Kingdom of Verin
Verintown

VELAMIR STORMED INTO the stables, ignoring the shouts behind him. The midday sun bored into his back before fading away as he found shelter under the roof of the reconstructed royal stables. He stopped at the stall at the far end, hearing an angry snort of greeting from the lancer horse within. Velamir entered the stall, not surprised to find Vandal in a mood. It had been weeks since he'd seen him. Weeks. Velamir couldn't remember the last time he'd been separated from his horse for that long. He ran his fingers over the soft shimmery coat. Vandal neighed, his head jerking up, his mane shaking, expressing his annoyance. Velamir patted his neck.

"I know, boy, I missed you too."

Velamir saddled him quickly, tightening the girth before reaching for the bridle.

"Velamir!"

Velamir closed his eyes at the shout. He'd thought he would have a few more moments before having to endure Finnean's attempts at swaying him.

"Four kingdoms, Velamir," Finnean exclaimed as he finally caught up. He leaned over, heaving in air. His new leather armor was rubbed to a shine, resting over a tan tunic. Brown breeches were tucked into well-constructed boots. Twin short swords crossed each other at his back. His black hair was trimmed close to his head, his equally dark beard groomed short. Velamir hadn't seen him looking so fine in all the time he'd known him. The badge on his chest was new as well. Captain of the Guard.

"I have no time to listen to your warnings, Finnean. I cannot wait any longer. Every moment is a chance of losing her. You should understand better than anyone."

Finnean flinched at the subtle reference to Krea's death and his grief over his lost love. "Velamir—"

"I know the roads are crawling with Tariqins. I know they could ambush me. I don't need to be told things I'm aware of."

Vandal sensed Velamir's agitated mood and dug his hooves into the straw-covered ground. Velamir took hold of the reins, turning to lead him out. Finnean stood in his path.

"I'm not trying to stop you, Velamir. I know you well enough to realize there is no possibility of that. I came to tell you the queen has called for volunteers to join you. They are gathered in the square."

"You know better than I do that no one will volunteer. They will call this a fool's errand."

Finnean's blue eyes shuttered as he looked down.

Velamir grimaced. "Tell me you didn't volunteer."

"I cannot allow you to go to your death. At least not alone."

Velamir reached out, placing a hand on his friend's shoulder. "You have a fresh start here. You have been promoted. Don't cast yourself aside for me."

"Velamir—" Finnean started.

"Goodbye, my friend."

Velamir patted his shoulder, and Finnean nodded solemnly before stepping aside. The clomp of Vandal's hooves echoed along the stone walkway as Velamir made his way to the square. A crowd was gathered before him. Velamir came to a stop, halting Vandal beside him. His horse shuffled uneasily at the noise coming from the restless people. Velamir peered over heads, focusing on the woman standing on a makeshift wooden platform. If there was one thing he admired about Queen Coralie, it was her dedication to her people. She wore the same modest apparel as the surrounding civilians. The only difference was the armor covering her chest and legs and the crown over her head of braided hair.

"Are there any others? Any other volunteers?"

Silence met her question as those gathered glanced at each other. They had lost enough in the war. Velamir knew they wouldn't bat an eye if he died. Some still saw him as an enemy. A former supporter of Prolus.

The crowd dispersed, and Velamir walked forward with Vandal trudging alongside him. The tall broad-shouldered man standing beside Coralie caught sight of him and nodded. After all the recent events, Velamir wasn't sure what to make of Mordon—*his cousin*—but it seemed one thing was clear: his loyalty was to Coralie and her alone. Velamir nodded back, holding his unrelenting stare. Coralie stepped off the platform, waving guards away when they moved to shadow her. She smiled as Velamir approached, though it was grim.

"Your Majesty." Velamir ducked his head in acknowledgment.

"I won't waste your time with talk, Alaric. I see you are prepared to leave." She eyed his horse. "Unfortunately, I could only secure two volunteers to assist you."

Velamir shrugged off the strange emotion his birth name evoked and focused on her words. "Two?"

Even that number surprised him when he hadn't expected a single person. Coralie jerked her chin behind him. Velamir glanced over his shoulder. Bear stood there, a grin pulling at the older man's lips. Velamir nodded gratefully. He should have known. Velamir scanned the young man standing at his former mentor's side, his eyes widening.

"Lore?" Velamir said, turning back to Coralie. "I cannot take him with me. He is so young, and this is dangerous. There is a possibility I will not return."

"I know," Coralie said. "But he is insistent. He wants to join you."

"Lore!" someone called, and Velamir turned, spotting Latimus pushing through the people drifting across the bridge into the town. His gaze was rooted to his brother. Velamir could see the worry in his posture. His eyes were reddened, and dark circles marked the skin beneath them. His face was sallow.

"You acted justly," Velamir told Coralie, "by not punishing Latimus for his father's crimes."

"Galva Blayton may have been a traitor, but that gives me no reason to harm his family," she responded. "Besides, I believe Latimus has tortured himself enough."

They watched as Latimus embraced his brother before gripping the younger boy's face and speaking to him lowly.

"And I handled the request you asked of me," Coralie said, and Velamir's attention snapped to her. "I sent a messenger to the Tariqin camp. We will negotiate for Jax's release. A prisoner exchange."

Velamir smiled for the first time that morning. He bowed his head. "You have my gratitude. I cannot tell you how much that means to me."

Velamir could not rest until Jax was rescued from that wretched camp. He couldn't live with that guilt.

"It is the least I can do. Without your help, Verintown would have fallen. This castle would not bear Verin's flag." Velamir followed her hand motion, seeing the green fabric billowing atop the castle towers high above. The imprint of an eagle with a heart dangling in its talons marked the flag. "Go now. Rest assured that I will do my best to save our friend."

Velamir nodded his appreciation and headed toward Bear. The Savorian flung an arm around Velamir's shoulders as he neared. His shoulder-length blond-gray hair rippled back in the breeze. Latimus was still speaking to his brother, clasping the young boy's shoulder, his face resigned.

"I will return before you know it, Latty."

Latimus swallowed. "I know." He lowered his head, blinking fast before pulling him into a rough hug. Lore returned it, his arms wrapping around Latimus, his expression vibrant and excited for the coming journey. Latimus looked up over his brother's shoulder and met Velamir's gaze. Velamir inclined his head. *I will take care of him*, he said wordlessly. Latimus nodded. He released Lore and stepped back.

"May your road be open and your journey swift," Latimus said, the farewell solemn despite the well wishes.

Velamir mounted Vandal. Bear and Lore did the same with horses provided by the castle mounts. Velamir clicked his tongue, and Vandal set off into a trot, riding over the drawbridge and through the reconstructing town. Once clear of the townspeople, Velamir nudged Vandal into a canter. The hoofbeats of the others signaled their presence behind him. They rode for hours, following the traces left on the ground. The melting snow made it easier to find the boot prints. Velamir glanced down at his hands gripping the reins, focusing on the bracelet circling his wrist. He recalled Natassa's saddened gaze as she told him how important it was to her, how her brother had given it to her. *I will find you, no matter what it takes, no matter how far I must go. I will find you.*

Natassa

Karalik Empire

NATASSA PEEKED THROUGH her lashes at the sleeping forms around her. Other than the occasional snore, the night was still as a corpse. The trees overhead blocked out the view of the moon and stars with their long spidery branches. The fire the Savagelanders crafted had sizzled to embers. Natassa rose to a sitting position, glancing at the Savagelander on watch leaning against a tree trunk. Sleep had overtaken him so deeply that drool escaped his mouth. That was her chance. She pulled her hands out of the rope she had loosened over the long hours of waiting. Her wrists burned, and she winced at their raw state.

Natassa climbed to her feet and held her breath as she took a step. Her boot squished into the soft snow. Natassa

froze, her eyes darting about. The Savagelander on watch rubbed a hand beneath his nose before the snores started up again. She exhaled, taking careful steps away from the sleeping group. Guilt turned in her stomach as she walked. How could she leave the other prisoners behind? Natassa turned back. She spotted Yalnos sleeping near the edge of the camp. His arms were propped up beneath his head, and his face appeared settled, as if he were having the most relaxing slumber in his life, as though he lay upon a bed of silk rather than twigs and cold snow.

Natassa's focus snared on the sword resting a heartbeat beside him. Her fingers itched to close around the hilt. She could use it to cut the prisoners' bindings. She calculated the time it would take and the amount of risk. There was a Savagelander lying near each prisoner. She wouldn't succeed in freeing them without awakening the camp. Natassa backed away, her fingers closing into a fist. *I'm sorry*, she thought as she turned.

She could barely feel her legs as she advanced with caution. The icy air bit into her hands and face. Tears of relief burned in her eyes once the red sparks of the dying campfire faded from view. She moved faster, escape her only thought. A stitch in her side slowed her pace. She pressed a hand to a trunk to catch her balance and inhaled deeply. *Keep going*, she told herself. *Keep going.*

A hand clamped over her mouth, and her resulting scream was muffled. She thrashed, her muted shouts useless.

"Shh. You don't want the others to hear. You know what happens to runaway slaves?"

Natassa closed her eyes. She knew exactly what happened to runaways. Even her father's practice had been to murder them. The hand dropped away before seizing her arms in a vicious hold and spinning her around. Yalnos peered at her. He tilted his head.

"I can give you away, or I can save your life. You're indebted to me."

A shiver shuddered through her at his calculating look. Natassa sucked in air and steadied herself. It seemed her shadows would be her only means of escaping. She focused on Yalnos while seeking her shadows' presence. The Lure, the shadow of persuasion, came to the forefront of her mind. She could almost feel the shadows' ghostlike hands brushing her neck.

"You will help me."

Yalnos frowned, confusion creasing lines between his brows.

"Help me escape."

A thick sweetness dripped into her voice as the Lure sent persuasion through her, smooth as honey. Darkness poured into her mind like water as she released the dam blocking the shadows' path. She sucked in a breath at the intoxicating sensation she'd been resisting. *More*, she thought, searching for a way to cross into Yalnos's mind. But a thick wall blocked her path, and try as she might, even the Lure couldn't tear it down.

Yalnos wavered. "I . . ."

"You will help me escape."

He looked uncertain, but he couldn't take his eyes

off her. Then he did something that surprised her. He laughed, an amused chuckle that put her on edge.

"You think I will fall for that? Shadow Manos do not affect me."

Natassa was stunned. How did he know? She touched her forehead, ensuring her hair still concealed the mark.

"I knew you were one the moment I set my eyes on you. I would be a fool if I didn't. One isn't raised by a Shadow Manos, experiencing all their tricks, to emerge gullible, do they?"

Natassa retreated a pace. She couldn't outrun him, drained as she was. She glanced around, searching for something she could use as a weapon.

"Your father was a Shadow Manos?" Her voice sounded panicked, but she had to keep him talking, place his focus elsewhere.

He clicked his tongue. "No, my parents were beggars. I abandoned them as soon as I stole enough coin and found refuge with a noblewoman. My Lady Guin raised me. I thought she was the most powerful Shadow Manos there was until I encountered you. You have an incredible draw, much harder to resist."

Lady Guin. It was a common name, yet something about it pulled at Natassa. She'd known dozens of Guins in the palace court. Leaves rustled, and Yalnos spun around, a hand falling to his weapon.

"We must return to camp. Now."

Natassa turned and darted in the opposite direction. He estimated her move and caught hold of her arm, then yanked her back. He placed a finger to his lips, his dark eyes flashing angrily. Then his expression settled, and his gaze narrowed on her head. He shoved her hair back. A sharp breath escaped him.

"You . . ." He paused. "The Golden Pheonix. You are the phoenix from legends."

Natassa forced a laugh. "I'm just a Shadow Manos."

"No, Shadow Manos marks do not glow like this." His smile grew wide, revealing all his teeth.

Revulsion crawled through her at the predatory way he was peering at her. He gripped her arm and pulled her back through the trees. Shouts broke out and grew louder as they neared the camp. Yalnos's fingers grasped her arm like a claw. As soon as the campfire came into view, Yalnos cursed. Mist-like forms clothed in white robes were attacking the Savagelanders. Their moves were so elegant, it almost seemed as if they were dancing.

Natassa looked down, spotting a thick branch resting near her feet. She leaned over and curled her fist around it. She moved fast, smacking the back of Yalnos's head with the wood. He dropped like a sack of potatoes. Natassa returned her stare to the camp, where the Savagelanders lay in bound heaps around the fire. The white-garbed figures were in the process of unbinding the prisoners. Natassa sensed they were harmless. Despite attacking the Savagelanders, they hadn't wounded a single one, instead knocking them out of their senses. She would have better luck approaching them for help than staying alone.

She walked toward them, and several of the robed figures turned to watch her approach. At the sight of one of them, she froze in her tracks: a woman wielding a dangerously curved knife. Natassa's heart almost stopped. Those eyes, that startling shade of green. They were Velamir's eyes.

Honzio
Karalik Empire
The Grand Palace
Dungeons

"Go, go, go," Draven barked out.

Honzio fumbled with the handle and shoved the lever down. Draven pushed past him into the dark void awaiting them. Honzio followed, with Svorgin just behind. Metal clanged as Svorgin shut the trapdoor closed. He crept forward, catching a glint of light ahead—the shine of Draven's blade. Honzio swallowed. Down here in these dark tunnels, no one would witness a thing if Draven murdered them in cold blood. Honzio remained light on his feet, waiting for the slightest movement from Draven showing his intention to skewer them. But if he were planning such a move, he would wait until they had left the tunnels. He couldn't make it out without a guide.

Draven halted, allowing Honzio to pass him. Honzio felt along the tunnel wall, trying to pinpoint their location through memory. He heard a sudden shout and spun around.

"What is this new blighted hell?" Draven groaned. "Something bit me."

"There is no time to waste," Honzio replied, amusement twisting the corner of his mouth.

He continued forward, holding his good arm against the wall. He counted his breaths and steps as he navigated his way to the exit. The sound of boots sloshing along the water-drenched ground echoed behind him. Honzio blinked, but it didn't make a difference. He was blind to his surroundings. Sweat trickled down his face, and his breath came quicker. That familiar tightness in his chest started, accompanied by the drum of panic. He had to be calm. He had to overcome it. He released the wall to touch the beads around his neck and exhaled.

"Why have we stopped?"

Svorgin's voice pulled him from his panicked state. He cleared his throat and wiped at the perspiration on his forehead. Instead of answering, Honzio forced himself to advance. Soon, he felt a little nook in the tunnel wall, indicating the approaching stairs. Honzio staggered his way up them. He pushed at the metal overhead, attempting to lift it. A groan slipped free, but the ceiling didn't budge. He retreated. The fear crawled back around him. He was cowering in the bottom of the tandoor oven once again. No sound except his sobs, no sight except shadows, no scent except that of lingering smoke.

He choked on a breath and dropped his hand.

"Lift this," he ordered the man closest to him.

The trapdoor lifted a second later, and light pooled onto them. Honzio inhaled a freeing breath. Sunlight shone on Svorgin. The Savorian paused, staring up at the brightness. His blond lashes glowed with the light, his midnight eyes shining blue as the Lagrima Sea. Svorgin hefted himself up and leaned down, extending a hand to Draven. The former prince accepted it and grunted on the way up. Honzio was next. Svorgin reached down. Honzio stared at the rough lines marking his palm. The Savorian nodded at him. Honzio took his hand and was up in an instant, leaving the dark tunnels behind. Honzio stumbled onto the snowy ground and shuddered. It didn't matter how many times he had traveled through the tunnels; they still carried the same heavy weight. The same taste of fear.

"Are you all right, *Mosori?*" Svorgin asked.

Honzio nodded, inhaling the freshness of the surrounding trees. *I am now.* The Savorian continued staring at him, making him uncomfortable.

"Of course he's all right. He wasn't the one bitten by a rabid creature."

Honzio glanced down at Draven sprawled out on the ground gripping his ankle. Honzio kneeled, motioning for Draven to remove his hands.

"Snakebite," Honzio said, examining the pronged marks.

"What?" Draven's fingers edged toward the sword

resting beside him. If Honzio didn't play his cards right, he would end up on the end of that blade.

"The tunnel snakes are poisonous. Those who know of the antidote are scarce."

"My healers in Ayleth are skilled. They will know how to fix it."

Honzio smiled, hoping the man wouldn't see the bluff. "I wouldn't have such faith. Your teeth will rot. Your skin will yellow and come off in gruesome patches. You will fade, slowly and horribly."

"That's enough!" Draven grimaced, closing his eyes. "What is the antidote?"

"Ah. A reasonable question. It is not a knowledge parted with lightly."

"What do you want?" Draven ground out.

Honzio's first clear thought after exiting the tunnels had been to sneak into the city and seek shelter with Moralis. Go into hiding. The coward's route. But how long would he be able to do so? He would be putting Moralis's and Aylis's lives at risk; that is, if he even managed to infiltrate the city without being spotted. No, the day he entered Hearcross would be the day he took back his city, not cowered within it.

"Svorgin and I will accompany you to Ayleth, where I will share my knowledge of the antidote with your True Manos. In return, you will supply me with soldiers and swear fealty to me as the true emperor."

Draven shook his head before Honzio even finished speaking. Horrified laughter broke free from his chest as he stood, hopping on one leg. His chuckles drifted between the trees surrounding them. Draven's smile faded as he glanced between Honzio and Svorgin, who were both watching him without the slightest hint of amusement.

"You're serious," he realized.

Honzio nodded. "Very."

"I will allow you to journey to Ayleth and seek safety in my castle, but no more. I will not waste my soldiers on a ridiculous endeavor, and I surely won't bow to you."

"Your choice. Every moment is costing you."

Draven inhaled through clenched teeth. "Fine, I agree. Let's just get on with it."

Honzio wasn't a fool to believe Draven's empty promise, but at least this would get him to Ayleth and out of the lion's den. It would buy him time.

"First, we need horses," Svorgin said. "And I know just where to get them."

T**HE OPEN EXPANSE** of empty land faced him, but the image of the hundreds of corpses wouldn't leave Latimus's mind. His father had been the cause. Latimus's fist clenched. A man he'd respected, placed on a podium far above his head, had done something so despicable. He cursed every day he'd called him father. Galva Desor Blayton had ruined his family and honor, torn it to shreds in a travesty Latimus feared he could never repair. He'd made it a daily ritual to leave Verintown and the castle grounds and ride about the battlefield to remind himself of mistakes he could never forget.

The sound of hoofbeats drew his attention. His own horse's ears twitched at the noise. Latimus turned, spying a man clad in leather armor approaching.

The soldier halted when he neared. "Captain Blayton, Her Majesty, Queen Coralie, summons you."

Latimus winced. He no longer revered his family's name. He despised it more than he ever had anything. He longed to trample it beneath his feet until his disgust was vanquished. But he remained calm and gave the soldier a nod.

"I will be there."

Half an hour later, Latimus found himself outside the throne room doors, waiting for permission to enter. He stared at the scuffs marking his boots before darting a glance around the empty hall behind him. Everything was the same and yet changed. The same tapestries were mounted to the walls. The same floors were newly polished beneath his feet. But the air was different. Latimus recalled the old days when he'd come to the castle to visit his father. The arrogance and pride he'd carried upon his shoulders as he walked through the halls. Latimus never thought his father, the mountain of his world, would come to a crumbling heap. The doors swung open, and Latimus spotted Finnean exiting. Finnean paused, eyeing Latimus with concern.

"Everything fine?"

Latimus nodded, his mouth thinning as annoyance sprouted within him. He didn't want to be pitied or viewed as a wounded child. Yet he had no way of escaping the hellish pain his father had wrought.

"Yes," he said shortly.

"Queen Coralie is waiting to see you."

Finnean patted his shoulder as he passed. Latimus strode forward and entered the throne room. The queen wasn't sitting upon the throne as he'd expected but was standing beside a large window overlooking the castle grounds. Latimus made his way toward her and stopped a short distance away.

"Come," she said, beckoning him to her side.

Latimus crossed the remaining distance and joined her beside the window. The courtyard below was buzzing with life as the castle residents drifted about, minding their business. The clanging of a blacksmith at work could be heard even from the height they stood at. Latimus could see beyond the castle walls to the town below. They were recovering, healing from the brutality Prolus had inflicted on their land and loved ones.

Latimus felt Coralie's gaze on him and turned toward her. He placed a hand on his chest and inclined his head. "Your Majesty, you called for me?"

Coralie nodded, her expression unreadable as she scanned him. Latimus wondered what she saw when she looked at him. He wondered if she noticed the same things he did whenever he caught his reflection in the mirror, in the water, on any reflective surface: cowardly flitting eyes the color of wood, thin unsmiling lips, unruly hair drifting over his ears, and most of all, the fear that burned brighter than the candelabras in the palace halls. The fear that he would never overcome this humiliation.

"The town is coming together."

Latimus made a noise of agreement. "So are its people."

Coralie returned her knowing gaze to him. "Not all."

Latimus lowered his head. Shame burned his neck. He had no pride left to allow him to meet the eyes of those who knew of his father's betrayal.

"General Zenrelius is preparing to make the return journey to Ondalar. As you know, Ondalar is enduring a harsh trial. They lost their king, and a new leader must be crowned. They require the general's presence there."

Latimus remained silent, absorbing the information.

"You must know of the agreement Verin now has with Ondalar. Zenrelius is bringing my proposal of allying the kingdoms with a closer bond to his new king."

"Closer bond?" Latimus darted a glance at Coralie. The queen watched him carefully, her bronze skin glowing in the sun shining through the window.

"If accepted, High Lord Genvor's daughter will be given to a Verin noble in marriage."

"And forgive my question, but what does this have to do with me?"

"I want you to go with him. If the proposal is accepted, you will be the groom of the potential bride."

Latimus's jaw dropped open, shock causing him to stutter.

"You will be Verin's ambassador," the queen told him.

Latimus had wanted to be an ambassador for so long. But that had been before. Although he was being offered this chance, it didn't come with the sweet taste of victory he'd always expected. But Coralie was queen, and her orders weren't to be defied. He was already walking the plank because of his father. He had to do something, and this would earn him a chance to reclaim his family honor. To once again be a worthy and prominent Blayton.

"As you wish, Your Majesty."

Jax
Kingdom of Devorin
Castle Yakh

THE IMAGES PASSING before his eyes were hazy and swift. Velamir was there, standing before him and giving him that reassuring smile. Then he was gone. A pair of violet eyes peered at him. A woman called out to him. *Wake up.* Lissa's voice was soft as her hands cupped his cheeks. *Wake up!* Jax exhaled, trying to force his eyes open, but a dark wall blocked his vision. Voices drifted closer and closer until the inaudible mumbling formed coherent words. His lids were like impenetrable ice frozen together. Breath fanned his face, and the distress that filled his gut made him squeamish.

"How's your experiment coming along?" The familiar tone sickened him further.

There was no reply. A strange numbing cold seeped into his limbs. Jax struggled to move as the feeling spread over his chest and tangled around his throat. He shuddered, his lips trembling. A voice spoke, startlingly clear in his mind. *Awaken, pet.*

Jax's eyes snapped open, and the tight tension in his chest eased. He panted, focusing on the form leaning over him. Two clouded blue eyes watched him from over thin pale lips. Jax's horror returned as memories assailed his mind. The queen. The queen of Devorin. His new jailer. He attempted to move but found his wrists and ankles bound down with iron, fastened to the long board beneath him. She laughed, her mouth stretching wide, revealing a row of pearly teeth. Jax couldn't keep the disgust from his face. He'd never in his life found a smile to be horrifying, but in that moment, hers was the stuff of nightmares. Jax closed his eyes to the view and jerked his face aside until his cheek pressed to the wooden board.

"He's coming along nicely," she said. Her voice was much softer and harder to decipher when she spoke aloud. She rose to her full height and turned to face the other figure.

The person stepped closer, the light from the roof of the tower highlighting his features. It took Jax a moment to place him. Smaller build, average height, gleaming blue eyes, and graying wavy hair. General Winston. But he'd died, hadn't he? Jax swallowed as more memories came forth. Winston had fooled them all and broken their spirits, most of all Velamir's. He'd poisoned himself and planned his own death to urge them on a mission solely for revenge. He'd used them. Him, Velamir, even Quintus. And Lissa.

A sharp burning sizzled in his chest. The pain of his shattered heart. It had broken into too many pieces; it was too fractured to mend. He shivered, a soft sob racking his frozen form. He could see her so vividly, the last torturous image of her stored forever in his mind for him to relive over and over. Her body falling back, the sharp branch spearing her. The gasp slipping from her parted lips, the pain in her beautiful eyes. The snowflakes lingering on her lashes and jet-black hair.

Never stop being the hero, Jax.

Her last words to him. Jax squeezed his eyes closed, and a single tear slipped free. He clenched his shackled hands. How could he be a hero when he wanted to murder them? Winston, Quintus, Vykus. Every single one of them.

"Such rage."

The queen's eerie focus returned to him. She held a large goblet tucked between bone-like fingers. It was as if her skin were stretched beyond its limits to cover the skeleton beneath. She appeared to be a walking corpse. The fancy dress and overdone hairstyle were a desperate grasp at life and beauty. Her brows lowered. She seemed to sense his thoughts, or perhaps she was reading his mind. She leaned over again, bringing the rim of the goblet to his mouth. Jax resisted, knowing it was poison. She persisted until the contents slipped down his throat. He choked on the vile liquid. His vision blurred, and the two figures became dark dots. Then his thoughts receded until he returned to the numb absent state he'd awoken from.

Natassa
Kingdom of Devorin
Sok Town

Torches flickered in the darkness as the white-robed figures focused on her, wariness in their stances. Some of them moved to approach her, but the green-eyed woman lifted a hand. They halted at once.

"I mean you no harm," Natassa started, unsure if she should use her shadows to convince them. "I was taken prisoner by these Savagelanders and was attempting to escape."

"Well done. You freed yourself and left us behind," one prisoner muttered. "Why did you return?"

Guilt cleaved her, and she winced. She opened her mouth to answer when the green-eyed woman cut in.

"Any who seek shelter with the Elders are welcome."

"The Elders?" Natassa whispered. The secret order she had intended to find ever since she'd learned about them from Manos Xeni in the Grand Palace.

The green-eyed woman nodded. "We cannot linger here. Let us make for the town."

Natassa traveled somewhere in the middle of the large group. The other prisoners kept as much distance as they could from her, some shooting her dirty glances. Natassa avoided their stares and instead examined the woman in the lead. She wondered if she simply missed Velamir so much that she was seeing parts of him in others. Natassa wished she could see more of her features to dismiss her doubts, but like the other robed figures, a thick fabric covered all but her startling eyes.

The woman held up a hand, and they stopped. Natassa peered forward, spotting a gate ahead. The entrance to Sok Town. The Elders moved swiftly, removing their ghostlike robes. They appeared as common civilians beneath the robes in tasteless brown apparel with marks of Devorin blue. They kept their faces covered. A sword hung on each of their belts.

As the woman urged them forward, Natassa took in the houses rising crookedly through the gates. But the most eye-catching sight was far ahead: a winding tower that shot up so high, it looked like it could brush the clouds. Natassa blinked in amazement at the stone peak glittering under the moonlight.

"The queen's lair."

Natassa's gaze snapped to the green-eyed woman's and found her watching her.

"The highest tower in Devorin, if not the Empire."

Natassa had never been to Devorin. She knew what everyone else in the palace did. The queen of Devorin was a mysterious woman. She lived in darkness and mourning ever since she'd lost her husband. It was rumored she had a terrible illness, one that never seemed to go away. Natassa had never seen her in person, as the queen had attended none of the palace celebrations. Natassa wondered if she used her sickness as an excuse. But Emperor Malus had never batted an eye at her lack of appearance. Her representatives always brought the owed tax and plenty of glittering gifts to bury any resentment.

"Queen Guin has crafted quite a reputation for being a recluse."

The words startled Natassa. Queen Guin. Guin. Could it be the same Guin that Yalnos had referred to—the Lady Guin he said had raised him? But if that were the case, that would make the queen of Devorin a Shadow Manos. Natassa glanced behind her, searching for signs of pursuers. But the forest was still.

"Keep your heads down," the green-eyed woman instructed.

Once they'd crossed through the gates, the woman brought them to a secluded corner. The Elder members surrounded the group.

"We have delivered you safely into town. Now it is time for you to decide if you wish to go your own way or come with us. Whoever leaves will be given a pouch of gold."

Glances darted within the group before the former prisoners began nodding. The green-eyed woman nodded as well, and another Elder dropped coin purses into extended hands. Smiles burst across faces—a drastic change from their sullen expressions. The newly freed people dispersed into the town. Natassa watched them leave and then realized she was the only one who had remained. The green-eyed woman's careful gaze examined her.

"And why have you stayed?"

"I need your help. I've been searching for the Elders for a long time."

A thick brow shot up, almost disappearing beneath the fabric wrapped around the woman's head. "How did you come to know of us?"

Natassa hesitated. "Manos Xeni. Manos Xeni told me to find the Elders. That they could assist me with my predicament."

The Elder members glanced at each other after she said the name. The green-eyed woman's steel gaze never wavered.

"Come with us."

Natassa followed her and her companions as they led the way through twisted alleys and crooked pathways. They stopped before a small house with a smoking chimney. The woman rapped her knuckles on the wood. A deep voice spoke in reply.

"How does the world unite?"

Natassa shivered, tugging her arms around herself as a sharp wind ruffled her threadbare clothes.

"With justice," the woman replied.

"Where is justice?"

"With courage."

"Where is courage?"

The companions all placed their hands over their

chests. Natassa watched in fascination as the woman closed her eyes.

"In the heart."

The wooden door creaked open, and they were ushered inside. Natassa nearly sighed as the warmth from a crackling fireplace settled in her bones. A set of comfortable chairs took up one corner of the chamber, and a curtained window was positioned on the other. It was cozy.

"Where are we?" Natassa asked.

The green-eyed woman turned toward her, removing the cloth over her nose and draping it over her shoulder. Natassa was struck again by how much she resembled Velamir. She was slim and tall. Her skin was pale in contrast to Velamir's olive complexion, most likely due to the cold Devorin air and darker days. Her nose was thin and sloped up gracefully, whereas Velamir's was dented from being broken.

"The place you were searching for," the woman responded. "I am Aria."

Natassa dipped her head in acknowledgment. "And I am—"

The deep voice that had called to them from behind the door cut her off. "Well, well, welcome to the humble abode of the Elders."

She turned, mouth slackening at the familiar face. A sense of déjà vu washed over her as she recalled his last words to her. *I have a feeling we will meet again in the near future.*

Rost, the merchant she and Krea had rescued, smiled and inclined his head. "What brings you here, Natassa Hartinza?"

Velamir

Kingdom of Verin

THE TRACES WERE gone. The Savagelanders must have caught on to being pursued and removed the evidence. Velamir's hands fisted around his reins, and Vandal reared, his legs kicking into the air. Clumps of wet dirt shot off his hooves. Velamir dismounted. He kneeled in the snow and raked his hands over the ground, searching for something, anything. His fingers dug into the dirt in desperation as his eyes roved in endless motion for a sign.

"Lad," Bear said, his tone gentle. "Lad, we need to rest."

Velamir ignored him. Bear's voice was a dull wind pressing on him. He couldn't hear him. Instead, his thoughts turned elsewhere. They turned to the dark places he'd been avoiding. Glimpses of Natassa, bleed-

ing and wounded, sprang into his mind. He shook the images away, refusing to submit to them.

"I must have missed something. Somewhere." His frustration pushed him forward, and he returned to Vandal's side.

"Lad, look at me!" Bear yanked on his arm, turning him.

Velamir met his former mentor's worried frown.

"We cannot go any farther."

Velamir tried to speak, but Bear cut him off.

"We have traveled nonstop for hours, lad. The moon is high. Night has fallen. You will kill yourself this way. If you do not care for your own well-being, at the very least, care for the horses. For that wee one."

Velamir's eyes darted to Lore, who was watching uneasily. He was exhausted. It was plain to see in his hunched posture and sweat-soaked clothes. Guilt churned within Velamir as he looked at the horses. They were breathing heavily, clouds of air erupting from their nostrils. Perspiration drenched their coats. He returned his focus to Bear.

"I'm sorry," he said. "I lost myself."

Bear's blue eyes softened, and he squeezed Velamir's arm. "I know."

They set up camp. Velamir tended to Vandal and the other horses while Bear and Lore built a fire. They warmed themselves by the flickering flames, eating pieces of dried jerky. Velamir ate in silence, feeling Bear's worried stare on him. Lore filled the emptiness for them. His endless chatter was a pleasant welcome to escape the worries holding Velamir captive.

"Thank you for letting me come along, Galva—Captain—" Lore stopped. "What should I call you?"

"Velamir is fine."

Lore beamed. "Excellent. This is my first mission. I must say, I was a bit nervous, but you are an outstanding leader. Though, I haven't seen you in action much. Well, there was that time during the jousting tournament." He tapped his chin and then waved his hand through the air. "But that was over too quickly. We never even crowned a victor. Can you imagine? The first time in so many years, Verin's tournament had no victor. The castle folk were talking about it for days."

Velamir stoked the fire with a branch. "I'm sure they were."

"They were also talking about you and General Boltrex. His pain is no longer, his glory remembered." Lore whispered a prayer before continuing. "Is it true that he's your father?"

Velamir nodded, tracing the scar by his ear, and Lore's eyes shot wide open.

"So the rumors *are* true. I also heard your rightful name is Alaric."

"Lad," Bear started, noticing Velamir tense.

"I apologize." Lore winced. "I shouldn't have pried."

"Leave him," Velamir said. "I need to get used to the truth. Yes, my name was Alaric."

"I must say, I prefer Velamir. It's a heroic name. Alaric . . ." Lore shook his head, making a gagging noise. "Too common, and I used to have a friend named Alaric until he stole my apple pie. My mother makes heavenly apple pies." Lore lifted his eyes to the sky and sighed before glancing back at them. "What was I saying?"

"The lad stole your pie," Bear provided, sharpening his axe with an amused smile.

"Ah, yes. But the point was that the name Alaric gives me a foul taste in my mouth whenever I hear it. No disrespect, Galva—Velamir."

"None taken. I'm not much of a fan of it myself."

"It must have been terrible losing General Boltrex right after reuniting," Lore said, his features downcast. "I lost my father too. I hear people talking in the castle and the town, saying vile things about him but falling silent when I pass. He may have been a traitor, but he was still my father." Lore wiggled his boots. "These were his. They were a gift from a talented cobbler. I admired them from the moment he got them. He told me once I was big enough to fit them, they would be mine."

Velamir's heart ached at the solemness in his tone.

"They still don't fit properly. But at least I have a part of my father with me. Do you have something from your father?"

Velamir opened his mouth to reply in the negative when he remembered the letter tucked in his tunic. It had been hidden away ever since Coralie had given it to him. He wasn't brave enough to see his father's last words, his final goodbye.

"So, this girl must be mighty important," Lore said, when Velamir didn't answer. "Who is she? A nobleman's daughter?"

"She shouldn't have to be a nobleman's daughter to be deemed important enough to rescue. Her being in danger and requiring our aid is reason enough. Titles and crowns are meaningless. What truly matters is our love for each other, for our fellow brothers and sisters. Our rescue of her shouldn't be determined by if she is the richest or poorest person in the Empire."

"Whoa," Lore said, awestruck. "That was some poetic thing you did there." Then he leaned forward, his eyebrows tilting conspiratorially. "Are you sure you aren't in love with her?"

Velamir chuckled at the boy's enthusiasm.

"Oh, he's in love all right." Bear snickered.

"Is it a secret?" Lore asked. Then he winked. "I promise I won't tell."

Velamir shook his head, finishing the jerky in his hand. "Get some sleep. I will take watch."

"Be sure to wake me," Lore said, but he was already yawning.

The boy settled down, curling on his sleeping roll, and in just a few minutes was fast asleep. Velamir watched him, a strange fondness growing inside him. If he'd had a brother, would he have been like Lore?

Velamir leaned back, his eyes darting down to the corded bracelet around his wrist. He stared at it, wondering how Natassa was. Was she cold? Was she in pain? His eyes closed at the merciless images tugging at his mind. If even one of those Savagelanders laid a finger on her, he would be their reckoning.

"You will find her, lad."

Velamir glanced at Bear, who was lying on his back, his hand gripping tight to a small figurine. Velamir recalled him holding that same carving many times in the past. During moments when he'd thought he was alone, sadness pulling at his features, he'd held the carving like it was the only thing keeping him from falling to pieces.

"What is it?" It was the first time he'd dared to ask.

Bear sighed a deep rumble of breath as he passed the carving to him. Velamir took it in a light grip, tracing the worn edges of the figurine. Velamir wondered how many times Bear had polished it, kept it smooth. The carving was of a Savorian warrior brandishing an axe and a lethal-appearing roar.

"My son made it for me," Bear said softly. "The month after he was apprenticed. He told me I was the bravest warrior he'd ever seen."

Velamir's mouth tugged downward as he listened to the sorrow burdening his former mentor.

"Who knows what he's had to face? If he's even alive." Bear's gaze filled with the flickering flames from the fire. "I had no choice but to leave them all behind. He promised me he would protect them in my absence. It's too much of a burden on such a young lad."

"You will find him," Velamir said, gazing into the night. "We will find them."

Honzio
Karalik Empire

"WHAT PRECISELY ARE we doing here?"

Honzio's question lingered unanswered in the evening air. He glanced at the two men on either side of him. Both stared at the empty land below. Draven seemed annoyed, and Svorgin looked focused, a muscle ticking in his jaw as he waited. Honzio sighed, peering over the sloping hill peppered with bushes they were crouching behind. A small farmhouse with a larger barn stood planted on the land below, and animals dotted the area. Honzio grimaced as he took in the sight of the underfed horses.

"Those are the horses we will be *taking*?" Honzio refused to say *stealing*.

"The older the horses get, the less he has use of them and the less he feeds them," Svorgin spat. His arms were

buried in the melting snow, his belly flat to the ground as he watched the land below. "He keeps his prized stallions in the barn."

Before Honzio could ask whom he spoke of, Svorgin suddenly let out a jumble of harsh-sounding words in Savorian. Over the hours in his company, Honzio had pinpointed his favorite swear word. *Goshsta*. He'd asked him what it meant, and the Savorian had scratched his neck, appearing uncomfortable before translating. *Mittens.*

Mittens, Honzio had repeated.

They weren't ordinary, and neither was their owner. They belonged to a kind nana who had a devious side no one expected. She used to rob the villages, leaving only an allusive mitten. Svorgin had grimaced. *It's a bit hard to explain, but you grasp the essence of the fable.*

Honzio and Draven had been speechless.

"There he is." Svorgin nodded his chin forward.

Honzio squinted his eyes, trying to focus on whoever Svorgin was seeing. He wondered at the man's sight. He had heard Savorians had stronger eyesight—something to do with the enchanted lake water in the center of the island. Honzio had assumed it was a myth, but he was realizing that the things he thought to be stories were all coming true.

"There, by the barn."

Honzio spotted a grizzled older man carrying a scythe.

"My old master," Svorgin said bitterly, his mouth curving into a sneer. "He bought me a few years ago. Chained me for days to his barn. In the dead of winter."

More swears passed through his lips. "I nearly froze to death. The wood chopping he made me do probably saved my life. Kept the blood circulating."

"Such a devastating tale. Should I spill a few tears to add to the heartbreak? You aren't unique. Most Savorian slaves go through similar treatment," Draven grumbled. "I'm not sure if you two are aware, but I currently have poison spreading throughout my body."

Svorgin's lips thinned in response, sparks erupting in his eyes as he seemed to keep himself from strangling Draven.

"Don't worry, Draven. It's a slow-acting poison. You should be able to arrive in Ayleth intact. Well, you may be missing a few fingers, but—"

"Barinson," Draven hissed, interrupting Honzio. "Whatever your plan is, I suggest you do it now."

"The sword," Svorgin replied. "Give it to me."

Draven gripped the hilt, refusing to budge.

"Give him the weapon," Honzio said. "If you die because of your stubbornness, what use will it be to you?"

Draven slowly extended the sword, and just when it touched Svorgin's waiting hand, the false emperor's grip on it tightened. "If you deceive me, know that I will do everything in my power to destroy you."

"You need to come up with more original lines, Draven," Honzio said. "You are starting to sound cliché."

Draven glared at him before releasing the weapon into Svorgin's hand. The Savorian glanced at Honzio as he rose to his feet.

"Follow me, *Mosori*."

Honzio moved as quickly as he could to keep pace with Svorgin. The farmer became clearer the closer they came. He remained by the barn, still holding the scythe. He seemed to be examining the sharpness of the blade. Honzio's muscles tensed as he glanced at Svorgin, who was stalking toward the farmer with no intention of stopping. Hearing the thuds of their shoes against the ground, the farmer turned.

"Who's there?"

He stilled at the sight of them. Honzio and Svorgin slowed, stopping a short distance from the farmer. The man glanced between them before returning his wide eyes to Svorgin. His bloodless fist tightened around the scythe.

"What are you doing here?" the farmer whispered, paling.

"Good. You remember me," Svorgin said harshly. "I told you I would return. The day you kicked me until I was black and blue, the day you finally removed those chains in the second stall of your barn, the day you sold me as if I were worth less than a dog. I promised you I would return."

Honzio's gut turned at the hate emanating from Svorgin. Every word escaping the Savorian's lips carried a burning passion. The anger from years of torment. Torment Honzio had allowed to rein free in the Empire. Torment he had been unable to prevent because he had been too weak to stand against his father. He was a coward.

Svorgin advanced a pace, and the farmer raised his scythe. "Don't come any closer."

Movement by the barn snared Honzio's attention.

Then he caught sight of two small figures creeping closer—two dangerously thin Savorian boys with their hands and feet chained together. Honzio swallowed the fury that burned in his throat at the obvious torment they were receiving. The boys were bruised, their hands rubbed raw from who knows what menial tasks they had been forced to do. Honzio tore his gaze from them to look at Svorgin. Whatever Honzio felt at the sight of the Savorian boys must have been multiplied by a thousand for Svorgin. His face turned a dark shade of red, and he charged forward, uncaring of the farmer's murderous-looking scythe.

"Svorgin!" Honzio called out.

The farmer swung the scythe. Svorgin dodged it and roared as he crashed into the farmer and shoved him to the ground. The scythe dropped into the melting snow. Honzio's heart hammered. He could almost feel the blood charging in his veins. Svorgin and the farmer rolled across the ground. He wrapped his hand around the farmer's neck, squeezing tight. The man grasped at a pointed rock.

Honzio rushed toward the abandoned scythe. He heard a thwack and saw Svorgin fall with blood gushing down his face as the farmer claimed high ground over him. The farmer wrenched the sword from Svorgin's grip and attempted to bring it to the Savorian's neck. Svorgin grasped the farmer's wrists, keeping the lethal edge of the blade inches from his throat.

Honzio sprang forward. He thought of slashing at the man but decided to hold the sharp scythe to the farmer's throat. The man froze.

"Drop the sword and stand."

The farmer rose, hands in the air. Svorgin jumped up and reclaimed the sword. He held it up, intent on ending the man, but Honzio prevented him by gripping his shoulder. The chained Savorian boys stepped closer, watching the scene.

Honzio pressed the scythe closer to the farmer's neck. "You will free them. Now."

The farmer gulped. A sliver of his skin sliced along the edge of the scythe, and blood welled forth.

"Hurry!" Honzio said, his arm and hand shaking. He wasn't sure how long he could keep up the façade of strength.

The farmer nodded, grimacing as he reached into his trousers and produced a silver key. Svorgin gave him a rough shove to his back, and he stumbled toward the Savorian boys. He unlocked the chains with shaking hands. The boys appeared scared and uncertain. Svorgin spoke in their tongue. Whatever he conveyed seemed to calm them down.

"The horses," Honzio told Svorgin.

The next minutes went by swiftly. Svorgin rummaged through the house, packing several bags of sustenance, half of which he gave to the boys. Honzio kept watch of the farmer, ensuring he didn't move. The man was fuming, anger turning his face purple. Svorgin returned with the saddled horses. He provided the boys with a mount before speaking to them further. Honzio gathered from what he could put together that the Savorian was instructing them where to go. They seemed wary and glanced at each other before slowly trudging away, looking back several times as if it were all some sort of cruel joke.

The farmer hissed at Honzio. "You will pay for this."

"I highly doubt you have the power to make that happen. The era of slavery in the Empire is over. If you are caught with one again, you will be executed."

The farmer's brow furrowed. He glanced at Honzio's misshapen arm and then back at his face. Honzio lowered the scythe and turned away, grabbing the reins of one of the horses.

"Where will they go?" Honzio asked Svorgin, nodding his chin at the boys in the distance.

"There was an old woman who treated me after one of my escapes. She takes in the wounded and helpless as much as she can. I gave them directions to her town."

Honzio nodded. As they walked, taking the scythe with them, the farmer called after them.

"I recognize your face!"

Honzio paused, the horse nickering at the sudden stop.

"You are Prince Honzio."

Honzio turned, looking over his shoulder to pin the man with a look. "And you best not forget it."

CORALIE
KINGDOM OF VERIN
VERINTOWN

CORALIE STARED AT the intricate engravings along the wooden council table. She followed the swirling lines with her eyes, drowning in the spirals of waves they formed, drowning in her doubts. They had saved Castle Verin and the town from Prolus's grasp, but for how long? How long would this resistance last? How long until Prolus returned with an even mightier force? And what of the other towns currently seized and under the control of the Dark Army? Her fingers dug into fists. Without the unity and support of the other kingdoms, there was only so much she could do. Ondalar's aid kept them from submitting, but they needed more than that. But how could she possibly receive more when

Draven Valent had claimed leadership as the emperor? She grimaced, recalling the disturbing letter he'd sent.

I've longed to see my sister.

Those words had troubled her, along with the gift he'd sent with the messenger: a thick journal inscribed with countless entries. Ever since she had sifted through the pages, ever since she had read the entries of the Uluzar woman, Kolesta-na—her mother, her *true* mother— she'd been plagued with sleepless nights.

The wolf women are born with birthmarks on their necks, have been for centuries, and if they aren't, the symbol is burned there. A half-moon. My girl had one, a perfect crescent. She has the blood of wolves in her. My job is complete. Even if I fall, I won't be the last to howl.

Those words in the final entry had struck her with clarity. A perfect crescent. Coralie's fingers drifted to her neck, an almost unconscious motion as she traced the curved birthmark there. She'd wanted to deny it with all her might, but the evidence pointed in one direction. Prince Irox and Princess Mari may have raised her, may have taught her, may have spilled their blood and hopes for her, but they hadn't been her true parents. They had been the father and mother she'd loved and always would love, but that didn't change the fact that the deceased King Joster and Kolesta-na, an Uluzar, were her birth parents. Draven, the monstrous former prince of Ayleth, was her half-brother.

"Your Majesty? Queen Coralie?"

Coralie blinked, the voice pulling her focus to the present and the troubled features of her personal advisor, Alesto.

"You haven't heard a word I've said, have you?" He placed the stack of parchments on the table. The chamber was empty except for the guard by the door. All the council members had filed out at the end of the meeting minutes before.

"My mind was elsewhere," Coralie said.

"Clearly." Alesto's wide brown eyes could have rolled with that statement, and she wouldn't have been surprised. "You've been toiling in the town endlessly and are too tired to focus on political matters. Leave the work to your subjects. Your role is to lead them out of the mud, not dirty yourself by pulling them out."

"I will give you credit for that clever metaphor, but as queen, I have no right to remain unsullied. A true queen works alongside her people. A kingdom is made together. If it is to last, that is."

Alesto clapped his hands together. "A wonderful speech, but it fails to impress me. Building a stable or an inn could lift the civilians' morale, but failing to address matters such as these"—he motioned to the papers—"that is how kingdoms collapse, a lack of focus from within. Your people need your mind, not your strength."

"Alesto, I did not make you my personal advisor to berate me at every moment."

"I'm *advising*, Your Majesty."

Coralie released a soft chuckle at the innocent smile he wore.

"And if you've forgotten, we have a more pressing matter. Emperor Draven's letter. When will you set out for Hearcross?"

Coralie flinched. "Verin is still too weak to be left leaderless. I will send an ambassador in my stead."

"But, my queen—"

Coralie lifted her hand. "That is enough advising for the day, Alesto. I need some air."

She stood from her chair and swept past him. Alesto lowered his head in respect and placed a half heart on his chest. Coralie left the castle and went to the place where she would find peace. To the person she could find peace with.

A short distance from the castle was a large fenced enclosure. Coralie stopped, watching from afar the thrashing rumloks within. The ruthless beasts were devouring the fresh meat being thrown inside. Coralie's gaze drifted to the large man speaking to them. He laughed as one beast whined for more meat. Coralie smiled and started down the hill toward him. Mordon threw the remainder of the meat over and leaned against the fence. His back was tense, and his hair rustled in the gentle wind. The rumloks prowled, but their viciousness had receded. Around Mordon they were calm, intelligent creatures, but even he needed a break from them. And when he did, they turned bloodthirsty. Hence the fence.

Coralie stopped behind Mordon. He stiffened, sensing her presence, but didn't turn. He breathed in, and when he spoke, she could hear the smile in his tone.

"Coralie."

She tucked her hand into the crook of his arm. His

posture softened, and he turned his head, smiling at her over his shoulder. That soft side smirk tugged at her heartstrings.

"How are they?" she asked, and he followed her gaze to the rumloks.

"Wild, but I'm getting to them. Slowly. Inat is taking orders from me, and as he is alpha of the pack, the others naturally obey him."

"Inat?"

Mordon nodded. "The name of the rumlok I bonded with. He nearly killed me in the camp."

"But now you know his name. That's a splendid development."

He rubbed his temple, and Coralie noticed the gauntness in his features. He was suffering. It wasn't just the rumloks draining him. Ever since Boltrex's passing, perhaps even before then, there had been a darker weight lingering on him.

"Sixteen days." The words slipped from his mouth. "He's been gone for sixteen days."

Coralie's hand tightened on his arm, hoping to convey her understanding. "I know."

"I still cannot process it. General Boltrex Vaz was invincible, undefeatable. I never imagined I would see him that way. On the tower. Broken."

The tower. Coralie exhaled, detesting memories of that day. The day secrets were unveiled. The day Mordon had hung from the crenelations. He'd nearly died battling Velamir and received a ruthless scar that cut down his face. He'd changed that day and not just outwardly.

"I despised him," he admitted, and Coralie listened in silence. Mordon hadn't spoken of Boltrex since he'd passed. He'd bottled up all his emotions instead. "For loving Velamir, for opening his arms to him after everything. And I detested Velamir solely for being his true son."

Coralie saw how much that had wounded him—Boltrex's clear affection for Velamir. Boltrex had admitted why he'd denied Mordon warmth during the last conversation the two had had. Coralie knew that learning the truth about Boltrex, the reason he'd withheld his affection, had affected Mordon more than he let on. Despite all his harshness, Mordon had loved Boltrex. Even after learning he was Velamir's father, he still loved him.

"I'm always here for you." She squeezed his arm gently. She could help him. Lift his spirits even for a little if she revealed her feelings for him. Returned his passion. But she couldn't. She wasn't strong enough. Not yet.

She dragged her hand back, but he reached up, snaring her fingers in his. He brought their tangled hands to his chest, drawing her closer to his side. Closer to his warmth and the heady scent of cinnamon and clove that emanated from him.

"I hope one day to return the rumloks to Savoria," Mordon said, changing the subject, his deep tone rumbling. "Maybe there, their wild ways will be tamed." She could feel his heart beating against their joined hands. "Home." The longing whisper drifted into the wind, a hope, a promise, a plea. Mordon turned to face her. "Coralie, I—"

She stepped back, snatching her hand from his. "The town is looking better. We rebuilt the inn."

He nodded, his features resolved. His thick black waves brushed his shoulders. Coralie found herself admiring him without intending to. The hard angles of his face that softened in rare moments, his dark eyes, black as a raven's wing. The proud tilt of his head. The broadness of his shoulders that held up so much more than a person had any right to bear. She blinked when she saw a soldier racing down to them.

"Your Majesty, news from the capital."

Coralie turned toward the man, worry building when she saw the panicked expression he wore.

"The Savagelanders. They have taken over the Grand Palace in Hearcross."

"What?"

"Draven Valent has been imprisoned."

Coralie glanced at Mordon, seeing his jaw flex.

"The Savagelanders have asked for obedience from all the kingdoms or else . . ."

"War," Coralie finished.

VELAMIR KEPT WATCH until dawn crept over them before stirring the others. Bear shook awake, his blue eyes glancing about before focusing on Velamir.

"Lad," he said. "Why didn't you wake me to keep watch?"

"I wasn't tired."

Bear's mouth tightened, but he didn't comment further. Lore passed around dried fruit from the saddlebags. The boy's wavy hair was tousled and tangled, and he ran his fingers through it to even it out. Velamir smiled, recalling Latimus's similar habit of making himself presentable. The more he examined Lore, the more he noticed the brothers had in common. Velamir didn't waste any

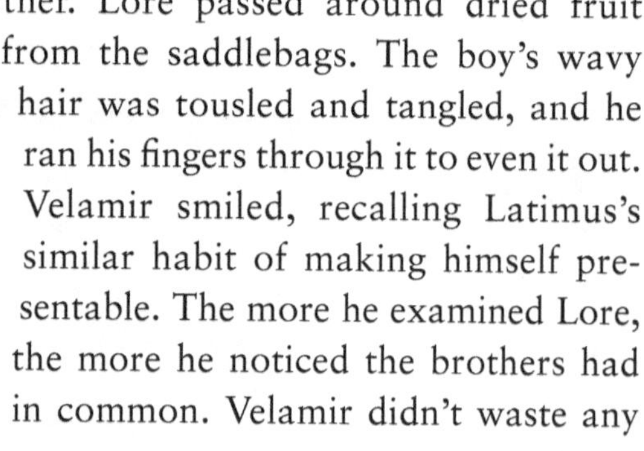

time, downing one of his water flasks and finishing the dried fruit. They hadn't a moment to spare. He reached for his sword belt, which he'd kept beside him during the night, and slung it around his hips. The familiar weight of his sword settled against him, instilling in him that sense of comfort it always did.

"Your sword is unique," Lore pointed out, munching on dried fruit. "I've seen nothing like it."

Velamir gave him a small smile and unsheathed the blade. A low hiss accompanied the weapon as it slid free from the scabbard. Velamir held it in a light grip, admiring it as he had the first day he'd seen it—the wolf's head adorning the pommel and the engravings fanning into wings on the cross guard.

"Neither have I," Velamir said. He glanced up, seeing Lore watching with wide longing eyes. "Here, try it."

Lore raced forward and took it in a hesitant grip. Velamir frowned when Lore gasped, his arms shaking and brow knit in concentration. The sword slammed toward the ground. Velamir jumped back just in time. Lore heaved over the blade, both hands gripping the hilt. He locked eyes with Velamir.

"How do you wield this so easily? It's so heavy."

Velamir shrugged. "It feels light to me."

Lore examined Velamir's arms with a dubious look. Bear's chuckle drifted to them.

"No need to show off, lad."

Velamir waved him off before focusing on Lore. "It is made from derinium, a Savagelander metal. Perhaps that is why it carries so much weight." Lore opened his mouth, but Velamir answered the question he sensed was coming. "A Shadow Manos mentor gifted me the blade in the Chishman Academy I used to attend in Tariqi."

"Frumgan," Bear said.

"Frumgan," Velamir repeated, recalling the old man. He'd been Jax's mentor. Everyone in the academy had been wary around him, but Velamir remembered his fondness for Jax, although Jax hadn't quite seen it himself. With the memory of Frumgan giving him the sword fresh in his mind, he addressed Lore. "Even he had trouble carrying the blade. He was the one who told me about the metal."

Lore nodded, though he seemed disappointed at his own lack of strength. Velamir retrieved his sword and sheathed it along with the conversation. Before long, they were back on the road.

"If the traces are gone, where are we going?" Lore asked.

"I have a few places in mind," Velamir replied. "The closest being Sok. If they were to seek shelter, they would have gone there."

"To an Imperial town? But they wouldn't be allowed inside."

"Times have changed, Lore. The Empire has weakened."

Lore frowned at his brief response but fell silent, focusing on guiding his horse. Velamir stroked Vandal's neck, and his horse snorted in response.

"Good boy," he whispered.

He broke off the road and delved deeper into the forest. He sniffed, the scent of a campfire brushing his nose. The Savagelanders might have camped nearby.

Velamir held up a hand, and the others halted. Velamir dismounted, carefully treading forward. His heart pounded a little harder, and his breath escaped a touch faster at the thought of what scene would confront him. He muttered a prayer for Natassa's safety. He didn't know what he would do if something had befallen her.

His breath caught as he came upon the fire—now a heap of ash—and the pile of bodies around it. Fear pumped through his blood at the sight of so many limp forms.

"Look for survivors!" he called to the others.

He moved fast, searching through the bodies. Lifeless dark eyes haunted him as he felt for heartbeats. But it was in vain. They were dead, all of them. A sharp slice of the neck had drained each of them of their life source and painted the snow with their blood. Velamir glanced up at the other two from his kneeled position beside a corpse.

Lore had seen his fair share of death during the attack on Castle Verin. No one had been spared the gruesome sight of the lifeless piles of corpses collected after the war. The endless funerals. Despite that, the boy looked on with a green hue to his face.

"All Savagelanders," Bear stated.

Velamir had noted that as well. The tattooed arms and gaping mouths with sharpened teeth gave it away. But what had befallen them? As far as Velamir knew, according to the older woman who had informed him of the Savagelanders, they'd had at least three prisoners with them, Natassa, the woman's daughter, and her intended.

"Do you think they . . ." Lore started.

Bear shook his head. "They could not have defeated such a large group of Savagelanders."

"Then who? Who could have done this?" Lore asked. "Imperial soldiers?"

"Aye, and possibly even Tariqins," Bear surmised. "They both despise Savagelanders well enough."

"No," Velamir said as he examined the angle and deepness of the cuts. All by the same blade. "This was done by a single person."

Their heads whipped toward him.

Velamir frowned, noticing the Savagelanders had all been bound by rope. Why would the killer bother to tie them up if they were going to eliminate them? Something was off. He stood up. "These are fresh traces. Going this way." He motioned to a pair of bootprints leading farther into the forest.

"But that makes little sense," Lore said. "One person? What about your sweetheart? What happened to her? Unless you think she is the one who slayed them all."

Velamir shook his head. "She would never slaughter so coldly. This was a skilled warrior who used that blade like it was an extension of their arm. And it seems they are the one who left these tracks." Velamir glanced up, peering through the gaps in the tree branches. He held up a hand, a flurry of snow cascading into his open palm.

Bear and Lore still appeared perplexed.

"Following these prints may be our only chance of finding her. The answers to our questions lie with the one who slayed the Savagelanders."

They remounted their horses and moved into a trot, following the traces in the snow. Lore still looked queasy.

"Are you all right?"

Lore nodded, forcing a smile. "Yes, Cales."

Velamir shook his head at the boy's determination to call him by a title. He was not a captain, but Lore wanted to feel the full experience of a mission, so he didn't reprimand him. Their horses' hooves dug into the soft clumps of snow as they continued forward, following the tracks to where he hoped they would find Natassa.

Honzio
Karalik Empire

THEY RODE THEIR newly attained horses for hours until the sun sank low in the sky and darkness shadowed their path. Svorgin led the way, informing them that he knew of a less traversed road to Ayleth, one that was not guarded by soldiers. It seemed he had been in every dungeon the Empire had. Draven called for a rest, complaining of the ache in his ankle.

They made a small fire Honzio hoped adversaries wouldn't notice through the cluster of trees.

He stared at the flickering embers before looking up, finding Draven's gaze on him. The familiar disgust rose within him as he watched the former prince of Ayleth. Draven had started this war between them by murdering Hesten. He had always planned to take over the Empire. To steal what became Hon-

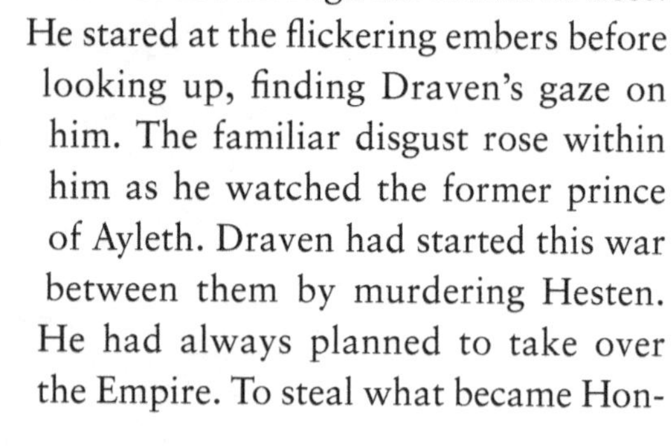

zio's birthright. And for what? What had he planned to accomplish when he took the throne?

"Why did you want it?" Honzio asked.

Svorgin, who'd been playing with a piece of wood, using a small knife to chip at it, froze as he glanced up between them.

Draven smirked, leaning back on a fallen tree. "Why does anyone want it? Power, might. The Empire is the heart of the world. If you capture the heart, the body is in your control."

"And that went so smoothly for you."

Draven's mouth twitched. "It's of no matter now. The Uluzar reign has begun. Our survival depends on if we surrender to them or bow to Prolus for protection."

Honzio leaned forward. "How easily you have given up. Don't forget you promised to help me, to accept my rule."

Draven scoffed. "First, honor your word and rid me of this poison. I have had quite enough of that stuff."

Honzio chuckled. "She gave you some of your own medicine, did she?"

Draven flinched, hands fisting at Honzio's indirect mention of his late wife. Natassa's decoy. "Do not speak of her."

Honzio recalled the way Draven had murdered her. Such a brutal end. The girl and her twin had resembled Natassa so closely even Honzio had moments when he couldn't tell them apart. He swallowed. It was too easy to picture the slaughtered handmaiden as his sister. It had nearly been her. If her handmaiden hadn't taken her place, it would be his little sister's head on the stake Draven had planted outside the palace gates.

"She will be avenged. *Everyone* you have wronged will be avenged."

Draven's pale eyes shadowed, and he slumped down, bundling his arms beneath his head. His blond lashes fluttered closed as he proceeded to ignore Honzio.

"I wouldn't sleep with my eyes closed if I were you," Honzio warned. "There are far too many people who want your neck."

Draven didn't move as he mumbled, "And too many people who need me more than they want me dead."

Honzio rolled his eyes and turned away, glancing at Svorgin and admiring the design he was tracing into the wood. The intricate pattern flowed into itself—a bow twisting into an arrow, the arrow gliding forth, the tip turning into a circular target before the target drooped into a single drop.

"You have talent."

Svorgin didn't look up as he replied. "As soon as we were old enough to pick up an axe, we chose a trade. Shadow Manos Seers oversaw the ceremonies, peering into the minds of the young ones. Some became black-smith apprentices, some sailors, some hunters, some soldiers, some healers. I became a carver."

"Is that a common practice?"

Svorgin shrugged. "It was boring to most children. The carvers were what you would call historians here. Preservers of our past. They kept the past alive with their art. Their art became the stories we told our youth."

"And what of your carving now? Is it a story?"

Svorgin nodded, and Honzio leaned closer, examining it better.

"Many of our letters are formed this way, as objects." Svorgin shaved off more of the wood. "This story is engrained in my mind. My mentor made me shape it so many times, I could do it in my sleep."

Honzio's brow rose. "So, it's a well-liked tale."

"It is about the coming of the hero." Svorgin motioned to the bow. "He will take up his weapon and shoot it into the hearts of the oppressors. He will free the people of Savoria."

"Like the hero of legends," Honzio murmured.

He recalled Natassa's song during his father's birth celebration. A time that seemed so long ago. She had recited from the banned tome and awakened something in him. She had reminded him that there was hope, even if it was hard to see.

"There are many tales of heroes. Every culture has a prophecy. I believe we simply rely on these myths as a way to cope, to continue forward. There are no true heroes."

Honzio nodded. He had thought the same way of the Golden Crown. The legendary crown's ability was known far and wide, whereas the object itself was nowhere to be found.

"And the crown? You were imprisoned because you knew its location."

Svorgin laughed. It was harsh. "I lied. I have been on the run since I was fourteen years. Ever since the Tariqins set foot on my home soil. I did it to protect my family. I allowed them to imprison me so they would spare them."

His face contorted, and Honzio knew he was thinking of them. He remembered Svorgin's fury when he had mentioned his sister.

"Aylis is safe. If all goes well, you will see her soon."

"You seem a good man, *Mosori*. I hope you will keep your promise to save my people."

"I will do my best."

Draven's soft snores filled the quiet air until Svorgin spoke again.

"The snakes weren't poisonous, were they?"

"They weren't."

Svorgin smiled. "I thought not." He examined Honzio with a thoughtful expression. "You held back when we faced the farmer. Why?"

Honzio fell silent, darting his eyes toward the fire instead of responding.

"Your arm doesn't make you frail," Svorgin said. "It's overcoming your shortcomings that makes you stronger." He stood suddenly, tossing Honzio the knife.

Honzio barely caught it. "What are you doing?"

"Attack me."

"I can fight. I was trained before the accident."

Svorgin nodded. "Then this should be easy."

Honzio grumbled under his breath and swiped at the Savorian, aiming for a gut wound. Svorgin jumped back. Honzio swiped again and again, sweat trickling down his face, the cool air heating the more he moved until he grew unbearably hot. Svorgin stopped retreating, instead grabbing Honzio's arm and slamming it over his knee. Honzio cursed, the knife falling from his hand onto the ground.

"That's enough."

The Savorian wrenched him around. "You will not forfeit without even trying." He retrieved the knife and slapped the hilt into Honzio's palm.

Honzio sneered, throwing it down. "You must find this amusing, but I do not. You can effortlessly overpower me and have just done so. I don't see the point of this."

Svorgin didn't back down. "I have known many Savorians who lost things—their limbs, their eyes. The blacksmith in my village had one hand and only four fingers on it. And he was a blacksmith."

Honzio motioned to himself. "Do I look like a blacksmith? I am not a Savorian. I am not one of your courageous countryfolk."

"You are right." Svorgin nodded. "You are Honzio Hartinza. Prince of the Empire. And you, out of anyone, should not concede."

He ducked down, picking up the knife. Honzio looked at the gleaming weapon, uncertainty settling in the pit of his stomach. After his mother passed, his father had turned more malicious, and his punishments became crueler than ever before. Honzio had given up on begging for mercy, on searching for freedom. He'd accepted the invisible chains shackling him to his position in the palace court. He'd accepted his role in the Empire. The role of a coward, a forsaken prince who did nothing but bow.

He'd kept his father content by competing in tournaments, by battling the best Galvasirs in the Empire, by wielding the heavy lances in the jousts. He'd poured his soul and pain into training. And it helped him forget for a while. It helped him focus. Until the accident. The joust that destroyed his arm for good. The irreversible moment that transformed him from a prince with the slightest bit of potential to a useless fool in his father's eyes. He could still hear him, as if Emperor Malus had risen from the grave to taunt him.

You foolish twit.

What use are you? You can barely lift your spoon.

I'm young yet and can produce a proper son—one worthy of my place. A son who is capable of riding and fighting and obeying without question.

I am ashamed that you are of my blood.

You are a disgrace to the Hartinza name.

If you weren't my sole heir, I would have removed you from the palace long ago. Looking at you disgusts me.

Honzio blinked, and the horrible words faded away. Svorgin was still watching him, still holding the knife out to him.

"A true leader is not one because of the power in his arms or his array of possessions and wealth. A true leader fights not with a sword, but with the strength in his heart," Svorgin told him. "What you deem a vulnerability could be your strength. Your weakness *can* be your strength."

The Savorian extended the weapon again. This time, Honzio took it.

15

"You can stay in here."

Natassa followed Aria into a quaint chamber. A bed settled in one corner of the room, and across from it was an organized desk. The room was lit with flickering candles shielded by glass encasings. Natassa's eyes caught on a rack of wickedly curved knives, and she approached them. She lifted one in a careful grip, awed by the lethal shimmer.

"A karambit," Aria said. "The most dangerous weapon you can find. Double-edged and able to spill guts with a strategically placed slash. Many underestimate them because they are small, but that's where they make their mistake."

Natassa allowed Aria to take the karambit from her, watching as her deft fingers flicked the blade around her hand in lightning-fast movements. So precise and skilled. Natassa noticed two karambits sheathed on either side of Aria's belt.

"This is your room," she realized.

Aria nodded, setting the weapon back on the rack.

"I don't want to impose on your privacy."

Aria shook her head. "Any who seek shelter with the Elders are never turned away. And besides, it would be an honor learning more about the courageous princess who saved *Biyodar* Rost's life."

Natassa blushed, looking down. Rost had praised her nonstop after seeing her. He'd filled Aria in on their meeting, leaving Aria staring at Natassa curiously as they led her on a tour of the Elder shelter. Though the shelter appeared similar to the other homes in the town, it was far more than it seemed. The Elders had dug tunnels underground, building a small city of their own. The number of people she'd seen down below had astonished Natassa. All had welcomed her with smiling faces and warm greetings. The Elders had a strange glow about them. A soft natural light to their features. The same glow she had noticed while watching Rost all that time ago. Aria had given her a tour of a beautiful library full of books Natassa had thought she would never see again. She had taken one from the library with permission from the Elder librarian.

Natassa glanced down at the book, smiling at the words carved into the leather. *The Book of Prophecies: The Hero's Call.* She blinked away the sudden sting blurring her vision as her fingers brushed over the cover. She recalled her father tossing it into the flames, the hungry red shadows devouring the pages.

Aria cleared her throat, and Natassa's head snapped up.

"I will introduce you to the head of our order in the morning."

There was a knock at the door, and Aria opened it and stepped out of the chamber. She reentered moments later carrying a large bowl of steaming water.

"I thought you might want to wash off some of the travel dust."

"Thank you," Natassa said gratefully.

Hours later, Natassa settled onto Aria's bed, guilt pulling at her for intruding. But no matter how much she protested, Aria wouldn't hear a word. The Elder settled on a long cushioned mattress she placed near the bed.

"Why did you join the Elders?" Natassa asked, curious.

Aria was quiet for a moment. "It was long ago. My home was attacked, and we were under siege. I can remember it so clearly. The smell of burnt skin, the screams of the dying, the fear in my mother's eyes. I lost my entire family in one day. The Elders found me. They saved me. I had vowed to avenge my family, but the Elders made me realize revenge is a road without an end. A road that would have destroyed me."

Natassa propped up on an elbow, glancing down at Aria. The woman's green eyes were far away as she spoke.

"So, instead, I dedicated myself to helping others in need. I dedicated myself to serving."

"That is truly admirable," Natassa said.

"And you?" Aria glanced at her. "You are the princess. You must have plenty of loved ones waiting for you."

"Just my brother, Honzio, and . . . Velamir."

"Velamir, hmm?" One of Aria's brows shot up. "I don't recall a prince with that name."

"He's not a prince."

"A nobleman? I didn't realize the law for the emperor's children's marriages had changed."

"He's not a nobleman either. Well, he is . . . but it's complicated."

"I see the Imperial princess is rebelling." Aria smiled. "Good for you."

Natassa couldn't hold back the smile stretching her cheeks. "He was actually a Chishman warrior from Tariqi when I met him."

Aria gasped, sitting up on the mattress. "You are jesting!"

Natassa shook her head, laughing softly. Her heart warmed at the whispery conversation they were sharing. It had been so long since she'd conversed with someone this way. She missed those days with Krea and even Kasdeya. Natassa closed off the somber thoughts threatening to burst through and focused on Aria.

"It turns out he was manipulated by the man who took him when he was a child and raised him. Velamir is actually the general of Verin's son. He only found out recently that Boltrex was his father."

Aria paled. She reached out to grip Natassa's arm. "Boltrex?"

"Yes?"

"No, it can't be . . ." Aria was trembling. "This man, Velamir. Did he have a different name before the Tariqins took him?"

Natassa watched her carefully before revealing, "Alaric."

Tears bloomed in Aria's eyes. "Please, tell me everything from the beginning."

16

LATIMUS

KINGDOM OF ONDALAR

ZARDSARI

THE REINS SLACKENED in Latimus's hands as he observed the city. His horse's hooves clomped on the cobblestones. An irritated snort erupted. Latimus found he agreed with his horse. He wasn't exactly thrilled about being squished between two Ondalarian warhorses. General Zenrelius peered down at him from atop his enormous mount.

"I never tire of seeing the awed faces at the view of the city."

Latimus nodded, agreeing at once. That was one thing to be pleased about. He could ignore everything if it meant he would have a few moments to be the center of the famed general's attention. He glanced about at the surrounding buildings once again.

"It is a grand sight."

And it was. Far grander than Verintown, even before it had been destroyed by the Tariqins. The Ondalarian homes were lined up, made of the thickest stone known to man. Sangor, the stone was called, unique to Ondalar. The Ondalarians were known for their architecture just as much as their horsemanship. The stones were as beautiful as they were strong, veins of gold running across the pale blue.

Citizens milled through the street in the finest clothes. Children tossed yellow petals in the air as Zenrelius and his returning cavalry passed. Cheers of welcome greeted them. Latimus had never felt so seen, despite not being seen at all. He was just another man on a horse. The true respect belonged to the legendary general riding beside him. Latimus snuck another glance at him, still in shock that he had managed to see him in person, let alone speak with him. When General Zenrelius had first arrived at Castle Verin during the battle, Latimus had almost died from the shock, narrowly avoiding a sword swinging at his neck.

"If you wish to be led to your resting quarters, I can inform Gallaxos of your visit."

Latimus pondered for a moment before shaking his head. "It is best I see him myself. I am arriving as an ambassador, after all."

The general stared ahead. "As you wish."

They dismounted before the castle, a gigantic fortress of white stone that shimmered the slightest shade of gold in the sun. He had never imagined it could be so beautiful. Zenrelius moved fast, and Latimus had to close his gaping mouth to catch up with him. As they crossed into the castle, seven gates had to be opened. Latimus was impressed with the precautions they were taking. Zenrelius pointed out things as they passed. He waved a hand in the direction of the most majestic stable Latimus had ever seen. Embarrassment sifted through him at how proud he'd been of his own stables when they were nothing compared to this grand sight. Ondalarian warhorses were led in and out by stable hands. The colts were the size of a normal lancer horse. The size of Latimus's horse.

They led their horses into the stables, and Latimus watched as Zenrelius waved off the stable hands rushing to assist him. The general tended to his horse himself, from removing his tack and brushing him down to filling the awaiting buckets with oats and fresh water. Latimus half listened to a stable hand assuring him of his horse's well-being, the other half of his focus taken by the general's precise movements. He had every stable hand at his beck and call, and yet he preferred to do it himself. Latimus's respect rose another notch.

Finally, they took the steps up to the keep doors. Once inside, Latimus was greeted by enormous paintings of the previous Ondalarian rulers. The canvases hung in the corridors, filling the walls from top to bottom. Centuries of talented artists' touch in each of them. Latimus's feet dragged as he craned his neck to stare and keep up with the others.

Zenrelius's pace didn't lessen in the least, his confident strides unrelenting until they reached the throne room entrance. Latimus fidgeted beside him, fighting the urge to touch his hair and straighten his cravat. Would she be there? His future intended, Lady Sardala, daughter of High Lord Genvor? He raced through the mental list he'd learned about her. She was the sole child of Lord Genvor, who was right hand to the new king. She was fast and could wield a sword with precision, but then again, most Ondalarian noblewomen were trained to do so. She was described as an average beauty and very tall. The height was an assumption on his part since he'd heard she had become so angry once that she had stepped on a servant with one thick boot. Latimus swallowed the sudden lump in his throat just as the doors swung open and the herald announced their presence.

"General Zenrelius and company!"

They were swept into a large crowd. The loud voices turned to cheers, swallowing the tinkling music Latimus had heard before the doors opened. Heads turned, and teeth shone as lips pulled into wide smiles. Latimus inhaled, the cloistered air filling his nostrils with high-quality perfumes that smelled of riches. His stomach rumbled as he caught another scent, and his mouth watered at the thought of the prepared food. The deafening cheers continued, and several hands reached out, grazing his arm. Latimus flinched. Zenrelius's second barked a command, and the people cleared a path for them. Latimus fell into step beside the general.

"Is it always like this?" he asked. What would it feel like to be this loved, this admired, this praised? He found himself envious.

General Zenrelius smiled. "You get used to it."

They walked farther, the Ondalarian soldiers and

Asilles, the shieldmaiden, paces behind them. The thick crowd parted before them, revealing a floor covered in intricate patterns and a shiny sheen. Latimus's mouth was dry at all the probing eyes. He wasn't the type to shy away from attention, but *that* much was enough to make even him wary. He focused instead on the markings on the floor indicating the starting positions for dance partners.

Zenrelius came to a stop, and Latimus focused ahead of him. A large man sat on the throne. The perfectly proportioned features of his face were similar to Zenrelius's. Latimus racked his mind to place how closely they were related. Zenrelius's father, the deceased king of Ondalar, was succeeded by his nephew, who had then passed the mantle to his son. That made Zenrelius and King Gallaxos first cousins once removed. Latimus frowned. By right, Zenrelius should've been upon that throne, and judging by the endearment showered upon the general, Latimus thought the Ondalarians would have preferred it so. But his illegitimacy had denied him that right.

Latimus sniffed, snapping a hand to his chest and bowing before King Gallaxos. It wasn't fair to the rest of the population. The Ondalarians were gifted with natural fighting prowess, well-off lands, *and* an unusual number of good looks. Zenrelius simply inclined his head to the king.

"Welcome back, Cousin." King Gallaxos nodded, a sneer marring his handsome features. "I thought you might not make it."

Zenrelius remained composed despite the obvious friction between them. He motioned to Latimus. "Ambassador Blayton from Verin has accompanied us."

"Ah, yes." Gallaxos eyed him. "The lucky groom."

Another man stepped out of the crowd. Long robes hung from his broad shoulders and dragged across the floor, gold thread embroidered throughout.

"Genvor." Zenrelius and the man shook hands, clearly pleased to see each other.

Lord Genvor turned to Latimus. "Sardala has been looking forward to meeting you."

"She has?" Latimus grimaced.

Lord Genvor's brow lifted, and Latimus forced a smile. "As have I."

Zenrelius leaned closer to Lord Genvor. "Why don't we have a drink and discuss the recent happenings?"

Genvor nodded just as King Gallaxos waved his hands about. "Let the festivities resume."

Couples wove onto the floor. Zenrelius and Lord Genvor faded into the crowd, their heads tilted toward each other as they fell into a deep conversation. Latimus stood uncertainly, peering over the gathering in search of a tall woman. The problem was most of the Ondalarians were giants. He grumbled under his breath. He was of average height but felt the size of a child among these folk. A throat cleared to his right, and he spun to the source. A young woman with wide brown eyes and lanky braided hair regarded him.

"Would you like to dance?"

The forwardness startled Latimus. She tapped one sandaled foot against the floor, her fingers drumming against her hip as she waited for his response. Latimus had only begun to nod when she yanked him onto the dance floor. Latimus caught on to the music at once and gripped her hands in his. He took a step back, and she took one forward before releasing one of her hands and twirling under his opposite arm. She giggled, laughing giddily as the pace of the dance quickened. Latimus bobbed to the beat of the music. It was a song he'd learned to play during his first lute lessons.

"So, you are the ambassador?"

He nodded at the woman in his arms. Her large brown eyes regarded him. Their hands clasped together again before Latimus tugged her toward him, and then his fingers lightly held her waist.

"Hmm, so what do you think of Ondalar?" She waved a finger before his face. "You think it's beautiful. I can see it in your eyes."

Latimus cleared his throat before saying, "It is a fine place."

"They all say so. When they first arrive. All they see is the sparkling city, the richness of the clothing, the stone walls, the endless amounts of charm."

"When they first arrive?"

"If they give you a tour of the city, ask them to take you to the Pit. You will see the true Ondalar there."

Latimus frowned. "The Pit? You mean where the traitors are thrown?"

The woman shook her head. "I thought so at first too. But then one day I went. And it was like a veil had been lifted from my eyes. Carts and carts of dead are taken there. Not just traitors. Savorians, children killed in the mines." The woman paused, swallowing. "People who'd done nothing but be deemed worthless in someone's eyes."

"Why are you telling me this?"

"Because I can do nothing to change it. You are an ambassador. You can share this knowledge with your people. With your queen."

"And start a war with Ondalar instead of achieving the peace we so desperately need in these times?"

She looked disappointed before speaking again. "I'm sorry to have bothered you with such a trivial matter, Ambassador."

She broke off into comments about the weather and remarks about the people dancing nearest them. Her chatter never seemed to stop, and Latimus winced, a headache beginning to form.

"Can you tell me what you know of Lady Sardala?"

Her lips froze mid-sentence as he interrupted another long dump of information.

"What do you wish to know?"

"Any information would be valuable to me."

"She's a shieldmaiden."

"A shieldmaiden?"

The fiercest of Ondalarian women. The maidens were trained from their youth to wield a weapon with precision. They were the daughters of high lords and the king.

"She is a fearsome warrior. Her sword skills rival the best."

Latimus's nerves jumped. He was starting to abhor the idea of encountering her. "I've heard many rumors."

She leaned in, curiosity flaring on her face. "Oh?"

"I heard she—that she—" Latimus grimaced, lifting a hand from her waist to scratch his neck. "Well, it sounds ridiculous repeating it."

"Please! Please! Please!" the woman pleaded, foregoing the dance and bobbing up and down.

"I heard she tortured someone to death with a metal boot solely for irritating her."

The woman nodded, surprising him. Latimus's stomach twisted as she confirmed his words. "It's true." Her face turned downcast. "His family mourned for days. But, alas, they could do nothing against her wrath." She patted his shoulder. "Ah, but I worry for you, young man. Her last fiancé was found dead. Some say poison; others say strangulation."

Latimus forced a smile. "I can handle myself."

"Ah, there she is! Over there!"

Latimus turned in the direction she motioned, and his breath stuck in his throat. A woman well over six feet, perhaps nearing seven, was tossing a tray of food onto the floor. She shouted something, and people granted her a wide berth. She looked several decades older than him, her hair sheered short and trimmed close on the sides.

"That's her?" he managed.

The girl batted her lashes at him. "Yes?"

She darted away before he could question her further. A giggle reached his ears even as she disappeared into the throng of people. Latimus tugged at his collar, wondering what sort of disaster he'd become part of.

17

Natassa

Kingdom of Devorin

Sok Town

Elders' Shelter

As Aria led Natassa to the head of the Elders' order first thing the next morning, they passed a room Aria had referred to as the Room of Memories during the tour the day before. Natassa had a quick glance about the room, taking in the hundreds of pendants hanging from the walls honoring the Elders' martyrs. She thought of Velamir when she saw them, recalling when he'd told her about the old man he'd encountered in Castle Verin's dungeon. He'd been with the man during his final breaths and promised to return his pendant.

After we finish this business with Verin, after we stop Prolus and rescue Jax from their clutches, let's go together.

Natassa smiled as she remembered Velamir's hopeful words, his promise to find the Elders together. Her smile crumbled when she switched to wondering how he was. He must have been devastated when he couldn't find her. He would be searching for her—of that she was certain. Her throat bobbed. He had too much on his shoulders. The pain of losing Jax already weighed on him. She couldn't imagine the pressure he carried.

Aria knocked on the chamber door before them. Her face was tense, with shadows beneath her eyes. She hadn't had a wink of sleep, Natassa knew, because she'd heard her tossing and turning after their conversation. Velamir was her brother. Natassa was as certain as she was of her name that he was. What were the chances that she would find Velamir's sister? It was a miracle. Natassa thought of the question she'd asked her, the first one that had come to mind as soon as she learned who Aria was.

Why didn't you go to Verintown? Why didn't you go to General Boltrex?

I thought I lost them all after the siege. When the Elders took me in, I thought I was an orphan because my father—the father I knew—would never leave us.

Aria's emerald gaze had glossed over, and Natassa gripped her hand.

When I grew old enough to join missions, I had hope. Some part of me wanted to believe that they were alive. I searched and searched, never stopping to breathe. Then I learned he had become the general in Verin. General Boltrex Vaz. Every syllable of his name had been coated in sarcasm. Not only that, I learned he had a son. A son who wasn't my brother. He'd moved on. That was the day my father died for me.

Natassa blinked, the conversation dissipating as the door creaked open and Aria motioned her to follow her inside. The room was lit by candles, similar to all the other chambers. A heavy air of mystery and a cozy orange glow decorated the room. Thick volumes lined a shelf on one side. An intricately crafted rug pulled the chamber together, darting over the rough ground beneath.

An older bearded man sat cross-legged upon a cushion, his eyes closed and his mouth moving inaudibly. Large smooth beads rested in his hand. His fingers pulled at each one, tugging them until he made his way around to the first bead. Natassa had never seen such a dedicated prayer before—the passion in his posture, his focus somewhere else entirely. Aria moved closer to the older man, tilting her chin down in respect.

"Master Dunya?"

The man's eyes popped open, startling Natassa. His intelligent gaze focused on them.

"This is the head of our order, Master Dunya." Natassa followed Aria's lead by bowing her head slightly.

Master Dunya smiled, wrinkles creasing his eyes. "Welcome, Child. Rost informed me of your arrival. What brings you to the Elders?"

"I am here for your help. I am a Shadow Manos." Natassa brushed aside her hair to show her mark.

The older man seemed to take in a breath at the sight of the Golden Phoenix. He motioned to the cushions across from him. Natassa glanced back at Aria, who reassured her with a nod. Natassa settled down, smoothing the fabric of the dress Aria had lent her. The material was rougher than she was used to. Natassa had never appreciated the softness of the palace apparel until she no longer had it. Even so, Aria's clothes had a unique beauty to them, a viciousness that suited her. Natassa glanced at her, noting the dark green skirt pulled in by a belt laden with a karambit on either side. Something told Natassa those weren't the only weapons the woman carried. A brown vest fit snuggly over a green undershirt that cuffed around her wrists. She wore a different headpiece, a brown band circling her head and holding a long green scarf in place over her braid. Dangling beads framed her face in various shades of green and brown. The outfit was completed by her confident posture and that familiar smile Natassa had seen on Velamir's lips so often.

"We will do our best to assist you," Master Dunya said. "But you will only be freed from the shadows by your own will."

Aria retrieved a teapot from the table by the shelf and sat beside Natassa before placing three cups between them and Master Dunya.

"How?"

Master Dunya leaned forward, his amber gaze focused on her shadow mark. "Your mark differs from all others that I have seen. Not merely the color, but also the size."

Aria tilted the pot, pouring the rich orange tea into the cups in generous amounts. Natassa focused on the steam rising from them as she hesitated in responding to Master Dunya.

"Manos Xeni told me I have two shadows," she finally said.

Master Dunya was silent for a long moment. "You came to us seeking our aid, and we never refuse calls for help. But I want you to be certain of what you are asking. You are a rare case, Princess. You are the first I've heard of to be afflicted with two shadows."

"Please, call me Natassa." From what she knew, Draven was the current emperor, and if he had his way, she would never be referred to by that title again. "And yes, I'm certain. I want to remove these shadows. It is torture living with them every day. I'm so tired."

"Removing the shadows is a tricky process. We are the only ones in the Empire who have succeeded in doing so."

"How many shadows have you expelled?"

"Fifty so far."

Natassa smiled. "That is a good start."

"Out of those fifty, only five Shadow Manos survived the purging."

Her smile dropped, and she felt Aria's stare probing into her.

"If you wish to rethink your decision, no one will fault you." Master Dunya lifted the tea and sipped it, heedless of the burning heat.

"No, I want to do this. I must do it," Natassa said, firming her resolve.

"There are four steps to the removal. The first is to withdraw the mental shield you have built to prevent them from fully penetrating your mind."

Natassa frowned. "But that shield is the sole thing keeping me protected."

"That is why it is the hardest step. Once the shadows enter your mind, communication becomes easier."

"You want me to speak with them?" The idea horrified her. Their whispers were more than enough. How could she converse with them?

"It is essential to get to know them. Only then can we advance to the next stage, which is urging them to leave. You must convince them they have no place there."

Dread built within her.

"They rarely comply, which is when we move to the third step: believing something is greater than them. Prey on their arrogance. You must have a light stronger than their darkness. Faith. Love. Strength. The shadows are afraid of this power."

"And if that doesn't succeed?"

"The final thing that could work is pain. We've noticed excruciating pain can also remove the shadows. When they have no spirit left to feast on, they leave to find another form to inhabit. But it is perilous and something we do not practice here. Something you would have to risk yourself."

Natassa nodded, falling deep in thought before she asked him the question she'd had ever since she'd learned of her shadows. "I could never find information on the shadows. There were no tomes, no knowledge of them in the palace. Could you tell me where the shadows come from?"

Master Dunya stroked his beard. "A fine question indeed. There are many tales of how the shadows first came. But according to my research, the most truthful accounts come from those of your ancestors. Emperor Vesopa and Empress Leoni."

"Accounts," Natassa repeated. "You have their journals?"

Master Dunya shook his head. "I have the journals of their advisors preserved carefully and passed down for generations until they ended up in our hands here."

Natassa was stunned by that knowledge. That such an important part of history was still intact and that the Elders had it filled her with joy. Her father and grandfather had attempted to erase all history relating to the shadows, burning and desecrating any material referring to Shadow Manos.

"When the war with the Savagelanders began, your ancestors knew they would lose the battle. According to the journals, they tampered with dark magic and opened a gateway to the spirit world. They opened a door for spirits to enter our realm. The spirits became known as shadows.

"The shadows agreed to help your ancestors in exchange for remaining a part of the dynasty. So, Emperor Vesopa and Empress Leoni promised their only child, their daughter, as the bride of the most powerful shadow they had released. The vow was to be upheld as soon as the Empire had victory. The Savagelanders were defeated, and your ancestors turned their back on the shadows. They double-crossed them, closing the gateway with the hopes of sealing the shadows back."

Master Dunya peered into his glass, the tea resembling his amber eyes. "But they had underestimated the shadows, who prevented the gateway from closing entirely and placed a curse on the royal line. A never-ending curse. Your ancestors despaired but still attempted to remove the shadows. Their plans failed, and their daughter became the first victim of shadow possession, bringing forth a lifetime of cursed children. Shadow Manos.

"Over time, the Shadow Manos spread throughout all the kingdoms. Of course, the royals are known to dally about. Bastards carried the curse. Families grew. Soon Shadow Manos were everywhere. They have plagued us humans since then. And until the gateway is sealed, they will continue to do so."

Natassa's features turned downcast. "Why are we burdened with such a darkness? Why do we have to pay for the sins of our ancestors?"

"Because this is your destiny, Natassa Hartinza. Your destiny is to fight."

18

LATIMUS TOSSED AND turned the entire night. The unfamiliar guest room and horrifying future he no doubt faced kept him awake until the sun crept through the curtained window. He tossed the stifling covers off and dressed, dread hanging from every part of him. Latimus glanced in the mirror and grimaced at his state. He wasn't the typical handsome man, at least according to the whispers he'd overheard from the maids in Castle Verin. He didn't have the fashionable closely shorn hair or the cut-from-stone face or the height and bulk, but he'd always thought he was average at least. With his land and wealth and family reputation, better than average. But with his father dragging their name through the

dirt, he had bigger problems to worry about. He'd been concerned the entire journey to Ondalar that Sardala would find him ugly, but since he'd seen her, he could only hope he wouldn't be her next quarry.

Latimus stepped out into the hall, blinking at the golden décor glaring at him. He was certain the entire castle was made of gold. The halls were empty except for an occasional guard. It seemed the Ondalarian nobles slept late as well. Latimus ducked into a spacious room. Sizable shelves filled it, circling around comfortable-looking chairs. He ran his fingers along the thick volumes, stopping on one titled *Zenrelius, The Tale of a Legend*. His lips twitched upward as he pulled it free and took a seat in a chair. As he filtered through the pages, he found them far more detailed than anything he'd managed to obtain about the Ondalarian general in Verin. Until the recent alliance between the kingdoms, most Ondalarian materials had been banned in Verin.

He turned his head at movement on the balcony along one side of the library. Latimus leaned forward, spying two men conversing. Zenrelius and High Lord Genvor. Latimus tilted his head and shifted closer, hoping to catch a snippet of their conversation.

"They smuggled more in?"

Lord Genvor nodded. "From the Docks. Do not fret. No one is aware. What are you intending to do with the substance?"

"You will see. Foremost, we must handle Gallaxos."

Handle? What did they plan to do? Latimus lost his balance, the chair careening to the side and crashing to the ground. Latimus groaned, pulling himself up. He froze as both heads turned toward him. He leaned over, picked up the book, and brushed off the cover.

"It's a lovely morning for a little reading. General." He smiled, tipping his head with respect. "My lord."

They both stared.

"I didn't mean to intrude."

Lord Genvor stepped into the library. "No, no, you weren't intruding. I trust your first day on Ondalarian grounds was a pleasant one. Did you have a chance to meet my daughter?"

Latimus flinched. "I glimpsed her, but she appeared . . . preoccupied."

"Well, well. That won't do. After all, the wedding is to be held on the morrow."

"Morrow?" Latimus repeated, blanching.

Lord Genvor nodded. "She is currently training. You don't want to miss seeing her in action. Why don't you have a servant lead you to the shieldmaiden training hall, and I will come along shortly?"

Latimus grimaced. "Of course."

He soon found himself outside the training room door, fingers drifting over the handle. The guard who had escorted him returned to his duties, and Latimus wondered if he should use that opportunity to disappear back to his chamber. He could make the excuse that he had lost his way or was unable to find an escort. Weak reasons but an escape all the same. Latimus inhaled, pushing back the thoughts, and thrust the door open. His jaw promptly dropped. Lady Sardala held two thrashing women by their collars and rotated in a circle. She then flung them toward the wall, and they crashed into a pile of armor.

"Again!" she screeched.

Blood drained from Latimus's face, and he took a step back. Someone grabbed his arm and yanked him forward, then slammed the door shut behind him. The girl from the day before beamed at him, releasing his arm.

"You came to watch the training?"

Her high-pitched voice echoed in the large room, and all eyes shot to them. Latimus's smile was strained.

"I was actually just passing by."

The girl pouted and lowered her tone. "But you must greet Lady Sardala."

Latimus faltered, every fiber of his being screaming at him to flee. Lady Sardala was staring him down from across the room, breathing fire through her nostrils. He would have to confront her at some point. He nodded reluctantly, and the girl latched onto his arm again and dragged him forward. She listed off the names of fellow shieldmaidens as they passed. They wore matching uniforms: light armor buckled over a tan dress that split down the sides, allowing for free movement of their leather-encased legs. A large belt pulled the look together, a dagger and sword hanging from it. Bronze bands clasped their upper arms. All the women watched him with lowered brows and fierce stares. He fought the queasiness in his belly when he reached Lady Sardala.

"It is . . . a *pleasure*," he emphasized, "to finally meet you."

Lady Sardala peered down at him. "And you are?"

The food he'd eaten the day before twisted in his gut. Was she unaware of the betrothal?

"I am Latimus Blayton."

"Ah." She sneered. "I see."

Latimus nodded, forcing a small laugh as the silence progressed.

"Then we must whip you into shape."

"Pardon me?"

She clapped her large hands together. "No one comes in here and leaves without emerging stronger than before. You may be an ambassador, but I will give you a solid pounding without caring."

Latimus's mouth slackened, and Lady Sardala reached out and gripped his shoulders, positioning him sideways. She eyed him as she worked, adjusting his footing and raising his arms. She closed his fingers into fists and nodded approvingly.

"Much better."

Latimus stood frozen, maintaining the position.

"Let us see what the men in Verin possess. Throw a jab."

"Why don't we head to the hall for some breakfast instead?"

Those lethal eyes settled on him with a murderous look. "Hit me."

Latimus winced, hesitated.

"HIT ME!"

The shout sent him into action, and he threw a weak punch toward her face. She didn't even move as his fist connected with her cheek in a light smack. Her posture was solid, her face unreadable, and his knuckles had left slight red marks on her skin. He pulled his hand back, regret coursing through him.

"I apologize, my lady," he said, glancing at the shieldmaidens witnessing the proceedings. They all watched without even a twitch. "I should have—"

Knuckles connected with his chin, throwing him backward and closing his teeth on his tongue. His palms slammed on the floor, absorbing the impact. He groaned and tasted blood welling in his mouth.

"Again." Lady Sardala beckoned him with raised hands.

Latimus bit back his pain and struggled to his feet. He touched his aching chin. The door to the chamber opened, and Lord Genvor entered. Relief rained over Latimus as the man strode up, glancing between them. Lady Sardala straightened her posture and stood in a firm stance, slamming a half heart to her chest.

"High Lord," she said, her tone laced with respect.

Latimus continued to be baffled. The woman spoke to her father as if he were her superior officer. With them standing so close to each other, Latimus saw no resemblance between them at all. Lady Sardala towered over her father. Her face was harsh and angular, and she appeared far too close in age to him.

"I see you've met Instructor Korso," Lord Genvor said.

Latimus nodded before stopping abruptly. "Who?"

Lady Sardala let loose a bellowing laugh. "Me, you fool."

Latimus closed his eyes in slow blinks as he waded through his confusion. High Lord Genvor's brows crinkled as he watched Latimus.

"She oversees the training of the shieldmaidens."

Oversees the training of the shieldmaidens. The words repeated in Latimus's mind.

"Oh." *So, who is Lady Sardala?*

The answer came to him as he looked over his shoulder at the gathered shieldmaidens whispering to each other. They chuckled, not bothering to conceal their disdain for him. Latimus focused on the girl from the night before. The one he'd danced with. She threw him a saucy wink and waved her fingers at him before swiping them over her lips in a telling gesture. Latimus could only stare back as he followed her motion and wiped away the blood trickling down the side of his mouth. She giggled behind her hand, and he winced, wondering if he'd been dealt an even worse fate with a minx such as her.

Honzio

Kingdom of Ayleth

THE ENDLESS DAYS of travel were accompanied by sparring sessions that had left Honzio covered in bruises and Draven in fits of laughter. The former prince's favorite pastime seemed to have become watching Svorgin hurl Honzio to the ground. Honzio glanced up at the arched gateway as they crossed through. The guards posted at that gate were more lenient since they were entering the kingdom through the common gate. Like Hearcross, Ayleth had several entrances—some for normal civilians, some for visitors, and some for royalty—making it easy for each to reach wherever they needed to go in the city.

"This is the first time I'm passing through this gate like some sort of peasant," Draven grumbled.

Honzio snorted. "Ah, I apologize, Your Supreme Majesty. How much heartbreak you must be enduring to forfeit your glorious entry through the main gates."

Draven glared at him. The man looked the worse for wear. His beard was fully grown, covering his jaw and extending up his face into his oily strands of white-blond hair that peeked out from under his hood, and his apparel was streaked with grime. Honzio had no right to judge, not when he was sure he looked just as filthy, if not worse.

"Even if *Lsrar* wanted to, I doubt it would have been glorious," Svorgin added as they walked through the city.

"Oh, shut—" Draven stopped mid-sentence as he caught sight of what the Savorian was staring at.

Rows upon rows of Tariqin soldiers were marching ahead of them. Draven went still. Even his breath seemed to cease. Honzio eyed the black-and-red uniforms, the symbolic mask blazing across each flowing cloak.

"They are marching toward the castle."

"I see that," Draven muttered. "Follow me."

They moved after him, keeping their heads down and profiles shadowed in the hoods of their cloaks. After weaving through countless alleys, Draven paused before motioning to their left. Honzio grew uneasy as he noticed they had shadows on their tail. He locked eyes with Draven, who nodded, pausing in the middle of the road. They turned as the three men closed the distance between them—toughened men who knew exactly what they wanted. And by the glint in their eyes as they fastened their gazes to Honzio's and Draven's belts, it was coin they were after. Mercenaries.

Honzio glanced over his shoulder, seeing two more mercenaries block the way forward—a woman with cracked teeth and a thinner man with a decisive eager stare.

"What've we 'ere?" the tallest of them said.

Honzio looked about, realizing with a start that Svorgin was nowhere in sight.

"Rat," Draven hissed. "He abandoned us at the first opportunity."

Honzio didn't respond, his thoughts occupied by how they would escape the throng of hungry mercenaries. The tall one, evidently the leader, slapped the head of a club against his shoulder.

"Hand o'er yer coin, and no one gets hurt."

"Oh, I don't think so," Draven responded. "Even if I were to have anything in my purse, I wouldn't give it to you scum."

Growls vibrated around them, and Honzio winced.

"Perhaps try *not* to antagonize them."

"Not sure what they got in those rags," the female said. "They look like they just broke outta prison."

"You have no idea," Honzio muttered.

"Worthless or worth, I smell somethin' un'er those layers of grime."

"How dare you?" Draven said. "I'll have you know only the most blessed of eyes have seen under my clothes." He cast the woman a wink, which broadened her scowl.

"I can't believe you." Honzio placed a hand to his forehead, blocking the sight of the once-grand prince of Ayleth flirting with a mercenary.

"Well, you better start believing, *Your Majesty*," Draven muttered back, "because there is only one way we will get past them."

By fighting. The words settled in his mind, along with resignation.

"I won't lay a hand on a woman," Honzio said, unsheathing his dagger and glancing again at the mercenary woman glaring at them.

"No worries. Leave her to me," Draven replied with a cruel smile.

The mercenaries launched at them. Honzio ducked just as the club sailed toward his head. It whooshed over him, ruffling his hood. He darted forward, wrapped his good arm around the mercenary's waist, and tackled him to the ground, losing his dagger in the process. The stench of sweat assaulted his senses as the mercenary attempted to shove him off. In the struggle, Honzio found his nose buried in the man's armpit, and a bout of nausea rolled through him. He couldn't breathe. Through his watery eyes, he made out the sight of Draven knocking two of the mercenaries flat out, and then the woman jumped onto his back and yanked at his hair. The former prince cried out and stumbled back, batting at her.

An elbow stabbed Honzio's gut, and he wheezed. The tall mercenary shoved him off, and Honzio collapsed onto the ground, struggling to regain his breath. The mercenary leaned over him and pulled back a fist in preparation to strike. Honzio vaguely noticed that one of the other mercenaries had collapsed a short distance away. The mercenary above him stepped back a pace. Was he attempting to give more strength to his punch?

Honzio blinked as a hand clasped the man's shoulder from behind. The hand patted his shoulder, and the mercenary's fist lowered as he started, then looked behind him. A punch greeted him and sent him flying against the alley wall and crumpling in a defeated heap.

Svorgin stood before him, and Honzio grinned.

"Well done. Your stance is much improved," the Savorian remarked.

"Where did you disappear to?"

"I trailed around back. I thought I would give you a few minutes to train."

Honzio pushed to his feet, spotting the unconscious mercenary he'd noticed before and knew it was Svorgin's work.

"I've got your back, *Mosori*," Svorgin said.

"And you have my thanks."

A loud screech caught their attention, and they turned, seeing Draven fling the woman off his back. A thump followed as she slammed on the ground, out cold. Draven heaved for air, a hand on his knee and the other waving at them.

"And my gratitude as well." The sarcasm was clear. "I was over here battling for my life, and you two are chatting like a pair of gossipy villagers."

"It doesn't appear as if you needed help," Honzio said, eyeing the three unconscious forms around him.

Draven sighed, flinging back the hair dangling before his eyes. "We cannot delay further."

Honzio nodded, and he and Svorgin stepped into place behind Draven as he led them onward. They had barely taken three paces when a shout came from behind them.

"You there! Stop at once."

They froze, and Honzio glanced back at the Tariqin soldiers entering the alley.

Honzio grimaced. "*Goshsta,*" he muttered.

Svorgin nodded, repeating, "*Goshsta.*"

❧

Half an hour later, after several close calls, they had evaded the Tariqins and stood before a stone house in the middle of a street crowded with vagabonds. Draven rapped on the door with quick fingers. The door swung open and closed behind them as soon as they stepped inside. They stood in the home's narrow entryway.

"What is it you need?" a gravelly female voice demanded.

Honzio adjusted to the darkness and glanced at the speaker standing before them. The poofy curls caught his attention first, colored a startling shade of purple. Her hands were planted on her hips, thick red paste darkened her lips, powder bronzed her cheeks, and her wide eyes were shadowed with black powder. She wore so much makeup, it was impossible to determine what she truly looked like. Her dress was the opposite, plastered tightly to her form and leaving nothing to the imagination. Honzio cleared his throat and averted his gaze. Draven threw back his hood.

"Hello, Marcella."

There it was—the arrogant brogue that had been

missing for days. It seemed being on his home soil had brought some of Draven's old habits back.

The woman stared at Draven as if she were struggling to place him through the layers of beard and filth before she gasped and chuckled. "My dear King Draven, to what do I owe this pleasure? Which unfortunate courtesan needs assistance?"

Honzio and Svorgin exchanged a bewildered glance. Draven shook his head.

"No courtesans. Surely you have heard the happenings."

"Yes, of course, your attempt at taking the Imperial throne. The rumors of your imprisonment. Then the Tariqins showing up in Ayleth in the blink of an eye." She paused. "But you only visit me when one of your women has troubles."

Honzio joined the conversation. "By troubles, you mean with child?"

She nodded. "Though I heard rumors about Princess Natassa carrying your heir. Is that why you killed her?"

Draven flinched.

Honzio turned a horrified gaze on him. "Tell me that is a falsehood."

"I wasn't aware she was with child. I realized the fact after I killed her, but that is beside the point. *That woman*, Kasdeya Vosta, wasn't some saint. She attempted to take my life on multiple occasions. She was nothing more than a con woman with her eyes set on my throne." Draven sneered. "Why am I even discussing this with you?"

Honzio grabbed him by his collar, clenching the material of Draven's cloak within his fist. White-blond hair slipped forward, blocking the prince's features. "Because you are a vile imbecile whom I would rather see buried in the ground than roaming free on these lands. You ruined that girl and . . ." Honzio shook his head, disgust tainting each word. "You've destroyed so many people, and yet you can speak as if nothing affects you."

Draven's features shifted, and Honzio could have sworn he saw sadness in his gray eyes. But then that almost sorrow dissipated, and he shoved Honzio back. Honzio stumbled. Svorgin reached out to balance him.

"Yes, that is one of the biggest misfortunes in my life. Being unable to feel. But I regret what I did to her. At least that much is real. The realest truth I can tell you." Draven's jaw clenched. "I don't want to discuss this again. Don't you dare mention her to me."

Honzio shook his head, distaste burdening his tongue with words he wanted to shout.

Marcella butted in. "If you do not need my concoctions, what is your purpose in coming here?"

Concoctions. Honzio stared at the woman again, that time forcing himself not to look away. There, right at the edge of her jaw, was a birthmark. A phoenix birthmark. It disappeared under the pasty makeup she wore.

"She's a Shadow Manos," Honzio whispered.

Svorgin nodded. "I noticed."

Honzio glanced at him. The man had a keen eye.

Draven rubbed a hand over his face, as if trying to wipe away his frustration. "Where did the Tariqins come from? When did they come?"

"From seemingly nowhere. They weren't here a week

ago, and then they were marching through the city. Your soldiers didn't stop them. They weren't fit to even try doing so."

"Smells of dark magic," Svorgin said. "I wouldn't doubt Prolus would dabble in it."

Draven snapped his fingers at the Savorian, nodding. "There is only one way the Dark Army could travel so quickly. By using the traveling serum. Zamanin Sulari. It seems Prolus's Shadow Manos have mastered it if they can transport forces this large."

"There's more," Marcella said, hesitating. "There are rumors that the Dark Lord Prolus is here. That he's sitting on your throne."

NATASSA
KINGDOM OF DEVORIN
ELDERS' SHELTER

NATASSA SAT ON the floor in Aria's chamber with her eyes closed to the outside world. She lingered within her mind, struggling to communicate with her shadows. It was fear holding her back, keeping her from bringing down the wall between her and her shadows. She'd spent days listening to Master Dunya's advice and trying her best to heed it, but no matter what he told her, it wouldn't change a thing. She had to do it on her own.

Natassa walked through the darkness of her mind until she felt that familiar barricade. Whispers taunted her, brushing her ears. Natassa braced herself. She inhaled and pushed through the wall without any further delay, stumbling into a circular area with white mist pooling around her feet. Figures formed from amid the mist, rising and drifting toward her.

Princess. Princess Natassa.

Natassa flinched, straining to keep both figures in her line of vision. This was far different from her previous experiences with the shadows. She had simply used their powers before, never fully viewing them. She'd used them to see into the minds of the Karakan and the Sirchoba. Both had been troubled animals she wanted to help. But this . . . she was dealing with something entirely different.

Princess, one said, *you have come to your senses at last.*

The figure had a feminine voice, soft with a poisonous edge.

Natassa grew wary as the shape flowed over the mist and toward her, closer and closer.

We've been waiting for this moment for a long time, the other figure said, a male tone, deep and threatening.

"What do you want?" Natassa asked.

They chuckled, circling her.

We crave the same thing you do, Princess, the female hissed. *Freedom.*

Natassa sensed the persuasion in her voice. So she was the Lure, leaving the male to be the Seer.

And you have the key to that freedom, the Seer said.

You used us. We answered you every time you called on us. We did whatever you asked of us. Natassa could feel the Lure's anger. *Now you must keep your promise.*

The figures drifted to her sides, one by either ear, the brush of their lips lingering over her hair. Natassa shuddered. A trail of sweat trickled down her brow at the pressure in her mind as she struggled to maintain herself.

"What do you want from me?"

There are many paths you can take, but only one will lead to the future you seek, the Seer said.

"How can you know what future I want?"

The Lure's translucent fingers snared around her wrist and yanked her forward and into the mist. Natassa stumbled, her heart thudding wildly. She emerged into a wide green forest. Trees rose around her. Natassa turned in circles, trying to find her way out of the maze of vegetation. She stepped into an open valley and spotted a small home. Curls of smoke rose from the chimney and into the air. Natassa gripped her skirt and ran toward the home. She turned the knob and entered. A man leaned over a fireplace, where he stoked the flames. He rose to his full height, a loose tunic draped over his form, the fabric of his sleeves bunched up over his forearms. He turned to look at her, and a wide smile creased his eyes.

"My phoenix? You are back early."

Natassa couldn't stop her smile from blooming, and Velamir opened his arms. Natassa darted forward and rushed into his hold. She gripped him tight, her arms circling his middle. She heard an intake of breath, and then his arms enfolded her.

"You missed me, did you?" She could hear the laughter in his voice.

"So much," she whispered.

She savored the warmth and safety of his embrace. She'd missed his beautiful green gaze and his comforting words. But most of all, she'd missed *him*. Natassa wanted to brand that moment to memory so it would never end.

"You want your happiness, just like all humans."

Natassa stiffened as Velamir's voice grew hard. She tried to extricate herself from his hold, but his arms were like iron. She looked up. His face was stony, and then his form dissipated into mist. Natassa gasped, feeling so alone.

But happiness cannot come so easily, the Lure whispered. *If you want your freedom, you will help us.*

Cold hands shoved her forward, and she stumbled, crashing to the ground. Her palms smacked the stone floor. Stone? Natassa lifted her head. She was in a castle corridor. A figure drifted down the hall before her. Natassa found her footing and followed. They entered a wide chamber, where a throne sat centered on a raised podium. She frowned, blinking as the air shifted and a large doorway appeared in the middle of the throne room.

This is the gateway to our world, the Seer said. *Until it is fully opened, we are trapped here as mere shadows.*

Opening the door will set us free, will reunite us with our true forms, the Lure whispered. *We will no longer need humans to sustain us.*

"And when I open the door, the curse will be broken."

You will set us free, the Lure said again. *You must destroy the barrier.*

"If I do so, I will let your destruction loose on my people. That is not what I want," Natassa responded. "Leave my head. Leave me!"

A soft breath touched her neck, and she flinched. *We are at your side always, whether you like it or not.*

Natassa forced her eyes open, and she was back in the Elders' shelter, in Aria's chamber. Her chest rose and fell as she gasped for air. Sweat drenched her. But the horror wasn't over. Two shadows appeared before her, looming over her.

"Get out!" she screamed. "Get out of my head! Get out of my life!"

She heard maniacal laughter in return, pounding inside her skull. She clasped her hands over her ears, trying to block out the noise. *Faith, love, strength.* Master Dunya's words drifted to her. *You must have a light stronger than their darkness.* She thought of her mother. The image of her love-filled eyes, the soft timbre of her voice, the gentle touch of her hand. Natassa thought of her brother Thorsten, his smile that always warmed her heart, the way he used to tweak her nose when she was little. His kindness and strength. The shadows' laughter faded. She thought of Velamir. Of his courage, his adamance to follow justice, his green eyes that shone with emotion. Tears slipped down her cheeks, and when she removed her hands from her ears and looked up, she no longer saw the shadows. But she still heard them, far back in her mind.

We are not leaving, Princess.

The door to the chamber opened, and Aria entered, her brow furrowed.

"Natassa? Are you okay?"

She tried to nod, tried to speak, but only garbled words emerged before her vision darkened and she slumped over.

Velamir

Kingdom of Devorin

Sok Town

The long stretch of land ahead was covered with rows of stone houses. The homes looked identical, each one a square box coated with layers of snow. Velamir tugged his cloak over his head, trudging through the thick blankets of white toward the gate. The others' footsteps were muffled behind him. An involuntary shiver went through him. He was growing accustomed to the cold. It hadn't been this way in Tariqi, where the drizzling weather lasted all year round. In the Empire, it was biting heat in the summer, blissful wind in spring, and freezing cold in the winter. At least, that was if you lived in Verin. But up here in the mountains, Devorin was called the Kingdom of Snow for a reason.

"Halt!" the guards called as they neared.

Velamir raised his hands, showing his lack of weapons. The comforting weight of his sword still rested on his hip. If Velamir truly wanted to, he could unsheathe it in less time than it took him to blink. But he had to portray a harmless look.

"State your name and business in this part of town."

"We are here for market week," Velamir replied.

"Papers?"

"No papers. Our prisoner here destroyed them."

He nodded behind him toward Bear. Lore held the rope binding the older Savorian's wrists together. Velamir's heart twisted. He hated putting his former mentor in that position, but they wouldn't be allowed past any other way. Bear snarled in Savorian—curses, most likely—his nostrils flaring as he rushed toward the guards. They flinched, recoiling. Lore yanked on the rope, and Bear stumbled back. There wasn't enough muscle on Lore's gangly arms for such a move, but Bear made it look real. His right eye closed in a subtle wink as he brushed against Velamir.

"You made it just in time," one guard said after clearing his throat. "The auctions are about to begin. You can sell off this monster."

The guards allowed them past. That part of Sok had a far damper atmosphere than the rest of the town. The people observed them walking past with eagle eyes, watching for anything suspicious. Velamir had noticed several wanted posters of runaway slaves hanging about. The queen was on a hunt and the civilians after a reward. Velamir's boots rang out against the cobblestones. He'd been searching for Natassa and the slayer of the Savagelanders for days, but it was as if they had disappeared without a trace. There was no sign of them anywhere, although the tracks had led to the town. If another enslaver had taken Natassa prisoner, Velamir estimated they would make an appearance on market day. His hopes were hanging on this assumption.

It was oddly quiet despite the many people grouping around and setting up raised platforms. The only sounds were the clinking of chains as the bound prisoners were escorted toward the platforms. A desperate suffocating air lingered around the captives. Velamir wanted nothing more than to level the town and release the poor souls. To cut the ropes binding their wrists and lead them to freedom. But he wouldn't. He couldn't. Not without finding Natassa.

"Any ideas?" he asked Bear.

"From what I know, they sell oldest to youngest. I think we will have to wait a fair bit."

Lore glanced about with wide eyes, his youthful features stricken. "But slavery is illegal."

"Aye, lad," Bear said. "It has no place in the Empire. But it brings in a great deal of money, and some people decide that's of more value than their morals. They bring them in through the Docks and ship them around."

"Why doesn't anyone stop it?"

"No one's strong enough. Those who don't like it do their best. The only one who could ensure the elimination of slavery is the emperor. But, you see, the deceased Emperor Malus himself had many Savorian slaves he called servants. He turned a blind eye to what happened in the Empire. I doubt Emperor Draven will change that."

Velamir scoffed. "He doesn't even deserve that title."

Velamir looked away, spotting a hooded man leaning against the stone wall of a house. He was watching them, and something about him seemed familiar. Velamir took a step toward him, and the man shot off, disappearing between buildings. Velamir was after him in an instant, calls of his name swallowed by the dust behind him. He spotted the end of the man's cloak flapping as he disappeared into another alley. Velamir gave chase and soon came upon an empty road. He swiveled around, but there was no sign of the cloaked man. Then he noticed the house across from him. The door trembled as if it had just slammed closed. The gray curtains barricading the window stirred, and Velamir could have sworn he saw eyes peering at him. The rush of boots approached.

"Empire's sake, what happened?" Lore asked.

Velamir turned. Bear was first, his hands twisted in an awkward position because of the rope, which was still held fast in Lore's hands. The boy trailed behind Bear, looking the worse for wear. It appeared as if Bear were dragging Lore forward rather than the other way around. Velamir contained a laugh and threw his hands up in defeat.

"Lad? Where did you run off to?"

Velamir motioned to the house. "There was a man watching us. He's inside."

"Do you know him?" Lore asked.

"I feel like I do, but it's more than that." Velamir hesitated. "I think he wanted me to follow him."

He moved forward, but Bear stepped beside him. "Careful, lad. It may be the person who killed the Savagelanders. He might have caught on to our pursuit."

Velamir nodded, patting his arm before stepping up the stone stairs to the door. He knocked briefly. No answer. He unsheathed his dagger from his boot and stepped back, angling his body and preparing to ram the door open with his shoulder. Just as he launched forward, the door flew open, and he stumbled into a dimly lit room. Thick hands grabbed him. Velamir resisted the hold, freeing his arm and shoving his assailant toward the wall with the edge of his dagger to their throat.

"Velamir!" Bear shouted, barging inside.

"I'm fine," Velamir called back. He pressed his lethal blade deeper into his attacker's skin. "Who are you?"

Through the darkness, he could make out a portion of the face. The man reached up, removing his hood.

"Calm down, young Velamir."

The accented voice struck his memory. But it was Lore who placed the man first.

"You are the master of the joust! Koseer-ja, what are you doing here? We all thought you were killed in the battle at the castle."

The Savagelander smiled, teeth glinting in the darkness. Other than his braided hair, he was almost unrecognizable. Gone was the outlandish apparel he'd worn during the jousting competition. Velamir frowned. He had completely forgotten about him after the Tariqins attacked the castle.

Koseer-ja must have read his mind, because he said, "As soon as I heard word of the Dark Army's imminent approach, I set off from the castle. Not as a coward, as you are no doubt thinking, but because I had important news to deliver."

"So you were a Savagelander spy, just as I expected."

"Uluzar, and yes, I was a spy, just as you were a spy for Prolus."

Velamir flinched.

"But a few years ago, I came across another order. One whose goal aligned with mine. Changing this world for the better. So just as you abandoned being a Chishma, I abandoned being a spy for my Uluzar chief. Instead, I changed my loyalties to serve the Elders."

Velamir's grip on his dagger loosened. "Elders? You are part of them?"

"Yes, and I would appreciate speaking without feeling as if my throat will be severed in half."

Velamir stepped back, glancing at Bear and Lore.

"Was that not the order you were searching for?" Bear asked.

Velamir didn't answer, but his thoughts immediately went to the pendant resting above his heart. He'd made a promise to deliver it to the Elders.

"That is good to hear, because the Elders have been searching for you as well," Koseer-ja said. "They've been looking for the one who will unite all opposing lands under one banner. The one who will unite the Uluzar and the Empire."

"And who is that?" Lore asked.

"Young Velamir right here." Koseer-ja smiled.

A long moment of silence passed before Velamir started laughing. He exchanged a bewildered glance with Bear.

"I mean, I believe Velamir is a good man—a great man even—but you are asking him to join two warring countries together. I don't think anyone has the strength to do so," Lore said.

"The boy's right. I'm not the man you are searching for."

"Aren't you, though? Are you not the wielder of the blade?"

"I don't understand."

"Your sword, Velamir. Have you ever wondered why anyone else struggled to wield it?"

Velamir racked his mind, recalling Lore's failure to hold the sword. He remembered Mordon's face back in Prolus's camp when they had taken their weapons. Mordon had struggled with the weapon. A man as large as him should have had no problem with a blade like Velamir's. He recalled the moment Frumgan had first given him the blade. The Shadow Manos could barely carry the sword to him. Velamir had blamed it on his age, but had that truly been the case?

"That sword was forged in the Savagelands, in the Uluz, made with derinium metal by the greatest smith of our history. It was given to the khan of all the chiefs, the leader of the Uluzar."

Velamir's mouth parted, and he slowly shook his head.

"From khan to heir, it was passed down. No one except the khan could wield the sword. And then one day, it disappeared. The Uluz fell to darkness, as suddenly no one could become the khan. No one had power over anyone. The Uluzar broke into tribes. The final khan's son set off in search of the blade. The last trace of the weapon was found in the Empire. That is the reason the Uluzar are trying to take the Empire. They are attempting to reclaim order, leadership. They want to reinstate their previous glory. And to do so, they need that weapon." Koseer-ja nodded. "The blade that caused the death and bloodshed of countless is in your hands. You have the sword."

"But that makes little sense," Velamir said. "If only the khans could wield the blade, why can I?"

Koseer-ja gave him a pointed look. "Who was your father, Velamir? Who were your forefathers? Who are *you*?"

"But Boltrex was . . . Imperial." Velamir glanced at Lore and Bear, who stared back with disbelief. "He was Imperial, wasn't he?"

"I never even thought about it," Lore said. "I mean, he was General Boltrex Vaz. He was always there."

Had no one known him? Who was Boltrex Vaz? Velamir recalled the letter the general had written him, hidden and unread in his pocket. He sheathed his dagger and pulled the letter free. The paper crinkled as he smoothed it over and stepped outside into the light. The cloudy sky above him and the biting wind seemed far off as he stared at the looping letters on the page.

Alaric,

Though the moments we shared were few, they were the greatest treasure this world could have given me. We didn't have time to speak about many things, but some secrets cannot remain concealed. For years, I served under King Dale's rule. I maintained the guise of a loyal Imperial. At first, my accent and behavior gave away my true identity, but King Dale rewarded my loyalty with silence. No one knew the truth. They would have killed me if they had.

The reality is that I am what the Imperials call a Savagelander. My father was the great khan of the Uluz. But after a series of irreversible events, everything changed. I was forced to flee to save my life. But I couldn't allow my brother to take over the Uluz. He would have brought war on the world to attain the power he sought. So, I took the one thing that could have granted him the right to rule. I took the sword you now carry. The weapon of khans.

My brother has hunted me since that day. I kept the sword hidden in my fortress, but the moment it was overtaken, I thought it was lost for good. When I saw you carried the sword, confusion plagued me. I wondered how you could wield it, how you possibly found it. I formulated countless tales to explain it. That you were my brother's son, that he had somehow claimed the sword when the Uluzar took my fortress and passed it down to you. I thought of every possibility other than the truth. That you were my son. That was why I said the sword was meant to be yours, Alaric. I see the goodness in you. You are what this world needs. I wish I *could have been there to guide you. But know that I will watch over you from afar. I will watch over you with all your ancestors.*

Your father,

Boltrex/Boldrix-ja

Jax

Kingdom of Devorin
Castle Yakh

Icy cold water splashed over him, startling him awake. Damp curls stuck to his face. Jax gasped for breath, his hands and legs still bound to the wooden board beneath him. He breathed in. His teeth chattered, and the hairs on his arms rose from the cold. Where was he? What was he doing there? They were familiar questions. That wasn't the first time he'd thought them, he realized. Jax struggled to sit up. The muscles in his abdomen clenched as he pushed himself up.

"Don't strive for naught." The voice was close, so close.

Jax flinched, glancing around. That voice was also familiar, haunting him every time he awoke. He closed his eyes, and his wet lashes threaded together.

It will only tire you further.

When he opened his eyes, she was there, standing above him with a sinister smile. She reminded him of the stories the children in the Chishman Academy used to whisper at night. The ice witch of the Empire. Stealing the hearts of the young. Jax inhaled as she leaned over him. Strands of icy white hair fell over her shoulders. Her pale, colorless eyes examined him. Despite how she appeared blind, she saw far more than he wanted her to. Her long skeletal fingers grasped his chin, forcing him to meet her gaze.

"What do you want from me?" he mumbled through purple lips.

You aren't the Shadow Manos Prolus promised me.

Jax flinched. He had felt empty since the day Quintus delivered him to the ice queen. The thought of that bastard brought fire to his bones. The flames broadened as he recalled Lissa's lifeless body. His fingers formed into fists.

That's more like it.

The whisper grated on his nerves. The snow queen's thin lips widened in approval. She was unnervingly beautiful. The kind of beauty that kept you awake at night in terror, if such a thing existed.

They killed your love. They abandoned you.

Jax frowned. Quintus was the reason Lissa was gone, but he didn't understand her implied abandonment.

Your friends.

He heard the ominous voice in his mind.

Your friends abandoned you. You have no one now. Nothing but what I can give you.

Her eyes were locked with his, and a memory flooded through Jax's mind with sudden force. Deedans hauling him back to the Tariqin camp. He'd been wounded, weakened by blood loss, his eyes shuttering closed as he focused on the figures he'd been dragged away from. Velamir and the others. Velamir had been shouting, attempting to get to him. Jax shook his head.

"Velamir was trying to save me."

But he didn't. He left you. He left you to rot.

Jax refused to believe it, though panic struck him. Not Velamir. Never Velamir. He could picture him across from him at the Chishman Academy, gripping forearms. *Brothers.* They were brothers. Velamir would never leave him behind.

"He's my brother." Jax was adamant.

The queen's eerie chuckle washed through his thoughts, and then she whispered, *You may not be a Shadow Manos, but I will do everything I can to use you. To make you my warrior.*

"How can you speak to me this way? In my mind."

You don't think I've lived to the ripe age of a hundred years without a few tricks up my sleeve?

Her hissing laugh echoed.

Come, girl.

A woman with a lowered head neared. When she lifted her head, Jax sifted through the deep places in his mind to his childhood memories and remembered why he hated the queen even more. Lilly, his cousin, stood before him, her lips sealed together with a thick black cord. Sewn to keep her silent. And yet he heard her too.

Yes, my queen.

Her voice echoed, softer than he remembered. Barren and lost. The queen extended her hand, palm up. Lilly dropped a vial into it. Jax's stomach lurched at the sight of the golden liquid.

"No!" he screamed. "No."

But as always, the queen probed his mouth open, and the contents slithered down his throat. He gasped for breath, for strength, tears seeping out from the corners of his eyes. The fog came slowly, blocking his pain, and soon his thoughts faded away. He blinked as the soft incantations of a woman's voice recited around him. He blinked again. Where was he? And then a more pressing question arose. *Who* was he?

Latimus
Kingdom of Ondalar
Zardsari

Sweat plastered the collar of his fine robes. It might as well have been a noose. Latimus was signing his life away for the good of Verin to regain his family's honor. He was accepting marriage to a woman he wasn't sure was in her right mind. The woman who was grinning widely across from him. She reached out, pinching him.

"Smile," she hissed from the corner of her mouth. "You look like you are attending a funeral instead of your wedding."

But it *was* his funeral. The grand death of Latimus Blayton's days of being a man on his own, captain of the lancers, dashing hero. The dashing part might have been an exaggeration, but

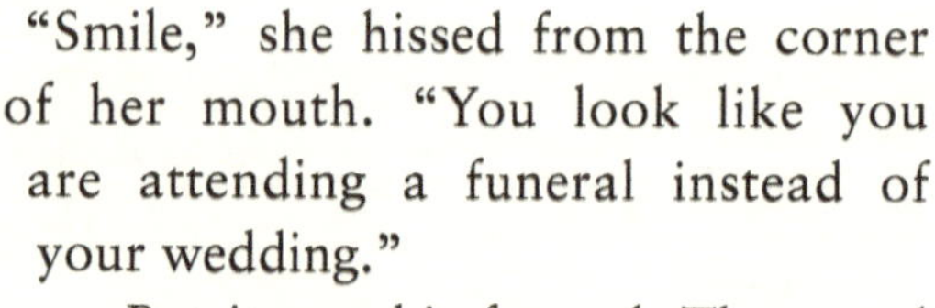

the point was that all of his hopes and dreams were crumbling to ash right in front of him. And he was supposed to smile. He forced one, but it must have looked worse, for the true Lady Sardala rolled her eyes and pressed fingers into her cheeks, emphasizing her own smile. Latimus exhaled a pained breath.

The officiator spread his hands wide. "We are honored to witness the joining of young Captain Blayton and Lady Sardala Genvor. As well as the joining of two kingdoms, Verin and Ondalar."

Several mutters of anger rang out from the rows of witnesses gathered behind them. Many Ondalarians weren't pleased with the peace agreement. If they'd had their way, he would've worn a funeral shroud instead of golden robes. King Gallaxos was behind the officiator, staring down at them from his throne. A large crown nestled into his perfect hair.

"Bring forth the veyer."

A shieldmaiden stepped forward, extending a tray laden with the thick paste. The officiator stepped closer to Latimus and Sardala, dipping his fingers into it. Latimus examined the greenish gunk. He recalled the Shadow Manos Jaxon Tana speaking about it.

It's made from dung and leaves.

Dung? Latimus had exclaimed. *There's another reason I will never marry.*

Jax had rolled his eyes. *You have a bigger problem. You would have to find a person willing to marry you.*

Latimus chuckled at the recollection. A throat cleared, and his humor receded at the glares the audience, Sardala, and the officiator were pinning him with.

"I apologize. Please continue."

"Before all these witnesses, you shall be bonded till the end of your days, connected by the beat of your hearts, the air in your lungs." The officiator spread the paste across Sardala's pale wrist, tracing the blue vein running up her arm.

Latimus peered at Sardala. She wasn't bad-looking. In fact, if he saw past her strangeness, she was even beautiful. Dressed in a glowing golden gown that draped over her form. Her brown waves done up in a crown around her head, soft tendrils hanging loose about her flushed cheeks. Her brown eyes gleaming with happiness. But that was the thing about beauty. It was misleading. He was marrying an Ondalarian maiden who might one day kill him in his sleep, if not by driving him mad before then.

Sardala beamed at the veyer covering her veins. The officiator turned to Latimus, dabbing the paste across his wrist. Latimus recalled the first wedding he'd attended as a boy. He'd asked his mother why the officiant had spread the paste onto their veins.

Because the vein travels to the heart. It's a promise to love each other with every heartbeat, she'd said.

It was almost as if he were watching from far away as the officiator lifted their arms and pressed them together, skin to skin, pulse to pulse.

"They are now linked forever. Until their last breath."

Latimus's eyes locked with Sardala's as applause rang throughout the throne room. Sardala's fingers tangled with his, and she thrust their hands into the air, jumping up with a cheer. Latimus's shoulder was nearly ripped out of its socket.

Sardala dragged him over to the high seats intended for the couple. Papers rested beside the delicious plates of steaming food. Things they had to sign to make the matrimony official. The basics, such as promising their first child as their heir, their second to becoming a True Manos, their third a prospect for the emperor's Cadellion—the reason his parents had stopped conceiving after Lore—and so on. Latimus sat beside Sardala. She chattered nonstop, throwing out facts Latimus had never even cared about knowing, hardly stopping to breathe with the exception of bites of food. Well-wishers and non-well-wishers stopped by the table. Latimus nodded at each one, hoping the torture would end soon.

"Did you know next month I will be elevated to a full shieldmaiden? I will wear the graduate armor and patch." Sardala smiled dreamily. "Though I'm not so fond of the shine on the shields. They are too bright. Oh! Maybe you can wear something to match. Or not . . . Judging by your expression, you don't seem fond of that idea." She tapped her chin. "Let's do this, then. Let's—"

"Do you ever stop talking?"

Her eyes filled with hurt, and she fell silent. Her features were stricken. Something shifted in Latimus, and he turned his attention to his plate. He hadn't intended to offend her, but he needed a second to think, to breathe. Minutes passed. Soft music filled the throne room. Couples twirled around the intricately carved marble floor. Latimus glanced at Sardala. She was staring at her food aimlessly, her fingers gripping her fork so tightly, he could see the strain on her skin.

"Look," he started. "I'm just getting accustomed to everything here. I didn't mean to upset you."

She continued staring down.

"You must see, everything is so foreign to me. I've come from Verin. Our customs are different. I just pledged to spend the rest of my days here as your husband, leaving my old life behind."

Sardala dropped the fork and spun toward him, her lips flat for the first time. "This is strange for me too. It's not as if I get married every week."

Latimus tilted his head. "So, it's a peculiar experience for us both. Perhaps we can tread this path slowly, learn to understand each other?"

As soon as the words slipped out, he regretted them. He didn't want to know her better. In fact, he wanted to build a wall between them. He felt nothing for her. Latimus didn't want to mislead her. Soon there would be eyes on them, questions. Where are the heirs? Latimus shuddered inwardly. He would have to overcome that, but for that moment, he would take one thing at a time.

Sardala nodded. "I would like that."

Latimus managed a small smile and returned to eating. It took ten seconds, only ten seconds, for her to start speaking again. Latimus's eyes fluttered shut as he suppressed a groan.

"I grew up an only child abandoned to the care of nannies. The silence was overbearing in that empty manor. I would always try to fill it with words or songs."

Latimus's ears perked up. "Songs?"

"My aunt oversaw my teaching after my mother passed. She loved hearing me sing, so she ensured I had the best tutors."

"You can sing?"

She nodded. "I love to sing. Songs are like a secret language. They transport me to a different reality with their secretive phrases. When the world becomes too dark to bear, I sing, and the way through seems clearer. You look surprised."

"I'm only shocked that we have something in common."

"You sing too?"

Latimus shrugged. "I don't mean to brag, but I have some talent."

"We should sing together sometime!" she exclaimed.

Latimus glanced at her. She was beaming again, and for some reason, he felt lighter at seeing her giddiness return. And . . . she had dimples. He hadn't noticed them before, one on either cheek.

"I would like that," he said softly.

The hall fell into a sudden hush, and Latimus turned to see what had captured everyone's attention. Standing at the entrance of the throne room was General Zenrelius, garbed in full armor. King Gallaxos rose from his throne.

"You are late, Cousin."

"Or perhaps I am just on time."

Zenrelius strode forward, eyes following him the entire way until he stopped at the foot of the grand stairs leading up to the magnificent throne. The realization of how drab Verin appeared in comparison struck Latimus again.

"What are you insinuating?" Gallaxos peered down at Zenrelius.

"Your uncle, King Calias, had many children but bequeathed his crown to his nephew, your father."

Gallaxos glanced around, shifting uneasily. "Because his children are illegitimate and can never attain beyond their shieldmaiden status. Has the zat gotten to your head, Cousin? You are spouting nonsense during this joyous gathering."

Zenrelius chuckled. "If you truly knew me, you would know I have never touched a drop of zat. That poison destroyed everyone I knew. Returning to the conversation at hand, King Calias also had a son."

Soft whispers flittered around. He was speaking of himself. It was common knowledge. His relation to the deceased King Calias was as renowned as his prowess as a general.

"Your father never should have sat on that throne." Zenrelius motioned toward the grand chair.

Gallaxos snarled. "How dare you speak ill of my father!"

"I am only speaking the truth. It is time for the rightful line to rule once again. You shall not sully the throne any further."

Loud gasps rang out. Latimus was frozen in his seat as he glanced between the two men.

"I see you are longing for your death. Koru Komak formation!"

Men and women in golden uniforms jumped before the king, forming a protective barrier in front of Gallaxos. Zenrelius raised a dark brow at all the weapons pointed at him.

Gallaxos laughed. "What will you do now, *General*?"

"You are so naïve to believe I would walk in here without a plan. While you spent all your years drinking zat, I was forming allies."

Lord Genvor stood from his table. *"Haler Yeer jovel!"*

The golden-armored bodyguards switched positions at lightning-fast speed. Their glinting weapons were aimed toward a paling Gallaxos. Zenrelius's thin lips quirked up. He walked up the stairs, and the golden sea parted for him. He unsheathed his sword, pointing it at the king of Ondalar.

"Now, what will you do, *Cousin*? Surrender or lose your head?"

Natassa
Kingdom of Devorin
Sok Town

IT WAS THE first time she had seen the sun in days. A chilly breeze brushed her skin, and she inhaled, savoring the feeling. The sounds of bargaining townspeople faded. Then the Seer spoke, his voice piercing through the momentary peace.

Your time is fleeting, Princess.

A hand grasped her arm, and she jumped. Aria apologized, watching her with concern.

The Elder was dressed in a long beautifully embroidered dress. A thick fabric shielded her face and hair, and a thin chain of dangling coins rested beneath her eyes, the sparkling copper bringing out the green of her irises. Natassa was garbed in a similar outfit. They were attempting to stay out of sight.

Natassa grimaced. "It's the shadows."

Aria nodded, patting her arm with sympathy. "The fresh air making it any better?"

At Master Dunya's urging, Aria had taken her out of the Elders' safehold.

"It is helping," Natassa said. "It's good to focus on something other than them."

"Why don't you stand here for a moment? I'm going to head into this shop and purchase some wares for the shelter."

Natassa hesitated before nodding.

"I'll be back in a moment," Aria reassured her.

Natassa watched her duck inside the shop and crossed her arms over her chest against a sudden chill. A boy ran up to her, looking distraught.

"Miss, please help me."

Natassa grasped his hands. "Calm down and tell me what's wrong."

"My little brother, he's hanging from the roof."

Worry struck Natassa, and she motioned for the boy to lead her to his brother. She followed him through a narrow alley, looking up at the roofs for his brother. A warning thudded in her chest the farther they went. The boy stopped.

"Where is he?" Natassa asked.

The boy didn't answer, instead staring at something ahead of them. Natassa's heart went cold. Standing across from her and leaning against the stone alley wall was Yalnos. He watched her with a smirk.

"Thought you could escape me, girl?" He tossed a coin to the boy, who caught it and scurried away.

Yalnos strode toward her, and Natassa retreated, but he caught her easily, grabbing her arms and shoving her against the stone wall. Natassa gasped, pain shooting through her back at the impact. Her heart quickened as fear filled her mouth. Yalnos smiled that wide disturbing grin.

"Where are you off to?"

Natassa fought against his brutal grip. He towered over her, his eyes flashing with menace. Natassa breathed through her panic.

Princess, we are at your command, the Seer whispered.

Natassa felt them on either side of her. Dark spirits drifting about her.

"Help me," she said through gritted teeth.

Yalnos's face scrunched in confusion. Natassa closed her eyes, feeling the shadows guiding her forward until she saw into Yalnos's mind. They held her there, forcing her to bear his memories and see his intentions. She saw a tall bony woman with pale eyes and an eerie appearance. The queen of Devorin. Yalnos was kneeling before her in the memory, his expression desperate as he asked for forgiveness. The queen pointed a long finger toward the door and cast him out. Natassa sifted through other memories and realized what he wanted. The queen of Devorin was searching for the phoenix. She was searching for her, and Yalnos had planned to bring her before his queen in return for clemency.

Natassa gasped, jerking out of his mind. Yalnos's eyes rolled. His hold on her slackened, and he fell back several paces. He touched his brow, groaning.

"What did you do?" he muttered. "What did you do to me?"

Natassa reached forward and unsheathed the man's dagger. She waved the weapon at him. "Stay back."

But he didn't heed her warning and launched forward again. Natassa stabbed him in the leg. Then she tore away, leaving him screaming in agony. Natassa's vision grew blurry; her mind ached. She stumbled out of the alley and continued through the streets.

We have aided you and received nothing in return, the Lure hissed.

"Be silent," she said.

The time for our glory has come. You must open the gateway and undo the betrayal of your ancestors, Natassa Hartinza, the Seer told her.

Natassa glanced back. Yalnos emerged from around a corner, appearing enraged as he scanned his surroundings in search of her. He clutched his leg. Blood spilled from the wound, and the limp slowed him. Natassa searched in desperation for somewhere to hide. She dashed toward a cart with a linen draped overtop it and hopped inside, then pulled the linen forward to conceal herself. Folded fabrics lay around her. She peered through the linen and watched Yalnos staggering about, his gaze wild.

Natassa's headache grew. She blinked against the haze. Using her shadows had exhausted her. Natassa forced her eyes to remain open. She had to wait for Yalnos to leave.

⌁

Natassa blinked at the bright light as the linen was flung aside. She scrambled up, glancing around in confusion. She was in the middle of an empty road. The town and Yalnos were nowhere in sight. It took her a moment to realize what had happened, and she suppressed a groan. She'd fallen asleep. Natassa gripped the edge of the cart. A wide-set woman with an angry scowl glared down at her.

"What are you doing in my cart?"

The woman slapped a long whip into her palm. Natassa winced, looking over the cart to see dozens more carts ahead of hers. All had stopped, and the horses pulling them pawed at the ground. The drivers were looking back, watching Natassa and the woman.

"I-I am sorry. I didn't mean to stay."

The woman's mouth thinned, and she pointed the whip toward her. "Well, you have. And now that we have taken you this far, we demand payment."

"Can you take me back to town? My friends there can compensate you."

"We can either leave you stranded here with no one to help you but the next group of thieves that come along, or we can take you with us to our destination. Either way, we will require payment."

Her shadows whispered, and she contemplated using them to persuade the woman into taking her back to Sok but dashed the thought away at once. The shadows were bad enough as it was. Every time she used their powers, they seemed to gain more advantage over her. And it took too much of her energy. She couldn't risk losing consciousness and having the woman's caravan guards kill her for being a Shadow Manos. There were too many witnesses.

"I have nothing to give you."

The woman's eyes gleamed. "That piece will do nicely."

Natassa glanced down, touching the bracelet circling her wrist. "This?"

The woman nodded, extending her hand.

Natassa gulped. "Please—"

"I won't hear any more excuses. Hand it over. Or I will have my guards tear it off."

Tears blinded Natassa's eyes as she unclasped the bracelet. After the Savagelanders had captured her, she noticed the absence of the bracelet her brother Thorsten had gifted her. It had pained her so much, but she'd clung to the one that remained—the one Velamir had given her. The stone in the center shone as red as it had when he'd fastened it around her wrist. It had kept her spirits up, knowing he was alive because the promise he'd made continued to be upheld. Natassa removed the bracelet, a tear slipping free as she watched the stone dull to its original color. The woman snatched it and tossed it in her palm, nodding in appreciation.

The caravan continued forward as soon as the woman hopped back onto the seat at the front of the cart. Natassa did not know where they were going, but she could no longer receive help from the Elders. She had to cast the shadows out herself.

Latimus

Kingdom of Ondalar

Zardsari

Latimus sat dazed in the chair. General Zenrelius stood before him, peering at him with dark eyes. The general's words from the wedding feast rang fresh in his mind. Following his bloody removal of King Gallaxos, Zenrelius had turned to address the crowd.

"For years, Ondalar has lain back. When Emperor Malus demanded our aid, we were there. When Ayleth demanded our aid, we were there. When Verin was at the depths of destruction, who came? Who stood by them? We did. What do all these kingdoms have in common?" Zenrelius scanned the crowd of open-mouthed spectators. *"They owe us. They owe us, but we owe them nothing. Verin and its treacherous monarchy took our dear*

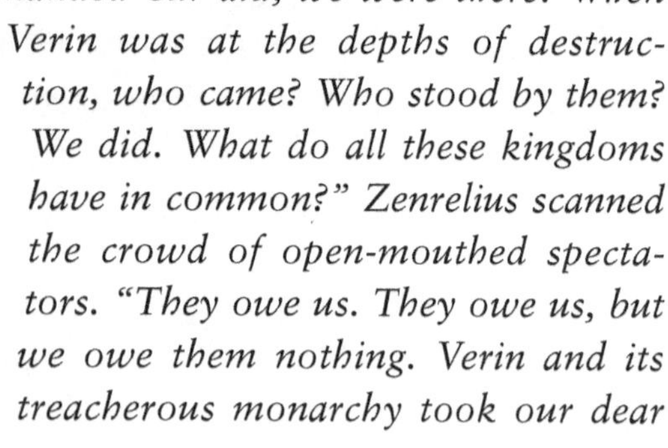

*princess from us. They took my sister, Princess Adela-
nia, from us, murdering her and her child. Will we leave
that unanswered?"*

The crowd rallied, screaming their denial.

*"Our next step is to march to Verin. We will exact
our revenge. At long last." A wide unnerving smile
spread across his face at those words.*

"All hail King Zenrelius!" Lord Genvor shouted.

"Long live the king!"

*The chants filled the throne room so loudly, it
seemed as if the castle trembled from the passionate
cries. Zenrelius stood before the throne before slowly
lowering himself onto it. His forearms settled onto its
outstretched arms.*

The general had broken rules that day. He'd changed
them. As the bastard son of an Ondalarian king, he had
no prospects, yet he'd become a general. As the bastard
son, he never had a chance of becoming king, yet the
halls were filled with shouts of his sovereignty. It was
proclaimed in the Book of Codes. A bastard had no
place on the throne, yet on it he'd sat.

Latimus glanced up at Zenrelius, unsure of how to
respond to the question he'd asked.

"Will you assist us, Blayton? You are our dear
ambassador. You can convince your people to surrender
and avoid more bloodshed. They cannot defend against
our cavalry. You know that."

Latimus wondered what he'd missed, what he hadn't
seen. Was this truly the man he'd admired? Respected?
Zenrelius was planning to conquer *his* kingdom. His
home. To erase Verin. That had been his plan all along.

And Latimus had naïvely fallen for his charm, for the entrancing aura that surrounded him. But not again.

Latimus stood. "I will not help you. I will not allow you to destroy Verin."

Zenrelius clicked his tongue. "Such a shame."

He motioned to the guards by the door, and they grabbed hold of Latimus. He grunted, struggling against them. They dragged him out of the room to where Sardala was waiting in the hall. As soon as she saw him, her mouth dropped open, and then her hand covered her lips.

"Let him go! What are you doing?" She lunged forward, but her father, Lord Genvor, held her back.

"Ambassador Blayton has chosen his path," Zenrelius said. "He may rot in the dungeon until his death or a change of thought."

Latimus swore at the general. The guards didn't relent, shoving him through the castle until they reached the lower levels and the dungeon. They threw him into a cell and banged the iron bars shut. Latimus grumbled under his breath. Rat droppings littered one corner, and what appeared to be human feces decorated the other. Latimus grimaced, swallowing the bile rising in his throat.

"What did you do, mate?" a hairy man in the cell beside him asked.

"I refused your wicked general."

"Huh?"

"I suppose it was his first rejection, since he threw me in here like a petulant child."

Laughs barked throughout the cells as other prisoners pointed and chuckled at him.

"I don't see what is so amusing about this."

Several hours later, the dungeon door screeched
open. Latimus grasped the cell bars. He was past the
point of caring about his cleanliness. Silk slippers came
into sight and then the hem of a skirt brushing over
them. Latimus drew back, surprised when the rest of the
person came into view.

Sardala rushed toward his cell, carrying a tray with
a bowl of soup and a thick piece of bread. "I brought
food."

"I don't want food. I want my freedom."

She glanced behind her, toward the guards waiting at
the top of the stairs, before lowering her voice. "I am on
your side. Zenrelius is doing wrong. I tried to convince
him to change his mind, but it was futile. He is determined to conquer Verin."

"And your father?"

"He refuses to listen. It's like he's changed. He obeys
everything Zenrelius says without batting an eye."

"Queen Coralie has no idea of his plans. I have to
warn her," Latimus said, desperation making him grip
the bars tighter.

Sardala's eyes conveyed her sympathy. "I brought
you a wedding gift."

Latimus huffed. "I'm not in a humorous mood."

"The bread, dummy," she whispered. "I placed a
key inside of it."

Realization dawned on him, his gaze rooted to the

bread. Footsteps thudded down the stairs, and Zenrelius appeared along with Lord Genvor.

"Father?"

Lord Genvor ignored her. "We received word from the cooks that there was tampering with the prisoners' meals."

Sardala paled as Zenrelius snatched the tray from her. He poured the soup, and the thick liquid splattered onto the stone. Latimus's heart thudded, hoping against hope that the man would not search further.

"She only came to give me food. Lady Sardala has done nothing wrong."

Zenrelius gave him a skewering smile before grasping the bread. He tore it to shreds, and the pieces fell, leaving in their remainders a solid metal key. Zenrelius looked up, meeting Lord Genvor's gaze.

"I expected better of you, Lady Sardala," Zenrelius said. "You aided a traitor. You betrayed Ondalar. Put her in a cell."

"No!" Sardala screeched as the guards grasped her arms and shoved her toward the empty cell across from him.

"Get your hands off her!" Latimus roared.

"Your Majesty, we are speaking of my daughter," Lord Genvor finally said. "She is naïve. Perhaps you can overlook this slight mistake."

Zenrelius shook his head. "This *slight* mistake could have ruined our entire battle plan. If the boy had escaped and given word in advance to his queen, all would be for naught. Lady Sardala must remain here, at least until we take Verin."

"But—"

Zenrelius patted Lord Genvor's arm. "I'm sorry, dear friend, but it must be this way."

Latimus's breaths came out in angry pants as he watched the cell door slam shut on Sardala's tearful face.

"Father!" she cried out. "Father!"

But Lord Genvor only gave her a regretful look before following the new king of Ondalar from the dungeons. Silence descended. Even the other prisoners remained quiet. The only noise was the snuffles Sardala emitted. She sniffed, sinking down on the cold stone. She pulled her knees into her chest and hid her face from view. Latimus's fist clenched around the bars. He knew exactly how she felt. He'd experienced firsthand how devastating a father's betrayal was. His father hadn't just destroyed his family; he'd sold out the entire kingdom. Latimus sank down and pressed his head back against the stone. He glanced over at Sardala, whose body shook as she attempted to silence her sobs. The other prisoners looked on, some even appearing remorseful.

Sardala's words during the wedding came to Latimus's mind.

When the world becomes too dark to bear, I sing, and the way through seems clearer.

"They say if you see danger, close your eyes." His voice emerged hoarse.

All gazes swung to him. Sardala's head lifted the slightest bit. Latimus cleared his throat and tried again.

They say if you see danger,
close your eyes.
They say if you feel anger,

keep it hidden inside.
They say if you see darkness,
turn around.
But then I saw you.

Latimus's voice broke for a moment. He didn't dare look at the others. He bolstered his courage and continued.

In you, I saw something.
I saw hope.
In you, I sensed something.
I saw light.
In you, I found the strength.

Latimus halted, pausing for breath. A soft feminine voice flitted over to him, and he turned, stunned. Sardala stared at him with red-rimmed eyes, her lips moving as she joined in the song.

The strength to face danger,
the strength to bear anger,
the strength to forge through the dark.
In you, I found the strength to hope.

Their eyes remained locked together. Latimus began to smile, and Sardala did as well. The prisoners cheered, hands clapping. Sardala's smile grew until her dimples revealed themselves. Latimus's chest warmed at the sight of them. He had hope. They would get through it. They would find a way.

Velamir

Kingdom of Devorin
Sok Town

"You are the heir of the Savagelands?"

Lore's stunned whisper was the only response to Velamir's revelation. The boy looked up from Boltrex's letter that he'd snatched from Velamir's hands minutes before. Bear attempted to read it over his shoulder but gave up soon after. Imperial wasn't his first language, and he'd never tried hard to master reading it. Instead, his focus was on Velamir, worry gouging his face.

"Are you all right, lad?"

Koseer-ja stepped out of the house they had spoken in.

"I—I need some air." Velamir strode away, walking until the others were indiscernible forms behind him. He climbed onto a low wall and sat on

the edge, his legs dangling over it. His heart twisted. When he'd thought life couldn't get any worse, Koseer-ja had revealed his true heritage as the wielder of the blade that decided the next khan of the Uluzar.

He used to sit like that with Jax, side by side. Talking about their day, their classes, their training. From the biggest things to the smallest, anything and everything. And he didn't even know where his best friend was. Was he still alive? Velamir had no choice but to have confidence that Jax was well, that Coralie's plan to retrieve him had worked.

He heard a shuffle of movement and turned to Bear, who pulled himself up onto the wall beside him. They sat in silence for endless moments.

"When will this end, Bear?" Velamir asked. "This pain, this uncertainty?"

Bear peered ahead at the rows of homes before them. "Well, lad, that's a question I used to ask myself. The truth is, it never does. Pain reminds us we are living. Uncertainty reminds us we are human."

"The guilt doesn't leave me. I feel responsible for what happened to Jax, to Natassa. I could have prevented it. I should have."

"You put too much on your shoulders, lad. You cannot blame yourself for everything that goes wrong in the world. No one is able to carry that kind of burden, not even you."

Bear pulled out the Savorian warrior carving his son had made for him from within his vest pocket. "I spent so many days working, trying to create a better life for my family, that I forgot to live life with them." Bear sniffed. "The day the Tariqins came storming in, killing, pillaging, attacking, enslaving, was the day I regretted my actions."

A tear slipped from his blond lashes. Velamir's sympathy rose at the sight of his agony.

"I blamed myself. Why hadn't I done more, tried harder?" He shook his head. "But that changes nothing. I am one man against an army. I had no chance."

Velamir placed his hand on Bear's shoulder. "Prolus took everything from us. Let's return the favor."

Bear chuckled through tears. "Agreed."

"Velamir!" Lore called, approaching. "I found someone who knows something about your girl."

Velamir's heart leaped, and he hopped off the wall and took rapid strides toward the boy. A woman emerged from behind Lore. Her face was concealed, leaving only her eyes exposed. She froze at the sight of him.

"Alaric?" she whispered.

Velamir stood rooted to the ground, watching the woman before him. Her green eyes filled with tears as she closed the gap between them. Her hand lifted into the air, stopping inches from his face. She stared at him as if he'd sprouted up from the dead.

"Alaric," she whispered again, the dark fabric crossing over her nose and mouth muffling the name.

"Who are you?" Velamir asked, wondering how she knew his former name.

"This is Velamir." Lore shifted, looking uncertain as he glanced between them.

"I know. Natassa told me about you."

"Natassa? You've seen her? Where is she?"

The woman gestured for him to calm down. "Please, come with me."

Velamir's breathing quickened, and his heart thudded—just at the mere thought of seeing Natassa, at reuniting with her. He couldn't rest until he did. No meal, no sleep, no company could ease him until he saw her whole and well. Velamir followed the woman, and Koseer-ja fell into step beside her. They conversed in low tones, and Velamir derived that she was also part of the Elders. They walked in the shadows, away from the prying eyes of the townspeople.

The woman led them to a house, and before long, they were underground with torches to guide their way. It reminded Velamir of his time in Castle Verin, when Coralie had sent him off on the mission to retrieve Mordon and ruin Winston. Velamir's lip twisted at the thought of his mentally unstable former mentor. The man he'd considered a father had turned out to be the Dark Lord Prolus himself. Velamir still couldn't comprehend it. The masked figure he'd always pictured when hearing the name didn't match his jovial, caring mentor. Or at least, he used to be that way before he showed his true colors. Before the mask came crashing down.

The Elder woman and Koseer-ja snuffed their torches and bade Velamir and the others forward into a large circular room. "You can speak at normal levels in here," she said. "There is Master Dunya, the head of our order."

An older man turned toward them as they entered. He regarded them with amber eyes seeping with knowledge. Koseer-ja stepped to his side and leaned in, whispering something in Master Dunya's ear. The older man's gaze settled on Velamir. Koseer-ja retreated a pace, and Velamir stepped forward. He glanced at the woman, itching to know where Natassa was but holding himself back from losing control again.

"So, you are the proclaimed hero of legends," Master Dunya began.

"Not a hero. Simply someone attempting to right wrongs."

The old man smiled. "All heroes deny it. Welcome, Velamir. Koseer-ja has told me much about you."

Velamir glanced at the Uluzar, who stared back, unperturbed.

"You have a dark future ahead, young one. Are you ready to face it? Do you have enough strength to bear what is coming? The three lands are entangled in war. The Uluzar, the Imperials, the Tariqins. One brave soul must stand up to stop it. One brave soul must speak so others will finally listen."

"I cannot lead," Velamir replied. "I am not cut out for that."

The old man laughed softly. "So you say. And yet when you walked into this chamber, all eyes were upon you." Master Dunya motioned toward the others standing behind Velamir. "They look to you for guidance. You may be lost, but you are a light for them. You may not know where to go next, but they will follow. Even to doom, they will follow."

Velamir searched for words as he glanced about the room. All eyes were fixed on him, just as Master Dunya had said, and it wasn't just because he was having a conversation with the old man. Velamir had noticed it before. Stares burning into him wherever he walked. Even Bear, his old mentor, looked at him differently.

"I brought something. I was entrusted to return it here." Velamir lifted the pendant over his head and let it dangle between his fingers.

Master Dunya's face turned sorrowful for a moment. "Ah, Bendir Coros's medal of honor. He served the cause till his dying breath. May he rest in peace. Aria will show you where you can place it."

The green-eyed woman nodded at Velamir, and he followed her out of the chamber after inclining his head in respect to Master Dunya. Aria continued walking until she turned into another chamber. Rows upon rows of pendants hung within. Hundreds, thousands, perhaps. People had given their lives for the order, for the change it vowed to bring to the world. Velamir stared at the metal within his palm, brushing his thumb over the pendant. He slid it onto an empty hook.

"Rest now," he whispered and released it.

Aria's head was bowed as she held her hands up in prayer. When she finished, she smiled at Velamir. "I had long given up hope you were alive."

Velamir's brow knitted in confusion, and Aria stepped closer to him.

"I know this must be strange. You might not even remember. You were so young."

"What are you speaking of?"

"Fifteen years ago. A brutal attack on a fortress. A ruthless never-ending siege. The day a family broke apart."

His thoughts snapped to the vague memories he'd

stored in his mind. Smoke, confusion, anger. The day he'd earned a thirst for revenge. The day he'd stopped being a child at the mere age of four years. Velamir blinked, severing his connection with the glimpses of his past. Aria stared at him, nodding as if she knew exactly what he'd been thinking of. As if she'd lived those moments herself. But how could she have?

"When the Uluzar came"—she sniffed—"it was sudden panic. The first time I saw someone die right before my eyes. My mother's first instinct was to protect us. She hid me and went back to search for my brother. I never saw either of them again."

Velamir was motionless. He listened to her, watched her eyes glisten, absorbed her words, but couldn't understand. Couldn't believe her.

"But I never stopped hoping to find you. Some part of me"—she pressed a finger to her chest, over her heart—"right here, believed you were alive. I'm your sister, Alaric."

All the air seeped from his lungs. He was frozen as he put the pieces together. That was the reason she had reacted the way she had when she'd seen him. The reason she called him by his former name, Alaric. Why her name had seemed so familiar.

I was content at the time with Serana and the baby we were expecting. Your sister, Aria.

Boltrex's words from so long ago rang fresh in his mind.

"Aria." Velamir whispered the name aloud for the first time since he was four years of age.

She nodded, closing the distance between them

and throwing her arms around his neck. "I thought I'd lost you."

Velamir's arms lifted, hovering in the air inches from touching her. He was still numb with shock. That day in the fortress, the day Winston had taken him away, Velamir's old life had faded from memory. Any recollection of his family was gone. Only recently had he started recalling bits and pieces of his past.

"Though my mind told me you died there, my heart didn't want to believe it." Aria gripped him tighter, and Velamir's arms drifted around her, hesitant and uncertain as he returned her embrace.

"I did, in a way," he intoned, "and was reborn a loyal warrior for the Dark Lord Prolus."

Aria pulled back, nodding. "Natassa told me everything. We encountered her in the forest when we freed some captives held by the Uluzar."

Velamir stiffened. "Where is she?"

"She accompanied me to the market today, but then she disappeared. I had been searching for her for hours before I came upon your boy."

Velamir released a frustrated breath. "How could she have disappeared?"

"I can take you to the spot I last saw her."

Velamir nodded, and she patted his arm before stepping back. She wiped tears from her eyes and led the way from the room. "Just a warning, Alaric, the girl is much changed."

Velamir's blood went cold. "What do you mean?"

"She's faced her darkness. It may take her a long time to overcome it."

⚶

They searched the market in vain. Velamir ran a hand through his hair. Despair drove him insane. He leaned against a merchant's booth, trying to regain his focus. A loud voice shouted nearby, coming closer and closer until the words registered.

"Did you see a woman around this height with shoulder-length hair?"

Velamir spun, his eyes narrowing on a tall man leaning over the counter of another booth.

"She's a pretty little thing."

Velamir's heart pounded, and he started toward the man, fury pumping in his veins.

"Alaric." Aria followed, urging him to remain calm. He heard Bear and Lore exchanging words behind him as they hurried to catch up.

"Your slave?" the stall owner asked.

The man scratched his head. "You could say that. I captured her, and she got away. And just when I'd caught her again, she slipped through my fingers."

The stall owner pondered for a moment before saying, "I recall seeing a girl jump into the cart of a passing caravan. Could it have been her?"

The man was about to reply when Velamir grabbed his arm and flung him around.

The man freed himself, drawing his sword. "Who do you think you are?"

Velamir examined the man's stance and the tight grip he had on the hilt of his weapon. He knew how to wield it. That much was apparent. Had he been the one who slayed all the Uluzar?

"It was you, wasn't it?" Velamir muttered. "Why did you kill them?"

The man frowned. "What are you talking about?"

"The Uluzar. I'd been tracking them for days. Then I found them dead. It was your work, wasn't it?"

The man scoffed. "What's it to you? They were providing me with a sum I needed, and then I found a more worthy prize. Why would I have loyalty to them?"

"A more worthy prize?" Velamir hissed.

The man smiled. "I see I've struck a nerve. I'm speaking of the girl. There are those who would pay for someone as *gifted* as her."

Velamir lunged forward, uncaring of the witnesses gathered around.

"Get him, Cales!" Lore urged him on.

The man was a good fighter, but his injured leg gave him no chance. Within seconds, Velamir had dispatched him, and the man's limp bleeding form slumped to the ground. Velamir faced the open-mouthed stall owner.

"The caravan?"

Aria leaned closer to the stall owner, unsheathing a curved blade and flicking it around her fingers in warning. The man paled further, his eyes darting between her and Velamir.

"Where was it heading?"

Zenrelius

Kingdom of Ondalar

THE WIDE GRASSY field and colorful flowers were a welcome view after the weeks of endless snow in Verin. Zenrelius breathed in the warm breeze, nodding in appreciation. He walked forward until he heard the rush of water, and the river came into view.

"You have three days to mobilize the army," Zenrelius said, glancing over his shoulder at Lord Genvor. "Three days should leave me with enough time in Verintown."

Silence followed his statement, and Zenrelius turned. "Do you understand what you must do?"

Lord Genvor's fingers darted to the high collar of his robes. His hesitance was as clear as the sun shining above them. Zenrelius's irritation built. Once his goals were achieved, Genvor would

have to be removed. Zenrelius only had use for soldiers with unshakable loyalty.

"And this substance . . . this magic is trustworthy?"

"Not magic." Zenrelius's eyes flashed. "There is no such thing as magic. If you spread word along those lines to the cavalry, everything will be destroyed. All our plans shredded." He pulled a vial from his pocket, the contents swirling within. "Zamanin Sulari, the greatest invention of our time. It is the weapon that will allow us to conquer any kingdom we wish." Zenrelius peered into the vial, sensing Lord Genvor shift in discomfort. "Do you know how much we could accomplish with this manner of power?"

"But you accepted this . . . Zamanin Sulari from Tariqi. You bargained with the Dark Army. Does that not go against everything we stand for?"

Zenrelius's head whipped toward the man. Lord Genvor was pale, as if it had taken every ounce of courage he possessed to challenge Zenrelius.

"Your recent actions have been alarming me, Genvor," Zenrelius said. "If you have changed your mind and no longer wish to support me, inform me at once."

Genvor seemed taken aback by the strength pouring from Zenrelius's tone. He lowered his head. "Of course not, Your Majesty. I simply wished to know if it was wise to accept materials crafted by our enemy. What if the Tariqins tampered with it? What if they are lying to us? Could this"—Genvor waved to the vial—"essence truly transport an entire army to another location? It doesn't seem feasible."

"You will see with your own eyes in three days, High Lord."

Zenrelius uncorked the vial and poured the contents over the flowing river. The water sprang up into the air, freezing into a circle. Zenrelius slammed a fist through with a grunt. The frozen water shattered, flinging back into a swirling portal. Zenrelius felt Genvor's wary gaze upon him as he stepped forward. Without a backward glance, he launched through the portal. The familiar heady rush overwhelmed him as he shot through. Moments later, he landed in a pile of melting snow and cursed.

"Verin," he muttered, already missing the warmth of Ondalar. The kingdom was behind, as usual.

He stood, brushing himself off and taking in his new surroundings. He squinted, spotting the towers of Castle Verin in the distance, and gathered his location.

Hours later, he found the place he was looking for: a camp of rowdy mercenaries bumping tankards of zat together to celebrate their newfound wealth. Zenrelius strode through the camp, feeling stares probing him. He paid them no mind and stopped before the largest group. A man reclined on a makeshift chair, his head tipped back, and a golden eye patch covered a good portion of his face. He examined Zenrelius, his single eye narrowing. A bulky man stood behind the chair wearing a protective glare. His bald head was adorned with tattoos, and his arms were crossed over his chest. *Some things never change*, Zenrelius thought as he took in Vykus and his henchman Salvador. Zenrelius smiled before addressing the renowned mercenary king.

"I have an offer for you."

❦

DRAVEN
KINGDOM OF AYLETH

Draven watched the streets of Ayleth from the window of Marcella's home. The marching of Tariqin soldiers hadn't slowed as more and more of Prolus's deedans poured into the city. *His city*. Draven fisted the curtain, anger thrumming within him. He couldn't believe it had come to that. In a matter of days, he'd gone from being the ruler of everything to a runaway hiding in his own kingdom. Draven yanked the curtain closed.

The sounds of low conversation caught his attention. Honzio and Svorgin were sharing bread on Marcella's kitchen table. The two men were chuckling. *Chuckling*. Draven wanted to storm over to them, yank the bread from their hands, and smack it against their heads as he questioned their intellect. Draven's lip curled. Honzio still hadn't provided him with the cure for the poison running through his veins. Honzio claimed he could only receive treatment in the castle with the True Manos and their supplies. Draven wondered if the man was hoping he would die from the poison.

Draven strode away and headed up the stairs to Marcella's chamber. After he quickly knocked, the woman bade him to enter. He stepped inside. The familiar chaos of the chamber greeted him. Shelves of ingredients, rows of books, and a table covered in materials filled the room. Marcella glanced up, her hands gripping her mortar and pestle as she ground something.

"What is it you need, Majesty?"

Draven approached the table. "You have helped me with many things, but have you ever dabbled in poison?"

Marcella's eyes widened before she burst out laughing. "Poison? Your Majesty, I was crafting poison in the womb. It is in my nature as a Doer Shadow Manos."

Draven smiled, pleased to hear that. "I was bitten by a snake. Honzio told me it was a poison with a rare remedy."

Marcella nodded. "Let me take a look."

Draven took a seat at the table and propped his leg up. Marcella hummed under her breath as she examined the area. At last, she looked up at him.

"It has healed well. The fang marks are hardly noticeable."

Draven stiffened. "Healed? What about the poison?"

She shook her head. "If you were poisoned, you would be long dead now. It seems, my dear king, that you have been deceived."

Draven snarled, muttering Honzio's name and every curse he knew along with it. Marcella watched him with raised brows. He stormed from the chamber and ducked out of Marcella's home through the back door. The streets of Ayleth looked so desolate as evening descended. Draven was done hiding. He walked up to the castle gates, and deedans swarmed around him. He spread his arms wide, allowing them to search him. It was time he paid Prolus a visit.

Deedans boxed him in as they led him through his castle. The corridors gave him a pang of homesickness. Even if he was in Ayleth, even if he was in his own castle, nothing was the same anymore. The deedans made him wait by the throne room until their lord allowed them entrance. As soon as the heavy doors swung open, Draven caught sight of the masked figure reclining on the sole throne at the far end of the chamber. He bit back the irritation swelling within him and shook off the deedans' grips. He marched forward, and the deedans launched after him. The Dark Lord lifted a gloved hand, and his soldiers retreated, permitting Draven to continue.

"This is not what we agreed upon," Draven said.

Prolus's icy blue eyes peered at Draven through the mask. "Draven Valent." The threatening whisper of his name brought him to a halt. It was the closest Draven had been to the Dark Lord, the first time he'd heard his voice. He'd planned accordingly so he would never have to be in such a dangerous position.

"*King* Draven Valent," Draven said. "I see you've made yourself comfortable."

"We made an agreement, yes. We aided you, didn't lay a finger on you as long as you didn't assist Verin. As long as you kept your distance. If you recall, we sent you word in Verin when we attacked the castle. That is the only reason you remain breathing."

Draven ignored the tension building and took another step forward. "And yet you are here."

"You lost Ayleth the moment you set out to Hearcross." Prolus chuckled. "We have come to restore order. Besides, I believe we assisted you far more than you did us. The shipment of poisonous substance we sent you was what you used for your father, was it not?"

Draven flinched, picturing the late King Joster losing

his mind. It had taken time, but it'd been worth it in the end. The satisfaction of seeing that old bastard succumb to death at his hands had been worth it.

"This throne is not our focus," Prolus said in that low sinister tone.

Draven filled in the rest in his mind. Prolus wanted the throne in the Grand Palace. He wanted the entire empire.

"All I want is my kingdom back," Draven said.

"We may be willing to allow you the position of king in the new empire. But you must prove that you are with us. You must show your dedication to our cause."

Draven hesitated. "I can help you remove the one thing that may bar your way to the throne."

Prolus tilted his head, the smiling mask a chilling image as he awaited Draven's next words.

"Prince Honzio. I can give you Prince Honzio."

NATASSA

KINGDOM OF AYLETH

THE VIBRATION OF the moving cart didn't unsettle her any longer, and after days of bearing the bumps of the roads and jerky movements, Natassa had no trouble sleeping on the pile of fabrics. Her stomach growled. Her hunger had been partially satiated when the caravan members had spared some water and stale bread. She curled into herself, pressing her wrist to her middle, pretending it wasn't so bare.

"Get up, girl. You are soiling the fabric." The smack of a whip sounded, and it lashed against Natassa's arm. She inhaled sharply, the stinging pain sinking through her skin.

Don't allow her to treat you this way, the Lure demanded. *Stop her. Make her pay for it.*

The shadows were loud in her

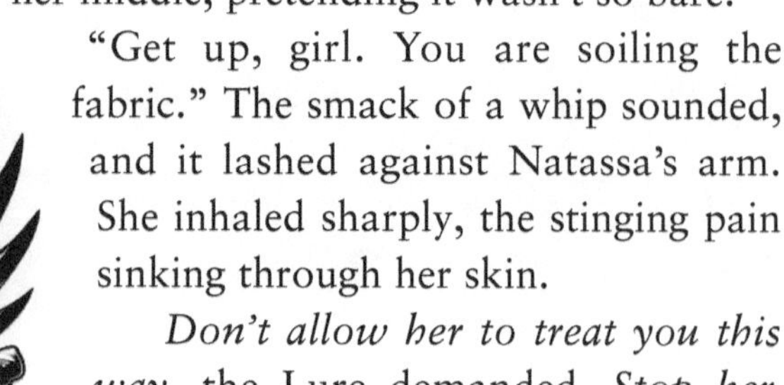

mind. She was starting to be unable to discern her own thoughts from their whispers. Natassa heaved herself up and glanced ahead, looking past the caravan at the approaching gates. The domed purple towers seemed like something from a nightmare. Natassa had been forced years before to memorize every section of the kingdom. Ayleth. The home of Prince Draven, her once-upon-a-time betrothed. Natassa grimaced at the reminder of those terrible days.

The carts rumbled through the gates. Natassa's brows furrowed at the uniforms the inspecting guards wore. Those weren't the normal violet shades. They were a distinct black and red. Tariqin colors. Deedans. What were Prolus's soldiers doing there?

"A change of power." The caravan woman glanced back from her seat at Natassa and snorted. "Matters nothing to us as long as we can sell our wares and get our coin."

But Natassa sensed something was wrong. A thick tension filled the air. Wariness tightened every muscle.

You must leave the cart. Go, Princess, the Seer ordered. *Get out.*

Natassa scrambled from the cart, her shoes slapping along the ground as she rushed away, leaving the screeches of the caravan woman behind her. Fire blazed in the sky above, highlighting the beautiful domes of the city before descending. Natassa looked back in time to watch the fireball crash into the carts behind her. A wave of heat blasted forward, flinging Natassa into the air. She screamed, her throat parched and arms raw as she scraped across the ground. Her ears rang. Though her body felt numb, she gripped at the ground with her fingertips and dragged herself up. She looked behind her, a startled gasp escaping her at the sight of the entire caravan in flames. The merchants screeched and patted themselves in desperation as the flames licked at them. They shouted at the tops of their lungs as they slowly turned to ash.

Natassa blinked, horror clogging her throat. Then her horror was replaced by fear; the gates that had just been swarmed with deedans lay in shambles, and a group of howling Savagelanders rushed inside, snarling and swinging their weapons at anyone in sight. Natassa stumbled, found her feet, and ran, not daring to glance back. She heard the pound of boots and knew she was being pursued. She continued running until she reached the end of an alley. Natassa exhaled, spinning around. Two ruthless-looking Savagelanders stalked toward her. Natassa had no weapon. Nothing except . . .

She locked eyes with the closest Savagelander and raised her hand in a placating gesture. "You don't want to do this."

Her shadows drifted on either side of her. Their presence was so powerful, she could see their silhouettes and feel their ghostly fingers.

The Savagelander tilted his head and chuckled, taking a step forward.

"Stay away!" she roared, and shock froze her. Because the shout hadn't been her voice. It was something else, something far darker speaking through her.

The Savagelanders glanced at each other then, uncertainty holding them in place. Natassa inhaled, focusing on her shadows. The Seer gripped her shoulder, and she suddenly saw herself before her. A violent, horrible-looking Natassa. Her hair was flitting about her face, her mouth twisted in a harsh frown, her eyes burning with unquenchable flames. Natassa realized she was seeing herself through the Savagelander's gaze. Natassa was afraid. For the first time, she was afraid of *herself*. She blinked, and the dark version of herself was gone, leaving her watching as the Savagelander retreated.

One of them barked in Savese, and their voices filtered through her mind, her shadows translating them.

"She's just a girl. Why are you being such a child? Attack her!"

At his companion's goading, the Savagelander collected his wits and swung his blade at her. Before Natassa could move a muscle, a large figure jumped before her, and the clang of weapons drummed in her ears. The new arrival disarmed and finished the Savagelanders within seconds. He swung a rusty-looking sword in his hand and glanced back at her.

"Doesn't work as well as an axe, but it'll do."

"Thank you?"

Strands of hair escaped the long braid hanging to his mid-back. He gestured for her to follow him. "Let's get to safety."

Natassa hesitated, unsure if she should trust him, but something in her gut told her to follow him. He led her to a house nearby. As soon as the door shut, a man called out.

"Svorgin, you've returned?"

Tears welled in her eyes at the familiar voice. A man

stepped into view. He looked so changed. A thick beard covered his jaw, and his hair crept over his ears. His brown gaze caught her, and he froze.

"Natassa?"

Her lips formed a trembling smile. "Honzio?"

≪

HONZIO
KINGDOM OF AYLETH

Honzio almost pinched himself. But there she stood, his fierce little sister. Natassa stared at him, tears in her large eyes. Then she ran toward him, and Honzio braced himself for impact. She launched into his arms, and he stumbled back a few paces. Honzio hugged her as best he could, an odd wetness affecting his vision.

"How?" he managed. "What are you doing here?"

Natassa squeezed him tight before pulling back. "It's a long story. But I will shorten it for you. I found the Elders, but I wasn't able to stay with them long. I ended up in Ayleth by journeying with a caravan. We were just attacked by Savagelanders. This man helped me." Natassa motioned behind her.

Honzio glanced over her shoulder and saw Svorgin watching them with a small smile. The Savorian had left the house to search for Draven, whose disappearance didn't bode well. Honzio nodded his gratitude to him, and the Savorian nodded back.

"And you? What are you doing here?"

"You must have heard the news." Honzio swallowed, searching her gaze. "Our father . . ."

"Emperor Malus is dead," she said. "Yes, I heard."

"And your handmaiden. I'm sorry, Natassa, but she's gone."

Natassa winced. "I heard that too."

"She told me something, right before she died," Honzio said, flinching as he recalled her brutal manner of death. "I don't know what occurred between you, but in her final moments, she conveyed her last wish. She wanted me to tell you she was sorry."

Natassa's features turned sorrowful. "Thank you for passing on her words." She squeezed his arm. "I was so worried when I heard Draven had proclaimed himself emperor. I feared he would harm you."

"He attempted to, but I managed to escape."

"That worthless—" She breathed in, steadying herself. "What happened after?"

"I—I did something foolish, Natassa." He grimaced. She watched him with a furrowed brow. "I made an agreement with the Uluzar, the Savagelanders. But they double-crossed me."

He explained to her how he'd shown Grongar-ja the entrance to the tunnels and how they'd planned to remove Draven. Natassa's brows lifted higher the more he spoke.

"There isn't much to tell after that." Honzio shrugged. "The Uluzar imprisoned us."

"Us?"

Svorgin joined in. "Your dear brother and his *friend* were lively company."

"You look exhausted, Natassa. You should get some rest," Honzio cut in, attempting to swivel the conversation. And with the circles beneath her eyes and the dirt staining her clothes and face, she *did* seem tired.

Natassa gripped his arm. "What friend, Honzio?"

He shifted his stance, hesitated, and, seeing no other way through it, admitted the truth. "They imprisoned Draven with us."

Natassa paled. "What?"

"We had no choice but to take him with us when we escaped. Or we wouldn't have made it this far."

Natassa swallowed, and Honzio could see the words sinking in as she realized the man she feasibly hated most in the world had accompanied them.

A bang against the door startled them all, and Honzio reached for his dagger. Alarm shot through him when he realized they hadn't locked it. Natassa grabbed the dagger from him before he could blink and moved toward the entrance just as Svorgin placed his weight against the door, attempting to prevent the intruder from breaking in. The bangs grew louder, pounding in time with their hearts.

29

Velamir

Kingdom of Ayleth

Velamir pulled on the reins, and Vandal neighed, tossing his head into the air. Gentle wind blew his mane back. Velamir's eyes were rooted to the gates ahead, on the smoke billowing above the stone and sifting into the air with a note of forewarning.

"There are no guards at the gate," he muttered.

Bear and Lore halted on either side of him, taking in the sight awaiting them. The flagpole had been decimated, leaving the purple colors of Ayleth hanging in tattered strands. They rode toward the gate, and the silence gripped them with unease. As they crossed through, the remainder of the flag slipped free and drifted onto the blood-soaked ground. Velamir ignored the sense of forebod-

ing welling in his chest and urged Vandal onward. The path ahead was devoid of people. Velamir could only hear the horses' hooves ringing against the cobblestones. He continued the slow pace until he caught sight of a row of carts piled together in burned shambles. Velamir froze, shock seizing him at the view of the charred corpses along either side.

Bear gasped. "Gah! The smell." He lifted his tunic to cover his nose.

Lore coughed, and his face twisted with repulsion. Velamir had smelled burned flesh before, but it had never been that bad. It had never been that many. He dismounted, taking hesitant steps toward the wreckage.

"The caravan?" Bear said aloud.

Velamir nodded, worry twisting his gut.

"Maybe she escaped." Lore's hopeful optimism was wasted on Velamir.

He glanced over each body, forcing himself to look past the gruesome burns and examine what he could make out of their features.

"Velamir." Bear grabbed his arm as he circled back to the first body to start again. "Lad, she's not here."

Velamir pulled free and continued his feverish search. His fingers stilled when he spotted glinting metal. He crouched beside a fully burned corpse and reached down, his hand brushing what remained of the wrist. Horror settled deep within him as he recognized the bracelet he'd given Natassa. The bracelet she'd worn above the one her brother had gifted her. Velamir touched her other bracelet tied around his own wrist. He'd been keeping it for her. Until the bracelets reunited where they belonged.

"No," Velamir whispered. His voice trembled. His fingers shook. "No!"

Tears filled his eyes until the corpse was a blur below him. The world could have crumbled around him, his chest could've been ripped open, his heart could have been clawed from within, but it wouldn't have grieved him as much as the anguish he felt at that moment. The weight of the pain brought him to his knees. He held her wrist, his tears slipping free. His head bowed over her still form.

"Lad," Bear said hesitantly, placing a hand on his shoulder.

Velamir didn't register the touch. His entire focus remained on the beautiful woman who lay lifeless, who had become ash and memories. He would never again see her smile. The smile that had brought out the sun on rainy days. He would never again breathe her scent. The scent that was as familiar to him as the sword on his hip. He would never again touch her skin, her face, hold her hand in his. More tears slid free, burning a trail over his lips. The world would be deprived of an angel, and he would be deprived of his light. Every moment without her had been spent breathless, on short painful gasps for air. How could he ever breathe again? How could he stand?

He heard Bear speaking, the older man's voice rumbling with understanding. Velamir recalled the orphaned children in the academy whispering fables that kept them awake late into the night. Tales of the love between a courageous warrior and a princess. An uncertain but true love. Velamir wished he'd never known it. Carrying that love in his chest was a scar he couldn't bear. Without Natassa, it was agony. He leaned closer to her form, reaching out with a shaking hand to touch her unrecognizable face. His fingers skimmed the air above. He squeezed his eyes closed, lashes clamping together with tears. He couldn't restrain himself. He grabbed hold of her and lifted her into his arms. Velamir rose to his feet, turning to see the others staring at him with pity.

"Velamir—" Bear began.

"I will not leave her here."

A burning arrow flashed past them, smacking into the charred wood of a cart. Bear pulled his axe free, and Lore unsheathed his short sword as their eyes darted toward the source. A deedan appeared. He lifted a horn to his mouth and blew loudly, again and again. Their horses reared up at the noise and charged out, Vandal leading the other two out of the city through the gates. Lore chased after them, but Bear hauled him back, hefted his axe over his shoulder, and flung it toward the Tariqin. It slammed into the Tariqin's chest, propelling him backward.

"He called for reinforcements," Lore said, agitated. "We need to get out of here."

Bear nodded and retrieved his axe. "We must hide in the city. If we leave through the gates, we will be in clear sight of the archers."

They started forward. Velamir's every step was weighed down by the ache ravaging his chest and the corpse in his arms. He couldn't bear to look at her, at the horrible reality.

"You need to leave her, lad," Bear ordered. "We have to go."

Boots pounded behind them. The other two were ahead of him, running through the alley when another arrow struck. Velamir gasped as it smashed into his shoulder blade. Then came the next, a few inches lower. Velamir stumbled, the air leaving his lungs. But he refused to let her go. He refused to drop her.

"This one is open!" Lore called as he attempted to shove open a door to a house. "Come on!"

Bear swiveled and grabbed Velamir. "Don't be stupid, lad. You're killing yourself. The lass wouldn't have wanted you to do this."

Velamir slowly lowered her. Brutal pain tore through his back at the movement.

"Forgive me," he whispered in regret.

Another arrow whipped through the air, striking Bear's chest. The Savorian grunted.

"Bear!" Velamir shouted.

"I'm fine, lad. Follow Lore."

The boy was desperately trying to shove his way into the home. The door was being held closed by someone from within. The Tariqins were nearing. Velamir brushed Lore aside and kicked the door open. A man on the other side stumbled back from the force. Velamir stormed inside, waving his hand for the others to enter. Lore rushed after him, followed by Bear. Velamir slammed the door closed and slid the multiple locks into place. He pressed his forehead to the wood, heaving in breaths. Several seconds later, he heard the pounding of boots as their pursuers rushed past the house in search of them.

He turned, and steel bit the skin of his throat. A

pair of hazel eyes peered up at him. The woman's eyes widened, and she lowered the dagger.

"Velamir?"

He laughed, a harsh broken laugh. Was he dreaming? It had to be a dream. Natassa threw her arms around his neck, hugging him tight. Velamir's hands hung useless at his sides before he overcame his astonishment and gripped her with all his strength.

"You died," he said in disbelief. "I was holding your body in my arms just like this."

"Velamir . . ." She sobbed, her form quaking with tears as she shook against him.

"I thought I'd lost you," he whispered, pulling back.

He stared at her face, her eyes, her lips, every feature. Memorizing them so he wouldn't ever forget. He brushed her tears away with the pads of his thumbs.

"I'm here," she whispered back.

Sudden pain tore through his back, and his vision dimmed. He grimaced, fighting to keep his balance before falling to his knees.

"Velamir!"

Natassa's screams faded as darkness took him under.

30

MORDON COULD ALMOST taste the joy in the air. The upbeat jovial music spilling from the main square of town grew louder with each of his strides. He spotted the crowd ahead and slowed his pace. He made his way through the onlookers and stood at the edge of the crowd, catching sight of what had them clapping their hands in beat with the song. His Savorian friends, allies, brothers. Brave men who had joined him against Prolus stood in the center of the square, moving in a passionate dance he'd never seen before. They lunged into the air, hefting axes up with a shout. As soon as their feet came back to the ground, they spun on the heels of their boots and fell to their knees, pounding

a fist into their chest with another shout. They danced in unison, just as they fought together, ate together, protected each other. They saw each other as family. Savorians gave their life for their loved ones willingly, without a bat of an eye. Mordon had grown accustomed to their boisterous ways and saw the warm souls beneath the harsh exteriors. Despite everything Prolus had done to them, they remained standing.

The song drifted to an end, and the crowd cheered along with the Savorians. Mordon glanced toward the chairs set up on the wooden platform, and his focus was overtaken by the queen watching the proceedings with a wide smile. Mordon's chest thrummed as his heart beat in an endless thump. The organ never failed to surprise him. He'd always thought it a cold broken thing, yet as soon as he laid eyes on the queen of Verin, it revived, and he started living. The civilians whispered of his miraculous survival against the ovaline poison. Little did they know he was returning to life every time he saw their queen.

A Savorian approached her, Silopar, and extended a hand toward her. Coralie's brows shot up before she lowered her chin in a regal nod and laid her hand on his palm. Mordon roved through the crowd, stopping under the overhang of the local bakery, and leaned against a wooden post. He tracked Coralie's movements as she joined the Savorians for their next round. She'd told him several days before of her intention to have the citizens warm up to the Savorians. It seemed to be working. Several people joined them. Coralie's bright laugh enhanced the entrancing music. She stumbled as she attempted to keep up with the Savorians. Mordon spotted Eris near her, his eyes scanning the crowd for any sign of danger. Mordon had handpicked him to be Coralie's new bodyguard from among the castle guards. Eris was strong, reliable, and, more importantly, happily married.

Mordon pushed off the wooden post and entered the ring of Savorians near Coralie. They hooted in approval when they saw him, slapping him on the back. Coralie was facing away from him as she twirled a young beaming child in circles. Mordon exhaled, taking in the sight of everything around him. The sun shining above them, pouring heat onto their skin. The rich green flags planted at the top of the castle battlements, flapping in the breeze and proclaiming the kingdom's freedom. The civilians wore wide grins as they watched their queen with adoration. The scent of soft freshly baked bread was accompanied by the fragrance of the recently planted flowers beginning to bloom. A moment couldn't be more infinite than that.

Silopar stepped beside him and gave him a shove toward Coralie. Mordon stumbled forward several paces, shooting him a backward glance to share his irritation, but the Savorian only gave him a wink in return. Mordon shook his head and closed the distance remaining behind Coralie. She wasn't even attempting to keep up with the Savorians' rhythm any longer, simply swaying in gentle motions as she spoke to the little girl. Mordon stood behind her, waiting for her to notice him. That intoxicating aroma drifted off her. Lilies and mint. As familiar to him as the birthmark on her neck.

The curved crescent that defied the moon in beauty. He reached out, grasping her waist and spinning her toward him. His queen staggered into his arms. Her startled eyes met his as her dagger met the fragile skin at his throat. Mordon lifted his hands, a grin spreading across his face.

"I feel like we've lived through this moment before."

Coralie lowered her weapon, pressing a hand to her chest. "Mordon! You startled me."

He leaned in, whispering in her ear so the music wouldn't swallow his words. "Is your heart racing, Your Majesty? It can't seem to control itself when I'm around."

She rolled her eyes and pushed at his shoulder. "Arrogant as usual."

But he could see the relief in her gaze, the softening in her posture. She'd been worried about him for days, always attempting to alleviate the blow of the past months with her company. Mordon was still struggling with himself, his new plans. His life had always been directed by someone else. Boltrex, Winston, society. One grand goal. Power. Ownership. A throne. A crown. He had to leave the past behind and look ahead.

Mordon grasped Coralie's hand, entangling their fingers as he drew her away from the square. She gave him a questioning look while he scanned for Eris behind them. Mordon nodded, and the bodyguard fell back.

Mordon took Coralie to an empty space between two shops and released her hand. They stood across from each other. The music still slipped to them, brushing their ears from a distance.

"What are you trying to do?"

She tilted her head in response. "What do you mean?"

"This celebration. There's more to it than having the people accept the Savorians."

She looked down, playing with the hilt of her dagger—the dagger he'd gifted her after they had rebuilt the smithy. He'd made it himself, inscribed the words decorating the blade with molten gold. *Koral, Kahri, Kralis.* Defender, Hero, Queen.

"You spoke of returning the rumloks home. Will you ever go? To stay." She looked up, her thick lashes shielding the true emotions in her eyes.

"I have intentions of traveling there, to see Savoria."

Mordon assumed she wished to travel to the Uluz, to see the land her mother had been raised on. She'd revealed the details of Draven and her mother's journal. Mordon shared her disgust for the former prince, but he also shared her curiosity for the past. The history of the land of his forefathers. Coralie nodded, looking away again. She was concealing something from him.

"You will leave with Silopar and the others." It was more of a question than a statement.

Mordon frowned. "When the war ends, I will assist them on their journey home."

"When the war ends," she repeated.

"Don't say it as if you don't believe it," Mordon said. "It will end. Have faith."

A small smile tugged at her mouth. "What became of my sullen general?"

"I'm not always grumpy. Perhaps you are an excellent example. Perhaps I've started to hope."

But she still wasn't meeting his eyes. Mordon attempted to root out the problem.

"Don't you wish to visit the Uluz one day?"

"When they stop seeing us as enemies?" She shook her head. "Even if they rule over Hearcross for now, they will always view me as Imperial. Once we defeat them and send them back, they will never allow me on their lands. And I *always will* be Imperial. Nothing can change that. Kolesta-na may have birthed me, but this land, this soil, is my home. I may have Uluzar blood, but it's Imperial rivers that run through my veins." She glanced at him, searching his face. "But you will go. The Empire was never a home to you. You will go in search of answers, in search of the power and position you've always longed for. You will go to find your place in this world."

You will go. The three words struck him as he grasped the dread in her words, and he recalled her admission after the battle with the Tariqins, when it had been just the two of them in the stables. *What if one day you're gone? What if one day you leave? I'm better alone.*

And he knew that was why she was withholding her feelings from him. She was afraid that if she confessed her love, allowed herself to show her love, he would destroy her. That he would leave her when she depended on him most.

She looked away again, depriving him of her eyes. He reached out, grasping her chin, and tugged her face up. She exhaled as her gaze tangled with his. Coralie stared at him with those siren eyes, a question burning in them. His attention drifted down. The black fabric of her dress hugged her waist before flaring over her hips. Green embroidery decorated her shoulder pads and her belt. Her sword was in its usual place, hanging at her side. Her braids wound down her upper back. Several strands of her hair had slipped free from the exuberant dancing and drifted over her cheekbones in soft, wispy curls. Mordon swallowed, tucking a curl behind her ear.

"Dammit, Coralie." He swallowed the lump in his throat, the words slipping free. "You are so beautiful."

Surprise lit her features, followed by pleasure, but he watched as she doused it away, as she always did. She continued to hold up that wall between them. Her wall of protection. But he was breaking through it. Brick by brick.

"The Empire was never home. It was a land that chained me. Bound me by orders and hatred," he said. "It was a land that promised me nothing but pain."

She nodded, turning to move, but he stepped forward, placing his hand on the alley wall behind her, preventing her from leaving. She stared at his arm before releasing a soft sigh of exasperation as she swiveled to give him the look that would send any of her other subjects scurrying to obey her. But he wasn't any of her other subjects.

"But the Empire is simply land. Just as Savoria and the Uluz are. I've broken free of my chains. No *place* can hold me captive. But a person—" He paused, his other arm shifting as he placed his hand on the alley wall, caging her between them.

She inhaled a sharp gasp and backed away until she was pressed to the stone. But her eyes didn't release his. There was his unyielding queen.

"A person?" she echoed.

"A person," he said firmly. "One person in particular that I cannot live without. Who can command me, and chain me, and root me to any soil and make it my home."

"And who is this *person*?" she whispered, her lips tilting up in that mischievous smile he was so fond of.

He leaned closer, lifting one hand free and running his fingers over her cheek. Her lids shuttered closed, and his chest thudded. He loved that he had that effect on her. But she did not know what she did to him. For a single tear of hers, he could bring the world to its knees. She made him as rabid as the monstrous untrained rumloks remaining in Prolus's camp.

"Coralie," he said hoarsely. "I will always return to you. You are my Savoria, my Empire, my world." His hand lowered until his fingers brushed over the crescent birthmark at her neck and the pulse thudding beneath it. "You are my moonlight."

She expelled a shuddering breath, and when her eyes opened, a tear slid free. Mordon saw the acceptance in her gaze and the careful wall she had constructed collapsing. Her mouth opened, and he waited, eager to hear her answer to his devotion laid bare.

Then pain slithered through his mind, and Mordon flinched, hearing a distant voice calling for him. Agony followed through the link, blaring heartbreaking suffering.

"What is it?" Coralie gripped his arm. "What's wrong?"

"The rumloks," Mordon managed. "Something is harming them."

He stumbled out of the alley with Coralie paces

behind. When they returned to the square, they were met by a sea of frozen onlookers. All citizens' gazes were fixed on a man equipped with golden armor and the pile of dead rumloks behind him. The man dragged one forward and released it in a motionless heap before them. Zenrelius looked up, his eyes locking with Mordon's.

"General, so kind of you to join us."

31

HONZIO

KINGDOM OF AYLETH

"WHAT IN THE four kingdoms is going on?" Honzio's question was met with a blank look from Svorgin. The Savorian pulled himself up from the floor, appearing winded after the door had blasted open and thrown him backward. It had all happened so fast. Natassa snaring his dagger, Svorgin rushing forward to hold the door closed, Honzio grabbing a vase full of flowers he hoped Marcella wouldn't miss since they currently lay in crushed stems by his boots. The newcomers had burst in and locked the door behind them.

Honzio had held the vase like a weapon and marched forward to protect his sister, but the sight that confronted him had fastened him in place. Natassa had dropped her dagger—*his*

dagger—and threw her arms around one of the newcomers' necks. She had sobbed. His sister had *sobbed* for some strange man he had never seen in his life.

Honzio blinked, returning to the present. Natassa kneeled on the floor near the entryway, tears streaming down her cheeks as she held the unconscious man in her arms. Arrows stuck out of his back.

"True Manos? Is there a True Manos?" asked another newcomer, a young boy with panicked eyes and urgency in his tone.

An older man was slumped against the boy, his face lowered and sweat slicking long strands of his graying hair to his face and neck, rendering his features unrecognizable. But his pale skin and blond streaks of hair marked him as Savorian. Honzio sputtered, searching for words, when Marcella stepped out of the kitchen, wiping her hands over a battered apron. Her violet curls stuck up in a frizzy mess.

"Take him up the stairs. First room on the left."

The boy nodded, placing his shoulder under the Savorian's, and assisted him up the stairs.

"You two," Marcella ordered, hands on hips. "Take this young man here."

Honzio paused, still utterly bewildered, before following Svorgin.

Natassa stared at them, her fingers gripping her skirt and worry in her gaze. "Please, hurry."

Honzio jumped into action then, grabbing hold of the young man with one arm. Svorgin lifted most of the weight. They staggered up the stairs and into the room Marcella had directed them to. Natassa was one step behind them. Honzio recognized the room from the tour Marcella had given them during their stay. She rented the space to those who needed more privacy than an inn could provide. Thankfully, there weren't any tenants about. Two beds bordered either side of the room, mirroring each other, covered with homey squares of fabric that had been patched into quilts. A roaring fireplace took up a section of the wall, and a dresser faced the door, devoid of belongings other than the mirror hanging above it.

Sweat trickled down Honzio's brow and into his beard. His jaw clenched, and a labored breath slipped free as he helped deposit the wounded man onto the free bed. The other had already been taken up by the Savorian, and the young boy hovered over him wearing a panicked expression. Marcella barged inside, carrying hot water, linen, and what looked like metal rods. She placed them on the dresser and spun around.

"Who has experience in healing?"

Honzio shook his head at once. He didn't know the first thing about healing. Only that others had failed to heal his arm. He glanced down at the mangled limb. A True Manos had set it wrong. His father had suspected someone paid him to do so and had him drowned in the moat, regardless of whether his suspicions were true. The True Manos had made his prized son lame. *Useless.* True Manos after True Manos had been summoned to repair the damage, but they had all failed, and Honzio's hopes had been dashed. Honzio grimaced, closing his eyes against the memory.

"I've sewn my own wounds before," Svorgin offered.

"Good. Get to work on his leg. He has a gash there," Marcella ordered, appraising the injured Savorian as she spoke.

"I-I have some experience as well," the young boy blurted. "I was training to be a True Manos."

A second son, Honzio thought.

"What level?" Marcella asked.

"Third lesson." The boy hesitated.

Marcella spared him a glance before tossing him linen. "It will have to do. Get ready to cover the wound as soon as I pull this arrow free."

The boy nodded, and Honzio could see he was firming his resolve as he took his place beside Marcella. Svorgin was already hard at work. His brows furrowed in concentration, and his dark blue gaze never wavered from the gash in the Savorian's leg as he wove a provided needle and thread back and forth with steady fingers. Honzio glanced around, searching for a way to assist.

"The iron rods," Marcella barked, and Honzio nodded, springing into action.

He approached the fireplace at the corner of the room and placed the ends of the metal rods into the flames, watching them glow orange as they heated. He turned as he waited, seeing Natassa placing linen around the arrows stuck in the other man's back, stemming the blood seeping free. He heard a crack, and his gaze shot over to Marcella. The Shadow Manos had broken the arrow shaft before wrenching it free. She tore the tunic covering the man's chest.

"The linen!" she shouted, but the boy only watched with an open mouth as blood drained from his face.

Marcella rolled her eyes, yanked the linen from his hands, and pressed it to the Savorian's chest. Honzio took one rod from the flames and approached her. She grabbed it deftly, as if she did that sort of thing every day. Honzio admired her tenacity. She tossed the linen aside and pressed the rod to the Savorian's skin. Though the man had lost consciousness, the heat of the rod brought him back, filling his muscles with tension and his mouth with shouts of pain. Honzio attempted to hold him down as best he could, and Svorgin did his part on the other end, his work with the stitching finished. Honzio tried not to look, but his eyes kept darting back to the rod. Steam rose into the air as the flesh on the Savorian's chest roasted. Honzio swallowed his bile and continued holding him down.

Moments after Marcella finished, the young boy slapped a hand to his mouth.

"I think I'm going to be sick."

She waved at Svorgin. "Take the boy downstairs before he retches on my floor and get him something to eat."

Svorgin urged the boy from the room, and they disappeared from view. Marcella set to preparing her equipment for the other man, and Honzio approached his sister's side. Natassa trembled over the young man.

He didn't ask the questions burning in his mind. Who were these people? Why was she so worried about that particular man? Instead, he forged past them to the pressing matter at hand, being there for her, as he should have been long ago. "What can I do?"

"I can't steady my hand enough to break this," she

said, her fingers shaking around the arrow shaft. "I fear I will hurt him."

Honzio nodded. "Allow me."

He took her place, closing his good hand around the wood and using his thumb to crack it. Natassa held her hands down around the shaft, pressing against the man's back. A roar slipped through the young man's mouth as the arrow snapped. Honzio tossed away the broken end and grabbed hold of the next arrow. Tears continued to travel down Natassa's cheeks. Her face was pale and eyes red.

Marcella bustled over, waving him away, then proceeded to yank the arrows free and cauterize the young man's wounds. Honzio winced at the sizzling flesh. Natassa helped her spread ointment over the fresh burns. Marcella gave them each a tonic, and both men drifted into a feverish sleep.

Honzio leaned against the wall, watching his little sister rest her head against the edge of the young man's bed. Her hands were wrapped around his. A sudden remembrance gripped Honzio. Natassa had kneeled in that exact position months ago at Thorsten's bedside. Honzio's heart clenched, and he couldn't stand being in the room a moment longer. He stepped out of the chamber, taking a deep breath, and gripped the railing of the staircase. After he managed to get ahold of himself, he made his way to the kitchen. Svorgin and the young boy, Lore, sat facing each other at the wooden table in the center of the chamber. Both grasped a tankard and downed its contents as swiftly as they could. The young boy slammed his tankard down and pumped a fist into the air in victory. Honzio spied Svorgin hiding a smile. He determined the drink to be milk by the white mustaches they both were sporting.

"That's a good lad," Svorgin praised, ruffling the boy's hair.

"Hold there!" Lore shouted, yanking Svorgin's hand away. "One, I'm not a lad. I'm fifteen, I'll have you know. Two, don't ruffle my hair. It makes me feel like a child. And three, I'm not a child."

Svorgin held his hands up in surrender, and Honzio chuckled at the boy's indignation. Lore glanced toward the doorway where Honzio stood and frowned. He stood up, rushing toward him. Honzio backed away in confusion. But the boy moved past him to kneel on the ground and pick something up from the floor.

"This is Bear's," Lore said.

Svorgin walked toward the boy and kneeled beside him. The Savorian opened his mouth to speak and then froze at the sight of whatever was in Lore's hand. Svorgin stared at it as if he'd seen a ghost.

Honzio treaded closer, sending him a questioning glance. "What is it?"

Svorgin took it from Lore and lifted a miniature figure wielding an axe. "I carved this for my father when I was eight years of age."

Honzio's heart dropped. "Your father?"

They all turned, glancing up the stairs to the chamber where the other Savorian lay.

MORDON
KINGDOM OF VERIN
VERINTOWN

"WHAT HAVE YOU done?" Mordon couldn't recognize his own voice, the broken whisper that shattered the awful silence.

"I saved Verin from Prolus's scourge," came the reply.

Mordon stared at the lifeless rumloks. Pain, stronger than he'd ever felt before, crashed into him. It was coming from the mind link. Inat. Where was he? Mordon couldn't take his eyes off the limp forms of the slaughtered animals. Crossbow bolts protruded from a few of them.

"What—What is the meaning of this, General Zenrelius?"

Coralie's tone wavered as she took in the horrifying scene. Her hand wrapped around Mordon's arm, as if she feared what he would do next.

Mordon looked up, meeting the general's cold eyes. The townspeople whispered behind their hands as they watched with fright. That was when he noticed the other faces amongst the civilians. Mercenaries. Vykus's mercenaries, to be exact. The ringleader himself strode up beside Zenrelius, wielding a crossbow over his shoulder and proudly holding his head up, brandishing the golden patch over his eye.

"We meet again, Your Majesty." Vykus's gold teeth flashed as he smiled. "Your coin sustained us for a while, but there's always room in my trove for more."

Mordon held in a curse. Zenrelius had bought the mercenaries to assist him in the cowardly trap. He'd paid them in their favorite currency: gold and the promise of blood.

"Verin is under Ondalar's control," Zenrelius stated calmly, turning his gleaming eyes over the townspeople.

Coralie scoffed. "Have you lost your mind? With what right do you stake such a claim?"

"With the knowledge that I have an army of thousands on its way here. You decide, Your Majesty. How will you surrender? With or without bloodshed?"

Mordon remained motionless, empty. He'd spent hours with those rumloks, to the point that he'd felt one with them. To see them so still, so brutally slayed as if they were nothing, infused him with molten anger.

"We had an agreement. We sent an ambassador for this cause. Latimus Blayton married High Lord Genvor's daughter so we could make peace. I don't understand why you are doing such a thing now, but I'm sure I can reason with King Gallaxos."

"Gallaxos is no more."

A hush followed his words.

Zenrelius spread his arms out, a proud smirk tugging at his lips. The golden cape hanging from his shoulders shuddered in the light wind. "The king of Ondalar stands before you."

Coralie's brows shot up.

"As for your ambassador, he is languishing in the dungeon. If you don't want to end up in the same predicament, I suggest you surrender."

"You vile bastard," Coralie spat. "I would rather die than give my kingdom to you."

She unsheathed her weapon. Coralie's guards closed in around them, following their queen's lead. Swords rasped free from sheaths. Growls emitted from the Savorians present. Silopar emerged from the townspeople and stopped at Mordon's side.

"Steady," Captain Finnean said, holding a hand up to the tense guards.

Mordon burst through the haze curtaining his vision and clenched his fists. "You will pay. You. Will. Pay."

He'd barely uttered the last word when an enormous shape shot straight at Zenrelius. Screams filled the air as the rumlok howled, narrowly missing Zenrelius with his razor-sharp talons. The rumlok slammed onto the stone ground, his talons raking across and raising sparks. Glossy black fur covered the rumlok's muscular body, which moved with lethal power as his red eyes focused on his prey.

"Inat!" Mordon shouted, rushing toward them.

Run, he begged through the mind link. *Run.*

Zenrelius kicked the rumlok with his metal-plated boot. Inat fell back, mewling pitifully. Zenrelius lifted his sword to bring down the killing blow, but Mordon was there, blocking his weapon with his own. They stared at each other with heated animosity. Inat darted away, disappearing down an alley. Mordon shoved Zenrelius back and continued attacking. Zenrelius met him blow for blow. Panic and terror filled the square as chaos erupted.

"Stop!"

At Coralie's shriek, Mordon froze. He pulled back from Zenrelius, the urgency in her voice petrifying him. Coralie was staring at someone in the crowd. Vykus. He held the little girl Coralie had been dancing with. She was crying, writhing in his muscled arms. The edge of a knife rested at her throat.

"Keep fighting, and the girl dies," he warned.

Coralie met Mordon's eyes, hopelessness overtaking hers. Mordon scanned her for injuries, and his heart left him for a moment when he saw her tucking her arm into her side, blood trickling over her skin. She dropped her sword, the metal clanging at her feet.

"Do what you want with me, but don't hurt my people. Spare the citizens."

Sweat rolled down every plane of Mordon's face, and his breaths came harshly. No, they couldn't give up. They had to fight. They couldn't stop. But then he turned, seeing what Coralie saw. They had lost too many and were too few.

"And you? Vaz? Will you surrender?" Zenrelius's mouth twitched in distaste.

Mordon knew the moment he dropped his weapon, he was a dead man. If he continued fighting, he would force Coralie to make a choice to sacrifice more of her people. He couldn't allow her to live with that guilt. For her, he would gladly lay down his life. Mordon met Zenrelius's eyes and spat out a curse. His weapon clattered to his feet.

⌁

CORALIE
KINGDOM OF VERIN
VERINTOWN

Coralie's heart was lodged in her throat. She gripped her arm, forcing herself to ignore the agony spearing through it. Horror crashed through her as Vykus's mercenaries arrested her guards and the Savorians who had followed Mordon's example and abandoned their weapons. Two of them approached Mordon and wrapped his hands in a thick cord. Mordon's jaw clenched. Trails of sweat trickled through his beard. Zenrelius watched him with a devious gleam, and Coralie knew then that he planned to eliminate all threats, starting with her and Mordon. She grasped for something, anything, as mercenaries approached her.

"Rule 106, in the Book of Codes." The words flew from her mouth.

Zenrelius turned to stare at her, raising a dark brow.

"To rule a kingdom, one must be of noble blood. If the kingdom possesses a current leader, that leader must be vanquished on the battlefield."

The onlookers hushed, their gazes darting between them.

"Vanquished?" Zenrelius repeated. "I believe that has just happened here."

Coralie shook her head. "What you did was an ambush. This was not a true battle."

If she knew Zenrelius the slightest bit, dishonorable was the last thing he wanted to be known as. Coralie watched the fire flicker in his ebony eyes. His lips thinned as he managed to maintain his calm demeanor.

"Are you suggesting to battle me?"

"In order to take Verin, you must win in an honorable battle. A battle for the throne. No might or power from others. One-on-one. Solely with the strength of will."

"Coralie," Mordon started, fear tamping his voice.

Coralie met his gaze and prayed for him to understand. He searched her features and nodded slowly.

"You against me," Zenrelius mused. "What do you expect would be the outcome?" He seemed to be containing a laugh. "You may be a fearsome warrior, but you are no shieldmaiden. You will not last three minutes. And definitely not with that break in your arm."

Coralie fought the disgust that curled inside her at his blatant arrogance.

"Who said *I* will be against you?"

Zenrelius's mouth clamped shut, and his face twisted in confusion.

"Book of Codes, rule 107. And the leader may choose a champion in their place."

Her eyes found the man who had seen her at her

worst, who had urged her to pick up a sword, who had trained with her until she was bloody and defeated, over and over. The man who had turned his back on the Dark Army and returned to her side, the man who had grown out his hair, wearing it long despite what the fashion dictated simply because of her. The man whose heart she carried. The man who possessed her own heart. Every thump, every beat. She stared at the only man who could defeat her in combat.

Everyone turned to follow her gaze.

"I choose General Mordon to best you."

NATASSA

KINGDOM OF AYLETH

NATASSA WATCHED VELAMIR sleep. Counting his breaths was difficult, given he was lying on his chest. Over the past days, she had forced herself to accept that she might never see him again. The fact that he lay before her, even in his wounded state, seemed unreal. She leaned closer, examining him. His cheek was pressed to the pillow, concealing a portion of his features. He was thinner, his cheekbones more prominent. She observed his shuttered lids, the dark crescents circling beneath them, and hated that they hid his beautiful emerald gaze. She scanned his jaw blanketed in a thick beard that didn't lessen his appeal in the least. Natassa reached out, caressing the thick brown waves brushing over his brow. His locks had grown quite a bit, enough to get tangled.

"After he heard of your abduction, he was a different person," Bear said, startling her.

Natassa yanked her hand back, sitting upright on the edge of the bed. She'd thought Bear was still unconscious, but it seemed he had been privy to her appraisal. Embarrassment bloomed through her, and she cleared her throat, eyes darting everywhere but at the older man.

"There's always talk of grand love in folktales. But they seemed just that. Tales. Not possible in the real world. But then I watched Velamir. The lad would go days without sleeping, without breathing. It was like he couldn't allow himself to think until he found you."

Natassa's heart melted into a puddle. "He's been through too much. He was already destroyed when Jax was taken. No one deserves that kind of pain."

She met Bear's piercing gaze.

"And I would say most don't deserve this kind of love."

Natassa ducked her head. The Savorian shifted on his bed. Before Natassa could speak, a hiss sounded by her ear.

Natassa, the Lure whispered. *Princess, your time is waning. You must open the gate.*

She jerked up. They crept closer, their silhouettes growing brighter.

Natassa, they crooned. *There is no time to waste.*

"Leave me alone," Natassa said.

"Sorry, lass? I didn't catch that." Bear's concerned gaze lingered on her.

"I'm sorry. I need some air."

She stepped out of the room, leaned against the door,

and inhaled a deep breath. The shadows cackled from what seemed like every direction. Natassa looked up at the sound of movement. Svorgin rushed up the stairs, and Honzio was directly behind him. The Savorian appeared strained, his jaw tense as he approached. Natassa moved out of the way and stared after him as he entered the room. She grabbed Honzio's arm and gave him a questioning look.

"He found a carving. Something he made for his father."

"His father?"

Natassa and Honzio watched Svorgin through the door as he frantically glanced at Velamir and then turned his attention to Bear. Svorgin approached with slow steps before falling to his knees before the bed.

"Da." The word was broken, whispered with such a hope, Natassa's heart ached to hear it. Svorgin held out the carving. His fingers trembled around the Savorian warrior. "I'm here. Your lad is here."

Bear shifted, a sheen of tears creeping over his blue gaze. "Svor? *Vesir oeer orise?*"

Is it truly you?

Though they spoke in Savorian, the translation came easily to Natassa as her shadows whispered it in her mind. Both men looked at each other in disbelief before Svorgin reached for Bear's hand, placing it over his head in what must have been a Savorian custom. Svorgin's shoulders shook, his chin pointing down and tears openly flowing over his face. Bear's hand trailed down and tugged his son against him, hugging him like he'd never let him go. A tear slipped down Natassa's cheek at the reunion. Honzio glanced at her.

"Are you all right?"

She nodded and leaned into him, pressing her face against his chest, inhaling the scent of ink that always permeated him. It wasn't as strong as usual since other odors were overpowering it, but it brought her a sense of comfort because it reminded her of home. It was never the parties or dresses or riches that had made the Grand Palace home. It was the people. The people she cared for.

"You smell awful," she whispered, even as she snuggled closer to him.

"I know," he muttered back, lifting his arm and draping it around her shoulders, tucking her against him.

Natassa smiled. It was an action she never would have expected from Honzio. He was the cold one, the withdrawn one. Natassa peeked up at her brother through her lashes as he watched the reunited father and son. His throat bobbed, and Natassa realized he needed the embrace as badly as she did. She wrapped both arms around his middle and held on tight. They only had each other in that mortal world. Their brothers were gone, their mother was gone, even their father, who had been worse than an enemy, was gone. They just had each other.

"I love you," Natassa said.

He stiffened and glanced down at her. For a moment, he was silent, and then his arm squeezed her just a bit tighter. And she knew. She knew that was his way of telling her he loved her too. He simply wasn't prepared to say the words aloud.

❦

VELAMIR

KINGDOM OF AYLETH

Velamir opened his eyes, first noticing the soft pillow beneath him and the strange bed he was strewn across. He attempted to push up onto his elbows but stopped when pain tore through his back. Where was he? He glanced beside him, spotting Lore sleeping in the chair near his bed. His head was tilted in what had to be an uncomfortable position. Bear was across from him, talking animatedly with an unfamiliar man. Velamir blinked, trying to comprehend what was happening. The door opened, and Natassa entered. Velamir's chest flooded with relief.

She hadn't been a figment of his imagination. She was alive.

"You are awake." She smiled, rushing toward him. "How are you feeling?"

She sat on the edge of the bed and assisted him in turning over. He ignored the burning anguish the movements caused and drank the tonic Natassa handed him on Marcella's orders, feeling a buzzing sizzle over his skin as the pain faded to an ache. Natassa reached out and placed her hand over his forehead. Velamir closed his eyes, focusing on her comforting touch.

"Your fever is gone."

"I must have died and gone to Alaris," Velamir managed to say, his voice coming out hoarse and scratchy.

"Then I must be there too." She laughed, retracting

her hand and lowering it to his. She wrapped her fingers around his wrist and felt the veins there. Her eyes met his. "Your pulse is so fast."

"You are with me," he said, as if it were the most obvious explanation.

She blushed, her hand sliding back, drifting over his skin in the most captivating way. Velamir exhaled a shaky breath, knowing she had no idea of her power over him. He caught her fingers in his before she could extract them and twined their hands. He glanced up at her, memorizing her features. Her hazel eyes, made up of all his favorite colors, called on him to drown in them. Her nose, slanting into an upward point, tempted him to follow the slope. Her cheeks, burning with life, asked him to caress the soft skin there. Her lips . . . He broke his stare, forcing himself to focus back on her eyes.

She raised her brow. "What is it?"

"You look different," Velamir realized. "Your hair. You are no longer covering your mark."

Her hair was bound back, the top braided and the ends brushing her shoulders. She nodded and touched the phoenix mark absently. "I'm tired of hiding, Velamir. And besides, you were the one who helped me overcome this fear. I am who I am. A mark won't change that."

Velamir tugged her closer until she was resting on his chest. "There's my phoenix."

He ran his fingers through her hair. Natassa's eyes drifted closed, and she sighed in contentment. Velamir glanced at Bear and the other man. They gripped each other's shoulders, their foreheads touching.

"Who is that man with Bear?"

"His son," Natassa replied.

Velamir's mouth parted in shock, and then he smiled, happy for his former mentor. Another miracle, a blessing. Bear had reunited with his long-lost son.

Velamir and Natassa remained holding each other until a sudden pounding shattered the moment. Sounds of the door on the lower floor breaking were followed by an enraged roar.

"Honzio Hartinza! Where are you?"

Natassa

Kingdom of Ayleth

NATASSA FROZE AT the voice. The blood drained from her face. The last time she had seen Prince Draven was the last time she'd seen Kasdeya, when they had ridden off together under the moonlight. She could still picture his skepticism when he'd looked at her. She'd been so sure he'd seen through Kasdeya's bluff and realized she wasn't the true princess. She remembered his pale gray eyes glinting with suspicion and Kasdeya's proud smirk as he lifted her onto his horse. Natassa blinked, raising her head from Velamir's chest. She'd forgotten Draven had traveled with her brother. Seeing Velamir had dispelled her worry of his return.

"Honzio? You coward! Where are you?" The silky, slithery tone was brimming with anger.

The young boy, Lore, who had arrived with Velamir and Bear, was startled awake, his russet hair sticking up at odd points as his wide eyes scanned them. "What is it?"

Svorgin stood up, shrugging his father's axe onto his shoulder. Bear attempted to pull himself up and grimaced.

"That would be *Lsrar*," Svorgin grumbled and, seeing the boy's confusion, added, "The prince. Draven."

"He cannot know we are here," Natassa said, apprehension filling her. He would kill Velamir if he saw him. And her . . . she didn't want to imagine what he would attempt if he knew she was there.

Svorgin nodded. "I will go see what his problem is."

The door shut softly behind the Savorian, but it didn't mute the shouts still emerging from the lower floor. Unease for her brother consumed her. She couldn't sit still. She stood from the bed, but before she had taken a step, warm fingers darted around her wrist, stalling her. She glanced back, seeing Velamir staring up at her with desperation.

"Don't go," he said, fear radiating in his eyes. Fear for her.

She tilted her head, urging him to understand. "I have to check on Honzio. I will return at once."

She could see he didn't want to release her, that he wanted to hold her there with everything in him, but at the pleading look she bestowed upon him, his posture softened, and the fingers caging her wrist loosened. He nodded.

"All right," he said in almost a whisper.

She slid her wrist from his grasp, leaving his hand

hanging in the air. Natassa almost shuddered at the coldness she felt at the loss of his touch. She forced herself not to look back or she would crumble under his beseeching gaze. Natassa grasped the handle of the door, drawing a breath as it creaked open, and she looked down over the railing at the lower level. Urgency pulled at her at the sight below, and she rushed forward, gripping the railing with all her might, forcing her anger into the wood rather than releasing the shouts building in her chest. Red and black, colors she had been raised to despise and fear, cloaked a line of soldiers who stood guard before the entryway, blocking the exit. Marcella, the Shadow Manos, was on her knees, her hands bound behind her. Tariqin weapons were aimed at her from either side. More deedans sifted about the floor, upturning Marcella's belongings in a search of the house.

"They're gone," Marcella spat, blowing a wild violet curl from her face. "They left a short bit ago."

"Do not lie to me! Don't you dare lie to me."

He came into view, and Natassa gasped. Draven was unrecognizable, looking far more manic and disheveled than Natassa had ever seen. His ragged blond hair hung in oily strands about his face, an unkempt beard hugged his jaw, and a mustache covered his top lip. In fact, his mustache hair slipped between his lips as he shouted. Natassa's fingers dug into the wooden railing, observing the man she had almost married. The man who had devised countless plans to destroy her family and succeeded in doing so.

"We found him!" someone barked.

Natassa shook her head in denial as deedans emerged

from a side room, dragging her brother into view. Draven's pacing came to a halt. A sneer coated his features.

"Well, well, well, thought you could hide? Your end has come, dear Brother-in-law."

Honzio laughed in return, his arms gripped back by the deedans and his knees pressed to the wood floor. Even through his bravado, Natassa saw his wince and knew his arm was paining him from the position he was in. Draven stalked forward and promptly silenced him with a backhanded blow. Honzio's head snapped to the side, and blood trickled from his nose. He sniffed, shaking his head as though to clear it. Draven lifted his hand again; his fingers trembled with visible rage.

"Stop!"

Natassa hardly recognized her own voice. Her heart beat in her ears, a harsh thud that deafened her. At her shriek, all gazes swung upward. Draven's wild gray eyes locked on hers, and he froze, feet planted to the ground as his lips parted.

"Kasdeya?"

Natassa wasn't sure what astonished her more—that he'd said that name or that he was staring at her with longing and disbelief.

"Release my brother."

Those three words shattered his hopeful features, and he stiffened. That awful grin, the one she had become accustomed to over the years, spread across his face. "Welcome back, Princess. I was wondering when you would join us."

"Natassa, get out of here," Honzio muttered, then spat blood from his mouth.

Natassa stood tall, refusing to break under Draven's odious stare. "Not without you."

"Prolus's orders. Kill him," Draven said without taking his eyes off her.

"No!" Natassa screamed.

Marcella snarled, spitting curses at Draven as a deedan approached her and Honzio. The deedan raised his blade, and the kilisham glinted, the whip jolting into a solid sword. Time slowed as the sharp edge neared her brother's head. Then a figure sprang forward and crashed into the deedan, sending him stumbling into the wall. Svorgin swung his axe in a wild arc, creating space and pulling Honzio and Marcella behind him.

"I will protect him. Get the others to safety," Svorgin called to her.

Natassa hesitated. As the deedans mustered their courage and collided into battle with Svorgin and her brother, Draven's cold gaze remained rooted to her. He mounted the stairs, closing the distance between them. She chilled at the icy look in his eyes as his long legs ate up the steps.

"Go!"

Honzio's voice propelled her into action. Natassa staggered back, running to the door. The sounds of clashing metal and swearing filled the air behind her, along with a screech as Marcella slammed a metal pan over a deedan's head. Natassa banged the door closed and shoved the wooden wedge down to bar it. She spun, pressing her back to it, and breathed out. Three pairs of eyes watched her, worry in each one. Bear stood beside his bed, and Velamir was pulling himself from his. Lore reached for Velamir's arm to assist him.

"Draven came with Tariqin soldiers." The words rushed out of her.

A force slammed against the door, making her flinch, the wood rattling behind her.

"Come here," Velamir said, urgency pulling at his features.

She stepped away from the door. Velamir exhaled, clenching his jaw in a way that told Natassa he was doing everything he could to conceal his weakened state.

"Velamir," she whispered.

Lore's gaze darted between them. "What should we do?"

She glanced back at the door after another bang. It wouldn't take long for Draven to break through.

"We have no way of leaving the house through this room. And we won't abandon our companions." Velamir squeezed Lore's shoulder. "We must fight."

Tears filled Natassa's eyes. "You don't have the strength to fight."

Another bang. Another flinch. Velamir reached out and cupped her cheek in his calloused palm, a tenderness in his gaze that she adored so much. "I won't leave anyone behind. We rise and fall together."

"Together," Natassa repeated, forcing herself to feel the same hope.

"Together," Lore added, unsheathing his short sword.

She grasped the dagger Velamir extended to her, holding the heavy metal in her palm. Velamir reached for his own sword, which had been resting at his bedside.

Perspiration made his tunic cling to him. He wasn't even wearing his armor. They had removed it while tending to his wounds. Natassa glanced at Bear. He seemed a meager amount better off. A body flung against the door, and wide cracks appeared on its surface.

"Stay behind us," Velamir said to her before his gaze slid to Lore. "If something goes wrong, protect her and get out of here."

Lore hesitated and glanced at her.

"All right," she whispered to relieve Velamir. But there wasn't a chance they could survive that. They would fight to the death together.

One last smash and the wood gave way. The door flung open, and Natassa's heart rate spiked at the sight of the man filling the doorframe. No, not a man. Draven Valent looked like a monster. Red-rimmed soulless eyes, white-blond hair hanging limply over his forehead. His clothes were ragged and hung loose on his form, as if he'd lost weight. The once put-together shiny prince was nowhere to be seen. What remained was something unrecognizable.

"Ah, the little slum rat." Draven eyed Velamir. "I'm amazed you're still alive."

"Sorry to disappoint you, Your Highness," Velamir shot back. "I guess it was in my fate to end you."

Tariqin guards flanked Draven, and when he stepped inside, they spilled in behind him. The sound of clashing weapons could be heard from below. Natassa could only pray her brother was all right.

"You allied with Prolus," Velamir said. "I can't say I'm surprised."

"That's startling. With your meager brain, I would expect you to be astonished by most things." Draven glanced back at the deedans. "Attack!"

They flew into action, charging toward them. Velamir parried the first blow and ducked under the second. His movements were labored and slow, but within seconds, he had a Tariqin on the end of his blade. Bear was equally struggling. Natassa rushed toward the Savorian and jumped onto the back of a deedan attacking him. She stabbed the man's shoulder before pulling off, watching him stumble away.

"Princess!" Lore shouted.

Natassa whirled around, seeing a deedan approaching her from the rear. She leaned back in time to avoid the hissing whip of his kilisham. Lore's short sword found its way through the man's back, and the boy stumbled as he pulled his weapon free, eyes wide and horrified when he saw the crimson coating his blade and the crumpled form of the deedan at his feet.

"Behind you!" Natassa said before intercepting a deedan swinging at the boy.

She managed three stabs in his chest in quick succession. She forced herself not to acknowledge the blood, the life leaving the deedan's eyes, the horror of it all, and instead focused on protecting Lore. She grabbed his shoulder, jerking him to awaken him from his horrified stupor.

"Stay with me," she pleaded.

Bear tumbled to the ground a short distance away with a gash in his forehead. Draven smirked, eyeing the effective pommel of his sword. Natassa searched for

Velamir, finding him surrounded by three deedans. She moved to assist him, but Draven blocked her path.

"We finally reunite, Natassa Hartinza."

Natassa trembled. The dagger shook in her palm. Draven lifted his blood-covered sword, pointing it toward her.

"I wonder what I ever saw in you. You're just a scared little girl. You would always put on such a brave face, but inside, you are a weak thing."

Even though they came from Draven, the insults still speared her.

His eyes lifted to her forehead and the mark there. "You are a Shadow Manos. What a shame. It's no wonder your father tried to rid himself of you. I will do the Empire a favor by freeing it of one more curse," he spat. "It is time for you to die just like the rest of your line—by my hand."

Natassa inhaled as he raised his sword. She prepared herself to retreat when Draven was thrust back. Velamir swung his blade at him, and Draven narrowly evaded it, ducking down as the blade sailed over his head. They exchanged blows, both men's skill evident as neither gave room for weakness. Velamir managed to disarm him, and Draven fell to his knees.

"You are a strong man." Draven held up his hands. "Even as clearly injured as you are, you've held your ground. But would you truly kill an unarmed man?"

Velamir hesitated, his gaze drifting toward Natassa. Draven took that moment to lunge to his feet and grab a metal rod they had used for cauterizing hours before, then smashed it against Velamir's head.

"Velamir!" Natassa screamed, covering her mouth with her hand. Her vision darkened as terror filled every part of her.

Velamir dropped, out cold. Draven leaned over to retrieve his fallen sword. The tip dragged across the floor as he approached Velamir's limp form. Before Natassa could move, Lore stood in his path, blocking his way to Velamir.

Draven waved a hand at him. "Move aside, boy."

"Make me." Lore jutted his chin out, standing bravely with his short sword.

"*Move*," Draven said, nearly freezing the word with the amount of ice his tone carried.

Lore raised his hand in reply, crossing his forefinger over his middle one in the symbolic Imperial curse. *Bastard*. Draven tilted his head, shock and surprise halting him before his features hardened.

"You asked for this."

Natassa rushed forward, but not fast enough. Despite Lore's bravery, Draven disarmed him in a moment and thrust him away with a sharp punch to his face. The boy groaned, collapsing beside Velamir.

"Draven," Natassa called. "Your battle is with me."

Draven pivoted, a horrible laugh breaking free. "And how will you battle me, Princess? I'm very intrigued to know."

Natassa approached him until they were mere paces apart. *Come to me*, she whispered. Her shadows appeared on either side.

"Don't do this, *please*. There is goodness in every person. I fully believe that. Don't do this, Draven."

As she stalled for time, she held his gaze, watching his posture soften. *Let me into his mind.*

As you wish, the Seer said.

In an instant, she was seeing Draven's inner thoughts. Disgusting, vile things. She inhaled, recoiling.

"What are you doing?" Draven snarled. His sword slipped from his fingers as he grasped at his head and gripped his hair.

Heat coated her skin, dots of sweat forming as she concentrated, as she forced herself to see. She saw Hesten, her eldest brother, riding into Devorin. Draven had been standing far off, watching as the crossbow bolt struck him through the heart. Natassa could feel his pleasure radiating in waves. She nearly heaved the contents of her stomach. Then she saw Draven speaking with a stable hand, paying him for silence and secrecy as he tampered with Thorsten's lance. The weight had been off. Tears rolled down Natassa's cheeks. Draven fell to his knees before her.

"Get out of my head!" he screamed.

Natassa saw him shoving his lance into her brother's chest plate. Thorsten's blood spilling on the ground. Draven's inner satisfaction. Her father's head smashing against the fountain. Draven had killed even him in a horrific manner. Her first maid, whose death had been made to appear a suicide. She saw Draven slicing her throat and setting up the scene. Natassa bit back sobs. She swallowed the lump in her throat as she sifted through more of his memories.

There were ones where he was happy—not in a sick, twisted way, but truly happy. As a child, presenting a flower to his mother, resting his head in her lap and her stroking his hair. Him, being praised for his talent with a blade by his first weapons instructor. And something that startled her to the core. Kasdeya. She'd made him happy. Natassa dug through those memories, her heart clenching at the image of her once dear friend. Kasdeya was smiling in a way Natassa had never seen before. Then she saw the heart-shattering memory of Draven murdering her as if she'd been nothing. Natassa yanked out of his mind, gasping for breath, for air away from his darkness.

Draven's head hung. Dark circles clung to the area beneath his eyes. Tears slipped freely from his lashes. He looked up at her.

"Please," he begged.

Natassa knew he'd viewed everything she'd just seen. Those memories she'd looked through had been brought afresh through his mind. His lips trembled, and when he pleaded again, she knew that he was asking for release from the torturous hold his actions had over him. For peace. So Natassa didn't hesitate when she approached him. Draven's eyes locked with hers as she stared down at him and plunged her dagger through his heart. Draven gasped, blood erupting from his mouth. She avenged them. All of them. Her brothers, Elise, Kasdeya, everyone he'd harmed, even Draven himself. He collapsed at her feet, his lips moving as he struggled to speak. Natassa crouched down, finally hearing him.

"Thank you," he said.

35

Honzio

Kingdom of Ayleth

Honzio gasped for air, glancing about at the deedans sprawled around his feet, their dull eyes staring listlessly above. He gripped his dagger. The sharp edge dripped red.

"Not bad," Marcella said, eyeing him with appreciation.

The Shadow Manos's curls were plastered to her skin and her makeup smudged, leaving her birthmark exposed. She dropped the pan she had been wielding against the Tariqins, and it clattered on the ground.

"Well done, *Mosori*," Svorgin added. The Savorian slung a bloody axe up, balancing it against his shoulder, his forehead shiny with sweat and chest heaving from the exertion of taking down the majority of the deedans.

"You did most of it," Honzio replied, but a sliver of pride made its way through him.

It had been so long since he'd felt any sort of power. But since he held a weapon in his hand and had a mind of his own and the attention of people who wanted to listen, he felt reborn. Crown Prince Honzio Hartinza was no longer the invisible shadow behind Emperor Malus. He was vivid and alive and prepared to revive the Empire.

A scream from upstairs yanked him from his thoughts. He exchanged a tense glance with Svorgin.

"Natassa," Honzio whispered and darted up the steps.

His boots screeched to a halt at the entrance of the chamber. He reached out, steadying himself against the doorframe as he peered inside. The door creaked as it moved back and forth in an ominous motion. Honzio's gut twisted. Motionless forms were scattered throughout the chamber, gaping wounds visible on most. But what caught his gaze was Natassa. His sister kneeled on the ground, staring down at the body splayed out on the floor before her. Honzio stumbled toward her. He dropped to his knees, grabbing her shoulder and turning her toward him. The look in her eyes immobilized him with fear. Her irises were golden, bright as the sun. She was facing him but looking through him at something far away.

"Natassa? Natassa, look at me."

He tapped her face, but she remained in another world, one where he couldn't reach her. Terror clutched him as he watched her in desperation. He'd only seen her like that once before. After Thorsten released his final breath. She'd let out a scream that still haunted Honzio's dreams. A golden light had showered the chamber, nearly blinding him. Her mark, the phoenix, had been alight, just as it was then. But it had been for a moment, brief and short, before she collapsed on his arm. The day he'd realized his sister was a Shadow Manos.

Honzio swallowed, shaking her, but it was to no avail. His eyes found the mark on her forehead, the lines making up the phoenix glowing hot and angry, pulsing with power. Honzio touched it and jerked his fingers away at once, the searing heat burning his skin. Gazes probed him as the others witnessed his sister's once closely concealed secret.

Honzio wrenched his gaze from her face. Draven lay flat on his back, his mouth parted and blood trickling into his beard. His gray eyes were empty, forever silenced. A dagger protruded from his chest, and a small river of his blood seeped into the wooden floorboards beneath him.

The older Savorian, Svorgin's father, groaned, regaining consciousness. "Velamir."

Svorgin was at his side in an instant, helping him sit upright with a concerned frown. He spoke in Savorian, and Honzio concluded he was asking if he was hurt anywhere based on the questioning tone of his voice. Bear waved him off. "Where's Velamir?"

The name seemed to snap Natassa into reality. She inhaled, her head slumping forward as she sagged onto Honzio. He tilted her back and watched in horrified fascination as her irises shimmered, fading from gold and returning to her familiar hazel. She blinked, looking up at him for a long moment, her brows slipping together in clear confusion before she broke out of his hold.

"Velamir!" Natassa scanned the chamber in an agitated manner.

She pulled to her feet, and Honzio rose with her, keeping his hand positioned at the small of her back. Natassa moved on shaky legs, giving him the impression that she may collapse at any moment. She clambered over bodies until she spotted the young man. Honzio grasped her arm, helping her down, but hesitated, wincing when he saw the swollen contusion near the man's temple.

"Natassa."

His sister didn't seem to hear him as she brushed the man's hair aside and whispered his name urgently. Worry for him tugged at Honzio, and he didn't even know him. Seeing his sister with tears streaming down her face disturbed him. He didn't want her to bear another loss. After several tense seconds, the man's lashes fluttered and opened, his green gaze focusing on Natassa. She laughed in relief, and her hands drifted to either side of his face.

Honzio turned away, giving them privacy. He spotted Lore in the corner of the chamber. Marcella was tending to him, nursing him with a tonic and proceeding to hold a linen to his nose.

"My first broken nose! I can't wait to tell my brother," the boy exclaimed with watery eyes as if he'd earned some sort of medal. Honzio smiled, shaking his head.

But that smile faded as his gaze caught again on Draven's still form. The man had broken into the house with deedans and Prolus's order to kill him. When Draven didn't return with news of success, the Dark Lord would send another troop to the house. They weren't safe there. But where could they go? How could they go? Honzio had no soldiers, no resources, nothing but his brains and the raggedy clothes on his back. He looked back at his sister, watching her converse with Velamir. Her earlier state alarmed him. The shadows still plagued her despite her visit to the Elders. If she didn't remove them, they would destroy her. He couldn't bear to see her that way again—possessed and distant, a stranger. Honzio had to prevent that before it was too late. And the only way she could receive treatment was if the war ceased. He had to end it, once and for all.

But for that, he would need an army.

"I need to send out word of my survival."

Conversation halted as all gazes swung to him.

"I will not hide any longer. I will not allow myself to be a pawn for Prolus or the Uluzar. I must return to Hearcross. Awaken the citizens. Break them out of their fear and unite the kingdoms. Ayleth may be overrun, but we still have Ondalar. We still have Verin and Devorin. They just need to know they haven't been abandoned."

They continued staring at him, as if not recognizing him. Hell, Honzio barely recognized himself. He was so used to speaking only when allowed to, so used to keeping his thoughts to himself that he wondered where that courage had come from. But as he looked at all the gazes watching him as if they saw more than a cowardly prince, he knew. Their belief had changed him.

"I will not force you to come with me. I will return

alone if I must. I cannot ask you to lay your life on the line for a mere grasp of hope, but—"

"Honzio." Natassa stepped toward him, reached out to touch his arm. "We have been surviving on a mere grasp of hope. We will fight for it as well."

He placed his good hand over hers, nodding gratefully. She gave him a soft smile in return. "We will defeat this evil. Whatever it takes."

"For the better," Velamir added, joining them as he declared his position.

"You gave me a promise, *Mosori*." Svorgin spoke up. "In the Grand Palace dungeons, you swore an oath to free my people. I didn't believe you then. You were Imperial, an enemy, a heartless dictator just like the rest of them."

Honzio flinched.

"But perhaps not all Imperials are the same." A grin pulled at the Savorian's lips. "I believe you now. And I will follow you."

"I'm with the lads," Bear said, slapping a hand on his son's shoulder as his eyes found Velamir.

"For what it's worth, I'm also with you, Your Majesty," Lore said, his voice muffled behind the linen still grasped around his nose. Marcella slapped his cheek, ordering him to remain still.

They all chuckled, and Honzio glanced around him. He'd never felt so light, so proud. All the glowing faces and smiling lips. And the belief that they could make a difference.

Marcella shoved back a runaway curl. "Well, I've

been thrown in with your lot, whether I like it or not. My home is marked."

Honzio grimaced. "You have my apologies."

She waved him off. "A load of crap that will give me. You want to send word around the Empire, to reach your people, don't you?" At Honzio's nod, she continued. "I can help you with that, but first I want your word. I have been living in hiding my entire life. Covering my mark just because I would be strung up and hung for existing as a Shadow Manos. Because of your father."

Honzio scratched his head, guilt gnawing at him.

"But I see you will change things, if not for your Shadow Manos civilians, for your sister."

Natassa shifted, and Honzio glanced at her. Her secret was long gone.

"Once this is over, I want a fancy house of my own in the capital with enormous windows that look out on a garden and at least two balconies." She drifted off for a moment, as if imagining the home, before jerking back to the present. "I've always wanted to be a healer—truly. Not just behind closed doors and in whispered alleys."

"Agreed," Honzio said. "How can you aid me?"

"Not only me. Promise to reward the others."

"The others?" Honzio repeated.

"The other Shadow Manos. We have been under such corrupt rule for so long that we had to create other means to communicate with each other. It was risky to leave our homes more than we had to." She paused, as if unsure she should divulge more information. "We use a specially crafted ink to communicate. If I can convince them of your sincerity, they will help us."

Honzio's brows rose. "You have that form of power?"

"We are Doer Shadow Manos. Crafting is our best trait." She smirked. "My acquaintances are all over the Empire. With their help, I can have a letter delivered to whomever you wish."

Honzio didn't see a better opportunity than that one. He nodded. "Consider it done. I will grant them what they desire once I regain my throne." He turned to the others. "Ready yourselves. As soon as we send the letters, we must leave."

"Where will we go?" Natassa asked.

"To Hearcross. We are going to retake the Empire."

36

CORALIE
KINGDOM OF VERIN
CASTLE VERIN

CORALIE PACED HER chamber, one end to the other, before starting again. The ache radiating through her fractured arm didn't faze her, as her focus was consumed by another source. She would have fought Zenrelius herself if she hadn't been so sure he would slay Mordon then and there. She had chosen Mordon as her champion to save his life. The thirst for blood had been evident in Zenrelius's eyes.

But still, doubt plagued her. Had she made the right decision? Zenrelius was a ruthless fighter. Some considered him the greatest in the Empire. She believed with all her heart that Mordon could defeat Zenrelius. But if he didn't, and she lost him in the risky bet, Coralie would never forgive herself. She com-

forted herself knowing that if he lost, her life would end shortly after. She would perish before she saw Zenrelius sitting on Verin's throne.

Knuckles rapped on her door, snaring her attention. Before she could even part her lips to answer, the door swung open, and Zenrelius entered. Irritation shot through her at his blatant disregard. She wondered why he'd even bothered knocking. His hired mercenaries blocked her doorway, preventing her from taking a step into the hall. She was a prisoner with fancy furnishings. Zenrelius closed the door behind him, and she stiffened. A closed door and two unmarried individuals alone in a chamber. Even under unusual circumstances, propriety was a must. Warning bells sounded in her mind.

He took another step into the room, placing his arms behind him as he glanced about her chamber. Coralie stood in silence, unease slithering over her. Many eyes had viewed her space—maids, bodyguards, family, advisors—but none of them had made her feel as exposed as he did with his gaze tracing over her belongings before settling on her. He examined her arm and the sling covering it before meeting her eyes.

"You must love silver," were the first words from his mouth.

Coralie started. "Pardon?"

"Most of your furnishing," he said, sweeping his arm about. "It's silver."

Coralie simply stared at him, refusing to fall into his trap of polite conversation. His lips curved when she didn't answer.

"How did you find your meals? I can have the cooks prepare something finer if you prefer."

"What are you doing in here?"

"I wanted to see if you had any needs."

Coralie almost rolled her eyes. "I want nothing more than for you to return to Ondalar and honor our agreement."

"I am afraid I cannot do that."

He was not dressed as he normally was. The heavy armor was gone, leaving him looking vulnerable in a long tan tunic and dark trousers. The sleeves were decorated in gold embroidery. He had to maintain some level of authority. But there were no weapons, no defense. He stepped closer and Coralie retreated, backing up against her vanity.

"I'm sure you are wondering about your people," Zenrelius said. "They are all being taken care of."

Coralie scoffed. "I'm sure. In the dungeon?"

Zenrelius sighed. "Do you view me as a beast, Coralie? Your people are moving about freely. Only the untamed ones are being held in the dungeon."

He meant Mordon, of course. Coralie swallowed her guilt. That was her fault. She should have prepared better. They were Ondalarians, after all, Verin's enemy of decades. She should have had precautions ready for when they stabbed a dagger into their back. Zenrelius loomed closer, eliminating the space between them.

"Don't do this, Coralie. What will this fight cause? Nothing but more lives lost. You know that boy will not defeat me."

"That *boy* will defeat you. I have no doubt about that."

Zenrelius clicked his tongue, peering down at her. The gray streaks in his hair were more prominent up close. "Why this stubbornness? You are a good queen, but you would make an even greater one at my side."

"What are you alluding to?"

"You lied to me. You are not betrothed. It was a falsehood to keep me at bay."

Zenrelius leaned in, his face inches from hers. The warmth seeping from his large form was overwhelming. Coralie's pulse skittered as she grasped behind her, her fingers curling around a long hairpin.

"But that was when I was the illegitimate general. Now I am the king of Ondalar." Zenrelius smiled, his eyes glittering with pride. "Imagine us ruling together. The world would bow before us. We start with Ondalar and Verin, and who knows how much farther we could go?"

For a moment, his plan seemed alluring. Coralie could almost see herself beside him, both with crowns of gold. But then she tore her eyes from his and breathed in. That wasn't what she wanted. She wanted to be queen to protect and uphold her people, not for glory.

"You came here to sway me to your side," Coralie said. "I'm afraid to disappoint you, General."

His expression changed, and Coralie spotted the rising anger before he concealed it behind his expressionless façade.

"Coralie," he breathed out. "That boy is nothing but a rage-filled tragedy. I am everything you could want in a spouse."

Coralie whipped out the pin just as his face lowered toward hers. He jerked back, surprise lashing his features. He stumbled back a few paces. Coralie covered the new ground, keeping the pin centimeters from piercing the skin over his heart. The tip of the pin poked between the laces of his tunic, brushing aside the hairs of his chest and drawing blood. That was when she noticed the odd lines darting across his skin, hidden by his tunic. Coralie pressed closer, moving the material aside, and a gasp slipped from her lips.

"You are a Shadow Manos."

Hidden for years behind layers of armor and secrets was a phoenix birthmark. It was the palest blue mixed with purple, like irregular veins twisting around each other. Zenrelius took in her expression.

"You are the first to know to have survived."

Coralie caught his implication, and everything fell into place. She made sense of that strange feeling she'd always experienced around him. The sense of comfort and the compelling aura—why she had wanted to comply with everything he suggested. He had been using his shadow's influence.

"You manipulated me," she said. "This entire time. And who knows how many others you have taken advantage of?"

Zenrelius shrugged. "I was born with it. Why not use it?"

Coralie shook her head, disgust welling in her chest. "You are sick."

He flinched, his genuine emotions revealed for the first time since she had known him. All those false masks of sincerity and adoration had been used to attempt to win her over.

"You will be defeated, and Mordon, who you call a boy, is braver than you could ever be."

Zenrelius's brows lowered in fury, and he spun around without a word, then slammed the door closed.

⋞

MORDON
KINGDOM OF VERIN

The damp dungeon air clung to his skin. Chains bound his wrists and ankles to the stone wall. The mercenaries had shoved him into the cell as if he were a wild animal, nearly stabbing him with their weapons as they did. He closed his eyes, a shudder passing through him as a gust of cold spread over him. It was chillier there than the rest of the castle, as if he were in the depths of winter once again.

The link connecting him to Inat remained. *Go,* he whispered, *go.*

He hoped the rumlok would leave, disappear far away, and never return. Mordon had been responsible for the rumloks. He'd taken care of them, ensured they and everyone around them remained safe. He leaned his head back against the cool stone, heaviness weighing him down. He'd failed. As usual, his attempts and goals went to the dirt. If it was the last thing he did, he would kill that blasted Ondalarian.

Eerie silence was his sole company as hours passed. The rest of the cells were empty, other than the ghosts of the many who had languished behind their bars. Velamir had been there once, locked away while Mordon fought to overcome the poison that had nearly taken his life. Perhaps he'd even stayed in the same cell.

He had viewed Velamir through a lens of hatred and loathing. He'd never seen past that barrier. But in an odd sort of way, Velamir was closer to him than he'd thought. The world had collapsed around them both. They'd found their true fathers at the same moment. And he had to admit, despite how much Velamir infuriated him, he respected the man. It wasn't often he battled someone who matched him for skill, speed, and talent. He hoped they would cross blades again one day, not as rivals, but perhaps as something closer to allies. He didn't know what to call their relationship. Some sort of twisted brotherhood.

The dungeon door swung open with a shrill squeal. Mordon lifted his head as footsteps crossed down the stairwell. Zenrelius came into view and stopped before Mordon's cell. The flickering torch he carried cast shadows over his face, but Mordon could still make out his features, twisted in wrath. The emotion surprised Mordon. He'd never seen the general act anything other than composed. Zenrelius unlocked the cell and stepped inside, not bothering to close it behind him.

"To what do I owe the honor of your visit?"

"I hear you will subdue me in the match." Zenrelius hung his torch on the wall and turned to face him.

Mordon eyed him, raising a brow when he saw the man's hands trembling and closing into fists.

"I will kill you, just as I slayed the rumloks. And no

one will remember your name. You will be a worthless pile of rubbish."

Fury boiled within Mordon. "You will pay for their deaths. I will avenge them."

Zenrelius scoffed, his mouth turning in distaste. "Of course, leave it to you to avenge vicious creatures. After all, you resemble them closely."

"I would rather resemble them than a two-faced traitor like you."

The punch hit him square in the jaw. Mordon's head snapped back. He blinked to clear his vision. Then he chuckled, tasting the metallic flavor of blood. "Such a powerless strike. The famed tales of General Zenrelius are nothing more than lies. You are simply a terrified coward who beats chained men."

The blows rocketed, slamming onto Mordon's jaw, but mostly his chest and stomach. The punches were deviously placed, enough to damage him but falling just short of breaking his ribs. When Zenrelius pulled back, his fists were coated in Mordon's blood. His eyes held a wild craze in them. Mordon wheezed as he inhaled. His head drooped, and he spat out the blood in his mouth. Zenrelius grasped Mordon's chained wrist and followed the metal until he grabbed hold of his little finger. Mordon's pulse skittered, knowing what was coming. The king of Ondalar's gaze was molten rage as he broke the finger without hesitation. Mordon roared, his agonized voice filling the dungeon. Tears blurred his eyes. Zenrelius released his finger, and another wave of pain overcame him, but Mordon withheld the scream burning his throat, unwilling to give Zenrelius any further satisfaction. Zenrelius reached out and gripped Mordon's hair, yanking his head up to stare him in the eyes.

"You will die, boy," he whispered. "You will die, and I will celebrate with Coralie at my side. She will remain queen of Verin. The only difference is that I will rule beside her."

Mordon's gut clenched. He exhaled countless labored breaths, and his vision grew dark as he struggled to fight against the torturous agony spreading through his body.

"I will make her my wife. When you are beneath the ground, covered in dirt without even a gravestone to prove your existence, she will be in my arms. She will bear my children."

Mordon couldn't comprehend the emotion he felt at those words or the horrifying images they conjured. He couldn't imagine or want to imagine a world without Coralie at his side. Zenrelius's grip on his hair tightened.

"While your body decomposes, she will crave my touch, and soon she won't even remember you. I will erase you from her mind."

"Shut your filthy mouth, you scum," Mordon spat, blood and saliva trickling over his lips. "Don't you dare touch her, or I swear I will tear every limb from your useless body."

Zenrelius chuckled and leaned in. "Farewell, Mordon Vaz."

Then he released him, strode away, and locked the cell behind him. Mordon shivered as the cold wrapped him in its vicious hold. But within him was a fire nothing could douse.

37

Latimus

Kingdom of Ondalar

L ATIMUS FORGOT THE passing time the longer he stayed in the dungeon. Not because of boredom. He forgot time because it disappeared as he spoke to his wife. They shared stories of their lives, smiling, laughing, and even shedding a few tears, though he wouldn't admit to it. They were heedless of the other prisoners looking on.

"That must have been so awful," Sardala said after he finished telling her about his father's betrayal.

"It was."

Latimus leaned against the bars, peering through them at Sardala sitting in the cell across from him. She watched him with a sullen expression, her round toffee-colored eyes filled with sadness. Latimus started. When had he begun to think her eyes resembled toffee?

He cleared his throat. "Often, I wonder how I will move on from it."

Sardala was silent for a long moment. "I read something once. A man was asked, 'After everything you've been through, how do you find the strength to stand?' and the man responded, 'I think of the world and its seasons. It changes so often, endures the heat of summer, the mourning of autumn, the harshness of winter, and yet it still has hope for spring. That is what makes me stand up. Spring has not yet arrived for me.'"

Latimus locked eyes with Sardala. She gave him a gentle smile.

"Spring has not yet arrived for you, Latimus Blayton."

"That is beautiful," Latimus said, the words touching him deeply. "Something to reflect on."

"Latimus." She paused. "May I call you that?"

"Of course."

"I heard my father speaking with Zenrelius before our wedding." She glanced away at the mention of their union, a blush touching her cheeks. "They were discussing a traveling serum. I assume that is how they will transport the army to Verin."

"The entire army?" Latimus mused. "How is that possible?"

"I don't know. But it sounds like Shadow Manos work. I also overheard something about the Tariqins. Do you suppose he could have procured it from them?"

Latimus shook his head. "He fought against the Tariqins. Why would he work with them now?"

"One thing we know for certain is that Zenrelius will attempt to take over Verin using this substance."

"And we have no bloody way to stop it." Latimus slammed a hand against the bars, rattling the iron.

Sardala flinched, and they both glanced up at the sound of someone approaching. Lord Genvor came into view, carrying a tray. He scanned over Latimus before focusing on his daughter. The high lord had started making frequent visits to the dungeon when he learned his daughter wasn't eating from the food the servants delivered to the prisoners. A line creased his brow as he stepped closer to Sardala's cell.

"My girl," he began, extending the tray toward her. "Sardala, you must eat."

Sardala jerked her head away, refusing to look at her father. Latimus watched as Lord Genvor attempted everything, including begging her to forgive him.

"Sardala, my girl, you know I cannot go against our king."

"You act as if he tortured you to obey him," Sardala said. "You chose Zenrelius, Father. You stood behind him and helped him attain the position of king."

"He will make a far better ruler than his predecessors." Lord Genvor sighed, using one hand to balance the tray as he leaned over and slid a metal key into the lock. He opened the door and stepped into Sardala's cell. "You must eat. For me. I had them prepare your favorite sweet. Rice pudding." Lord Genvor placed the tray on the ground beside his daughter. The high lord glanced about the cell. "It is cold here. I will have blankets sent for you."

Latimus's arms crossed as the man continued speaking of how he would make the cell more comfortable for his daughter instead of taking her out of it. Sardala shot up while her father was distracted with the inspection and raced from the cell. Lord Genvor spun around, but Sardala was already twisting the key, locking the door.

"Sardala!" Genvor shouted, rushing toward her.

She pulled the key free and stepped back. "I'm sorry, Father, but until we stop this war, I am afraid you will remain in there."

"Open this at once!" Lord Genvor demanded.

Sardala approached Latimus's cell and leaned in to unlock it. Strands of her wavy brown hair slipped free from her braid as she concentrated. Her lips pursed in the most adorable way. Latimus chuckled, and her head snapped up.

Her eyes narrowed. "What?"

"I am just laughing at the irony. My mother gave me a stern lecture before I left home. Enough of the recklessness, enough chasing danger, she said. Since, before that, I hadn't seen her in weeks, and during my absence, I had been in all sorts of life-threatening situations. She was pleased to learn I would be sent as an ambassador. If only she knew how quickly I had ended up in the dungeon."

The lock clicked, and Sardala swung the cell door open. "It seems danger is chasing you instead of the other way around."

Latimus stepped out of the cell, stretching his muscles. Lord Genvor continued shouting, but they blocked him out. "She wanted to be here for my wedding, but I advised against it. After all, I didn't want her to be disappointed."

Sardala's mouth dropped open, and she shoved his chest, nearly sending him sprawling back into the cell. "Disappointed by me?"

Latimus rubbed his chest and chuckled. "So touchy."

"You haven't seen anything yet."

"I didn't want her to be disappointed by the wedding. She'd always had these fanciful ideas for the ceremony. And . . ." He hesitated. "She expected me to marry a prim and proper lady, one who set me in place."

"And?" Sardala glared. "Am I not those things?"

"I'm not sure about the prim and proper part." He grinned when she huffed and blew a strand of hair from her face.

Sardala closed the cell behind him and moved toward the stairs. Latimus went to follow her but paused to watch Lord Genvor demand his daughter set him free. The other prisoners laughed at the scene he was making.

"Latimus?" Sardala stood at the foot of the stairs, extending her hand to him. "We have a war to stop."

He nodded and stared at her hand for a moment, examining the lines cutting across her palm. Then his fingers slid into hers, and something thrummed in his chest. It was as if he'd finally found his will to continue. It felt right.

⌁

It took quite some time to gather all the nobles in the throne room. They all appeared bored and dazed, as if just roused from slumber. They trailed into the chamber wearing silk robes of varying shades of gold. Latimus couldn't help thinking they resembled bathing robes. He forced down the laugh bubbling in his chest and watched them trickle to the table where he and Sardala were seated. Sardala had removed the king's chair so everyone would be on an equal level in rank. She nodded at each noble. No one was surprised to see them; just as Sardala had told him, it seemed her father hadn't allowed word to spread of their imprisonment. After everyone had settled, Sardala cleared her throat, but before she could talk, a nobleman spoke up.

"Lady Sardala, where is your father? Is he not to lead this meeting?"

Sardala shook her head. "He is not. Because he did not summon you here. I did."

Some tittered amongst themselves before a woman leaned forward in her seat.

"What did you wish to discuss, Lady Sardala? If this is about the interruption of your wedding celebration, we can surely gather another one."

Latimus felt Sardala's tension ripple forth. The nobles nodded and began discussing ways to make the celebration an even grander occasion. Sardala's fingers closed into a fist above the table. She stood, her chair screeching back.

"I did not call you here to discuss the colors of the table settings. We have a serious problem at hand. Zenrelius has gone to conquer Verin, or are you unaware of that?"

The nobles fell silent, glancing at each other until one, Asilles the shieldmaiden, spoke. "We know very well what our *king* is doing. He is exacting vengeance on those who wronged us."

"Are you certain? Or is he simply conquering land for his own gain? Do you not realize that if he takes Verin, he will be giving our true enemies an opening to invade?"

Latimus stood as well. "We wanted the kingdoms to unite peacefully. What Zenrelius is doing is creating chaos. The people in Verin are our brothers and sisters, not our enemies. We must stop him before it is too late. He plans to sacrifice Ondalarian troops to kill ours."

Asilles pushed to her feet and glared at them. "Do not speak ill of or address our king so informally. His orders will not be questioned."

"I know how much you care for him, but surely you must see how wrong this is," Sardala pleaded. "We cannot allow this massacre."

"What does Lord Genvor think of this?" someone asked. "Does your father agree with your treasonous thoughts?"

"My father has fallen prey to power. He cannot think clearly at this time and will not be of use to us."

The nobles began speaking at once. Their conversations turned to shouts as they tried to be heard over one another. Sardala was unable to regain their attention. Latimus attempted to intervene, but none of them listened.

"SILENCE!"

At the heart-stopping shout, all sounds ceased. Latimus glanced behind him. The weapons instructor, Korso, wore an intimidating glare as she stood in the chamber doorway. She marched toward the table, shieldmaidens streaming in behind her.

"My respect for Lord Genvor is endless," she boomed. "But I agree with Lady Sardala. For the good of the Empire, we must stop Zenrelius. The shieldmaidens will not assist in taking Verin."

The nobles hesitated, staring at the fearsome group of armored women with stony features.

Asilles shook her head. "Not all. I am with our king, and I will not stand by and allow traitors to speak ill of him."

Before Latimus could blink, the shieldmaiden flung a blade. The glinting weapon shot toward him, aimed at the skin between his brows. Someone shoved him aside, sending him sprawling to the floor. He pushed himself up. Sardala, wearing the fiercest expression he had ever seen on her face, stood in the spot he'd just been, the hilt of the thrown knife in her grasp. She tossed the blade away and unsheathed another shieldmaiden's sword. A gripping tension held the onlookers still. Asilles drew her own sword and stepped closer to Sardala. Worry tugged at Latimus, pulling him to his feet. He stalked toward them, but a large arm shot in front of his chest, blocking his way.

"Leave them to settle this," Instructor Korso barked.

At her command, the shieldmaidens retreated. The nobles stood from their seats to fall back. Sardala and Asilles circled each other, weapons perfectly still in guard positions. Then Asilles shrieked, swiping for Sardala's neck. Sardala slid across the floor beneath the sword, slicing her blade against the other shieldmaiden's armored side. The blade scraped the metal but couldn't penetrate it. Sardala returned to her full height and slashed at Asilles. Asilles retreated, kicking a chair to block Sardala's pursuit. Latimus's chest seized when Asilles threw another knife that sliced through a lock of Sardala's hair.

Korso's fist remained blocking his chest. "Patience, boy," she muttered, her own brows knit as she watched her protégés.

Asilles hopped onto a chair before jumping on the council table. She swiped her sword, shattering water glasses and knocking off a plate of refreshments. Sardala swung onto the table, lifting her hands in the air before slicing her sword downward. Asilles lifted her weapon in time. The blades connected, producing sparks. Both women stared at each other with fierce determination, the power in their arms on full display as neither allowed the other room to penetrate their defense. Asilles kneed Sardala and sent her stumbling back. She teetered at the edge of the table. Sweat trickled down Latimus's brow, his body itching to move. Sardala regained her balance in time to duck under another swing from Asilles before flinging her leg out, tripping the other woman. Asilles collapsed onto the table, grimacing as sharp remains of glass poked her. Sardala leaned over her and pointed her sword at her neck.

"Surrender."

Asilles hesitated, looked at the blade and then Sardala before the fight in her seeped out. "You have bested me."

Sardala removed the threat of the sword, tossing it

back to the shieldmaiden she had taken it from before offering a hand to Asilles. The woman took it begrudgingly. Sardala hopped off the table, a beaming smile crossing her face that made her look nothing like the terrifying warrior she was. Instructor Korso's fist dropped, and Latimus went to Sardala's side.

"Well done," he said, surprised by how proud he was.

The witnesses clapped politely as the dispute was settled.

"The cavalry will not be sent," Sardala said. "This is a time for the kingdoms to be united, not at war with each other."

The other nobles nodded, agreeing and putting Latimus at ease.

"Ambassador Blayton and I will set out with volunteers to stop Zenrelius."

She glanced at Latimus, and he nodded in acquiescence.

Instructor Korso neared them. "Do not worry about the state of things here. I will keep them in check."

Sardala smiled. "Of that I have no doubt."

HONZIO
HEARCROSS

IT WASN'T UNTIL six days of relentless travel later that Honzio found himself watching the path leading to the main gates of Hearcross, the capital of the Empire. He squatted down behind shrubs and the cover of overhanging branches. He could remember a time when the road was crowded with travelers from every part of the Empire coming to trade or see the grand city. But only birds flew past. Twigs crunched as Lore settled down beside him.

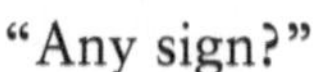

"Any sign?"

Honzio shook his head. They'd been waiting for an hour. He wiped the sweat dotting his forehead, gaze returning to the gate in the far distance where the small figures of Uluzar stood guard. Footsteps approached,

and Honzio glanced behind him, seeing Velamir and Svorgin returning. They'd gone ahead to scout.

"The cart is advancing this way," Velamir informed him.

Honzio's mouth formed a grim line. "Then let us be prepared to welcome it."

Velamir led the way, stopping beside a large tree where their horses were hidden. Honzio smiled, recalling the joy Velamir and Lore had shared when they'd reunited with their lost mounts, nuzzling their noses and hugging them. Lore might have gone a bit overboard by offering his horse nearly all the sugar cubes he'd snared from Marcella's supplies, earning the Shadow Manos's annoyance as well as Svorgin's, who they had discovered from Bear had an unhealthy sweet tooth he'd carried with him since childhood.

Velamir pulled his bow free from his saddlebag while Svorgin crouched down, glancing across the empty road to the opposite tree line. Honzio squinted, making out Bear's form on the other side, waving in return. Natassa and Marcella were waiting with him.

It was a risky plan, but one they had to take. After their escape from Ayleth, Natassa had foreseen an Uluzar merchant approaching Hearcross—their key to entering the city.

The clomping of hooves neared, and Honzio instinctively ducked down with the others. His breathing grew loud in his ears, and his heart pumped a touch harder. He scanned the road, relief sweeping him when he saw a bay-colored horse come into view. An Uluzar directed the steed, clicking his tongue and slapping the reins to urge it faster. The poor creature was weighed down by the large tarp-covered cart it was pulling. Two Uluzar rode on either side of the cart, armed with swords and fierce glares. The Uluzar sitting at the forefront of the cart unhooked a whip from his belt, irritation creasing his expression. He slashed the whip across the horse, and a pained whinny cut through the air. Honzio's mouth thinned at the sight. Velamir bristled visibly with rage. As the cart pressed closer, Honzio nodded at Lore and gestured to Marcella. The boy stood and rushed forward, raising his hands up. Marcella followed suit, both of them waving madly at the approaching Uluzar. The merchant sneered, slowing the horse but not stopping entirely.

Honzio raised his hand, and Svorgin readied himself, his hands tightening around his axe while Velamir nocked an arrow to his bowstring. Tense seconds elapsed before Honzio closed his fingers into a fist. In a blink, an arrow sliced through the horse's reins before another found its way into an Uluzar guard's shoulder. The man toppled off his horse. The other Uluzar guard looked about in fright, while the merchant stared at the remains of the severed reins hanging in his hands with mute shock. Bear emerged from the trees with a terrifying shout and yanked the Uluzar guard from his horse. The others charged onto the road, and the horses reared in alarm. Their hooves stomped the ground, raising dust. Velamir grabbed the nearest horse's halter, preventing it from bolting and running a calming hand over its coat. Svorgin wrenched the Uluzar merchant from the seat with a brutal grip. Honzio marched toward the abandoned cart and the Uluzar sprawled before it. The Uluzar glared up at him as he neared, spitting out words in Savese that couldn't mean anything good.

Svorgin was making good use of his father's axe, positioning it beneath the merchant's chin at a threatening angle and effectively silencing his insults. Honzio walked alongside the cart, finding Natassa had thrown up the tarp and was surveying its contents. He joined her, peering inside.

"Just as you said." He looked up, meeting his sister's gaze.

Food, weapons, and, most importantly, Uluzar uniforms folded neatly within.

"What are we gonna do with them?" Lore called, standing beside Svorgin and staring down at the wounded Uluzar, who were holding their hands up in surrender.

Honzio's eyes darted back to the cart, and he pulled out a long coil of rope. He tossed it to the boy. "We should make good use of that."

❧

NATASSA
HEARCROSS

The uniform was oversized, scratchy, and rubbed uncomfortably against her skin. She had never thought the day would come when she would be garbed as an Uluzar, yet there she was. The others stepped onto the road from the tree line, where they had dressed in the private cover of the branches. She held in her laugh at how uncertain and uncomfortable they appeared in the uniforms. Velamir approached her, his brows pinching even as a gleam of amusement shone in his eyes.

"What are you chuckling about?"

The uniform fit him to perfection, the sleeves and trousers not a touch too long or short. The smoky gray and black fabric blended, highlighting the sparks in his green gaze and bringing out the harshness of his bearded jaw. Silver spiked pads gripped his shoulders, emphasizing their broadness. Velamir lifted a matching silver helmet over his thick hair, hiding the brunette strands from view. The rim of the helm rested over his brows and protruded out by his cheekbones, leaving the rest of his face in full view.

"I was thinking of telling you how dreadful you look in enemy colors," Natassa responded, biting her inner cheek to hold her smile.

He raised a thick dark brow. "You were thinking of telling me? Why not say it outright?" Velamir stepped closer, his larger form blocking out her view of the others.

She tilted her head up, holding his gaze. "I cannot."

His mouth broke into a smile, and he leaned closer, his hands darting around hers. "You look quite a bit dreadful yourself," he said, his gaze warming and telling her a different story entirely.

"Is that so?" Why did she sound so breathless?

He tugged on her hands, and she glanced down, realizing what he was after. She relinquished her hold on her helmet, and he lifted it ever so slowly and placed it onto her head. His fingers slid back, brushing over her skin in a slow tantalizing motion, leaving a burning trail behind. His gaze remained rooted to hers all the while. He leaned down suddenly to dig in the ground, giving her a chance to regain her composure. When he rose to his full height, his hands were streaked with dirt.

"What are you doing?"

Instead of answering, he turned behind him, whistling to catch the others' attention. Honzio was already staring at him with a pointed look, scowling as he watched them.

"Smear dirt on your faces. I've seen some of the Uluzar wear paint, but we will make do with this," Velamir told them.

"Paint or blood?" she heard Honzio mutter.

Velamir turned back to her, brushing his thumbs over her cheekbones, coating the skin there in dirt. His eyes were dark, wholly concentrated. Natassa remained unmoving. Her lashes drifted shut for a moment as she cherished his tender touch. When she opened them, she saw him staring at her with what could only be described as desperation, as if he had been deprived of air and she was his source of breathing. He'd wanted her to stay behind, to not enter Hearcross with them, but they needed her. They wouldn't make it past the gates without her.

Natassa retrieved some dirt and returned the favor, spreading it across his warm skin. "I will be fine."

He nodded. Twice. "I won't lose you again."

He whispered the words so low, she wondered if he'd even meant for her to overhear them.

A short while later, they headed toward the gates. The cart's rickety wheels rolled over the pebbled road.

Honzio sat at the front of the cart, while Svorgin and Bear were hidden inside, away from searching eyes. Despite the dirt tracing their features, their unmistakable ice-colored gazes and pale features would give them away. Natassa and Velamir walked before the cart. They had left the other horses behind with Lore and Marcella, who were guarding the Uluzar they had tied to a tree. Velamir had made the call to have them stay behind, much to Lore's disappointment. He'd convinced the boy he was doing them a significant favor by watching the Uluzar, but Natassa had sensed Velamir's real reasoning. He didn't know what was awaiting them in Hearcross, and he didn't want the boy to be harmed.

Natassa glanced at Velamir striding straight and confidently beside her. He caught her watching and sent her a wink, his hand reaching for hers. His fingers had barely brushed against hers when a loud throat cleared. Natassa glanced back at Honzio, who stared at them meaningfully. She sent him a questioning look in return, simply to annoy him. It seemed he was taking his role as her older brother quite seriously.

"We are approaching the gates," he said.

Natassa's stomach bundled into a fit of nerves. If the Uluzar didn't allow them through, she would have to do the talking with the help of her shadows. She had forced herself to sound confident while they'd been forming the plan, but she wondered if she could accomplish it. There was only one way to find out.

The Uluzar guarding the gates stiffened at their approach, scanning their uniforms with narrowed eyes and pinched lips.

"Fifteen," she heard Velamir mutter, and she followed his gaze to the walkway above the gates where more Uluzar stood peering at them. After a quick count, she came to the same estimation.

"Keep your heads down," Honzio warned as they grew closer.

The gates loomed ahead, solid brass with a beautiful design to please the eyes. The main entrance into Hearcross was a show for newcomers, not as well stabilized but heavily guarded to compensate for the weakness.

An Uluzar barked in Savese. *Let them through*, her shadows translated in her mind.

The gates swung open, and Natassa's tightened muscles released as relief bloomed in her. They moved through the gates, sharp eyes probing them the entire way. They had nearly made it all the way through when she heard harsh Savese snap behind her.

Halt!

She froze, casting a worried glance at Honzio. He gave her a comforting look in return. His belief in her warmed her heart but didn't convince her that she could truly do this. Natassa braced herself and swiveled, facing the Uluzar approaching them with a frown.

"*Ki pochis astili?*"

Who is your chief?

Natassa's lips parted as she grasped for her shadows' assistance.

They chuckled. *What do we receive in return, Princess?*

"*Tuwa zabona kaybatis kazin?*"

You lost your tongue, woman?

Natassa hissed, snapping inwardly as the Uluzar continued to grow suspicious. He moved closer to the cart, reaching for the tarp.

If you do not help me, they will kill us. Who will open your portal then?

That seemed to snap them into focus, and their overwhelming presence grew on either side of her, the Seer manipulating her voice and the Lure transferring a convincing aura along with it.

"Pochis ova Grongar-ja."

Our chief is Grongar-ja.

"Maro burdis carop."

He called us here.

Honzio stiffened at the name of the Uluzar chief who had used him to infiltrate the castle. The Uluzar's hand dropped from the cart, and he examined her for a long moment, scanning her up and down. Natassa held his stare. She could not allow her doubts to surface. She had to seem entirely sure of herself. After what felt like a century of time had elapsed, the Uluzar dipped his chin.

"Meydoni gidi."

You may pass.

Natassa's breath rushed free as she exhaled. She turned, ensuring to relax her posture and keep her expression blank. As soon as the gate grew distant behind them, they picked up their pace.

"We've entered the city," Natassa called back to Honzio. "What do we do next?"

"We find Moralis."

Jax

Kingdom of Devorin

HE SHIVERED ON the table. He couldn't find the strength to attempt freeing himself. A figure approached from his peripheral, holding a bucket. He trembled, knowing what was coming. The masked soldier stared down at him before lifting the bucket with gloved hands. The freezing water splashed onto him, pulling a gasp past his lips. He writhed against the board, his torn clothes stuck to his skin, piercing him like ice.

"Who are you? What is your name?" a soft and cunning female voice asked from somewhere out of view.

He sputtered, searching for an answer to end the torture. But there was nothing.

"I don't know," he managed to say.

He looked up at the soldier holding

the empty bucket, focusing on the only part of his face that was visible. The soldier's dark eyes were soulless and empty. He wondered if his own looked the same.

"Your. *Name*."

Another figure stepped into view, and his gaze flicked to the woman. Her beautiful features were as striking as they had been the day before and the day before and the—

He stalled, attempting to remember, but he couldn't recall the first time he'd seen her.

"I don't know," he repeated, more power in his tone.

She stepped beside the soldier, smiling down at him. "You are prepared for the next stage. Your past no longer matters. The man you were before is gone." She ran a hand over his sopping wet sleeve, tracing his arm. "Despite the loss of your shadow, you lasted this long. You are strong."

He shuddered through another wave of cold. The freezing water continued seeping through his thin clothes, sending stinging pricks of cold into his skin. The woman's words spiraled him into confusion. What did she mean by them?

She nodded to the soldier and stepped back. The soldier unshackled him from the board and yanked him up. He gasped when his bare feet touched the ground and would have fallen if it hadn't been for the soldier. When was the last time he'd stood on his own feet? He had so many questions, so many blank spots in his mind that it was beginning to terrify him.

He was propelled down a long winding staircase and then taken to a chamber where he was washed in steaming water. Two servants assisted him, sponging his body. He stared down at himself, slightly alarmed by his protruding bones. Next, the servants dressed him before a mirror. Haunted blue eyes gazed at him through the wet curls dangling before them. He looked hard at his reflection, trying to remember something, anything. But the man peering back at him was as unfamiliar to him as everything else was. The servants brought forth shears, cutting through the thick locks of his hair. He stared at the fallen curls, knowing he should feel something at the loss but there was only emptiness. The servants dressed him in fine leather armor. Their lips were sewn shut, but it was such a regular sight that he didn't think about it.

He was then taken down to another floor and entered a wide hall set alight by hundreds of candles. His breath lodged in his throat at the view before him. Row upon row of men and women clothed like him. Half of them had their lips sealed shut by a thick cord. They were lined up, eyes forward, empty. Someone shoved him forward and placed him in the first row.

Welcome. The queen's voice washed through his mind. *My lethal warriors.*

He stared at her. She was his queen; he was her weapon. It was a whisper that had been driven into him for days and nights.

"The time has come. We will join Lord Prolus in his task of conquering the Empire. You, my ruthless soldiers, will assist in this effort."

She passed the first row, stopping in front of him.

"Who are you?" she whispered, her lips moving as she said it audibly.

He sank to his knee before her. When he spoke, his voice was raw and certain. "Your weapon, my queen."

Honzio

Hearcross

THE MIDDAY SUN heated his helmet as they navigated the city. They had abandoned the cart in
a vacant alley a bit ago. Honzio pulled a crumpled note from his belt, knowing the words written on
it without even looking.

Little Cousin, Madame Clion's Inn is a lovely place.
They would regroup at the inn, inform Moralis of
the recent happenings, and he would also have a chance
to check on his cousin. That fateful night
when everything had gone wrong, when
Draven had attacked them in the throne
room, forcing Honzio to escape—that
night had been his last glimpse of his
cousin and Aylis. He knew Moralis
could take care of himself, but Honzio
wanted to see him safe with his own

eyes. He'd gotten Moralis involved in the entire thing by entrusting him with Aylis.

"Madame Clion?" Natassa said, increasing her speed to keep up with him. "The presumed Shadow Manos?"

Honzio nodded, not sparing a word as he scanned their surroundings. The capital of the Empire was much changed. Buildings had been demolished, stores closed, and an eerie stillness reigned over the streets. Prying eyes watched them from behind curtained windows, making him uneasy.

"Perhaps we should have brought Marcella in case she corresponds with her. We would have gained her trust easily."

"*Presumed* Shadow Manos," Honzio reminded her. "We do not know if she is one. You realize many people say the things they do about her because her inn allows mercenaries and the like."

"Well, presumed or not, what does she have to do with Moralis?"

The others' boots clomped behind them as they followed in silence. Honzio briefly filled her in on Aylis. As he did, he noticed a poster hanging in the distance and ruffling in the breeze. He stopped as they neared it, his breath catching as he read the reward amount. The face above it was unmistakably his.

"Forty thousand gold." Svorgin whistled through his teeth. "You carry quite the price on your head, *Mosori*."

Honzio ignored him, his mind trailing to Grongarja, the Uluzar who had taken charge of the palace. The Uluzar still saw him as a threat. Even after imprisoning him and knowing of his impaired arm, they viewed him as a risk. He didn't think he should feel so gratified by that knowledge, but he couldn't help himself.

He pressed on through the streets, not making eye contact with anyone who did cross their path. At last, he stopped in front of a solitary building with a wooden sign dangling above its door. Words were carved in the sign, proclaiming a name in an elegant font. *Madame Clion's Inn.*

Honzio climbed the few steps and rapped on the door. He heard footsteps approach from within, and the door opened the slightest bit. A middle-aged woman with prominent features evaluated him through the gap before her eyes flicked to the others behind him. She focused on their uniforms, her fear unmistakable.

"Give me a moment," she said before slamming the door closed.

Honzio stood uncertainly on the top step, his mouth parted with words he'd been unable to say. He glanced back at the others, who waited on solid ground below him. Svorgin and Bear spoke in low tones, and his sister was leaning toward that Velamir fellow, their heads close together as they conversed quietly. Honzio shook his head and swung his attention back to the door as the wooden frame rumbled open. Fully that time.

The woman had an odd sort of smile pulling at her cheeks. "I'm afraid I do not understand Savese, but is there anything I can do to help you?"

Honzio nodded, leaning closer. "You can allow us inside."

Her features froze in surprise when he spoke in Imperial before she composed herself. "Your chief already did an inspection on my inn. There is no one here."

Honzio frowned. Madame Clion's Inn was never empty, according to the rumors that had flitted about the Grand Palace. Even if the noble folk didn't rent her rooms, it was always buzzing with noise and brawls.

"You must be Madame Clion?"

She nodded, appearing startled as he stepped closer.

"If you'll allow me?" He motioned toward the space behind her.

She seemed hesitant before stepping aside and allowing them through. Honzio glanced about the entry-way—a large circular chamber that didn't look peculiar in the least. Dark brown walls covered in paintings of flowers. The floor was tiled in mismatched colors of gray and brown. A candelabra hung on either side of an archway that led to a hall. Honzio spotted a staircase to another level at the end of the hall.

"Like I said before," Madame Clion said, her voice rising as she tried to retain his attention, "your chief did an inspection of my establishment. There is no one here. I have not been renting any rooms either."

"How about I simplify things?" Honzio said. "I am not here on behalf of any chief." He tugged his helmet off. "I'm searching for Galva Moralis Vane."

Her eyes swept over his features, dropping to his arm in its uncomfortable position, smothered by his sleeve. He no longer had tailored tunics fit for his mangled arm. He was a runaway, a hunted prince wearing the garb of his enemy.

"Prince Honzio," she breathed, recognition flickering in her eyes.

"No need to fret, madame," someone else said. "My cousin is of no harm to me."

Honzio smiled and turned as Moralis emerged from the hall. His cousin was looking much the same, albeit slightly worn out and quite sweaty, his plain tunic plastered to his muscled chest.

"Moralis?" The name emerged with a question hanging from it.

Moralis slung him into a hug, slapping him on the back. Honzio returned the embrace as best as he could.

"I expected you long ago," Moralis said in his ear. "Manos Cerel informed me of your escape from the dungeons. Where did you disappear to? And what's with the uniform?"

"It's complicated and far too long a tale," Honzio muttered back. "Forget about me. What happened to you?" He leaned back, making a show of looking him over. "You look like you've been in battle."

Moralis chuckled, giving him a sheepish grin as he scratched his neck. "You could say I was in battle. Aylis was teaching me a few maneuvers."

Honzio's brows shot up. "An Ondalarian Galvasir in need of training?"

Moralis must have noticed the look on his face, for he hurried to clarify. "Combat moves. Savorian tactics. She told me everything, Cousin. I know of her past. Of her search for her brother."

"It was bound to happen. You've spent so much time here together." Honzio changed the subject. "This

Madame Clion . . ." He glanced to the side, ensuring the woman wouldn't be privy to their conversation. "She said the Uluzar did an inspection of the inn. How did they not find you?"

"I procured her inn solely for us so Aylis and I could remain concealed for as long as needed. That is the reason the inn is empty. As for the inspection"—Moralis smiled—"the Grand Palace isn't the only place with secret chambers and tunnels."

A throat cleared, most assuredly his little sister's.

Moralis glanced over his shoulder. "And who are your companions?"

"Svorgin and Bear," Honzio said, motioning to them.

The Savorians nodded, eyeing him in a distrustful manner. Moralis was unfazed, smiling broadly at each introduction.

"Velamir, a . . ." Honzio paused, unsure where to start with the man's background and deciding to forgo it altogether. "And you know Natassa, of course."

Natassa beamed and launched into Moralis's arms. She gripped him tightly, squeezing her eyes shut. Moralis laughed at her impulsive embrace and tousled her hair.

"Good to see you, too, Cousin."

Natassa sniffed and continued hugging him with all her strength. Honzio knew she was remembering their brother. Perhaps she was even imagining embracing Thorsten. It was far too easy to believe so. It hadn't been uncommon for them to be mistaken for the other. And it wasn't only the looks. Moralis also carried Thorsten's outgoing and fierce disposition.

Velamir locked eyes with Honzio, understanding in

his gaze. Honzio wasn't sure how much his sister had told the man, but it seemed he knew quite a bit about their family. The two had been inseparable the entire way to Hearcross. Natassa saw something in him. From what Honzio had gleaned, Velamir was a Tariqin Chishma-turned-traitor and was discovered to be the son of an Imperial general. It seemed unreal, like something from a tale, but Honzio wasn't about to judge. The man might not be a prince or even of noble blood, but none of that mattered. If he was as honorable as he appeared and returned Natassa's love for him, that was more important than the damned royal protocol and laws.

Natassa released Moralis, and he gave her a tiny smile, tweaking her chin. Natassa laughed, her eyes shining.

"Honzio?" The deep female voice snared his attention.

Aylis entered the entryway from the hall, a smile breaking across her face when she saw him. She wore baggy trousers and a brown vest that left her muscular arms on display. Her dyed black hair was braided down her back. She frowned as she scanned his uniform, and Honzio gave her a grin.

"You've returned in one piece."

Honzio chuckled. "So little faith in me."

She punched his shoulder in greeting, causing his chuckle to come to an abrupt halt.

He rubbed his arm and grimaced. "With your permission, I would like to introduce you to someone."

She stepped closer before freezing, catching sight of the people behind Honzio. There was a rippling tension in the air, as if all breaths had been stolen away. All eyes were on the two immobile statues staring at Aylis. Bear and Svorgin were paler than normal, all the blood drained from their faces.

"As I promised," Honzio said. "I found your brother."

Aylis sputtered before a shriek of joy ripped from her throat. She flew past Honzio, crashing into the two large Savorians. Honzio couldn't keep his smile at bay as they hugged each other tight. They spoke in their language, tears streaming down their faces. Velamir and Moralis watched the reunion with smiles. Tears flowed down Natassa's cheeks again, and Velamir stepped beside her, setting his arm around her shoulders and tugging her into his side. Bear pressed kisses to his children's foreheads. Honzio had finally kept a promise. He had reunited them. If only Thorsten could have been there to see it.

An insistent bang shook the door, cutting the joyful reunion short. They exchanged glances. Honzio searched for Madame Clion just as Moralis grabbed his arm.

"We must go to the hidden chamber."

Honzio nodded and moved to follow his cousin. They had taken but two paces when the door flew open and a group of Uluzar swarmed in. The man at the lead wore a uniform similar to theirs, only his spikes were higher and he had no helm. His hair was woven back into a braid that crossed behind his head before draping over his shoulders, the ends fastened by leather cords. The Uluzar evaluated them, hesitating on Velamir before returning to Honzio. A shape emerged from behind the Uluzar. Madame Clion. Her sullen face wore a pleased smile, and in her arms was a heavy-looking chest that no doubt contained the price of Honzio's head.

41

CORALIE
KINGDOM OF VERIN

CORALIE SHIFTED HER arm in the sling, wincing at the stiffness. Cheers from the mercenaries stole her attention. Coralie looked up as Zenrelius stepped onto the melee grounds. The long expanse of land had been used for Verin's annual jousting tournaments. A sense of foreboding erupted in Coralie's midsection at the memory of the last tournament. The one that had remained unfinished. When Mordon had been poisoned and nearly lost his life. She inhaled, forcing herself to focus on the present.

Zenrelius wore full armor, including a sparkling helmet over his graying hair. He lifted his sword, waving it around the arena at the audience and then tapping the hilt to his chest, a common gesture of loyalty. Zenrelius was one of the most despicable men she'd ever had the displeasure of knowing. And after her recent discovery, she knew he didn't have a drop of loyalty within him. All those poor people who adored him did not know how little he valued them.

A sudden hush fell as Mordon was escorted onto the grounds by guards. His armor was far less secure than Zenrelius's and sparser. He wore no helmet. Coralie's heart lurched to her throat. Why was he walking so oddly? *He's injured.* Coralie rose from her seat, and Vykus, the mercenary king, clicked his tongue.

"Now, now, you were told not to move, weren't you?"

Coralie glared at him. Vykus was out for his own gain, as always. He'd worked for Prolus for a long period before changing sides to assist Verin in its defense against the Dark Lord. Afterward, he was with Ondalar, or rather, Zenrelius. The path he took didn't matter as long as there was a glittering chest at the end of it.

"No need for such fierce scowls." Vykus smirked. "Sit down, lady."

Coralie held in her retort and returned to her seat. There wasn't much she could do in her position. Zenrelius had her strategically placed far away from any of her people. Mercenaries guarded her every move—a warning to her guards that a sword was at her throat every moment. Just one mistake and they would lose their queen. For an extra measure of security, he'd even positioned the Verin soldiers and the Savorians apart from each other. Zenrelius was doing everything to prevent an uprising. And with her wounded arm, it was unlikely she could lead such an event. Coralie's nostrils flared as her wrath grew. She watched the despicable man below as he swung his sword in a dizzying arc before slamming it into a guard position. The handle was gripped in his gloved grasp, the blade resting on his raised iron vambrace, extending into the air, the tip pointing at his opponent.

Mordon stood opposite him, his fingers wrapped around the hilt of a shabby-looking sword. It was then that Coralie noticed he was using his left hand. Mordon was right-handed. True panic lanced through her middle. What had Zenrelius done to him? The herald spoke up, his loud voice reaching all ears.

"Dear spectators, today we hold the match of a century. The match that will determine the ruler of Verin. King Zenrelius against the queen's champion, General Mordon."

In response, what should have been a chorus of cheers was instead a muffled sort of horror as everyone watched with tense expressions.

"Begin!" the herald shouted.

Zenrelius and Mordon circled each other. Two of the greatest fighters she had ever seen locking eyes as they waited for the other to make the first move. Coralie knew Mordon as well as herself, if not better. Her eyes trailed his form. He was injured and attempting to ignore the pain. The stance he had taken was a defensive one. Coralie swallowed the lump in her throat.

Zenrelius rushed toward Mordon, swinging his broadsword high. Mordon jumped back at the last moment, and the sword slammed into the sandy arena ground. Zenrelius spun, directing his sword toward

Mordon's neck. Mordon ducked under it. He was moving slower than normal. Coralie could tell he was conserving his strength. Zenrelius was slower too. The broadsword was a heavy weapon, and it took a significant amount of might to propel it through the air. Mordon seemed to realize that, because when Zenrelius's blade dropped into the sand again, he took his chance. Mordon bolted forward, breaking into a Galvasir attack. His sword flashed faster than lightning. Zenrelius stumbled back, barely blocking the blows. He tumbled onto the ground, and his sword slipped from his grasp. Mordon heaved his blade downward. Zenrelius rolled over just in time, and the end of Mordon's weapon buried into the sand. Zenrelius kicked upward, his metal-plated boot slamming into Mordon's stomach, shoving him back. Mordon shouted, his features tense with agony as he stumbled away. Coralie squeezed the edge of her seat until she could no longer feel her fingers.

Zenrelius staggered up, yanking off his helmet. Sweat trickled down his suntanned face. He rushed Mordon, slamming him onto the ground. Mordon disappeared from Coralie's sight as Zenrelius's bulk and armor blocked him from view. Zenrelius launched blow after blow beneath him, his arms raining down with an alarming speed. Nothing could hold her back any longer. Coralie shot to her feet and propelled herself over the seats. Vykus and his mercenaries shouted as they pursued her, but she ignored them as she darted between the chairs.

She made out the figures of her guards breaking free of their own captors, shoving the mercenaries aside as they struggled to reach her. Coralie stumbled onto the sand-covered grounds. Zenrelius rose, blood staining his gloves. Crimson tainted his golden armor. His face was dark, monstrous. Rough hands grabbed hold of Coralie and yanked her back. She screamed her rage, angry tears slipping from her lashes. Her shouts were indiscernible even to her own ears as she begged Zenrelius to cease his brutal attack.

But Zenrelius didn't seem to hear her. He leaned over, retrieving his broadsword, and dragged it toward Mordon. Coralie made out Mordon's motionless form through her tear-filled vision. He was covered in blood, his face unrecognizable. She couldn't lose him. Zenrelius lifted the broadsword.

"No," Coralie whispered. She didn't even feel like she was in her body. She was somewhere far away, watching as Zenrelius held the weapon above Mordon's chest.

Mordon's head tilted toward her, and his eyes locked with hers. His lips twitched, the beginning of a smile. A farewell smile. Coralie yelled, her struggles to reach him returning full force. Blood trickled from his mouth and nose. She sagged against the forceful holds of the mercenaries.

I love you, she mouthed.

Mordon took in her face, reading her lips. The sword came down. Coralie's heart left her throat. A shriek that would haunt any who heard it escaped her. Her lids clamped closed. Then she heard gasps of surprise, and her eyes flew open. A dark shape hurtled toward Zenrelius, sending him stumbling back. Flashing red eyes and gleaming sharp teeth snapped at him.

"Inat," Coralie whispered, shock and hope gripping her.

Zenrelius swung at the rumlok with vicious swipes, but the rumlok evaded each one. Darting with lithe muscles through the man's defense, Inat sank his teeth into Zenrelius's calf, finding the exposed area in his armor. Zenrelius howled and fell to his knees, while Mordon rose on unsteady legs, his hand extended as he focused on Inat. Zenrelius's anger was at a boiling point. Coralie could see it as he roared, stood, and launched another attack at the rumlok. His sword sliced along the rumlok's side, and blood welled forth, coating his black fur.

Inat whimpered, falling back. Zenrelius swung again, but that time, Mordon was there. The two men were entangled in each other, their faces inches apart. And then Zenrelius staggered back, looking down at his middle. The end of Mordon's sword stuck out of his midsection. The former general crumpled onto the arena ground, gripping his stomach in horror. Coralie exhaled, but her chest heaved in panic as her attention remained rooted to Mordon, who stumbled back before he also collapsed. The clutches on Coralie loosened, and she rushed toward him.

"Mordon!" She slid across the sand, falling beside him, and pulled his head onto her lap. Her fingers dug into the soft waves of his raven-black hair. "Mordon." His name left her lips in a strangled sob. "Mordon, stay with me."

His eyes were unfocused, staring at the bright sky above them. His mouth parted, and blood trickled from it into his stubble. His lips were pale and trembling as he tried to speak. Coralie gasped, tears blinding her as her shaking fingers stroked his face, wiping at all the blood.

"I'm so sorry, Mordon. I'm so sorry," she cried. "This is all my fault."

"Coralie," he rasped, choking as more blood emerged.

"Tell me," she begged, gripping his face.

"I promised myself that when—when you were r-ready"—he coughed—"I-I-I would propose to you on a day like this."

Coralie shook her head, biting her lip as tears slipped from her lashes.

"The sun is shining," he mumbled. "No s-sign of rain or storm."

His words were garbled as he choked on blood.

"It is a beautiful day."

Coralie blocked out the sounds of battle around her as her guards and the Savorians jumped into action, fury driving them to clash against the mercenaries.

"Mordon," she whispered, stroking his cheek.

"I love you, Coralie," he said, blinking slowly. "I-I've always loved you."

"No!" She pulled him closer to her. "No, you can't leave me."

Inat whimpered, curling near Mordon and nudging him with his head. The rumlok's intelligent red eyes were filled with sadness.

Mordon forced his eyes open, searching her gaze. "Will you marry me, Coralie?"

Coralie's chest shook. She shuddered as she clutched him tight. "Yes," she cried, her chin quivering. "Yes, I will marry you."

He smiled, blood coating his mouth as he fell still.

42

Velamir
Hearcross

V ELAMIR REACHED FOR Natassa on instinct, pushing her behind him. She gripped his arm with tense fingers, and when he glanced back, he deciphered her unease with a single look. She was wordlessly asking him if she should use her shadows. Velamir surveyed her, taking in her pallid features and pale lips, the circles beneath her eyes. He'd seen what happened to her after she spoke to the Uluzar guarding the city gates. While it had been an amazing feat—one he doubted he would see again in his lifetime—it had also drained her of her strength. Even then he could feel the tremble in her fingers around his biceps and hadn't forgotten the way she'd sagged against him as they journeyed through the city to find Madame Clion's Inn. He couldn't allow

her to continue using her shadows and destroy herself in the process. They would fight their way out of it, like every time before.

Velamir gave her a subtle head shake, and she nodded in return.

"You sold us out," Honzio said, his voice dangerous as he addressed the middle-aged woman with wrinkles cutting through her brow. "Moralis's coin wasn't enough for you?"

Madame Clion shrugged. "I do not know what you mean. You broke into my inn, and I did my civil duty to the rulers of this empire."

The tall Uluzar standing before the rest of the armored warriors smiled. "Do you hear that, Prince Honzio? Your own citizens have no care for you."

The man's accent wasn't as thick as most Uluzar Velamir had heard speak. His Imperial sounded lilting, almost adding a flair of richness to the words.

"You have an advantage over me," Honzio said. "You know who I am, but I haven't the slightest idea who you are."

Velamir's mouth twitched as he held in a smile. Honzio had shown he was a true noble; only nobility knew the language of belittling others in a regal way. He'd first given the Uluzar a compliment by allowing him to believe he had the upper hand before crushing him into an unknown face unworthy of recognition.

"I can't leave you in the dark now, can I?" the Uluzar replied, appearing unfazed. "I am Chief Jinong-ja, son of Chief Troyi-ja, son of Chief Nara-na, daughter of

Chief Ylan-na, daughter of the last khan. Does that suffice?" An arrogant brow lift ended the list.

"I asked for your name, not a history lesson," Honzio replied, sharp as a blade. "If it takes reciting your dead ancestors to prove your worth, don't bother."

Jinong-ja stiffened, his muscles tense with rippling anger. Velamir wasn't sure what Honzio was planning, but the angrier the Uluzar became, the faster they would enter combat. Velamir wasn't one to complain. He examined the Uluzar, noting the scars crisscrossing his exposed arms and the unlaced front of his tunic that proudly displayed the wolf tattoo spreading across his chest. His face was youthful; he couldn't have been more than a few years Velamir's senior. Velamir thought over the man's ancestral line. Jinong-ja was related to the last khan. Even distantly so, he carried the man's blood. The khan, Boltrex's father. Velamir swallowed. If he entered a battle with the Uluzar, he would spill the blood of his own kin, as strange as it was to believe. Velamir was forever tied to the Uluzar. Boltrex had run away from his people, but no hiding, no merging with the Imperials could change the truth that he was an Uluzar.

"Perhaps if you had heeded your studies, you wouldn't need lessons."

Honzio chuckled. "And I will learn them from a boy?"

Jinong-ja bared his teeth, and Velamir was surprised to see they were unsharpened. He leaned forward, his bronze skin glowing gold from the candlelight. "Though I would enjoy it immensely, Chief Xan-ja will give you your lesson."

Jinong-ja motioned the Uluzar behind him and barked something in Savese. The Uluzar swept forward, gazes locked on their targets. Jagged blades found their way into their fists. The first Uluzar swung his sword up in a wild arc, and then it crashed down like lightning. Velamir flew forward, pushing Honzio out of the way. The sword sliced through air, and Velamir grabbed the Uluzar's arm, yanking him past him. He heard growls and knew Bear and Svorgin had gotten their hands on him. Velamir didn't glance back to confirm it, as another weapon was swinging toward him. He dropped into a crouch, unsheathing his dagger, and the weight of the Uluzar's weapon meeting nothing sent the man stumbling forward. Velamir swiveled out of the way, slicing along the Uluzar's leg before returning to his full height. Ten more Uluzar flew toward him. Jinong-ja stood behind them, watching the attack with an impassive expression, his eyes following Velamir's every move.

Flashing blades swept at him from too many places to defend. Velamir tensed, unsheathing his sword and flipping his dagger in his hand so the blade was angled backward. Then Moralis and Aylis were there, crashing against the Uluzar with brutal force. Moralis disarmed an Uluzar and shoved the man's head against his knee. Aylis swung over the bent Uluzar's back and flung her axe into another's chest.

"Leave some for us, Sister," Svorgin said before saying something in his language that made Aylis laugh.

She wrenched her axe out of the Uluzar's chest and threw it into the air. Bear caught it, slamming it into a helmeted Uluzar. Svorgin fought beside his father, wielding his axe with such prowess, cutting through the Uluzar like paper. Velamir sliced an Uluzar's arm before sending a powerful jab to his face. He ensured he didn't wound them too severely, just enough to knock them out. He glimpsed a flash of silver approaching his left side and moved to intercept it. Natassa was faster. She caught the sword on her dagger's cross guard. The metal dragged against each other before she lifted her knee, smashing it into the Uluzar's groin. The man groaned, looking down with a pained expression. A mistake. Natassa elbowed his chin upward before burying a strike into his throat. The Uluzar collapsed with a moan of pain. Natassa adjusted her grip on her weapon and turned to Velamir.

Velamir's mouth was slack as he watched in amazement. He believed he might have just fallen in love with her all over again. After a beat, his head swung toward the noise of Honzio and an Uluzar struggling against each other. The Uluzar was gripping Honzio's collar, and the prince's hand was wrapped around the man's throat. They were both roaring, veins popping from their temples. Then Honzio's fingers drifted to the back of the Uluzar's neck, and he yanked him forward, slamming his head against the man's. The Uluzar dropped out cold.

"Well done, *Mosori*!" Svorgin called out.

"You taught me that one." Honzio panted and ran a hand over his sweaty face.

The Uluzar lay in battered heaps around them, leaving Jinong-ja the sole force of opposition. Aylis and Svorgin grabbed each other's arms before shoving against each other with a cheer of victory. The Savorians pressed their foreheads together, wide smiles on their sweaty faces. Bear joined them, and the three wrapped their arms around their shoulders, creating a small circle.

Moralis clapped a hand to Honzio's back, and the prince smiled, his face red from exertion. Velamir looked down at his warrior princess. Natassa was staring up at him with her shining hazel eyes. He reached out to cup her cheek and ran his thumb over her soft skin. She exhaled, her warm breath touching the exposed skin of his wrist. For a single moment, everything was perfect. Then he heard a screech. All eyes spun to the doorway, where a murderous-looking eagle soared in, talons latching onto Jinong-ja's outstretched gloved hand. The eagle screeched again, an awful sound that made Velamir's ears ring. Jinong-ja stroked the eagle's long feathers before releasing a booming laugh.

"You are brave. I will give you that. But you cannot outlast the Uluzar army."

Before anyone could move, they heard thundering boots approaching.

HONZIO

*H*EARCROSS

*T*HE *G*RAND *P*ALACE

HONZIO WAS SHOVED through his ancestral palace like a common prisoner. The halls he'd once called home loomed over him as the Uluzar gripped him with calloused hands. He heard the others struggling, and concern for his sister urged him to continue resisting. They had fought as hard as they could, but Jinong-ja had spoken the truth when he'd said they couldn't outlast an army.

Hundreds of Uluzar had left the palace to ensure Honzio's capture, and Honzio wouldn't risk the lives of his sister or friends. He'd surrendered, pleading for the others to be set free. But Jinong-ja . . . the man was irritating to no end. He'd ordered them all to be strung up and taken to the palace.

"Release me at once," Honzio snapped.

"Soon enough, Prince," came Jinong-ja's reply.

The Uluzar walked before him, leaving Honzio with a view of the three short swords sheathed at his back and the midnight-black braids weaving over his shoulders. Honzio grumbled. Of course he walked as if he ruled the world, with a straight posture and long confident strides.

Honzio lost his balance, his boots slipping on the marble floor and his legs collapsing beneath him. The Uluzar on either side of him didn't budge in the least, dragging him to the throne room doors on his knees instead of returning him to his feet. Honzio swallowed at the sight of the majestic doors—doors he'd stepped through without properly examining them for years. Handles made of solid gold, elaborate engravings running along the top and bottom frames. Swirls of paint in every color illuminating a story on the entirety of the doors. The emblems of the kingdoms. Verin. Ondalar. Ayleth. And Devorin. The four kingdoms Prolus hadn't been able to attain. Honzio scoffed. The Uluzar had finished the battle Prolus started. *They* had taken the rest of the Empire.

Uluzar guards grasped the golden handles and pulled the doors open. Hundreds of eyes leveled on Honzio as he was yanked through. The sparkling marble floor was coated in blood. Lanterns hung from the archways along either side of the room. Uluzar mingled under them, peering with inquisitive looks as Honzio was dragged past. He noted how they were divided into ranks. The ones closest to the doors were common laborers. The tattoos of rats along their wrists betrayed their positions.

The following Uluzar had snakes inked around their hands and up their arms. Spies. Honzio's eyes darted over a group at the far end, their clothes open at the chest, proudly brandishing the wolves cutting through the hair. There were more groups, too many to count. A man or woman Honzio presumed to be the chief stood before each one. Only the laborers were left leaderless.

A whispered hush ran through the throne room. Honzio's eyes shot forward, stopping on the large seat at the end of the chamber. The seat that had been filled by his father and forefathers for centuries carried an enemy's weight. Honzio was deposited like waste before the throne. He fought the queasiness in his stomach, balanced on his palm, and pushed himself up. His gaze dragged from the tips of the scuffed boots planted on the dais up past the leather greaves and chest plate and broad shoulders to meet a pair of the darkest eyes he'd ever seen. Darker than the tandoor oven his father used to cage him in, darker than the night. A short beard speckled with gray hugged the man's face. Jinong-ja pounded a closed fist against his chest four times, bowing his head before the man.

"I bring to you Prince Honzio Hartinza."

The man stared down at Honzio, his gaze unwavering as he appraised him. He waved a hand at Jinong-ja, and the chief retreated, taking his place before the group closest to the throne. The wolves.

"Ah, the princeling," a familiar voice said, and Honzio's attention snapped to a man standing in a group farther down. Grongar-ja, the Uluzar who'd fooled him into leading them into the castle. Grongar-ja watched him with a savage grin. "I could recognize his pitiful cries anywhere."

Honzio snarled, shoving up to his full height. The Uluzar accompanying him grabbed him before he could stride forward. His short-lived struggle ceased when he saw Natassa and the others held at knifepoint in a line behind him.

"So, you are Prince Honzio," the Uluzar standing before the throne said in a deep and gravelly tone, his accent evident as he spoke in Imperial.

"I am," Honzio replied, keeping his head high.

"And I am Xan-ja. I lead the wolves, but I am also the chief of all the Uluz tribes. And now the ruler of this vanquished empire."

The Uluzar marked with wolf tattoos grouped beside the throne cheered, their shouts morphing into howls. Jinong-ja remained unmoving before them. In fact, he looked a bit irritated.

"My first action as the new ruler of the Empire will be to dispose of your body." Xan-ja leaned down, his mouth twisting as he took in Honzio's arm. "Tell me, Prince, how do you wish to die?"

"You cannot forcibly take the Empire. The Imperial citizens will never succumb to your rule. How long will you burn them, torture them? Eventually, a rebellion will rise, and you will collapse."

Xan-ja's jaw twitched. "They will accept us. They must. And when they see their prince's head dangling on a post in the streets, they will fall to our feet happily." Xan-ja's eyes raced over the others. "Should we start with you, or would you like to witness the execution of your dear friends?"

Honzio inhaled, tamping down his rising panic. He had to do something, stop it somehow. He sought for a plan, watching Xan-ja reach for a bow resting against the throne. Honzio's eyes caught on the long banners that had once hung behind the throne, red as blood with the symbol of the half heart. Only they hung no more. They lay in heaps across the floor, under the boots of the Uluzar. Xan-ja stepped down from the throne. Honzio couldn't hide the slight tremble that gripped him. He forced himself to remain stoic. It would be a gruesome end, but he would rather die with his honor intact than beg for his life. Xan-ja maneuvered behind him, lifting the bow over his head. Honzio swallowed as the bowstring brushed against his throat. Xan-ja's shadow loomed over him. Honzio inhaled, and the string tightened. Natassa's pleading cries faded into the background. All Honzio could see were the approaching hands of death.

"Chief Xan-ja!" someone called out.

The string loosened, and Honzio gulped a quick breath. Xan-ja turned, and Jinong-ja stepped forward.

"My chief," Jinong-ja said. "There is something you must know."

Xan-ja's brows furrowed, and the two's conversation continued, slipping into Savese. After a long moment, Xan-ja stepped away from Honzio, appearing dazed. His eyes flitted from Honzio to the others bound behind him.

"Which one?" Xan-ja whispered, his gaze holding a crazed gleam.

"The boy."

Honzio followed Jinong-ja's motion and stopped on Velamir. All other eyes were on the chief as he took measured steps. Velamir shrugged his arms free from the Uluzar guards' hold, meeting Xan-ja's gaze with a strong one of his own. The Uluzar on either side of him watched with wide eyes, but they didn't dare to interfere.

"You," Xan-ja began, but words failed him. "You have the blade, the—the Zemsar."

Velamir's expression twisted into one Honzio couldn't read before his fingers darted down, draping over the hilt of his sword. He unsheathed the weapon, tilting it so it glinted under the lantern light. "If you mean this blade, yes, I have it."

44

CORALIE

KINGDOM OF VERIN

"No, no," CORALIE whispered. She placed shaking fingers against Mordon's stubbled face, slapping him lightly. "No."

He couldn't be dead, couldn't have left her. Not him. He always came back to her. *Always.* Coralie sobbed, pressing her forehead to his. Her chest heaved with heart-wrenching unrestrained cries of grief. Hands grabbed hold of her, pulling her from Mordon.

"Release me!" she ordered, her throat raw.

"Your Majesty." The captain of her guard, Finnean, held her back. His blue eyes, far wiser than his years, pleaded with her.

Coralie couldn't see past her grief, but she allowed him to hold her back, sagging against him. A True Manos

kneeled beside Mordon and held his fingers to his pulse. He leaned over Mordon, placing a small mirror by his nose. Coralie grasped for the smidge of hope awakening in her. The mirror clouded over. Coralie gasped and laughed with relief. She gripped Finnean's arm tight. The True Manos looked up, smiling.

"He's alive."

Coralie nodded, salty tears rolling over her cheeks and ending at her lips.

"We need to move him to the healing quarters," the True Manos said.

"Help him," Coralie called, waving to the nearby guards.

They gathered Mordon up and carried him toward the keep. Coralie started to follow, but Finnean stopped her.

"The mercenaries?"

Coralie glanced at the surrounding arena. Her guards and the Savorians had overcome the adversary forces and had every mercenary on their knees under the threat of a weapon.

"Take them to the dungeon."

He bowed his head, slapping a half heart to the captain patch on his chest. Finnean barked orders, and the mercenaries were dragged away. A harsh chuckle erupted nearby, and she looked over to where Zenrelius lay in his blood, staring at something behind her with shining eyes. Coralie's gut twisted at his eerie expression, and she turned to see what had his attention. Her lips parted at the sight of riders approaching from the hill in the distance. Yellow flags wafted in the air. The Ondalarian army Zenrelius had promised would come.

They were done for.

"We will take Verin," Zenrelius spat, grasping his seeping wound. "I told you we would."

Coralie swallowed her disgust and motioned at him. "Imprison him. We can use him as a trade. We will give the Ondalarians their king in return for them leaving these lands."

"The man is dying. He won't last long," Finnean said.

"Have a True Manos see to him," Coralie ordered.

Once Zenrelius was out of sight, Coralie marched out of the arena toward the gatehouse. The riders had halted at the start of the drawbridge, the leader rearing up and staring at her through the lowered portcullis. Coralie's soldiers lined up behind her, and archers were positioned above the gate, arrows drawn and pointing at the newly arrived Ondalarians. With the riders close, Coralie could see that she had miscalculated. There couldn't be more than forty riders, nowhere near an army in size.

The lead rider nudged his horse's sides and clomped forward. Another rider joined him. Both wore helmets concealing their faces. The sun glinted on the golden metal. Coralie grabbed a sword from one of her soldiers and stepped closer to the portcullis.

"Stop where you are, or my archers will fire," she warned.

The lead rider halted, helmet tilting up to the arrows pointing down at him. He raised his hands in an innocent manner before lifting them to his helmet and tugging it off. Sweaty brown hair matted to a familiar face. Coralie lowered her sword.

"Captain Blayton?" she said, uncertain what stance she should take.

"Your Majesty." Latimus bowed his head.

The other rider, decked in full armor, stopped beside him and lifted their helmet as well. A young woman with flushed cheeks and hopeful wide brown eyes regarded her.

"Queen Coralie, we request an audience."

Coralie hesitated. "Your king has been subdued. He is in our hands."

The woman tilted her head. "We came for that reason." Coralie frowned, and the woman continued. "We came here to stop Zenrelius."

Half an hour later, Coralie sat at the round council table with Latimus and his wife, Sardala. They had filled her in on the happenings, leaving her speechless.

"The Ondalarians adored Zenrelius, but even they saw it was madness to take Verin and weaken our forces, in turn making it easier for Prolus and putting our kingdom at risk," Lady Sardala said. "We gathered the nobles and spoke to them. It took a bit of convincing, but we managed it." She looked at Latimus with a wide smile.

Latimus stared back at her, and Coralie noticed their hands on the table shifting closer to each other.

"None of the Ondalarian nobles want war. They were driven by the desire to avenge their princess, Queen Adelania, but in the end, they saw reason."

Coralie nodded. Verin and Ondalar's long enmity had begun with King Dale's wife's death. She had been Ondalar's princess, but also Verin's queen. Both sides sought to blame each other for her mysterious poisoning rather than find the source itself. A source that remained hidden to that day.

"How did you arrive so quickly?" Coralie asked them.

"We would have come even sooner had Zenrelius not caged us in the dungeon."

Coralie's lips thinned. "The man is obsessed with imprisoning those he cannot control."

Latimus nodded in agreement before saying, "Zenrelius was using what some call magic and others call science."

Sardala lifted a satchel, placing it in the center of the table with an ominous thud. Coralie watched as Latimus opened it and withdrew a vial containing a sparkling liquid. The color was odd, a light blue that almost seemed transparent.

"What is it?" Coralie asked, staring at it curiously.

"We didn't understand it at first, so we found and spoke with a Shadow Manos in Ondalar." Latimus glanced at Sardala, and she nodded. "She says it is an invention by the greatest Shadow Manos of our time. Zamanin Sulari, it is called. A traveling serum."

Coralie's brows shot up in amazement.

"The Shadow Manos told us it can transport you anywhere you wish in the blink of an eye—within its bounds, of course." He motioned to Sardala, and she continued.

"The serum must be made with a part of the land it will take you to. Crushed grass, clumps of dirt, river water. As long as it comes from that land."

Coralie absorbed the new knowledge. "A dangerous

material. You could enter a kingdom and take over from within," she said, recalling what Zenrelius had done.

"Exactly," Sardala said.

"Prolus bargained with Zenrelius and gave him crates of this serum. They are now in our hands."

"Prolus's work, hmm?" Coralie wasn't surprised to hear that.

"And the Shadow Manos gave us more news. A letter from Prince Honzio."

Coralie leaned forward. "He's still alive?"

"Yes, and he needs our aid." Latimus extended a scrap of paper with the prince's note scribbled across.

Coralie scanned the words.

I summon all those loyal to the crown to the heart of the Empire. As your Crown Prince, I ask for assistance in reclaiming our land.

Crown Prince Honzio Hartinza

She looked up, meeting their gazes. "It seems we will be needing that serum."

Latimus nodded. "We thought you would say so. We brought some with us."

"Good."

Before they could speak further, Captain Finnean entered the council chamber, bowing his head. "I apologize for the interruption, but you must see this, Your Majesty."

Coralie followed him to the gatehouse, spying a cart sitting in the courtyard. It was covered with cloth. She pushed aside her unease and started forward.

"A Tariqin delivered this. He said it was in response to your request for a prisoner exchange."

Coralie nodded, recalling the letter she'd sent to the Dark Army's camp with the hope of retrieving Velamir's friend Jax from their clutches.

"Our scout also informed me that the Dark Army camp is much diminished—a quarter of the troops it had before. There is word that Prolus is in Ayleth." Finnean scratched his head. "Though, I do not know how he would get his army there so quickly and effortlessly."

"The traveling serum," Coralie whispered.

"Pardon, Your Majesty?"

But Coralie didn't answer. She approached the cart and hefted the cloth over. A rancid stench filled the air, making her swallow bile and pinch her nose. She blinked, taking in the horrible sight within the cart. Corpses mutilated beyond recognition. Tears sprouted in her eyes as she examined their tattered clothes, seeing the Verin guard crest.

"Your Majesty." Finnean reached out as if to assist her.

Coralie held up her hand, and he pulled back. She had to see the bodies with her own eyes. She had to see how cruel the Dark Lord was. That was his response to her request, and she would give him hell in return. She wiped a fallen tear with a vicious swipe of her sleeve before forcing herself to scan the dead guards again, searching for Jax. But despite her endless scrutiny, there was no sign of him. She gripped the cart in frustration, a sense of foreboding washing through her.

"He's not here," she whispered.

45

VELAMIR
HEARCROSS
THE GRAND PALACE

VELAMIR HELD HIS breath as he pointed his sword toward the Uluzar chief. Xan-ja's eyes narrowed in disbelief, yet a longing shone in them as he peered at the blade like an old friend.

"The weapon of the khan," someone whispered. Jinong-ja. The Uluzar stepped closer to them, staring at the sword with awe. "The blade lost for years has been found."

The throne room was swept into chaos as the groups of Uluzar broke into arguments. Confusion and shock and skepticism hovered above them.

"Enough!" Xan-ja shouted, lifting his hand.

The chamber was swallowed in silence.

Xan-ja shook his head, his focus returning to the blade in Velamir's grasp. "It cannot be genuine. It is a forged replication, Jinong-ja. How else could this Imperial have come by it, let alone wield it?" His attention flicked to Velamir. "How much did it cost you to prepare this decoy, boy?"

Xan-ja had spoken in a loud voice, ensuring their audience heard every word. His rule was on shaky balance, Velamir realized. It was tilting, and not in his favor. Velamir had watched the other chiefs when Xan-ja announced his rule over all of them. Many of them hadn't looked pleased, including Jinong-ja. Without the blade, his rule was unstable. The Uluzar looked on, watching the interaction with rapt interest. Most were staring at the sword in Velamir's hand.

"This sword was my *father's*," Velamir said, lingering on the word.

"Your father?" Xan-ja's mouth twitched as he forced a smile. "What nonsense tale are you spouting? Your father had a false sword crafted?"

"My father was the son of the khan." A hush followed this revelation. "I am Velamir, son of Boldrix-ja."

A gasp rang about the chamber. Xan-ja paled, his mouth thinning as he continued shaking his head. But even as he tried to deny it, Velamir saw something flicker in his eyes. Recognition.

"It cannot be," the chief stammered. "Boldrix-ja is dead. I saw to it myself. The traitor perished."

"Clearly not well enough," Jinong-ja joined in. "He had a son, didn't he?"

Xan-ja sputtered before examining Velamir again.

"You have his features," he admitted. "His eyes and stance and build."

Velamir would never have thought being told he resembled Boltrex would make him stand a little taller. That it would fill him with pride.

"But you are a dead man with that weapon." Xan-ja leaned in. "I've been after that blade for years. I've sacrificed too much to allow you to wield it like a plaything. Give it to me."

"The Zemsar has chosen its wielder, Xan-ja," Jinong-ja stated.

"It was stolen, or else it would have been mine. Now I will finish what I started long ago. I will destroy what's left of my brother by killing his son."

Velamir processed the words. Xan-ja was his uncle? He stood in shock, remembering Boltrex's letter. He'd written that his brother had been hunting him. As Velamir scrambled to focus, Jinong-ja retreated and motioned the guards keeping hold of Natassa and the others to move back. Velamir found himself in the center of the throne room, facing his murderous uncle.

"Do you accept this challenge, young Velamir?" Xan-ja sneered. "If you lose this battle, you will give me the blade."

Uluzar watched them eagerly, leaning closer and hanging on to every word. The crowd on either side of the throne room was boisterous. Shamans appeared from the shadowy corners, beating their drums and increasing the tension.

"And if I win, we go free."

Xan-ja chuckled. "We fight to the death, Velamir. If I die, you are free to combat your way out."

To the death. Velamir glanced over at Natassa. Her wavy brown hair had escaped her braid and brushed against her pale cheeks. Uluzar held her arms back. Velamir gritted his teeth, wanting nothing more than to destroy them and all those who held the ones he cared for captive. He exhaled. He would fight the battle for her, for them. Natassa sent him a comforting wordless glance. Though her brow was creased with worry, her eyes shone with love. She didn't doubt him, not for a moment.

Xan-ja unhooked a long chain from his belt and dropped into a crouch. Attached to the end of the chain was what looked like metal formed in the shape of a clawed hand. Velamir shifted his feet into a battle stance. Xan-ja charged him, swinging the chain into the air and propelling it at Velamir. Velamir leaned away, the clawed ends narrowly missing his throat. Xan-ja heaved blow after blow. He was fast for an older man. Velamir overcame his surprise and fell into a defensive position, ducking and evading every swing. He leaned to one side, then the other, the tip of Xan-ja's chain whistling past his ear each time. Velamir ducked down and unsheathed his dagger before whipping forward. Xan-ja startled, retreating a pace, but he continued slashing at Velamir. Velamir caught the Uluzar's weapon between both of his. The blades screeched along the chain, trapping Xan-ja's weapon. Velamir yanked the chain from the Uluzar's hand, and it clattered to the ground. Xan-ja conquered his shock quickly, unsheathing two short blades from hidden sheaths at his sides. The blades shimmered in the light, moving at lightning speed, coming from what seemed like every direction. Velamir was forced to retreat as he avoided the swipes. Heat gripped him, and sweat dripped from his hair and stung his eyes.

Before long, he noticed a pattern in Xan-ja's attack—a narrow opening when he swung both blades in an overhead strike. Velamir counted under his breath. Then, as Xan-ja's arms lifted into the air, Velamir lunged forward, pummeling into the man with his shoulder. Xan-ja huffed, the breath knocked from him, his blades slipping from his hands at the impact and clanging against the floor. It was over in seconds. Velamir placed the edge of his sword at Xan-ja's throat. Xan-ja's face twisted, red-hot with humiliation.

The Uluzar ducked back away from the danger of Velamir's sword and withdrew yet another concealed blade. He lunged for Velamir's leg. Velamir lifted his boot, and the blade sliced through the air beneath. He stabbed his sword through Xan-ja's shoulder. The Uluzar blanched, lowering his head to look down at the wound. Horror plastered his features, and he roared as Velamir pulled his blade free, allowing the blood to spray. Xan-ja collapsed to his knees. For a long moment, no one moved. Xan-ja cast a desperate stare around the room, begging silently for assistance. One man stepped forward, but Jinong-ja lifted a hand, halting him in his tracks.

"Leave him. He is no longer the ruler of the Uluz."

An eagle screeched, soaring around the chamber before settling on Jinong-ja's shoulder and extending its wings over the Uluzar. Jinong-ja turned to Velamir, pointing at him. "Your new khan, by fair combat and courage. Wielder of the Zemsar is Velamir." He paused. "Velix-ja, son of Boldrix-ja."

After a long pause, the Uluzar pounded their fists on their chests four times before sinking to their knees. Jinong-ja stepped to Velamir's side, his menacing eagle gripping his shoulder, looking over the chamber with a lethal stare.

"Release Prince Honzio and Princess Natassa and my other companions," Velamir ordered.

The Uluzar holding them captive appeared uncertain, glancing between Velamir and Xan-ja, who was still bleeding out on the floor.

"You heard him!" Jinong-ja shouted. "Release them."

The Uluzar dropped their hold on them and stepped back. Velamir scanned them for injuries, but they seemed fine, looking around as if they couldn't believe what was happening. Velamir hardly believed it himself.

"Allow the khan's allies to rest in chambers of their choosing. They are now our guests, not our enemies."

Velamir's brow shot up at Jinong-ja's order. Natassa and the others were led from the room. Velamir moved to go after them when Jinong-ja spoke again, commanding more Uluzar.

"Take Xan-ja to the dungeon until we plan a just punishment for him," Jinong-ja said. "He attempted to kill our khan's father. He must be tried for treason."

Velamir frowned. Boltrex had been the one considered a traitor until a few minutes ago. Velamir glanced at Jinong-ja, wondering what the man was up to. Why was he siding with him? Lending his support?

"Why did you help me?" Velamir asked.

Jinong-ja watched the Uluzar drag Xan-ja away. "I didn't recognize you at first, but Koseer-ja told me about you."

Velamir startled, looking at the man in a new light. "You are an Elder member?"

"I was tired of the savagery of my people. The Empire was spared from us for so long after the last war because we were too busy fighting each other, slaughtering our own kin for power to lead all the clans with one iron fist." Jinong-ja looked down at Velamir's weapon. "That sword is essential for our unity. It is crucial to ending the bloodshed and bringing Uluz to its former state. You carry the key, Velix-ja."

"I believe you have too much faith in me."

Jinong-ja shook his head. "When we attacked you in the inn, you didn't wield your blade to slaughter. Even now, fighting the man who tried to murder your father, you struck him in a non-vital area. You didn't want to kill him. Why?"

"I don't like needless bloodshed. If I can avoid it, I will not take a life."

"And that is exactly why you must be our khan," Jinong-ja said earnestly. "The Uluzar need peace. We need it more than anything."

46

NATASSA
HEARCROSS
THE GRAND PALACE

NATASSA SAT IN the steaming tub, staring at the wall across from her. It was the first time in weeks that she had soaked in such an extravagant soapy bath. Something she'd once taken for granted was a luxury, and she wanted to bask in it every second. But despite how hard she scrubbed her skin, the blood wouldn't go away. The stains, the memories, they were all there, forever inked into her skin. The shadows were on either side of her, whispering, coaxing her to do what they wanted. Natassa screamed internally, clutching her head, holding her hands over her ears. She couldn't stand it. She couldn't block them out. Or the images. Krea's body, Thorsten's motionless form, Draven's limp corpse, their final words.

Natassa dragged herself from the tub and pulled on the nightdress draped across a chair in the bedchamber connecting to her former room. She sobbed in frustration, slamming her hand on the edge of the tub. She gasped at the pain. Blood welled forth from the tear in her skin. She stared at the drops as they leaked out, blinking at the crimson dripping onto the marble floor. There was a knock at the door, but Natassa couldn't find the strength to answer. The banging grew louder, incessant. Natassa sank down beside the bath, her thick nightdress clinging to her damp skin as the blood continued to leak.

She didn't know how much time had passed when the door smashed open. The wood that had been barring it split in half. She heard Velamir's voice in the distance, and then she was lifted in strong arms. Her head hung, her hair dangling in messy strands. She was carried from the room. She buried her face into the linen tunic, inhaling the woodsy scent. The arms tightened around her as a face swam above her, the features unclear.

"Natassa, you are not well."

The arms deposited her onto her bed gently, and all she could think was that she didn't deserve the silk sheets beneath her or the pillow soft as clouds tucked under her head. The blurry figure disappeared before returning to tend to her hand. His gentle words brushed her ears, but she couldn't hear them. They were simply buzzing noises. Warm fingers tied cloth around her hand. Natassa inhaled, trying to focus on his blurred form above her. She was underwater, drowning, fighting to return to the surface. She concentrated on the green eyes peering at her, and she broke through. His words snapped into focus.

"You don't look well. Let me fetch a True Manos."

Natassa reached out, grasping his arm. "Please," she begged. "Stay with me."

Velamir relented, and her hand slid down to his, urging him nearer. He settled on the edge of her bed, then lifted her up and tucked her against him. Natassa breathed in his comforting scent and placed her hand over his chest, counting each beat of his heart. He looked up, and Natassa followed his gaze to the canopy of stars stretching over her bed.

"I'm fairly certain your brother would kill me if he caught us like this," Velamir said.

Natassa smiled. "He would at least give us a stern warning. My father, on the other hand, would have killed us *both*—after torturing and shredding every layer of skin and tissue that we had."

"Pleasant man."

Natassa tilted her head toward him, examining the firm line of his bearded jaw. He must have cleaned up after the show in the throne room. He'd trimmed his beard, and his hair was still wet, slipping over his forehead in dark strands. "I'm glad you never met him, but I wish you had known my mother. She would have loved you."

Velamir searched her eyes. His emerald ones appeared dark in the lantern's light. "I am sure I would have loved her as well. I would have fallen at her feet and thanked her for giving birth to such an angel."

A snort of laughter erupted from Natassa, and she clamped a hand over her mouth. "Velamir!"

He chuckled, his gaze shining as he took her in. He reached out, drawing her hand down to reveal her smile. "There it is."

She stared at him curiously. "There what is?"

"Your laughter is healing, Natassa. I haven't heard one from you in far too long. I yearned for it."

"Who taught you how to flirt?"

He shrugged. "I think it was a born talent."

She rolled her eyes, and he tapped her nose. She snuggled into his side.

"A year ago, I would never have believed this would be happening. That I'd be allowing a strange man into my room."

"Strange man?" Velamir repeated.

She pushed his shoulder. "You know what I mean."

Velamir's expression turned serious. "I spoke to Honzio and received his approval. After we regain Ayleth and vanquish Prolus for good, we will have an intimate wedding ceremony like you wanted with only our friends present."

"I know. He came to me after your conversation and told me."

They shared a happy smile and then Natassa pointed up at the canvas stretched above them. "I would lie here every night and dream I was on an adventure. That I was out there in the world seeing the real stars and forests, not just the ones in my room. I didn't realize how much pain the real world had within it."

"The pain never ends," Velamir agreed. "But at least the world has people like you in it. Caring, kind, willing to risk everything to help."

"And people like you," she said. "You are the bravest man I have ever known."

"I should do so much more."

"And now you can. You are the khan of the Uluzar. You can make a difference."

He nodded. "I'm thinking of where to start. I have so many ideas." He glanced down at her. "I want to ensure justice is upheld. The Uluzar often resolve situations with a bout to the death or first blood. I want to hold trials that will ensure the guilty are found. So that the weaker of us are no longer oppressed."

"That is a wonderful idea," she said.

He leaned down to press a kiss to the crown of her head. "But I would love to hear the suggestions of those closest to me."

"I haven't yet seen the Uluz to give you proper feedback, but I believe all lands should abolish the horrid actions of those before us. For example, in the Empire, we must close the mines. No more children should suffer and especially not mining for something that isn't even there." Emperor Malus's obsession with the Golden Crown had sent him on a mad search for it.

She felt Velamir nodding against her head, agreeing with her statements.

"And I want to improve the conditions of the orphanages. Ensure they receive proper schooling and necessities."

Velamir tilted her chin toward him. His eyes were covered in a slight sheen as he stared at her with what Natassa could only call adoration. "You are a unique woman, Natassa Hartinza. The Empire is lucky to have you as a princess."

Her heart thumped, warming at his earnest words. "Though my father passed recently, I have felt like an orphan ever since I lost my mother."

"I understand," he said, his voice hoarse. And Natassa knew he did. He had lost his entire family as a young boy and then again as an adult.

"We may be orphans," she said, her hand sliding down to grip his, "but as long as we have each other, we are enough."

His fingers wove into her hair, tugging her head to rest under his chin. "We are enough," he repeated.

⹅

One week later

Natassa awoke screaming. She sat up, her throat raw as the images continued to race before her eyes. The dead, the murdered, the broken. Someone grasped her arm, and she fought against them, pleading for them to release her.

"Natassa, it's me!" The voice registered in her mind, and she ceased fighting, her posture sinking in defeat.

Honzio stared at her with worry. His hand remained clasped on her arm.

"You were right to call for me," he said, glancing over his shoulder.

Natassa peered into the darkness to see Velamir's tall form there. He was also watching her with concern. Natassa hated to see that look. It made her feel like some sort of weak, fragile thing. It didn't matter if she was on the last threads of sanity or that her throat ached from screaming for a way out of the horrible nightmares. Their gazes hurt her more. But she knew it was out of love, out of fear of losing her. She inhaled, forcing herself to calm down. Natassa sensed Velamir combating the urge to come close to her, his hands fisting and opening as he debated himself.

Honzio's hair was tousled, and dark circles ran under his eyes. He wore a thin linen shirt and trousers. Velamir must have awakened him.

"I dreamt of Thorsten," Natassa said, her voice breaking.

Her brother shushed her and pulled her into a one-armed hug—a movement that told her he understood what she felt. When would the darkness end? Far too soon, Honzio pulled back. He lifted her chin.

"Wipe your tears and come with me. I want to show you something."

He stood and went to Velamir, nodding at him in gratitude. Natassa lifted herself off the bed and pulled a robe over her nightdress. Honzio led the way. As they crossed through the dark hall, Velamir's hand found hers. They linked fingers without looking at each other, and he gave her hand a light squeeze of reassurance. He'd been checking in on her every evening since the night she'd injured herself. She had seen little of him besides that. His days were occupied with politics. He'd been doing his absolute best to unite the Uluzar and Imperials. Natassa had watched one of the council meetings from a balcony above the chamber. Velamir had looked so serious at the head of the table. He'd given the chair beside him to Honzio, putting them both at equal ranking. She never thought she would be so proud to watch a council meeting, but seeing them—her brother and Velamir—discussing peace routes and coming to agreements warmed her heart. They had become allies, and the Uluzar and Imperials joining them at the table saw it too.

They entered the sitting room. She glanced around. Far too many terrible memories lingered there.

"What are we doing here?"

Honzio didn't respond, instead giving her a candle. Natassa grasped it in her free hand. Honzio took one for himself and brought forth a match.

"Honzio," Natassa repeated. "What are we doing here?"

He motioned toward the balcony and started for the grand double doors. Natassa frowned. He pulled the doors open, and a chilly breeze rushed through, seeping into her skin. Natassa closed her eyes, soaking in the fresh air. When she opened them, she saw Honzio had stopped by the railing and was overlooking the city. Natassa hesitated by the doors. The last time she had touched that railing, she'd almost fallen. When Draven had shoved the betrothal in her face and she'd been so certain he was plotting to kill her. Velamir stood beside her, a strength in the crushing weakness she felt.

"After Thorsten passed, we never had the chance to hold a proper ceremony for him." Honzio glanced back at her where she lingered. "Father sent you off to marry Draven, and the burial was short and empty of any emotion. The mourning period wasn't held."

Natassa nodded. Her father had forced her to leave without even allowing her to attend Thorsten's funeral.

"I sent word out to the city. News about the crowning ceremony to be held tomorrow as well as my request to honor the fallen."

He waved his arm out over the city, and as Natassa joined him by the railing, her breath caught. Hundreds, possibly thousands, of gleaming lights lit up the streets, twinkling like stars and brightening the city. Emotion welled in her throat.

"Honzio," she whispered.

"He was a light snuffed too soon. But he will never be forgotten."

The Chirokhe Mordeh, light of the dead. A ceremony performed for kings and queens, emperors and empresses. The highest of the high. Emperor Malus had forbidden the ceremony after he'd been crowned. Natassa remembered when she'd been a little girl and seen a whole family sentenced to life in prison because they had honored their deceased family member in such a manner. Natassa wasn't sure why it had bothered her father so much. It might have been because of the trauma it had left on him after his own father's passing. Seeing the lights brought him pain.

Tears sprang to Natassa's eyes, and she laughed as she took in the sparkling lights. Honzio's first action. His first change since Emperor Malus.

Natassa recalled a night years ago . . .

She hugged the pillow tight, sobs racking her slight frame. It had been weeks since her mother passed, but the pain didn't lessen. Her father had banned every and all festivities since she had collapsed and her heart had ceased to beat. The days were longer and the nights darker. Her chamber door opened, and Natassa sat up, sniffling. Thorsten edged into the room before closing the door behind him. He turned and crept toward her, placing a finger over his lips.

"Thor? What are you doing here?"

He sat beside her on the bed. "I came to check on you. You haven't left your room for days."

She shrugged, looking down at her hands.

"Guess what I brought?"

Natassa couldn't understand why he was smiling so widely. Their mother had passed. What was there to be delighted about? He pulled out two candles from his bag. Natassa frowned.

"We will honor Mother's passing."

"No! Father banned this ceremony. If he catches us—"

Thorsten grasped her hands in his large ones, ceasing her attempts to shove the candles back into the bag. "No one will know. I ensured it."

Natassa searched his eyes before she finally nodded, trusting him.

"Now." Thorsten lit one candle and then the other.

They held their candles while staring at each other. Natassa was giddy. The act of rebellion felt like freeing herself from her cage of rules. At least for a little while.

Natassa smiled. It was a broken and brittle smile, but she was smiling nonetheless. She knew why Thorsten had come into her room so positively. He'd been trying to urge her to see the light; he'd been trying to pull her from her dark abyss. He'd been too pure for their world.

Honzio lit his candle and leaned over, placing the flame to light hers. Natassa watched as the flame flickered to life. Honzio moved over, doing the same for

Velamir. They all peered at each other as Honzio recited the customary lines for the dead.

"Their pain is no longer, their glory remembered. Their names stronger, their honor forever."

Natassa spoke when he finished, looking up at the sky. "For Krea, the truest sister I ever had. A sparkling star, then and now."

Honzio nodded and spoke of his bodyguard. "For Bronus, though he was a bit of a tough spirit, he was a good friend and saved my life countless times. May he rest in peace."

They looked at Velamir. He shifted uneasily. Natassa was sure Tariqi didn't have such a custom and almost told him he didn't have to participate if he felt uncomfortable, but he cleared his throat.

"For Boltrex, I never knew him as a father, but he was a strong and loyal man. May he rest in Aralis."

They went back and forth, sharing the names of those they had loved and perhaps not loved as much.

Finally, Natassa whispered, "For Thorsten, the kindest, sweetest person I have ever known." A tear slipped down her cheek.

"For Thorsten," Honzio repeated.

"For Thorsten," Velamir said.

Natassa glanced over the city, taking in the beautiful sight once again. "It is easy to extinguish a single candle flame. But no one can drown out the light of a thousand shining together."

Honzio raised his candle, and Natassa and Velamir followed his lead. The three stood shoulder to shoulder as they stared down at the grand city of Hearcross.

MORDON
KINGDOM OF VERIN
CASTLE VERIN

ORDON CLOSED HIS fingers into a fist, ignoring the pain flickering through his little finger. Then he opened it slowly, stretching his hand. The True Manos standing above him clicked his tongue in approval as he examined the recovery progress. The cast he'd placed on Mordon's pinky had been removed the day before due to the speed of healing.

It was unnatural, recovering so fast, and wouldn't have been possible without the tonic recipes the Shadow Manos Jaxon Tana had left behind in the castle. The Shadow Manos had assisted in healing many people after the Dark Army's attack.

The True Manos nodded. "Very good."

Mordon sensed Coralie's gaze on them. The True Manos fiddled with his finger again, and Mordon inhaled sharply. Coralie swiveled on her chair toward them, worry tightening her posture.

"Mordon?"

He tilted his head back, exaggerating his reaction by grimacing further.

"That's enough," Coralie told the True Manos. "He should rest now."

The True Manos frowned, giving Mordon a suspicious glance before collecting his supplies. "The rest of your wounds have healed quite nicely. In order to fully recover, you must stay away from stress, keep off your feet, and surround yourself with as much positivity as you can."

Coralie nodded. "We will ensure he follows your orders, won't we?" She speared Mordon with a look.

As soon as the True Manos closed the door behind him, Mordon leaned back on his sickbed. He glanced at Coralie, who was sitting at his desk, penning official papers and letters. She'd been at it for hours, but Mordon didn't complain. Her presence lit up his drab empty chamber. Mordon groaned and shifted under the blankets as he tried to emphasize his discomfort.

"I do not think the True Manos examined me properly. This blazing headache must be the beginnings of a fever."

Coralie sighed and stood from her chair. She leaned over him, touching her hand to his forehead. "You are perfectly fine," she said. "And do not think I haven't noticed your acting."

Mordon's mouth opened in mock offense. "Acting?"

"You know . . ." She smirked. "If you want to be swaddled, you can just say so."

She was trying to probe his manly pride. Too bad for her, that was exactly what he wanted.

"Only by you," he responded, giving her a crooked grin.

She laughed, rolling her eyes as she tucked the blankets in around him. Then she handed him a glass of herbal tea waiting on the desk.

"Drink up," she ordered.

His pained expression wasn't feigned that time.

"*Drink*," she said, bringing it to his mouth.

"That reeks!" He coughed, pushing her hand away. "What did the True Manos say? Keep me away from stress."

"You will see stress if you don't finish every drop of this."

Mordon shook his head, chuckling before downing the glass in one go. Coralie placed the empty cup back and pushed away the hair dangling before his eyes. Mordon sighed.

"I may have said this before, but I really need to get injured more often."

Coralie ordered him to rest and returned to her chair, but Mordon's chest thrummed when he spied the tiny smile pulling at the corner of her mouth. She started writing her letters again, and Mordon's humor faded as serious thoughts overcame him. Coralie had already issued orders for a large number of Verin soldiers to prepare. She was planning on heading with Latimus Blayton and the other Ondalarians to Hearcross.

"How can we trust these transportive vials?"

Coralie shrugged. "Latimus says they work well. They have used them and researched them. It is the fastest way for us to arrive at Hearcross. Prince Honzio needs us."

"As long as it isn't a trick. When will we set out?"

She glanced at him, hesitating. "Mordon, I think you should stay here. In Verin."

He leaned forward. "Wha—"

"You are still injured. And I trust no one more than you to remain in charge here."

Mordon shook his head at once. "You don't know what you will encounter in Hearcross. If you are worried about the prisoners, we can delay the trials until we return."

Zenrelius, Vykus, and his mercenaries were being hosted in their dungeon. As Mordon continued stating all the reasons Coralie needed him, he realized she was no longer responding. He sat up straighter, looking over at her. A smile crept over his face. Coralie's head rested on her arms, fast asleep at his desk. Mordon thrust the blankets aside, stood, and approached her slowly. He peered down at her, admiring her bold features and catching sight of blue ink staining her cheek. He reached down, wiping it away before tracing her jawline. Then Mordon leaned in, whispering so he wouldn't wake her.

"You cannot leave me behind, Your Majesty. Even if you go to the ends of the world, I will follow."

⤫

VELAMIR
HEARCROSS
THE GRAND PALACE

Velamir walked through the Whispering Forest. He stepped lightly, avoiding fallen branches and uneven terrain. The training instilled in him years before controlled his movements. Uluzar marched forward on all sides of him, trudging through the woods without a care of the noise they made. Jinong-ja led the way until they entered a wide clearing. The Uluzar accompanying Velamir drifted away, leaving him alone in the center. They sank to their knees, creating a circle around him. They pounded their chests before loud, ominous howls emerged from their throats. Chins jutted up toward the night sky. Velamir followed their gazes, viewing the moon high above casting its ethereal glow upon them. The chiefs of the clans stepped out from between the trees and made their way into the circle past the kneeling Uluzar. Each dressed representing their tribes.

He examined them as they stopped short distances away. One chief wore dark green, her wrists covered by thick dyed cord that wrapped up around her arms. Her hair was braided at the top before falling in jagged locks over her shoulders, and her mouth was painted a deep red that smeared across her fanged teeth. The chief of the snakes. The next chief wore a burnt orange vest over long dark trousers. Hair from a fox's tail was braided into his waves, the light blond apparent among the black. Chief of the fox tribe. Velamir looked over many more before coming to rest on Jinong-ja, who faced him. Though he was young, the man carried a lot of weight over the Uluzar. Velamir was grateful for his assistance and knowledge. He'd guided him over the past days, teaching him Uluzar customs and the duties of the tribes. Jinong-ja wore his open vest, his tattoo proudly visible to all who looked. Black paint smeared his chin and cheekbones. A large helmet resembling a wolf's head concealed his hair, lending him an even more terrifying appearance.

Shamans approached, beating their drums in a haunting fashion. One came to the forefront to stand beside Jinong-ja. Velamir examined him, wondering why his features seemed so familiar. Then he placed him. The Uluzar shaman he had encountered on his way to the Tariqin camp. The man who had left him with the haunting words: *You will wield the strength of kings.* How right he'd been. Velamir's fingers tightened around his sword hilt.

"Velix-ja, son of Boldrix-ja, son of the last khan, the blessed sword has chosen you." Jinong-ja's deep voice echoed around the clearing.

The shamans circled Velamir, their drumming growing faster and more intense, pounding in time with his heart. Despite the late hour, Velamir didn't feel a wink of sleepiness. The shaman watched him carefully, his mouth moving as he repeated Jinong-ja's words in Savese.

"For years, the Uluz has been a barren desert filled with injustice and greed. The promised prophecy from the texts of old has come true. The legendary hero whispered of in tales has come to save our people and unite the tribes under his rule."

Velamir heard the words but couldn't fully process them. Couldn't process that all those witnesses saw him as a hero of legends. The Uluzar howled again, and the wind blowing over them seemed to grow harsher, carrying the power of their voices with it. The shamans started chanting the prophecy. Jinong-ja stepped closer to Velamir, speaking to him as he translated the words.

From the sands of Jahar,

of wolf's blood,

bright as a thousand stars,

streaming in golden flood,

the hero returns

to bind the clans.

Hope for the oppressed,

uniter of lands

with courage blessed.

Destruction for the tyrants.

Of wolf's blood,

a hero for all.

Velamir swallowed. The words and chants and howls shifted the world around him. Jinong-ja kneeled on one knee before him, slamming a closed fist to his chest four times.

"My khan," he said, lowering his chin in deference. "The wolves pledge their allegiance."

More lingering howls spread about. The chiefs followed Jinong-ja's lead until all had sworn loyalty, completing the ceremony. Velamir bade them to stand. His body shivered with what felt like a newfound power, a tingling that raced over his skin with the weight of his new duty.

Velamir raised his hand to silence the drumming and howls.

"I may wield this sword. I may be a descendant of the khan, but that doesn't make me any better than anyone else. It doesn't give me the right to claim anything I wish. You have accepted me as your leader, and I will do everything in my power to serve. You are my people. I am your guardian."

"May your years be long!" Jinong-ja said. "May fate and fortune be in your favor."

"In your favor!" the witnesses repeated.

"May our khan's reign be glorious!"

"Glorious!"

"May the Uluz prosper under his rule!"

"Prosper!"

"May he change the fate of the land!"

"Change the fate!"

The chants buzzed against his ears. Velamir spread his arms out, his lids closing as he whispered, "For the better."

NATASSA
HEARCROSS
THE GRAND PALACE

WHEN HONZIO TOLD her she was about to see a familiar face, she hadn't thought it would be Manos Xeni. The old man looked up from the long cushioned seat situated beneath a window in the library's corner. His pale eyes were as mysterious and unnerving as they had been the last time she'd seen him. Natassa smiled, approaching him.

"Princess." He rose to his feet, his white ponytail falling over his shoulder.

"I will leave you two alone," Honzio said, nodding at Manos Xeni before ducking out of the library.

Natassa joined Manos Xeni as he retook his seat. They sat in comfortable silence for a while. Natassa felt his stare on her and glanced at him. It had

330

been so long since she'd seen him; she felt so changed. She was no longer the scared princess who didn't know which path to follow. She was a wiser princess, resigned to the path she hadn't wanted.

"You are far more powerful than before, Princess," Manos Xeni said in a grave voice. "*They* have become stronger as well."

They. The shadows. Natassa nodded. "I allowed them past my mental barrier."

Manos Xeni watched her with an impassive expression.

"Master Dunya told me to do so. It is the only way I can fight them."

"They are feeding off you. If you are not careful, they will overtake you before long."

Natassa grimaced. That was her entire problem, and she had no way of removing or destroying them. They nagged her mind at every moment. It was getting harder and harder to ignore them. She had noticed several maids giving her strange looks when they caught her whispering to the shadows. They must have thought her mad after everything that had happened.

"I couldn't stay long in Devorin with the Elders. Because of certain events, I had no choice but to leave. I have no option but to battle *them* myself."

"They were but glimpses before," Manos Xeni said, his white eyes unfocused. "But I can see them as clear as day now. Lingering behind you, latching onto you, and draining you to regain their power. Draining you of your life source."

"They cannot," Natassa said. "Not until I give them

what they want. They won't dare to kill me until then. But I fear they may drive me mad before."

"That is the fate of all those like us, Princess. The spirits steal our life, leaving us an empty shell of ourselves while they search for another source to possess." His ominous words made her shiver. "But yours is a more delicate matter. Two powerful spirits. Far more taxing than a common Doer. A Lure *and* a Seer plague you. They will destroy you far faster."

Do not listen to him, the Seer whispered in her ear. *The foolish man knows nothing.*

Natassa ignored him, turning a pleading look on Manos Xeni. He'd been attempting not to say the word *shadows* and alert them to their intentions, but the Seer and Lure were far too wise not to realize.

"What should I do?"

Manos Xeni fell silent, stilling on the seat across from her. His pale eyes crossed, and he began trembling. Natassa wondered if that was how she appeared when she received a vision. Endless minutes passed. Sweat trickled down the old man's face. Then he jerked backward, his gaze snapping back to their less alarming state. He exhaled a shaky breath, and his eyes found hers.

Natassa shifted in the seat, gripping her skirt. "You had a vision."

Manos Xeni nodded, peering out the window before turning once again to face her. "They want you to open the gate to their world."

She nodded. "I know."

"They wish to bring forth a wave of devastation. Starting with the Empire and, before long, the rest of the world." His white eyes widened, and his voice contained a terrified tremor. "If you open that gate, they may leave you without harming you, but the damage will be far worse than the good. If you open that doorway, you will unlock the destruction of the world."

Natassa swallowed, her posture tense as her gaze remained locked with his, the seriousness of the words taking root within her.

"In my vision, you were standing before a silver throne, a swarm of dark forces around you. The gate was before you. You faced dozens of shadows. I saw two paths you could take. The first would be to open the gate, and the second will risk your very life."

Understanding drifted through Natassa at the implication. If she closed the gate, she would save the world and doom herself in return.

Velamir
Hearcross
The Grand Palace

THE THRONE ROOM rippled with layers of emotions. Velamir couldn't remember the last time such excitement had surrounded him. The palace had spared no expense. The throne room was filled to the brim, not a single chair empty. Imperials and Uluzar were scattered around the space. A line of Imperial civilians drifted through the chamber doors. The line began in the palace halls and ended before the throne, where Velamir and Honzio stood. Uluzar were on guard, watching for anything amiss.

"Today is a historic day," Jinong-ja called out. "For today, we will crown two leaders. We have made peace between the Uluzar and the Imperials. A day many said would never come to pass, and yet here we are."

Polite claps drifted around. Velamir noticed many people weren't so thrilled about the prospect of allying with the ones they had seen as their enemies for so long.

"Everyone has come to pay their respects, but before they do so, I will proceed with the crowning." Jinong-ja turned to Honzio and lifted an emerald-and-ruby-studded crown. It was a legendary crown, passed down to each emperor. Velamir had seen it in drawings and sketches, but never fully in the flesh. The metal glinted. Intricately shaped hearts dotted the crown.

Honzio's mouth was tight as he stared straight ahead. Jinong-ja placed the crown atop his thick brown waves. Velamir attempted to read Honzio's emotions, but the man was solid as a wall. Velamir hadn't been able to decipher his mood since the moment he'd met him. He was cold from afar, unwelcoming. But Velamir had seen warmer parts of him emerge, such as the night when they had honored the dead. His stiff mask also cracked whenever his sister came into view. Honzio's weakness was Natassa. Velamir smiled. They had something in common.

Jinong-ja turned to the people, announcing, "Standing before you is the new Imperial emperor, Honzio Hartinza!"

At the shout, more scattered applause broke out. A man in the audience shouted, "How will you rule with your lame hand? How do you plan to lead us?"

A hush broke over the crowd as wide eyes bounced between Honzio and the man who had spoken. Velamir couldn't believe the rashness. To speak to your emperor in such a manner without any fear or respect . . . If it had been anyone else crowned emperor, Velamir was certain that comment would have granted the man the execution block. Honzio's jaw clenched, and his eyes burned with anger. Perhaps he shouldn't underestimate the new emperor. He might make killing the man his first action. Jinong-ja sent Velamir a questioning look, silently asking him if he should intervene. Velamir chanced another glance at Honzio, seeing his sizzling fury hadn't receded. Just as Velamir was about to nod at Jinong-ja, Honzio took a step forward.

"A wise man once told me a true leader is not one because of the power in his arms or his array of possessions and wealth. A true leader fights not with a sword, but with the strength in his heart."

Velamir followed Honzio's gaze to the Savorian sitting with Bear and Aylis. Svorgin wore a broad smile. The three were dressed in blue, bringing out the color of their eyes. The resemblance between Bear and Svorgin was unmistakable. Father and son wore matching tunics and trousers, large belts over their hips, where each had an axe hooked in place. Their strong jaws were more prominent since they had shaved down their beards to stubble. Their long hair was combed back into thick braids. Aylis looked just as fierce beside them. A midnight-blue dress clung to her waist and slid all the way down to the floor. Her collar flared around her neck, highlighting its length. Her black hair sat piled atop her head; braided parts slipped free around her face. Moralis stood beside her wearing a matching suit coat, his hand at the small of her back.

"I may not possess two capable arms," Honzio finished, "but I believe one heart is enough for all of you."

Svorgin stood from his seat, slapping his hands together in enthusiastic applause. Others slowly followed until the entire throne room was awash with noise. Jinong-ja approached Velamir's side as soon as the clatter died down.

"Uluzar khans always wore the mark of the wolf on their chest." A questioning look hovered in his eyes. "Your father had one."

Velamir was sent back to the moment he'd been staring down at Boltrex in Castle Verin. When Boltrex was recovering from Winston's attack and the stab wound he'd left him with. A large burn scar had covered a portion of Boltrex's chest, and Velamir had wondered how it had occurred.

"What happened to his mark?"

Jinong-ja ducked his head. "When he was sentenced to death, it was burned off as a sign of dishonor."

Velamir flinched. Boltrex had been scarred, and who knew what other burdens he'd carried. Velamir would put an end to it. He'd had enough marks, enough people attempting to use him, to etch their symbols into his skin.

"I will not accept a symbol that was taken from my father. I will be the first khan without the mark."

"As you wish."

Jinong-ja motioned for him to draw his sword. Velamir pulled the weapon free, relishing the lethal rasp of the metal against the sheath. Onlookers released awed breaths as they stared at the beautiful sword made from derinium. The Uluzar couldn't seem to get enough of the Zemsar.

"I present to you the Uluzar khan, Velix-ja!" Jinong-ja said with a sweeping hand motion.

The cheers that time were much louder and genuine. The people paid their respects until the lines dwindled, and the civilians started to mingle together. Soft music struck up, and couples took to the floor.

"Let's hope for the best," Honzio muttered beside him.

Velamir nodded and sensed the newly crowned emperor turn, appraising him.

"Do not think I overlooked your presence in Natassa's chamber or the fact that you moved into the room across from hers. You have not married yet. My eyes are upon you. I do not care to hear your excuses, but I do want your word. You will not hurt her through your words or actions."

"Natassa means more to me than anything in this world. I will never harm her."

Honzio's smile was grim. If it could even be called a smile. "I would like your oath to protect her. If a single hair on her head is damaged, you can be sure I will hunt you down and make you pay for it. I will strangle you with my one arm if I must."

Velamir held in a laugh at the image that conjured. His humor faded at the sight of Honzio's stern expression, and he cleared his throat.

"Rest assured, Your Majesty. You have my word."

"Good."

Their gazes remained connected—a show of power

as neither refused to give in. Someone stepped up beside Honzio and interrupted the tense stare down. Velamir excused himself and made his way through the dancing couples. Someone bumped into him, and he looked down, meeting Lore's excited smile.

"Velamir!" The boy grinned. "Or should I say Khan Velamir?"

Velamir patted his shoulder, looking the boy over. After they had taken control of things in the palace, Velamir had sent for Lore and Marcella to be retrieved, but he hadn't gotten a chance to see them yet. The palace affairs had kept him occupied. He spied Marcella in conversation a short distance away, wearing a colorful dress that matched her violet hair. Velamir looked back down at Lore. The boy had also dressed up. A pressed suit coat with a white shirt beneath. His pants were cuffed over shiny boots, and his hair was slicked back with oil.

"You are looking like quite a dashing fellow this evening," Velamir said.

Lore beamed, a flush covering his face at the praise. "That's what Java-na said—well, I'm not exactly sure what she said. I couldn't understand her, but—"

Velamir raised a brow.

"Well, her eyes said it," Lore justified.

Velamir couldn't hold back his grin. "And who is this Java-na?"

"I met her here. She was just—" Lore halted, glancing around them. "Where did she go?"

Velamir spotted a young Uluzar girl hiding behind a pillar, watching them with a mischievous grin as she bit into an apple. Lore continued looking around, and Velamir shook his head, smiling at the boy's growing panic. "I'm sure she's around."

A nervous server approached them with a tray of drinks. "Would you like a glass, my lord?"

Velamir reached for one, scanning over the crowd. The dancers slowed as the song came to an end. Just then, he saw her. She stood across from him, on the other side of the dancers. He froze, his hand hanging uselessly in the air, fingers brushing against the stem of the glass he'd been about to take. He took her in, from the pointy slippers up the voluminous layers of skirt. The fabric was fitted against her waist, studded with sparkling jewels that reminded him of stars in the night sky. The thin muslin fabric draped over her shoulders and flared around her wrists like a soft embrace. Then he saw her face. Her lips curved up, her doe-like eyes watching him watch her. He released the air that had been trapped in his lungs and realized two things: she was more dazzling than all the lanterns in the throne room, and since he'd met her, he'd forgotten how to breathe.

NATASSA

HEARCROSS

THE GRAND PALACE

NATASSA MET VELAMIR'S gaze across the room. His face had gone slack, his lips parted as he stared at her. The giddy girl she had once been flared to life, and she felt like floating up to the ceiling. Her feet moved of their own accord, and his seemed to do the same. The dancers parted for them, creating a path so they could reach each other. Velamir matched her pace, his long strides eating up the distance between them. Before she knew it, he was standing before her in the center of the floor. The hushed flittering whispers and curious eyes faded as she examined him. She hadn't thought Velamir could get any handsomer. He was dressed in formal wear that appeared tailored to him. The material

341

hugged his broad shoulders, and embroidery decorated the sleeves. His beard was trimmed close to his jaw, his thick lashes curtaining his brilliant green eyes.

"Natassa," he managed to say. "Dance with me."

At the hushed command that sounded more like a plea, she accepted Velamir's hand and allowed him to pull her toward him. Her other hand drifted to his shoulder as if it were the most natural thing in the world. His fingers lowered to her back, and he tugged her closer. As the music started up again, they danced slowly. Natassa held his gaze, lost in the green haze. If someone had asked, she wouldn't have been able to tell them what dance it was, what song was playing, who was there, where they even were. For her, there was just Velamir.

Velamir scanned her face. He lingered on her smile, on her hair, his breath catching. They didn't need words to communicate. They had an entire conversation with only glances. Strands of dark hair slipped over his forehead. Natassa tracked the movement and reached up, brushing them back. Velamir's eyes darkened, and he leaned closer, his nose brushing her temple. Natassa would never have dared to adjust someone's hair or anything so intimate in the past. But at that moment, she found she couldn't care less what anyone thought.

They stepped back, creating space between them as the dance dictated. While they circled each other, Natassa never broke away from his stare. She lifted her hand, and he followed suit, mere air separating their palms. The lilting music came into focus. It was one of her favorite songs, the lyrics telling the story of a forbidden love between a wanted criminal accused of stealing from a wealthy noble and the nobleman's daughter.

> *I hide from the sun. Moonlight shines my path.*
>
> *Chains around my wrists,*
>
> *only with you am I free.*
>
> *The rich can never be content*
>
> *if the poor starve.*
>
> *Chains around my wrists,*
>
> *they can beat me, silence me, imprison me, but*
>
> *as long as I am with you, I am free.*

They continued turning as more and more couples sifted onto the floor. Velamir closed the space between their palms, forgoing the rules of the dance to enclose her hand in his. Warmth rushed down her arm. His fingers captured hers, his hard-earned callouses scraping her skin.

> *Hunted in the night, your eyes guide me forth.*
>
> *Swords at my neck,*
>
> *only with you am I alive.*
>
> *They can only find my footprints,*
>
> *but they will never be content.*
>
> *If I draw breath, there are swords at my neck.*
>
> *They can stab me, wound me, wrench out my heart, but*
>
> *as long as I am with you, I am alive.*

They moved slower, each turn filled with an electric emotion that Natassa could almost see. She felt stares on them and realized how they must have looked to everyone else. Wholly in love. She smiled. Though Velamir's reign had just begun, they'd already made a drastic proclamation by choosing each other. Natassa wanted to laugh at the irony. He was the grandson of the last Uluzar khan, and she was Emperor Malus's daughter. From birth they should have been raised to detest each other. They never should have met unless it was on a battlefield. Velamir tugged her back against him, his hand settling on her lower back with a possessive grip. But here they were, proving that a union between warring lands was possible.

"You are beautiful." His thumb caressed her wrist where his bracelet had returned to its rightful place alongside her brother Thorsten's. Natassa had been shocked when she learned Velamir had saved her brother's gift, that he had kept the bracelet around his wrist during his search for her.

"There are many beautiful people here," Natassa replied.

"There may be," he agreed. "There are dozens of beautiful people in this chamber."

Natassa smacked his shoulder, scrunching her nose at him. He smiled in return.

"But if they were bejeweled in the latest fashion and dripping in diamonds, or if they wore shapeless sacks, it would not matter. It would not change that you are the only woman I see."

Natassa's breath caught at the heartfelt words. Her

hands trailed up his arms, settling around his neck. She rested her head against his chest. And they danced the night away under the light of the twinkling lanterns.

⁂

HONZIO
HEARCROSS
THE GRAND PALACE

An urgent knock startled Honzio awake. He rolled his neck, wincing at the discomfort. He'd fallen asleep at his desk. The maps and battle plans he'd been working on with Velamir and the Uluzar dotted the surface. Honzio reached for the waning candle flickering beside him and stood, heading for his door.

"Enter," he called.

The door creaked open, and a guard bowed his head in respect, slamming a half heart to his chest. "I apologize for disturbing you at this late hour, but the queen of Verin and an Ondalarian party have arrived at the palace. She wishes to speak to you immediately."

Honzio had been expecting arrivals to stream into Hearcross ever since he'd sent the letters with Marcella's help. He wondered what news Queen Coralie had that couldn't wait. Honzio looked to the chamber window, noting the night was fairly young.

"Escort them to the council room."

As soon as the guard disappeared into the hall, Honzio changed from his coronation robes. The heavy fabric felt as expensive as it looked. He laid it over his bed before scouring his closet. There was endless choice of apparel, yet each one sent a twinge through his heart. The right sleeves on the ceremonial suit coats were covered by a long cape that hung from one shoulder. Honzio's fingers trailed over the capes. He had ordered them himself long ago, so humiliated by the sight of his arm that he'd wanted to conceal it entirely.

Honzio exhaled, forcing himself to focus on the task at hand. He dressed himself in a simple tunic and trousers. Then he washed his face and ran a hand through his hair before exiting his room. Guards stood watch in the halls, lowering their gazes and saluting him as he passed. The council room doors opened before him, and he strode inside. A servant was just lighting the hanging lanterns, casting the chamber in an eerie glow. Four people stood conversing. Well, one broad and equally tall man was silent, focused on the words of a woman with braided hair and domineering posture. They didn't notice him at first, fully tuned in to their conversation. Another young man and woman stood side by side, nodding and adding to whatever she was saying. Honzio walked toward them, his steps drawing their gazes. They ducked their heads in respect. Hands slid to chests.

"At ease," Honzio said.

"Your Majesty." The braided woman spoke first. Honzio had seen her several times years before during the Grand Palace celebrations. She had been much younger but still carried that powerful presence.

"Welcome, Queen Coralie."

Coralie motioned to her companions. "My general, Mordon." The large man nodded, his mouth unsmiling, and from the way he stood beside his queen, Honzio got the impression the man was loyal enough to lay down his life in a blink to protect her. "Verin's ambassador, Latimus Blayton, and his wife, Lady Sardala of Ondalar."

The ambassador smiled. "My deepest congratulations on your coronation. May your reign prove fruitful."

"It is an honor to meet you, Your Majesty," his wife piped in.

Honzio motioned toward the council table. "Please, have a seat."

After they had all settled in, Honzio asked about the state of affairs in the kingdoms. They filled him in on the happenings, telling him about the former General Zenrelius's plot to overtake Verin and so much more.

"This is the traveling serum," Queen Coralie said, placing it onto the table.

Honzio examined the liquid within as Coralie explained how it worked and how they had used it to transport to Hearcross. Honzio's mouth went dry when he realized all the battle plans they had been working on were needless if they had this. It would change things. Without further thought, he summoned the council. That truly was an urgent matter. He called for refreshments as they waited, and soon, the others filed in. Velamir was followed by Uluzar. A few remaining loyal nobles who had returned to the palace for the coronation also entered.

After all had said their greetings, Honzio stood, proclaiming, "We have found a way to defeat the Dark Army once and for all."

51

VELAMIR HADN'T GOTTEN a wink of sleep after the coronation. He'd lain awake in his chamber, his mind spinning with doubts. When an Uluzar arrived and informed him of the gathering council, Velamir had been grateful for the distraction. He entered the chamber and was met by familiar faces. He approached them, smiling when Latimus rose and extended a hand. They clasped forearms in greeting.

Latimus wore a broad grin, quite unlike his typical broody expression.

"Velamir," Latimus said, "it's good to see you."

"And you," Velamir replied. "I hear you have become an ambassador."

Latimus shook his head. "Don't ask. You don't want to know what I've been through recently."

Velamir chuckled. "I am sure I don't."

"Won't you introduce me, Latimus?" a young woman said, appearing by his side.

Latimus tucked a hand around her waist. "My wife, Lady Sardala."

Velamir startled, then cleared his throat as he overcame his astonishment. So, that must be the reason for Latimus's drastic change in attitude. He'd gone from being the sulky man in Verin and transformed into a proud and content husband.

"Sardala, this is Velamir, an old friend of mine."

Sardala gave him a friendly wide smile. "I am pleased to meet you."

"And he's not just any man." Coralie spoke up from her seat at the council table. "From what we have heard, Velamir is now khan of the Uluzar."

The Uluzar seated around the table watched the interaction. Jinong-ja nodded at Coralie, affirming her words.

Velamir bowed his head. "Your Majesty."

She waved away the formality.

Latimus leaned closer to Velamir. "I am still in shock after hearing that news. I feel like it was only yesterday when little green Velamir came to Verintown."

Velamir smiled, recalling when they had met as boys.

"I wish you the best in your reign."

"Thank you," Velamir said. "And you have my congratulations for your wedding."

Sardala beamed, thanking him profusely.

"Lore will be excited to see you," Velamir told Latimus.

Latimus nodded. "And I him. You watched over my brother, Velamir. For that, you will have my eternal gratitude."

"It was nothing. You would have done the same."

Latimus clapped him on the shoulder before they all took their seats, Velamir and Honzio at the head and the others lined up on either side of the long table. Mordon watched him from Coralie's side with an imperceptible look until he finally lowered his chin in a nod.

"Velamir."

"Mordon," Velamir replied.

It was an odd sort of greeting, but it suited them.

Velamir looked to Coralie, lowering his voice as he leaned closer to ask her the question that had been weighing on him since he'd last seen her. "Jax?"

Her lips thinned as she slowly shook her head, sadness evident in her features. "I am sorry, Velamir. I tried, but he is still in Prolus's hands."

Velamir sat back in his seat, tension gripping his shoulders. Jax was still prisoner. Velamir had been attempting to reassure himself that Coralie had retrieved him and that he was safe in Verin. Who knew what he'd been through all that time? What Winston could have done to him . . . Velamir swallowed, burning memories of the mentor he'd once prized. The man he'd killed for. The chamber suddenly appeared so dark despite the flickering lantern light. Honzio was speaking, but Velamir barely heard him, his mind stuck on Jax. He reached up to loosen his collar and set several buttons free until cool air brushed his chest.

Honzio's words finally came rushing in. He motioned

to a vial resting in the center of the table. "Using the Zamanin Sulari, we will surprise the Tariqins. They have no idea about the incidents in Verin and Ondalar. They do not know Zenrelius has failed and that we now possess this serum. They will never see it coming."

The council listened with rapt interest as Honzio shared the information he'd received from Coralie.

"We need to rework the battle plan," Moralis said. He was seated farther down the table, along with Aylis, Bear, and Svorgin.

"What do you say, Khan Velix-ja?" Jinong-ja asked.

Velamir forced his conflicting thoughts aside and straightened his posture. "I have used this serum before. It works effectively, so there should be no doubts about that. If we arrive using this, the Tariqins will be taken by surprise, giving us a great advantage."

Honzio nodded. "We should be able to take the city with ease."

"*But,*" Velamir stressed. "We must not forget Tariqins are trained to battle from a young age. They will not surrender without a fight. They will group together and form a defense, though perhaps not as good of one as they would if they were prepared."

"And they have Chishmans," Latimus added, casting a glance at Velamir.

Velamir grimaced. The specially trained soldiers were the most skilled fighters in Tariqi. They could pose a dire threat. "They have Chishmans," he agreed. "We need to tread carefully."

"And we have a trained Chishma with us," Coralie

said, motioning to Velamir. "You out of anyone should know their tactics."

Velamir stood up and spread open a map of Ayleth. "There are several ways the Tariqins will defend themselves against a surprise attack."

He spent the next hour explaining Tariqin strategies. The others added to the conversation as they devised a greater strategy. A courier rushed into the council chamber and handed Velamir a note.

"An urgent message for the khan."

Velamir accepted it. The others carried on conversing, their voices fading as Velamir smoothed his hands over the paper, his eyes tracing the inked words.

We are expecting your presence at Castle Shikista. If you do not wish to put your friend Jaxon's life in jeopardy, you will come alone.

Winston

The cruel words blared as if the sun were blinding him. Velamir crushed the letter in his hand. Jax. Poor Jax. Velamir tucked the letter into his belt, concealing it from the curious eyes darting his way. He slipped his fingers into his hair, knowing the note for what it was. If he'd learned anything in all his years, it was as clear as day that it was a trap. But if it was the only way he could save Jax, he would take it. The council meeting came to an end, and Velamir motioned for Jinong-ja and Honzio to remain as the others filed out. Grongar-ja called to them.

"We best get moving with the attack. I am hungering for meat."

Honzio gagged, shaking his head. He glanced at

Velamir. "You need to do something about that cannibalism thing your people have going on."

Jinong-ja chuckled. "That is Grongar-ja's habit. The rest of us don't have such tastes."

"You cannot know how relieved I am to hear that," Honzio replied.

They both turned to Velamir, seeming to sense his serious mood.

"Why did you want us to stay?" Honzio asked.

"You will go to Ayleth without me."

They froze, and Honzio sputtered. "What do you mean? We need you. The Uluzar need you."

"And I will be there. But I will be inside the castle, destroying them from within." That was what Winston had trained him to do. What the Chishman Academy had instilled in him. He didn't plan to disappoint them.

"Who will you take?"

Velamir turned to Honzio. "You need to lead the army. I will use one of the traveling serums."

"You will go alone," Honzio said in a low voice.

Velamir nodded. "I must."

He reached out to grip Jinong-ja's shoulder. "I know you will lead the Uluzar in a manner befitting a chief. I have no doubt about you."

Jinong-ja's expression flickered, sadness warring with uncertainty before it settled into resignation. He pounded a fist to his chest four times. "As my khan commands."

"Velamir, the people listen to *us*. They will not follow me alone."

"They will," Velamir said. "You've already started changing so much for your people. You are not just a mere emperor. You are shaping a free land." Velamir leaned closer to Honzio. "Anyone can call themselves an emperor. But not everyone can lead."

Honzio nodded.

Velamir strode from the council room. In his chamber, he changed into his armor and gathered his gear. He pulled on his sword belt and sheathed the Zemsar in place. He wrote a letter for Aria and handed it to a guard to have it delivered. He hadn't been able to bid her a proper farewell in Devorin. He'd been racing to track Natassa, and they hadn't had time to spare. He knew the letter wouldn't be enough, but at least it was something.

Velamir left his chamber, walking to the one across from his. His pace slowed as he neared Natassa's door. He placed a hand on it, his heart aching to say farewell, but if he saw her, he might not be able to leave. Velamir leaned over, placing the second letter he'd written on the floor by the door. He forced himself to turn, closing his eyes as he continued forward.

"Leaving without saying goodbye?"

The soft voice froze him in place. Velamir tensed at the light patter of feet across the marble floor. Velamir braced himself and twisted to face her. Her large hazel eyes took him in, her mouth unsmiling. Her hair hung just past her shoulders in unruly locks.

"Natassa, I—" The words stilled in his mouth as she nodded.

"I had a vision of you leaving. Anything I say or do will not prevent you. I know that." She shivered, crossing her arms.

Velamir reached out. "You're cold."

She shook her head, and Velamir's chest clenched as a tear slipped free and trailed down her cheek.

"You will help your brother in my absence, Natassa. He needs you. The battle plans are nearly complete. The Uluzar and Imperials must remain united. Promise me."

She remained silent, another tear escaping.

"Promise me, Natassa." He gripped her face between his hands, needing to hear her acquiescence. He wouldn't be able to go in peace if he didn't.

"I promise."

Her whisper was low but sent a surge of relief through him. Velamir pulled her into his chest, gripping her tight. Her arms snaked around his back, embracing him just as firmly. Velamir placed his chin over her head and closed his eyes as he savored the moment. They fit together like everything that was meant to be, like stars fit the night sky. His fingers flowed through the silky strands of her hair. With a heavy sigh, he released her. He wiped the tears from her cheeks with his thumbs.

"I leave my heart with you," he said.

Her lips trembled as she smiled. "And I entrust you with mine."

He took several paces backward, his hand drifting from hers the farther he went until their fingertips broke apart, leaving a fervent longing filling the increasing distance between them.

NATASSA
HEARCROSS
THE GRAND PALACE

NATASSA WAITED UNTIL Velamir faded from view before returning to her room. She hunted through her closet, searching for her riding gear. She changed into trousers and pulled a split brown skirt over them before pulling a green vest over a beige long-sleeved undershirt. She swiveled toward the mirror, taking in her apparel. Her hands darted up, twisting her hair into a low bun. Several strands escaped at once, and she rolled her eyes. There wasn't any time to waste over trivial matters. She was still missing one thing.

Natassa returned to her closet and found her spare knife belt under a hidden panel. She hooked it around her waist and patted it with a smile. Then came the knives, six on either

side. She slid them into the tiny sheaths built into the belt and marched to her chamber door. The palace was still asleep. Well, most of it was. As soon as she stepped into the hall, she bumped into a pacing form.

"Oof!" the person exclaimed.

Natassa winced. "I'm so sorry."

The woman—Aylis, Natassa realized—waved her off. "No, it was my fault. I wasn't paying attention."

Natassa forced a smile, uncertain how to respond. She hadn't spoken to Aylis in so long, and they hadn't parted on the best of terms. Aylis's hair was black as tar, falling down to her waist, a change Natassa couldn't get used to. She still saw that vicious Savorian woman with golden hair.

"I was waiting." Aylis cleared her throat. "Waiting to see you."

Natassa translated that to her mustering up the courage to knock on her door. "Well, I am here."

An awkward silence commenced. Aylis moved closer, appearing resolved. She grasped Natassa's arm. Natassa looked down at the tight grip, and Aylis softened her hold.

"The last time we saw each other, we—I—" Aylis stammered. "I wasn't the kindest."

"You were experiencing so much. I can't blame you for that."

Aylis shook her head. "I was awful to you. We both were in a terrible state. If Thorsten was my love, he was your brother. Nothing excuses the way I acted." She steeled herself before appearing to force out the words. "And I apologize."

Natassa smiled. "There's nothing to forgive."

"Please, allow me to do something. To help you in some way."

Natassa took in the Savorian's earnest features and had just begun to reply in the negative when an idea sprouted in her mind. "Actually, there is a way you can assist me."

❧

Natassa made her way to Honzio's chamber. She caught sight of three individuals speaking just ahead of her. As she came closer, she made out the nearest woman, taking in the braids and confident posture. Natassa swept forward, calling out to them.

"Your Majesty."

She stepped beside them, and they all turned to her. Just as she'd estimated, the woman who had been speaking was none other than Queen Coralie. Coralie smiled in return. "Princess Natassa, it is good to see you again."

The queen stood in her regal stance. Natassa decided to bypass typical greetings and pulled her into a hug. Coralie exhaled, and her arms hung limply in clear surprise before she returned the embrace. Natassa pulled back, not wanting to overwhelm her. "It's good to see you too."

"Your Highness." Latimus Blayton lowered his head in respect. "I trust you are well."

Natassa nodded, pleased to see that the contempt Latimus had carried for her was nowhere in sight and he truly did seem happy to see her. A young lady stood beside him, practically bouncing on her feet as she bowed her head.

"Your Highness."

"My wife," Latimus introduced the woman. "Lady Sardala."

Natassa's brows shot up. She had missed several chapters, it seemed. "I'm very pleased to meet you, Lady Sardala."

"As am I." The woman was nearly sparkling with joy.

Natassa had never imagined whom Latimus would marry, but if she had, it would not have been Lady Sardala. Latimus was the stern sort, wholly serious, and always appearing like he was attending a funeral. Lady Sardala seemed the complete opposite, bubbling over with energy and wielding a smile as blinding as the sun. But as Natassa glanced at Latimus, seeing a fond look creep over his face as he watched his wife, she realized maybe they were perfect for each other.

"Natassa?" Her brother emerged from the connecting hall.

She excused herself from the others and approached him. "I wanted to speak with you."

Honzio motioned for her to follow him. After reaching his chamber and closing the door, Honzio turned, his eyes raking over her apparel. "Now, will you tell me why you are dressed like you're about to leave the palace?"

Natassa switched the topic, asking Honzio about Coralie, and learned that she had arrived in Hearcross with most of her troops. Latimus and Sardala had taken charge of Ondalar's army since the kingdom currently lacked a leader, and an entire cavalry was lingering outside the city gates in preparation to assault Ayleth.

"So, you will use the traveling serum?" Natassa asked.

Honzio shrugged. "It seems to work and guarantees to be the fastest way to reclaim Ayleth. We will finally bring the Dark Lord to the gruesome end he deserves." He paused, his eyes narrowing on her. "Why do I get the feeling you are evading my questions?"

It was Natassa's turn to shrug. "I haven't the faintest idea why you feel that way, but I do have something to tell you. Velamir left for Ayleth. I had a vision."

"I know." He ran a hand over his face.

"You must set out for Ayleth at once."

Honzio drifted off into thought before his gaze snapped to her. "You had a vision, Velamir left, and you are now in riding apparel. It all sounds a bit odd to me."

Natassa coughed, patting her chest as she wheezed. "I need some water."

Honzio's suspicion was replaced by worry, and he rushed to the jug in the corner of his room. Natassa used that opportunity to duck out of the chamber while he was distracted. She twisted the awaiting key and heard a satisfying click as the lock slid into place.

"Natassa!" her brother shouted and banged on the wood.

"I'm sorry, Honzio, but you wouldn't have let me go otherwise. And you are the sole person in this palace who can prevent me from leaving."

"You little brat," he growled from behind the door. "Let me out at once."

"I love you too, big brother," Natassa replied. "You know what you must do. I will see you in Ayleth."

She blocked out his shouts and turned to the person waiting beside her.

"I sent the guards away," Aylis said. "You have until the next shift, which doesn't leave you much time."

"Good." Natassa placed the large key in her palm. "I entrust this to you until then."

Aylis pocketed it before extending a glistening vial. Natassa thanked her, tucking the serum into her belt. She'd promised Velamir she wouldn't follow, but she had seen herself in the vision. She was there at the end. And when it came to her loved ones, not even her own promises could hold her back.

53

Velamir

Kingdom of Ayleth

Castle Shikista

VELAMIR STOOD WAITING before the throne room doors of Castle Shikista. When he'd arrived in Ayleth, he hadn't been stopped by a single deedan. In fact, they had welcomed him and escorted him to the castle. He hadn't expected it to be that easy, but it seemed Winston was eager to see him. The deedans hadn't even asked for his weapons, not even glancing at his sword, which still rested comfortingly on his hip.

Velamir braced himself as the doors swung open. It was the first time in weeks he would see Winston again. The doors slammed against the stone walls with a bang. Deedans probed spears into his back, urging him forward. Velamir moved into action, taking long strides into the throne room. It wasn't as grand as the one in Hearcross, but it was unique. Chandeliers dangled from the ceiling in a large circle. The floor was covered in a dazzling pattern of purple, which swirled into a giant sphere that mirrored the chandeliers. Velamir stopped in the center of the pattern, his gaze snapping to the man sitting upon the throne.

Winston reclined on the seat, his arms positioned lazily on either side of him, as if he hadn't a care in the world. His beard was longer than Velamir had ever seen it, and his wavy hair was trimmed above his ears. But his eyes remained the same, just as bright and blue as Velamir remembered. The mask dangled at the tips of his fingers. Prolus's mask, with the wide eerie smile cutting across and the empty eyeholes. The mask that had driven fear into countless men. A woman stood beside the throne, clothed entirely in white. The color was almost as pale as her skin. Her sinister eyes were focused on him in a way that made shivers race up his spine.

"The young man I told you about," Winston said. The familiar rumble of his voice brought a wave of pain over Velamir. It reminded him of different times. "He was perhaps the greatest warrior I ever had."

The woman's eyebrow lifted as she examined him. "We shall see."

Velamir's nostrils flared. "Where is he?"

Winston clicked his tongue. "Manners, Velamir." He smiled at the woman. "One of his major faults. He never had respect for his elders."

Velamir's anger simmered. He searched the corners of the chamber anxiously. Where could Winston be keeping him? But his search was futile, only uncovering the deedans positioned around the room, looking on with eagle eyes.

"This is the queen of Devorin." Winston motioned to the woman, and she waved her fingers in greeting. Her thin pasty lips rose in a smile.

"I don't care about your guests. You told me to come alone, and I did. Now where is he?"

"You should care, lad." The endearing term set Velamir's nerves on edge. "She was the one hosting dear Jaxon all this time."

Velamir's gaze flew to the woman again, finding her watching him with what seemed like satisfaction. Velamir refocused on Winston, nearly spitting out the words as he repeated them for the third time.

"Where is *he*?"

Winston gestured for him to calm. "Soon, Velamir, soon. You will be reunited with him. But first, you will spend a little time in the dungeon."

Velamir's hand inched to his sword hilt. He spied the deedans creeping toward him from his peripheral. Ten, he counted. He would defeat them, but not without a scratch. He kept his gaze on Winston.

"Face me, one-on-one."

Winston's brows shot up. "Why would I do that when I have you at my mercy?"

Before Velamir could respond, the queen slumped against the throne, clutching her head. She trembled, her pale eyes turning dark. She was a Shadow Manos, Velamir realized.

"No." She gasped. "No."

Winston stood from the throne. "What is it? What do you see?"

She jerked forward, white strands of hair floating over her shoulders as her irises faded to the pale color they'd been before. She heaved in breaths, slowly rising to her full height. Winston searched her gaze.

"There is an army closing in," she whispered.

Winston paled. "That isn't possible."

"Your time is ending," Velamir said.

The words turned Winston into a frozen statue before he sputtered, "You are bluffing."

The queen moved toward the balcony off the side of the throne room, and Winston joined her. Velamir followed them but kept his distance. Deedans trailed after him. They stepped through the glass doors and stood on the perilously high edge of the balcony. Velamir could see part of what they were viewing: a city in chaos; deedans assembling quickly; and a distance from the city gates, an army riding hard and fast. A smile tugged at Velamir's mouth when he spotted the flags flapping in the wind. Green for Verin, yellow for Ondalar, and the Imperial flag, bloodred. The Empire was coming together. More flags mingled throughout, different Uluzar tribe crests decorating each one. The figures at the forefront of the army were mere dots at that distance, but Velamir could imagine Jinong-ja, Honzio, and so many others. His friends and allies.

The throne room doors slammed open, and a deedan rushed inside, panting. "Lord Prolus!"

Winston swiveled, his panic apparent as he realized the situation.

"There is an army approaching. What should we do?"

Winston sputtered, "T-Take action! Heat the oil above the walls, gather the archers, block off the gates!"

His angry shouts sent the deedan scurrying away. Winston's harried gaze swung to Velamir.

"How? How could they assemble so quickly?"

Velamir shrugged, drawing his sword. "I think your concern should be your battle with me."

Winston glanced between Velamir and the blade. "So, that is what you wish."

Winston brushed past him, and the queen remained off to the side, expressionless. Velamir followed Winston until they stood across from each other in the center of the circle.

"An apprentice will face his master. A boy will attempt to kill the man who raised him. How pathetic."

Velamir lifted his sword, pointing it at Winston. "That boy was betrayed by the man who raised him. I trusted you. I *loved* you." His voice cracked. "But you never cared for me. You knew who I was the entire time. You knew Boltrex was my father, and you intended for me to *kill* him. How much more of a villain can you become?"

"Your time in the Empire gave you delusions. You weren't ready for your first mission. I gave you the opportunity to become the most powerful man in the world. You could have had a place by my side. You could have been the next emperor, Velamir."

Velamir chuckled, harsh and unbelieving. "You must think I am daft to believe that. You made me commit murders. You formed me into a monster. But I broke out of your mold. You are too selfish to place anyone else but yourself upon that throne. The rest of us are simply your pawns."

"You disappoint me, Velamir." He glanced at the mask still within his grasp. "But you are right, the time of cowering in shadows is over. Everyone will meet the true Prolus."

Winston tossed the mask, and it clanged across the floor. Velamir's gut twisted at the sinister smile on it. For so long, he'd seen that image; for so long, he'd fought for that wicked cause. It was time for it all to end.

Winston unsheathed his sword, and his head tilted, a question on his face. *Are you ready for this, lad?*

Velamir shifted into an attack stance and swung forward. Winston parried the move away. Velamir had always been calm during their practice bouts. He'd moved with lighter precision, usually on the defense. But just then, all the anger poured through his veins. All the hurt and pain he'd faced because of that man propelling him faster than he ever had moved before. His weapon swung in a blur of flashes. Rapid strokes Winston barely deflected. Velamir recognized the fear in those blue eyes.

Velamir continued slashing until his blade sliced through Winston's sword. The metal smacked the ground with a clang. Velamir's sword kept moving, piercing Winston's belly. Winston gasped, and Velamir pulled the sword free. Blood coated the end of the blade. Velamir's chest rose and fell in harsh pants. Winston stared wide-eyed at his weapon, a useless piece of metal. He tossed it away, looking at Velamir as if he didn't recognize him. Velamir held his sword tip at Winston's throat.

"Your blood deserves to be shed, but not by this sword."

Winston blinked, confusion lashing through his features. Velamir leaned down and unsheathed the dagger from his boot. He lifted the blade, the light from the chandeliers causing it to gleam.

"Do you remember this dagger?"

Winston swallowed, staring at the weapon. Recognition settled on his face.

"The dagger you gave to a child when you urged him to kill. To take revenge for his family. The family *you* destroyed." Velamir's breath trembled. "The family *you* broke apart."

"Velamir," Winston began, but Velamir pressed the dagger tip to his shoulder, silencing him.

"You are the reason for everything," Velamir whispered, his hair hanging in sweaty strands before his eyes. "The reason I never felt my mother's touch, my father's embrace, my sister's love. You destroyed me. That wretched day fifteen years ago, you destroyed me."

Winston watched him with pity, infuriating Velamir.

"You took everything from me, but I won't allow you to ruin Jax. I won't leave him in your hands. Where is he?"

Winston's fingers slipped over his bleeding abdomen, attempting to staunch the wound. Velamir shoved the dagger into his shoulder, and Winston roared. The veins in his neck throbbed as tears streamed from his eyes from the pain.

"It is only fitting that you die by this dagger. But not until you release him."

Winston panted, staring in horror at his gushing wounds. Velamir withdrew his dagger, and blood poured out in a sudden flow.

"WHERE IS HE?" The words ripped from Velamir's throat, raw and demanding.

Winston flinched, glancing over his shoulder at the queen, who continued watching with her pale stare. "Bring him."

The queen nodded at a deedan, and the man rushed from the room. Velamir kept his guard on Winston, his sword and dagger aimed at his former mentor. Another deedan entered, gasping for breath as if he'd run a long distance. His features paled when he saw his leader at sword point.

"The Imperial army sends a messenger."

Winston nodded, sweat trickling along his jaw, his breathing labored. "Let him in."

The doors opened, and the messenger rushed inside, eyes searching the room until they landed on Velamir.

"No," Velamir whispered, all the air leaving his lungs. "What are you doing here?"

Natassa ignored him as she took in the scene and focused on Winston. "I've come to inform you of two options: either you surrender and order your soldiers to stand down or face the consequences."

"Natassa," Velamir said.

"But I see Velamir has detained you, so there isn't much need for further discussion."

The doors opened once again, and figures clad in black swarmed inside.

Winston shook his head, a smile curling his lips.

"Velamir will release me in exchange for his friend, won't you, Velamir?"

Velamir's gaze caught on a man at the forefront of the newcomers. His clothes were torn and head lowered, exposing his short matted hair. The figures moved as one. There was something odd about them. A warning flickered in Velamir's mind, but he pushed it aside as he focused on the man at the front.

"Let him go," the queen ordered.

Velamir shoved Winston aside, distantly hearing him moan in pain. The figures allowed the short-haired man to go free. The man stumbled, his hunched posture and pallid features so changed. Velamir's breath trembled as he examined him. Natassa fell into place beside him.

"Velamir," she said in a low tone, her face twisted in apprehension. "Something's wrong."

But Velamir was so focused on Jax, he couldn't reply. His friend stopped before him and lifted his head. Jax was thinner than he had ever seen him. Gone were the golden curls full of life. He appeared sallow, as if all energy had been drained from him. His sparkling blue eyes were dull, murky pools. Haggard circles clung beneath Jax's lower lids, and his lips were thin and unmoving.

"Oh, Jax," Velamir whispered, guilt clawing through him. "What have they done to you?"

He pulled his friend into a tight embrace. Tears filled his eyes as he imagined the torture Jax had faced. His hands shook over Jax's thin frame. There was nothing but lean muscle and protruding bones.

"I'm sorry, Jax. I'm so sorry," Velamir repeated, his chest shaking in a sob.

Searing pain struck Velamir's side. Agony like never before stole his breath. Velamir released Jax, taking a step back. He glanced down, unbelieving when he saw a sharp dagger in Jax's hand. A sharp dagger coated in blood. Velamir heard Natassa screaming his name and saw her reaching for him, but he couldn't take his eyes off the weapon in Jax's hand. How? How could he have done that? Velamir's gaze drifted to the source of the pain wreaking through his side. Blood flowed forth through the leather of his armor. He pressed his fingers to it, attempting to stem it as he overcame his shock.

He looked at Jax, his brother, the one he could always count on. But an expressionless statue stood before him.

"Jax?"

The eyes that met his were someone else's entirely. The man standing before him was no longer Jax, his brother, his best friend since childhood. It was someone he didn't recognize.

54

Natassa
Kingdom of Ayleth
Castle Shikista

NATASSA SENSED SOMETHING was off as soon as the figures entered the throne room. She closed her eyes, her shadows tugging at her. Then she noticed the other shadows. So many of them, each one clinging to a figure garbed in black. They were all Shadow Manos, she realized with a start. What were so many Shadow Manos doing together? And why did they all have that lifeless expression on their faces?

"Something's wrong," she whispered to Velamir.

But he was staring at Jax. The two embraced, or rather, Velamir embraced him. Jax was motionless, his gaze far off. As if he weren't even there. Natassa glanced at the queen, who watched

with a wide smile. Winston collapsed at the foot of the stairs leading up to the throne. His hand was pressed to his wounds, but blood continued to seep through his fingers. But even through his pain, he looked on with a glint in his eyes. They were anticipating something. Natassa's attention swung back to Velamir just as she heard a gasp. Her heart jumped to her throat as Velamir stepped back. And she couldn't move, her legs rooted to the floor when she saw the red-stained dagger in Jax's hand, blood dripping from its lethal edge.

"Velamir!" She screamed his name and grabbed his arm, attempting to pull him back to see the depth of his wound. But he didn't move. He was still staring at Jax, hurt and disbelief cracking across his features.

"Jax?" he whispered.

Natassa shook her head. "Velamir, please."

Laughter echoed behind them, and she turned. Winston raised his red-tainted fingers in the air as he chuckled, joy lighting his eyes.

"I may not have been able to witness you kill Boltrex, but watching his son die at the hands of someone dear to him is a close recompense."

"You're sick," Natassa spat.

He smiled, slowly lifting himself. "You have no way out of this room, Velamir. You will die here, and I will witness your end."

The queen smirked. "My warriors, my weapons, attack!"

Velamir was still attempting to reach Jax. "Jax! Please! Look at me. I don't know what they did to you, but you don't have to do this."

But Jax wasn't listening. He dropped the dagger, and the other figures swarmed around him, unsheathing short swords. One of them passed a sword to Jax, and he took it in stiff fingers. They were cornered. The figures circled them. There was no chance Natassa could fight them off alone, and as injured as Velamir was, he couldn't battle in his current mental state either. They had to escape.

"Stay beside me," Velamir said with a pained tremor.

She nodded, unsheathing knives into both hands. Concern for Velamir filled her. He was breathing harsher, his posture hunched, one hand on his sword hilt and the other pressed to his wounded side.

"They are Shadow Manos," she told him.

The figures closed in. Her own shadows whispered, their silhouettes growing visible before her eyes.

You must accept the queen's offer, the Seer whispered, floating before her. *If you do not, your fate is certain.*

One of the Shadow Manos swung toward them, moving so fast, she classified his shadow as a Doer, granting him unnatural speed. Velamir yanked her back and blocked the attack. Natassa gasped, stumbling a few paces. Another Shadow Manos swiped at her, and she narrowly evaded him.

"If you don't help me, there won't be any offers I can accept," Natassa hissed at her shadows.

The Seer grumbled and merged with her mind, and Natassa saw the Shadow Manos's moves before they happened. She ducked and evaded every blow with ease before stabbing her knife into his shoulder. She shoved him away and threw a knife at a Shadow Manos creeping behind Velamir. He grunted as the knife connected between his shoulder blades and fell back. The Shadow Manos were the best fighters Natassa had ever seen. They were more vicious than the Uluzar and Imperial soldiers. It didn't matter how many blows they received; they continued returning with more fury.

Natassa was drenched in sweat, strands of her hair sticking to her face and mouth. She prayed for a way out as they forced their way toward the large throne room doors. The Shadow Manos continued after them, swinging blow after blow. A blade grazed her arm, and she flinched, blood welling forth.

"Natassa?" Velamir swung his sword in a wide arc, forcing their attackers back. "Natassa?" he repeated.

"I'm fine," she said, ignoring the blood. Velamir's wound concerned her far more. It was pouring blood since he could not put pressure on it. All his focus was set on battling. He was pale and perspiring. His chest rose and fell hard as he continued to fight. Natassa grew desperate. The doors were getting closer and closer. Then hands grabbed her and dragged her back.

"Natassa!" Velamir roared, rushing toward her.

Natassa shrieked, kicking her legs and trying to extract her arms from the harsh grips of her captors. Her knives were stripped from her, and then she was shoved to her knees before the queen. She could hear Velamir attacking behind her, shouting curses. Winston carried on laughing, pure joy on his face. Natassa wanted to rake her nails across his skin. The queen's gaze flicked over her, pity flattening her lips.

"What a shame. I heard the phoenix would be

something incredible, but you don't look like much. No matter. As long as you open the portal, I don't mind."

"Let me go," Natassa hissed, her voice hoarse, her bones aching.

Jax stood beside the queen, his face blank and empty.

"Jax!" Natassa cried out. "Jax, please."

But he didn't even flinch. Not a hint of recognition. Natassa's hopes were dimming. The queen reached up, fingers brushing a cylinder vial hanging from her locket.

"I spent years crafting in Devorin, brewing different concoctions and discovering many unique tonics. You must have heard of Zamanin Sulari? I created it, the only Shadow Manos alive who was successful." Her eyes gleamed with pride. "But it wasn't enough. It wasn't what I wanted. I traversed further into the dark arts, but still I was eluded. The shadows didn't deem me worthy."

Natassa's brows furrowed as the queen's hand closed around the vial and she yanked it free, staring at it with a crazed look.

"But finally, *finally*, I was able to master it. I was able to create a portal to the gateway of spirits."

Natassa's head spun, and she watched in helpless alarm as the queen uncorked the vial and tilted it. Smoke filtered free, filling the air and covering the marble tiles. The fumes rose, forming a dim archway. Natassa gasped as part of the smoke neared her, grazing her skin like cool fingers.

"A gateway to an invincible army," the queen said.

Natassa shook her head. "I will never open it for you."

"You don't have a choice."

She motioned behind her. Natassa turned, panic sprouting within when she saw Velamir surrounded by Shadow Manos, their weapons trained on his throat. He swallowed visibly as their gazes connected.

"Don't do it, Natassa," he said.

A Shadow Manos struck him across the face, and his head snapped back. Tears welled in her eyes.

"Stop!"

"I see you will decide to act wisely." The queen's fingers clasped together. "It is time for you to fulfill your destiny, phoenix. Your ancestors started this, and you will finish it. The shadows promised to end the curse as soon as the phoenix broke it. Once you open this gateway, they will no longer burden you." The queen smiled. "Isn't that what you want, dear Princess? You will be free, free to live as you wish with the companions you choose."

"Because the shadows will be living, breathing beings. No longer mere spirits."

The queen nodded. "Exactly, and they are far more powerful than us humans. Even the amount of power they grant us in their spirit form is enough to end lives. Imagine an army of them." The queen's eyes were dazed as she stared off into the distance.

Natassa trembled.

"Now come, Princess. It is time."

The Shadow Manos pushed her toward the gate. Natassa stood before the mist-covered doorway. Voices called to her from within. Her eyes drifted closed, but they only seemed to grow closer.

Open the gates, open the gates.

Her heart thumped in her ears. She extended her hand, her fingers drifting through the hazy smoke. She grew dizzy as hundreds of unfamiliar voices spread throughout her mind, begging her to allow them through. If she did so, she would save herself, but if she didn't . . .

Natassa reached out with her shadows. And she could sense all the other shadows within the throne room. They were all frozen with glee. All of them shouting one thing. A tuneless song, an endless chant.

Open, open, open.

Natassa could almost feel ghostly hands touching hers from the opposite side of the gateway. She forced herself into the minds of her shadows. They startled, alarmed at her intrusion. She had seen the world from their eyes before, but only when they had allowed it.

What are you doing? the Seer asked.

And that was when Natassa knew she was doing something the Seer had never seen coming. She used the two most powerful shadows in the land, the Seer and Lure, who had been bound to her since her birth, and forced their minds to join with the other shadows in the chamber. Her focus strained from the amount of effort it took. The air crackled as more shadows, shadows inhabiting the Empire and lands beyond were gripped by the pull. It felt like she was using all the force in the world. The queen looked on with unrestrained excitement.

"The curse is over," Natassa whispered. "Return home. Be free."

The curse had begun with a sacrifice, and it ended with one. Natassa used all her conviction, and the shadows couldn't fight against her determination. Their screams echoed in her mind as they slammed through the portal before the hazy archway collapsed with a snap. Natassa stumbled back, scrambling for breath. She felt so empty, so deprived of air.

"What have you done?" the queen screamed in despair.

Her Shadow Manos warriors collapsed around her, the separation of their shadows draining them of life. They had already been lifeless shells of humans; their shadows had been the only things sustaining them.

"What have you done?" The queen yanked at her white hair. "You've destroyed everything."

She quivered as her remaining soldiers pulled her from the room. Jax trailed after them, leaving without a backward glance. Natassa's gaze went dark for a moment, and she collapsed to her knees. She couldn't breathe, could barely see or hear, but she forced herself to crawl forward. She scrambled over bodies until she reached the one she had been looking for. Velamir was flat on his back, his fingers clutching his wound. His head tilted toward her as she approached, and he reached out with a bloodstained hand.

Natassa's lips trembled, and a sob broke free. She used the last of her strength to fall beside him. Her chest rattled as she struggled to breathe. Velamir's green eyes were full of love and tears as he traced the line of her jaw with his fingers. Wet blood trailed across her face with each stroke of her skin.

"You did it," Velamir murmured.

A tear slipped from her eye. "*We* did it."

He caressed her cheek. "My final view is the best I could have asked for."

Her vision was growing dark. "What?"

"You are the last thing I am seeing."

"Velamir." She tried to say more but coughed instead.

His eyes welled, and blood dribbled from his mouth. He ran his thumb over her lips before whispering, "I love you, Natassa Hartinza."

"And I love you."

55

THE CONQUEST WAS swift. The Tariqins hadn't been prepared to meet the full force of the Uluzar and the Imperials. For the first time in his life, Honzio had led the charge. His dear allies and, dare he say, friends rushed behind him as they broke through the gates. But like Velamir had said, the Tariqins put up a fight. Honzio rode through the gates, hearing the screams of his soldiers as hot oil poured from the battlements. He dropped the reins, drawing his sword and releasing a rallying cry. The Uluzar climbed the battlements with renewed vigor as Imperial archers picked off the deedans above. At the sight of the enormous army riding in, many deedans dropped their weapons and surrendered without a fight.

"Do not harm the ones who have

pleaded for mercy!" Honzio shouted, and several of his soldiers paused with their swords in the air, seconds from slaying Tariqins begging for their lives. They slammed half hearts against their chests as they followed his order.

The Imperials began binding the prisoners. Honzio turned his horse in a wide circle, scanning his surroundings. Fires sprang up in corners of the city. The Uluzar and Imperials scoured through, wielding burning torches against the lingering darkness. Honzio glanced up at the foggy sky. Light was emerging from behind the clouds. The sun was rising.

"To the keep!" Honzio ordered. "With me!"

The warriors closest to him followed. Honzio faltered when he caught sight of a horde of Chishmans emerging, but they were intercepted by Queen Coralie and her soldiers. Her general fought beside her, both equally skilled with a sword as they confronted the Chishmans. Honzio continued to the keep.

They entered the castle on foot as a small troop, Svorgin at his right and Jinong-ja at his left, a swarm of warriors just behind. Honzio's heart thudded, worry growing as he thought of his sister. He searched for the throne room, his soldiers picking off any deedan they encountered. He spied the large doors ahead, but just as he neared, figures dressed entirely in black slipped before him, blocking their way. An eerie silence descended. Honzio gripped his sword, a shiver racing over him at the vacant expressions in their eyes.

"Attack!" Honzio called and rushed forward.

A roar followed him as his soldiers charged. Svorgin passed him with ease, his stamina and endurance unmatched. He swung his axe at the first figure. But it was almost as if the man evaporated, slipping beneath the blade in a blink. Honzio frowned, then swiped at the black-garbed soldier closest to him. The man evaded his strike with ease before slamming a fist between Honzio's brows. Honzio staggered back, stars swimming before his eyes. He cleared the daze and slashed wildly before him. His opponent tilted his head, almost as if he were mocking him. Honzio growled, shifted his stance, and charged again. But no matter how much he tried, he could not land a blow.

Cries of pain echoed around him. Honzio glanced about, seeing his soldiers strewn about clutching mortal wounds. The black-garbed warrior swung at him, and Honzio ducked. He landed a kick to the man's midsection, creating space between them. Honzio darted away, regrouping with Svorgin and Jinong-ja—the only people remaining with him. They created a triangle back-to-back, weapons held before them defensively as the enemy circled them.

"This is unnatural," Honzio whispered. "I have never seen such warriors."

"They must be Shadow Manos," Jinong-ja replied.

Svorgin nodded, wiping blood from his busted lip.

"We cannot fight them alone." The realization struck Honzio.

They were only three men against what had to be more than twenty Shadow Manos warriors with unnatural prowess. They hadn't felled a single one.

"We have no choice," Jinong-ja said.

The Shadow Manos were creeping closer.

"Now!" Honzio yelled.

They jumped apart, swinging at the Shadow Manos. Jinong-ja slashed and stabbed beside Honzio. A Shadow Manos broke through Honzio's defense, and his sword went flying across the hall. Honzio retreated, leaving Jinong-ja to desperately fight off five Shadow Manos. A screech rent the air, and his enormous eagle soared through, claws raking over the Shadow Manos. The warriors screamed as the eagle tore through their skin. Honzio used the momentary distraction to his advantage, punching the Shadow Manos before him between the eyes. The Shadow Manos stumbled back, but there were several more to take his place. Honzio's strength was greatly diminished. He couldn't hold them off and definitely not without a weapon. A Shadow Manos pushed him, sending him sprawling on the floor. His back was pressed to the cold tiles as he stared up at the approaching warriors. He spied Svorgin a short distance away. He was out cold, his head dangling limply.

"Svorgin!" Honzio called, fear for his friend plaguing him.

The Shadow Manos dragged Svorgin away, disappearing from view. Jinong-ja continued fighting to the best of his ability, but it was no use. A Shadow Manos leaned over Honzio, lifting a sword. Honzio closed his eyes so he wouldn't see the point of the weapon when it came down.

But then it didn't.

The Shadow Manos began trembling before collapsing all around them. They convulsed with heavy seizures until finally falling still. Honzio sat up, locking eyes with

Jinong-ja, and they both looked at each other in confusion. Honzio got to his feet. The sound of boots neared, and Uluzar and Imperial soldiers rushed into the hall.

"Where were you?" With exasperation, Honzio wiped at the sweat and blood staining his face before ordering, "Find Svorgin."

As some of the soldiers went off in search of the Savorian, the rest followed Honzio to the throne room. A sudden unease closed in on him. His heart was heavy, but he pushed the doors open and faltered at the view that met him. Dozens of bodies lay scattered across the marble floor. Honzio stilled, catching sight of a man at the foot of the stairs leading up to the throne. The dark mask representing their enemy of years rested beside him. Honzio stepped closer, looking down at the man. The Dark Lord Prolus had been unmasked. Honzio checked him for signs of life, but there was no pulse. He was gone. Honzio spun away, searching for his sister. His panic took over, and he hurried to scan the rest of the bodies, searching each face, desperation overwhelming him.

"Find the princess!" he ordered the guards who had accompanied him. "Find Natassa."

He searched ceaselessly until he came across two bodies tilted toward each other. Both still, both lifeless.

"No," Honzio breathed.

He stumbled forward, falling to his knees. He gathered his sister in his arms.

"Natassa?" he said. "Natassa, I'm here. Look at me."

But she didn't. Her hazel eyes were empty. Honzio's

emotions swallowed him as he realized he had lost his little sister. She had been the last anchor keeping him ashore. He'd lost everyone, his mother, his brothers. But she'd remained. And she was gone too. Tears fell from his lashes and onto her face. Honzio trembled, then shook as he held her.

"Natassa, wake up."

He recalled when they'd reunited in Marcella's home and even before she left the palace. She had told him she loved him both times. She had always shown it. She had been an angel in his dark world, and he hadn't even given her a reply.

"Look at me," he begged. "One last time."

A hand clamped over his shoulder, and Honzio looked up. Through his blurry gaze, he saw Aylis, sorrow in her features. He heard more sobs, harsh cries. People gathered around Velamir. Coralie was there, and Latimus, Mordon, and Bear. All those who had known him and loved him.

Honzio didn't know how long had passed before he forced himself to release his sister. He put himself in check. He was the emperor. She wouldn't have wanted him to crumble. She would have wanted him to be the strength their people needed.

He spoke to Aylis. "We will bury the bodies soon. Any news of Svorgin?"

Tears hovered in her eyes as she shook her head. Honzio looked down, swallowing the lump in his throat as he registered what she couldn't say. Svorgin was most likely dead. Honzio squeezed her arm in support and then looked to Jinong-ja, who stood above Velamir's still form. He was holding a long blade. Honzio examined the weapon and recognized it as the Zemsar, Velamir's sword.

"We will bury it with him," Jinong-ja said. "End this greed for power."

"I think he would want you to keep it. And it seems the blade has chosen you."

Jinong-ja's lips parted as he stared at the legendary sword. His imposing eagle shrieked as it soared above him before landing on his arm. Its talons dripped with blood as it dug into Jinong-ja's glove.

"What do you say? Will you lead the Uluzar?"

⋞

HONZIO

KINGDOM OF AYLETH

The wind was gentle and the air somber as thousands gathered for the ceremony commemorating the fallen. The site had been constructed for those who had died fighting for the Empire. Hundreds of tombstones were placed beside each other, and at the forefront of them all were two inscribed gravestones.

The Hero and, on the opposite stone, *the Phoenix.* Beneath the titles were their names. *Natassa Hartinza, Princess of the Empire. Velamir Vaz, Khan of the Uluz.* Solemn faces looked on, keeping silent in respect. Honzio's hand brushed over Natassa's gravestone. He still couldn't believe his little sister had gone and left him behind. He rose to his full height and addressed the gathered crowd.

"We have entered a new era. From now on, I promise you an empire of peace, a changed empire. There is no room for cruelty, or slavery, or tyranny. I am Emperor Honzio Hartinza." He glanced over the gathering. "Every year on this day, we will celebrate. We will not mourn. We will recall our fallen with smiles because they sacrificed so we could have peace. They fought so we could live." He unsheathed his sword, thrusting it into the air. The cloak he used to wear over his right shoulder was gone, leaving his marred arm proudly displayed to all. "Let us dedicate this day to our heroes."

"To our heroes!" the people shouted, the entire area glittering as weapons pointed toward the sky.

"Heroes of the Empire," Honzio whispered.

High above, in a land where the sun never stopped shining, a young woman with golden-streaked hair ran across a grassy field. Her laughter carried around her. A young man chased after her, his grin wide and full of joy. Their fingers slid into each other's. They ventured forth, the brightest smiles sparkling on their faces. Green eyes met hazel ones. And up there, in the land of light, with their hands clasped together, no darkness or might could pull them apart.

56

CORALIE COULDN'T REMEMBER the last time she had been so nervous. She placed her hands over her queasy stomach, hoping to dispel the anxious fluttering there. She peered out the window of the guest room in the Grand Palace. Coralie could see well beyond the palace from that height to the streets of Hearcross, where delicate flower petals decorated the ground and giggling children tore past, each in their finest garments. Because today was a grand day.

"Your Majesty," her maid asked, "are you ready?"

Coralie turned, attempting to keep

her expression calm, but she couldn't stop the smile threatening to stretch her cheeks. At the knock on the door, Coralie nodded.

"It's time."

The maid opened the door, and Mordon entered. Coralie's nerves faded at the sight of him. Her anchor, her home.

"I don't believe the Grand Palace has ever been so full. There was—" His voice came to an abrupt halt when he caught sight of her. His mouth opened as if all the air had escaped his lungs.

Coralie's smile widened at his reaction. She wore a long dress with sleeves that hung from the shoulders and hugged her waist before flaring out at the bottom. Pearls studded the fabric along her collarbone, and gloves enveloped her hands to her elbows. A sheer veil covered her hair, which spilled to her mid-back in thick, unruly waves.

"Coralie," he breathed, taking a step into the room. "You look . . . ethereal."

She laughed. "You look quite handsome yourself."

And he did. His dark hair was brushed to a shine, falling to his shoulders. His broad chest and arms were covered in brocade, a cloud-colored undershirt peeking into view from the open collar. He wore pressed pants tucked into well-oiled boots. And he was wearing gloves, something she knew he detested.

He closed the distance between them and grasped her elbows, yanking her toward him. Coralie stared up at him as his hands slid down her arms until his fingers tangled with hers. Her skin warmed at the contact, even with the fabric between them. His eyes never left hers.

"Are you ready?"

"Never more," she replied.

He released one of her hands, and they headed toward the door. As they walked through the crowded halls, whistles and cheers followed them. They were bombarded with petals and even grains of rice as well-wishers chased after them. They reached the throne room, where two chairs had replaced the grand throne that hadn't been moved for centuries. Coralie stared ahead as she and Mordon passed rows upon rows of seated observers. They stepped up the stairs and stopped, turning to face each other. Never parting hands, even for a second.

In the front row seats sat their dear friends and allies. Coralie caught sight of Latimus and his wife, Sardala. They leaned into each other, wearing broad smiles as they looked on at the ceremony. Finnean sat beside them, seeming uncomfortable with the tender couple, if his tilting away was any indication. Moralis and Aylis took up the seats beside him, sadness coating their features, yet by their joined hands, it seemed they were closer than they ever had been before. The seat beside them was empty, reserved in the hopes that Bear would attend, but he hadn't been seen in months. He refused to believe his son was dead and had set out with the troops Honzio had sent to search for him.

"We are here to join two hearts," the officiator began.

The ceremony seemed to last ages. Even with all eyes on them, Coralie only saw Mordon's. A smile tilted the corner of his mouth. She blinked slowly, watching his pupils dilate.

"Do you accept Mordon, general of Verin, as your husband?"

"I accept him as the only ruler of my heart."

Applause broke out, and Mordon winked. Coralie's chest warmed.

"And you, Mordon, do you accept Coralie, queen of Verin, as your wife?"

"I pledge to serve my queen for the rest of my days," he said.

Coralie nearly rolled her eyes, and his fingers tightened on her hand.

"Before all the witnesses, you are now bound in love. May your home be filled with joy and peace."

Cheers broke out as the audience watched their passionate embrace. They pulled away from each other far too soon, and Latimus called from the audience, "Come on, Vaz! We were expecting more than that. Give us a good show!"

Laughter erupted at his teasing, and Mordon grumbled under his breath. He tore his gloves from his hands. "Damn these blasted things," he said, tossing them and successfully hitting his target.

Latimus groaned, receiving the gloves directly to his face.

"Hold those for me, will you?" Mordon shot back.

Several members of the audience hooted, and Mordon returned his hands to Coralie's cheeks. She closed her eyes as he placed a tender kiss on her forehead, his eyes containing the promise of so much more.

Coralie's attention was snared by Latimus and Lore fighting over the gloves as if they were some sort of trophy. Marcella—Coralie had recently become acquainted with her—leaned away from the boys, though she was chuckling as well, her violet hair shaking in its high bun. The officiator placed his forehead in his palm and shook his head. When the ruckus died down, Emperor Honzio stood from his seat and walked up the stairs to stand beside Coralie and Mordon.

"I wish the couple the happiest union," Honzio began. "As many of you know, these past months have been a struggle for all of us, rebuilding the empire, reclaiming friendships. The Uluzar, once known as Savagelanders, are now our allies. We will exchange goods with them openly, no longer in the black markets. The Tariqins have forfeited much land, returning to their side of the world. The horror the Dark Army wreaked across the Empire couldn't have happened without help from within. I am doing everything in my power to root out the traitors and eradicate them. The Tariqins no longer have Prolus at their head. Their troops are in disarray. Now is the perfect time to fortify and guarantee another siege will never be successful. We will honor our fallen by ensuring their sacrifice wasn't for nothing." Honzio swallowed at the reference to Natassa and Velamir, and all the others who had given their lives for the cause. "The king of Ondalar will be decided at the vote of the Ondalarian nobles.

"We have many more things to achieve, but first, I must honor an oath I made." Honzio's gaze flicked to the Savorian woman, Aylis. "I promised a dear friend of mine that I would free Savoria. That I would save those enslaved under Tariqi's cruel fist. I won't go back on my word."

Honzio stood straight, and any who saw him could see a changed man. His weaknesses were his strengths. He stared at the adoring crowd ready to follow his every command.

"We will march to Savoria."

EPILOGUE

S CREAMS PIERCED THROUGH the highest tower in
Devorin. But only the passing birds heard the desperate calls for help.

"More," the queen snarled, her sharp nails digging into the wood of her chair.

The whipping continued. Her conditioned nameless soldier held the lethal whip without an ounce of emotion as he lashed it across the back of the chained man. The man cried out, his knees pressed to the ground, his wrists raw from the metal encasing them.

"More," she whispered, her eyes alight with fury.

They had taken everything from her. She had researched and planned for years, but within moments, it had all gone to waste. She no longer had the power of an unstoppable army. All her Shadow Manos had withered away. That damned girl had closed the doorway and cut off the source of the queen's power. The whipping continued until the man fell silent, his back broken open and seeping with blood and pus. The queen rose from her chair and waved her soldier away. He followed her order at once. He was her commander. When all the Shadow Manos had faded, he'd remained. He was stronger than them all. He'd lost his shadow before, but it hadn't killed him.

Well done, she whispered in his mind, and then her focus turned to her new prisoner. She circled him, eyeing the bruises on his chest and ribs. His pants hung low on his hips, and his head dangled forward. Blondish brown hair hung in tangles. She reached out to grip his hair and yank his head upward. The Savorian's eyes were closed, keeping his midnight eyes concealed from view.

He groaned through busted lips. "What do you want from me?"

The queen smiled, running a nail along his cheek. She still had one chance at ultimate power, and the Savorian held the key.

"You will give me the location of the Golden Crown."

If you enjoyed this book, please consider
leaving a review. Reviews are so crucial in
helping spread awareness about the book.

ACKNOWLEDGMENTS

Book 3. I've stared at the front cover of this book and am still stunned at the sight of those two words. This is my third published book. Time is going too fast for me to believe it. The hours of writing and editing, the heart and soul and emotion poured into this series, are now in your hands. I hope these characters who have been dear to me for so long and the readers following their journey can forgive me for the torment I've put them through. And though these tragic last chapters may have seemed like an ending, trust me, the story is just beginning. As always, I couldn't have done this alone. First and foremost, I thank my family for supporting me in my dream and cheering me on. You are irreplaceable jewels that I will forever treasure. I thank my editors. Tanya, Chelsea, Lisa and Jenny. You are absolutely amazing, and I am infinitely grateful to you all for your meticulous work. Endless gratitude and love for my grandparents. Seeing your eyes light up when you hold my books motivates me more than you know. I am so grateful to have encountered wonderful authors and readers during this journey and hope to meet many more. If you read to this page, I want you to know how appreciative I am that you continued the series. Writing is pouring a part of yourself into your work, and sharing that with the world is like sharing a part of yourself. Thank you for reading, and I hope you will follow our heroes in the next one.

ABOUT THE AUTHOR

Israh Azizi resides in the land of ten thousand lakes with her family and five cats. Since she was a little girl, she has been a lover of words and fanciful tales. It was her dream to one day share a story of her own with the world. With sheer determination, lots of love, and a decent amount of caffeine, she managed to make that dream come true. Besides reading and writing, she has a dizzying number of hobbies, some of which include bossing around her younger siblings, experimenting with new baking recipes, and playing board games with her family and close friends. When life's plot twists don't cross her path and her fingers aren't dancing across the keyboard building a fantastical adventure, she can usually be found in a quiet corner with a good book and a steaming cup of coffee.